Patrick Quinlan was the youngest child in a big, noisy, New York Irish-American family. Ten minutes late to supper and the food was all gone.

Other kids in the neighbourhood wanted to become cops, or firemen, or crime kingpins. He wanted to become Jimi Hendrix. At an early age, he became an accomplished and incorrigible liar, eventually finding work that made good use of this talent - journalist, political operative, copywriter, and now novelist...

He lives on the coast of Maine with his wife, Joy Scott.

Smoked is his first novel.

SMOKED

PATRICK QUINLAN

headline
review

First published in the USA in 2006 by St Martin's Press

First published in Great Britain in 2006
by HEADLINE REVIEW
An imprint of HEADLINE PUBLISHING GROUP

First published in paperback in 2007 by HEADLINE REVIEW

1

ISBN 978 0 7553 3151 2 (A format)
ISBN 978 0 7553 2826 0 (B format)

Typeset in Fournier MT by Palimpsest Book Production Limited,
Grangemouth, Stirlingshire
Printed and bound in Great Britain
by Clays Ltd, St Ives plc

Headline's policy is to use papers that are natural, renewable and
recyclable products and made from wood grown in sustainable
forests. The logging and manufacturing processes are expected
to conform to the environmental regulations of the country of origin.

HEADLINE PUBLISHING GROUP
A division of Hodder Headline
338 Euston Road
London NW1 3BH

www.reviewbooks.co.uk
www.hodderheadline.com

For the real Lola,
with much love.

the great King of Kings
Hath in the tables of his law commanded
That thou shalt do no murder.

Shakespeare, *Richard III*

1

Nine years had passed since a gang of laughing boys raped Lola Bell at the back of a weedy and trash-strewn vacant lot. Pulling a train, they called it.

Now it was about to happen again.

Back then, sixteen years old, five of them had grabbed her in the late afternoon as she cut through the lot on her way home from the dance lessons her grandmother had paid for. She knew three of them. Tall, brooding, hostile – Brothers of the Struggle, they thought of themselves, young Gangster Disciples. They'd lounge on the benches, their hoods pulled down low over their faces, drinking out of bottles covered in brown paper bags. They had hit on her before, made comments to her, appraised her as she left her building and walked to the bus stop.

'Hey, shorty, where ya walkin'?'

'Honey, I'm liking that big black ass.'

'C'mere, baby, wanna make some green?'

Stupid, always taking that short cut through that back lot, never thinking of the danger. She remembered how the late sun was sharp and savage in her eyes as they held her down and took turns riding her. She remembered how the towering shadows of the Robert Taylor Houses grew longer as the time passed. She remembered the sound of cars speeding by on the Dan Ryan Freeway. She remembered the smell and taste of cheap wine on their breath. She remembered, after they left, lying there alone, the night coming on, rats starting to move in the bushes.

Now, twenty-five years old, she stood in a tiny orange bikini and high heels, in a small, bare office five stories above Congress Street, Portland's main drag. She cursed herself, her stupidity, that this could happen again. She had come here for a modeling 'try-out'. But now the man stood just behind her, holding her, twisting her arm against her back until tears nearly came. His other hand held a chunk of her hair, not quite pulling it, but tensed, ready to pull, controlling her like that.

Mr Blue Eyes, he called himself. He was tall and good-looking with a muscular body. He was clean-shaven and blond, and when she met him he was wearing a light blue Polo shirt by Ralph Lauren, and a pair of tan khaki slacks. His teeth, she had thought at the time – he didn't have model's teeth. That was what threw off his look. He had the snaggle teeth of a redneck.

'Hey, Shaggy,' he called across to his partner. 'You should see the tattoo she's got on her shoulder blade here. "Girls Kick Ass", it says, in a neat little curlicue. Well, ain't that cute?' He leaned close to her ear. 'You gonna kick my ass, honey?'

She could feel his erection against her back, pushing against the rubbery fabric of his Speedo shorts. They were standing on a plastic mat and behind them was a fake ocean scene. On either side of them were the bright lights and the black umbrella of a professional photographer. The lights were hot, and both she and Mr Blue Eyes had a fine sheen of sweat on their skin. She thought of the tattoo, the optimism it had represented for her, the dawning of a new day.

All lost now. All gone.

Across the office from them, maybe ten feet away, Mr Shaggy hunched behind a video camera on a tripod, viewing the action.

'Easy now,' he said. His words flowed like molasses, and his voice gave a taste of the Confederacy, as if he had come north as a ten-year-old boy and never quite assimilated. 'Let's just do this real easy. You're a beautiful girl, Lola. You got a future in this type of work, if you want one.'

Mr Shaggy was everything Mr Blue Eyes was not. A mountain man, husky, bordering on fat, with a bushy beard and long hair. He was a bear of a man in a black Harley-Davidson T-shirt. He had been stretched behind the desk when Lola walked into the nearly empty outer office, his feet up on a side table. He had conducted the interview.

Lola had liked Mr Shaggy. Despite his fearsome appearance, he had a disarming way about him, a gentle manner, one that had put her right at her ease. When she walked in, he had smiled, looked her up and down.

'Oh, yeah,' he said. 'Young lady, I think you're gonna do just fine.'

Mr Shaggy and Mr Blue Eyes. They were a perfect pair of con artists.

And Lola had walked right into their trap.

A week before, she had spotted a flyer tacked up on the public bulletin board in Monument Square: 'MODELS WANTED. Male and Female. Experience preferred, but not necessary. Fresh or exotic look, enthusiasm most important.'

Lola had done some modeling from time to time. A couple of years had passed since the last one, but she still kept her eyes open for opportunities. She didn't imagine anything would come of it, but decided to give it a try. A little extra money would come in handy. And with her long curls and brown skin, she figured she could pass for exotic, in any case. She pulled the flyer down and stuck it in her bag, glancing around as she did so. People sometimes got funny when you pulled down flyers.

That night, she called the number on the flyer. A brisk, businesslike woman's voice on the machine said to leave a message. Lola did. Two days passed and no one called her back. On the third day, a man called her in the evening. He told her the modeling agency was conducting interviews in Portland the very next evening for a catalog shoot. Could she make it? Friday night. She sure could.

He scheduled it for seven o'clock, gave her the address, said they would buzz her into the building. He told her to bring a head shot and a performance résumé, if she had these things. She said she did. He told her that would be great.

'No promises,' was the last thing he told her.

'None expected,' she said.

She tried not to get too excited after she hung up the phone. These things had ended in disappointment before. All the same, it might be something.

Now, her moist skin broke out in gooseflesh despite the heat from the lights.

'You cold, honey?' Mr Shaggy said. 'Need somebody to keep you warm?'

Her heart raced. Her breath came in rasps.

Mr Shaggy looked up from the camera. 'Mr Blue Eyes, will you remove those bottoms for Lola, please? If she's not gonna do it herself.'

Mr Blue Eyes brought extra pressure to bear on her arm. He let go of her hair and his hand strayed to the panty of her orange bikini. It was made of tight, grippy latex. He needed two hands to pull it down, but if he released her arm, then she'd be free.

'Come on, Lola, help me out,' he whispered into her ear. His breath smelled like those curiously strong mints, the ones that came in the little tin and used the spaceman in their ads. He smelled like he had eaten a whole handful of them.

'I promise I'll make this the best one you ever had.'

She had changed out of her street clothes and into this

skimpy bathing suit when Mr Shaggy suggested they take a few pictures, see what they had. She changed in a tiny bathroom. It looked like no one had used this office in months. When she came back out into the office, Mr Blue Eyes was already packed into his ice-blue Speedos. They barely contained him. He had thick neck muscles and a broad chest. His legs rippled with muscle and veins.

She had fanned herself with her hand, feigning a hot flash. 'Oh, my,' she had said. 'I didn't realize.'

'That's what I like,' Mr Shaggy had said. 'A girl with a sense of humor. OK, kiddies, let's shoot a little something, what do you say?'

Now he said, as he looked through the LCD screen that folded out from his camera, 'Yessir, like to break me open a little piece of that. Mmmmm-mmmm. That's what the doctor ordered.'

The things they said made it hard for her to think. The bright lights blinded her. She was in danger of freezing up. If she allowed her mind to lock, then they could do with her what they wanted. She had to get loose. Calm down, find the center, let everything go. Become soft rather than rigid.

She could scream. Yes, she could do that. What had she learned about screaming? Don't scream for help. Nobody responded to cries for help. If anything, cries for help scared people away. No. People responded to a different word. One that made them look out for their own self-interest.

Fire.

She took a deep breath, lungs gathering air for the effort.

It had to be loud, it had to be piercing, it had to rip through the calm and the quiet of an after-hours building, it had to rip through the walls, out to Friday night drinkers and diners and moviegoers – people walking by five stories below on the street. It had to rip through the world.

Mr Blue Eyes clamped a hand over her mouth.

He whispered in her ear, 'If you scream, then we're gonna have to hurt you.'

It was too late to scream. It was too late to do anything. She carried no weapon. The only weapon she had was herself. In a ridiculous orange bikini and high-heeled shoes.

Empty hand, she thought. Empty hand.

'You know what?' Mr Shaggy said. 'Let's have you folks head over to the examination table there. I'll just let this camera run, and bring the second camera over there and join you both. That'll make things easier on everybody, hmmm?'

Mr Blue Eyes turned her to the right and shuffle-stepped her over to an empty desk sitting near the wall. The wall itself was lined with floor-to-ceiling mirrors, as if this place had once spent time as a dance studio. He bent her over the desk.

He pulled her head up by the hair. 'I want you to watch.'

In the mirror, she saw him hovering behind her. His smile floated above his muscular torso. He still held her arm behind her back, but he had relaxed the pressure just a little. She felt him, erect now, monstrous, against her. Her eyes stared back at her. Was this what all that training was for? Was this what all the long hours of hard work had come to? To be easily manhandled by two jerks? By two rapists? No. The answer was no. All her hard work was so nothing like this would ever happen again.

Mr Blue Eyes giggled. He had become almost, but not quite, gentle. He stroked her hair, his fingers ready to clench again at any false move.

Nearby, Mr Shaggy fussed with the lighting, moving the big umbrella closer, a round light shining up into its maw.

'Please don't do this,' Lola said.

'What's that? What did you say?'

'Please.'

'That's a good girl. That's what I like to hear.'

What was she waiting for? She still had one free hand. Do it now.

In the mirror, she watched him.

He gyrated his hips against her, like a dance floor showoff. The sight of it might have been comical in some other circumstance. 'You are gonna come your brains out tonight, darling. You are one sexy bitch. I can't wait to put it to you, you know? I mean, I just can't wait. Fact is, I think I love you.'

Then Mr Shaggy's big body appeared in front of her, blocking her view. His meaty hands undid his belt buckle.

'You got a boyfriend, Lola?' he said.

He lifted her chin between two thick fingers. Strapped to his other hand, he had another small camcorder, its LCD screen folded out and facing her, displaying her own face back to her. Her eyes were wide and frightened and confused.

'Sure you do, pretty little girl like you. See how pretty you are? I bet you got yourself a nice boyfriend.'

Lola thought of her boyfriend, Smoke Dugan. Silly old Smoke, who had offered to come with her on this interview. He was afraid for her because scams like this were all over the place. He wanted to protect her. Smoke, always a gentleman, well into late middle age, who walked with a limp and carried a thick wooden cane everywhere — his shillelagh, he sometimes called it. Dapper Smoke, who had gray and white hair and wore an Irish touring cap of wool tweed in cool weather. Smoke, with his big workman's hands and his cats and his cigars and his long afternoon naps. Smoke wanted to protect her from animals like these.

'I'm a big girl,' she had told him. 'I think I can handle it on my own.'

'That's all right,' Mr Shaggy said now. 'We're gonna give you right back to him when we're done. Of course, that's if you even want to go back.'

DO IT, her mind shouted.

Almost ready.

Almost . . .

'All right if I put something in your mouth right now? Come on, Lola. Open up and say AAAAH.'

'OK,' she said quietly. She heard her voice shaking. Her chin had begun to tremble in his hand. Her whole body started to shake. She felt like she could vomit.

'What's that?' Mr Shaggy said. 'Not sure I heard you correctly.'

'OK. I'll do whatever you want. Just tell him to stop twisting my arm. It hurts.'

9

The two men exchanged glances above her head.

'Well, young man. You heard the lady.'

'Do I believe her?' Mr Blue Eyes said.

Mr Shaggy shrugged. 'Come on, kid. We're on camera here. It's not a conversation we're filming.' He undid the button of his green workpants and pulled down his zipper. 'What's it gonna be, Lola?'

She felt the first sting of tears and let them come.

'Whatever you want.'

'I believe her. Let's get down to business.'

Mr Blue Eyes released her arm. The numb arm flopped around in front of her like a fish and she planted her palm on the desk, next to her other hand. He released her hair. She was free, bent over the desk, her chin in Mr Shaggy's hand. Still, she did not move.

Mr Blue Eyes stepped back and bent over, peeling down his Speedos.

She had signed a waiver.

That thought struck her now with strange force. Mr Shaggy had handed the waiver to her right before she went into the bathroom to change her clothes. He had spoken with offhand nonchalance.

'Let's get you to sign one of these releases. You never know. Might get something tonight we want to use.'

She signed without even reading it.

Oh, they were smooth. They had it down to a system. Get the stupid girl to take off her clothes and put on a bikini. Flatter her some, tell her you'll pay her a hundred bucks an hour. Have her sign away her rights. Then rape her on camera.

Chances are good she never tells a soul.

If she does, you have it in black and white. Hey, maybe things got a little out of hand, but she *agreed* to it beforehand. It's all right here on paper.

Bastards. They had done this before. Of course they had.

'It's OK,' Mr Shaggy said. 'It's gonna be good. No need to cry.'

His voice came to her as if she were at the bottom of a deep well. He removed his shirt. He positioned himself in front of her, his big hairy stomach even with her face. Sometime today, he had sprayed his belly with cologne.

Now.

If she was going to stop this happening, it had to be RIGHT NOW.

'She looks tasty,' Mr Blue Eyes said somewhere behind her. His hands returned, roaming her body. He stood behind her, his erection poking between her thighs, rubbing against the fabric of her bikini bottom.

'Let's spread these legs a little,' he said.

She leaned down close to the desk, like someone doing a push-up. She turned her head to the side, cheek against the hard surface. From the corner of her eye, she saw Mr Blue Eyes, his attention consumed by what he was about to do.

'Uh, Lola?' Mr Shaggy said. 'We're playing both ends against the middle in this game. I'm gonna need some help up here.'

She placed her forehead against the desk. Her body tightened like a coiled spring.

'Lola?'

She thrust herself upward, legs planted, body pivoting at the waist. Ninety degrees to a vertical one-eighty in one second flat.

The back of her skull smashed into Mr Blue Eyes's face.

There was pain, but also the pleasure of feeling him cave in like a wet, rotten pumpkin. He grunted like a pig.

The impact reverberated like high-voltage electricity down her neck to the base of her spine, and across her small shoulders. Her whole body thrummed with the recoil.

For a long instant, the world went black.

Then white light streaked across her vision and Mr Shaggy stood across the desk from her, erection in one hand, camera in the other, eyes wide, mouth a great big O of surprise. She spun, bringing her right elbow up and around with the full force of her momentum. It connected, but not well, with the side of Mr Blue Eyes's head. He held his hands to his face. Blood flowed between his fingers.

She sidestepped from him.

A moment passed, the three of them standing in a triangle, each person's eyes darting between the other two end points.

Suddenly Mr Shaggy whooped and laughed. 'Damn. You let a little girl bloody you up like that? Shit. I've never seen anything like it.'

Lola backed away, kicking off the high heels.

Mr Blue Eyes stood nude, monster erection at half-mast now. He rubbed blood away from his face.

'Nose broken?' Mr Shaggy said.

'I don't know. I think maybe not. It sure hurts, though.'

Mr Blue Eyes looked at Lola. Then he did an odd thing. He smiled.

'I knew I shouldn't have let her go.'

'Look,' Lola said, 'let's make a deal. You let me leave, I don't call the cops.'

Mr Shaggy smiled too. 'Oh, that's funny. You're not going anywhere, Lola. We tried to do it the nice way. We *like* the nice way. Makes for better content. But we can do it the hard way too.'

Mr Blue Eyes grinned broadly, his face a swirled mask of blood. His teeth were jagged, like a row of shark's teeth. His eyes showed a simplicity, nearly a brute stupidity. He was enjoying himself. He sauntered toward her.

'You know I used to be in the ring when I was a kid,' he said. 'Had fifteen fights. Never once did I get knocked out. Probably not gonna start now.'

Mr Shaggy moved toward her from the left, buttoning his pants. He was a hairy son of a bitch. He even had hair on his shoulders. 'You know,' he said, 'it's gonna be awfully hard to make it in modeling if you won't do nudity.' He was still filming with the hand-held.

She backed toward the tripod camera, watching them approach.

'This is the most exciting one yet. You know, we've had

some get away, walk out before we ever got this far, but you're the first one who ever went this far and still showed this kind of spunk. Mostly, they just go limp.'

'Seem to enjoy themselves, some of them,' Mr Blue Eyes said.

And then Lola realized what was missing. She wasn't angry. Up until this moment they had scared her. Everything had flowed their way, their trap working perfectly. And she had gotten scared. But now she saw them clearly for the first time. They did this over and over, tricking young women who wanted to feel glamorous, wanted to feel good about themselves, wanted to be like the people they saw on TV. Wasn't that it? Yes, it was, and in a sense she saw herself for the first time too.

The exploitation, the degradation, the goddamn fucking lie of it all.

Somebody had to make them pay.

Well, if the past nine years hadn't been for a moment like this, then it had been for no moment at all. The high white buzz of adrenaline surged through her veins. Still shaking, still crying. That was OK.

A whistling sound seemed to shriek near her ears.

Mr Blue Eyes was almost upon her.

'Hey, take it easy now,' he said. 'Let's stop crying. Let's cut out all this nonsense and be friends again, OK?'

Her chin quivered.

He opened his strong arms to embrace her.

'Careful,' Mr Shaggy said.

'Oh, I'll be careful. I'll be gentle. We're gonna make Lola feel right at home.'

Lola planted her feet and rammed her forehead into Mr Blue Eyes's face. He was just as dumb as a stump, wasn't he? She drove it in hard, like she would hammer a nail into a log. The blow accelerated into the impact.

His nose felt sharp. This time she broke it. She heard a sound like a club pounding on a hollow gourd.

Mr Blue Eyes made a choking sound. Maybe it was a scream. He fell back.

She lunged forward. As she did, she delivered a punch to his throat with the edge of her right palm, the blade of it. The punch was part of the lunge, organic to it, not tacked on at the end. She had practiced just such a move thousands of times until it was seamless and flowed like water.

Mr Blue Eyes gagged and sputtered, his hands to his face. Blood soiled his chin and neck. His eyes seemed to peer at her from over the top of a bright red wall. She leaped into the air and delivered a front kick to his naked, helpless groin. He dropped to his knees, then fell to the carpet like the broken toy of a careless child.

Mr Shaggy was there, too late for his friend. He grabbed her from behind. She tried to use her head on him, but he sidestepped and her skull bounced harmlessly off the meat of his shoulder. He got both hands, strong hands, in her hair and spun her around. Roughly, he forced her to her knees before him.

He had put away the camera.

15

She stared up at him. He looked down at her. Their eyes locked.

She had two free hands, and he had none. With one hand, she reached up and grasped his testicles through his loose-fitting chino workpants. She got a good grip on him, measured the heft of him. She held him as she would hold a piece of fruit for inspection.

She smiled.

He shook his head. 'Don't.'

She squeezed and gave a savage twist.

He let go of her hair.

She sprang to her feet, phantom hands still yanking her hair, the pain there still bright. Shaggy was slightly bent, holding his balls with both hands.

She took one step and sidekicked him in the face with the ball of her foot.

He staggered away, lost his footing and fell over.

She glanced around for something to do next. The camera on the tripod caught her eye. She walked over and inspected it. It was a Canon XL1, a digital. It was still filming. She fumbled with the camera for a moment, then ejected the disk, a Mini-DV cassette. She flipped it onto the desk next to the hand-held camera. She ejected the Mini-DV from that one too.

Then she picked up the tripod, camera and all. She held it by the tripod legs like a baseball bat. It was heavier than it looked.

'Don't even think about breaking that,' Mr Shaggy said from the floor.

Now she was having fun.

'You know? I kind of liked you, Shaggy. I mean, like an hour ago, when I first met you.' She swung hard and smashed the camera against the wall. A piece of its hard plastic casing flew across the office. The force of the blow punched a hole in the painted sheet rock of the wall.

'Aw fuck,' Mr Shaggy said. 'Honey, I paid three grand for that.'

She swung again, punching another dent. The LCD screen broke off and hung by a wire. 'I guess you'll need a new one.'

He climbed heavily to his feet. She watched him.

He paused, staring down at Mr Blue Eyes, who writhed and squirmed on the floor, blood from his nose staining the carpet black. Mr Shaggy sighed from deep in his chest. He released a long exhalation. 'I think my friend is hurt.'

'Shaggy?'

He turned to look at her.

'Yeah?'

She swung the tripod and the shattered camera connected with his face.

'So are you.'

Alone now, Lola surveyed the wreckage.

She crouched between the two men piled on the floor. She was naked but for a bright orange bikini. No matter. Mr Blue Eyes had no clothes on at all and Mr Shaggy's belly hung out there like a giant hairy potato. She was still breathing hard, her hair was matted to her head and sweat dripped down her face. No matter. They were bleeding like twin volcanoes.

All those years of practice, women's self-defense, extreme self-defense, karate, grappling, several different styles, years of sparring, and she had never known if any of it would work in real life.

Worked? It had damn well rocked.

'Are we done here?' she said.

Neither of the men said a word.

'I guess that means yes.'

She climbed out of her crouch and glanced around the office. Nothing much to see.

'Listen, I want to thank you guys. That was the best time I've had in years.'

Later, fully dressed and back out on the street, she walked several blocks before she started laughing. She came to a corner and threw the two Mini-DV cassettes in the gutter. She stepped on each of them, grinding them with her heel, then kicked them into the sewer. All the while, she giggled like a lunatic.

Two couples out for Friday night drinks passed her, glanced her way and kept going.

A moment later the tears began to flow and she could not stop weeping.

Smoke Dugan lay awake in absolute darkness, thinking about death.

Across the room, he heard the furtive rustlings as two of his cats wrestled. A glass of port wine from Portugal sat forgotten on the table at his elbow. She hadn't called yet and that was not like her. Somewhere in his mind, he knew this, but the problem was he knew other things as well. He lay in his basement apartment, watching the visions imprinted on his brain.

The visions were memories.

For more than a year, he had been free of the things. Then last week, something had happened that brought them all rushing back. He had been walking in the Old Port, enjoying the bright fall day. In fact, just moments earlier he had been out on the Maine State Pier watching four harbor seals frolic in the bay. He had read his morning paper out there on a bench, watching also as the Peaks Island Ferry came in and out. Now he was walking back through the sparse crowds. He was thinking he wanted to have a bite to eat, and he was deciding about the many restaurants available to him along the waterfront.

A man was following him.

Damned if it wasn't so. Smoke had first noticed him on the pier. He was a fortysomething tourist in a gray fleece jacket, jeans and LL Bean boots. He wore a Brooklyn Dodgers replica baseball cap and dark sunglasses. Sure, Smoke had seen him there, registered him with his binoculars and his camera and his leather over-the-shoulder tourist duffel. He had registered him like he registered the Hispanic fishermen in their sleeveless T-shirts with their plastic bait-buckets, the floppy-haired teenagers with their skateboards, and the crusty old salts sitting on the benches, commenting and frowning about the state of the world. Smoke registered everything, scanned everything, and as long as everything stayed where it belonged and acted properly, everything was just fine.

But on the crowded sidewalk of Commercial Street, he felt rather than saw the tourist there behind him. That's when the antennae began to twitch. Was he really there? What was he doing?

Smoke bumped into a young woman passing with her girlfriend.

'Oh, my,' he said, turning to her. 'Oh, young lady, I am so sorry. Are you all right?'

He touched her shoulders and glanced to his left.

The man was there, following along, twenty feet back. He tinkered with something on his camera. Had he taken another photo just a few seconds ago? Smoke's grip tightened on his cane.

The young woman smiled. She was a pretty girl, blonde. Her friend had a ring through her nose like a bull in a field. 'I'm fine, really. It's my fault. I should have been paying attention.'

'No, I insist. It was definitely my fault.'

'Well, no harm done.' Both ladies laughed.

The man found something fascinating in a storefront window.

The young lovelies moved on. So did Smoke. He walked along, heavy midday traffic flowing to his right. Abruptly, he turned and stepped into the flow. A car screeched to a halt. The driver leaned on the horn as Smoke waved his cane. He hurried across the street, glancing behind him at the driver who still hurled epithets. The tourist watched him go.

Now, Smoke peered into the dark. He reached and took a sip of his wine.

It didn't prove anything.

Half the street had watched him. After all, he had made a suicidal plunge into heavy traffic. People must have thought he was senile.

Maybe the man really was a tourist. Maybe he wasn't. But Smoke couldn't stay here – couldn't stay anywhere – for ever. That's what he realized now. He had always known it, but this past year had been so good that he allowed himself to forget. The day would come when the man behind him wasn't a tourist.

Perhaps the time had come to explain himself to Lola. Tell her the whole story. Ask her to run away with him. There was nothing keeping either of them here.

Would she come? Would she even believe him?

She wouldn't. It was that simple. Lola grew up in bad circumstances, but she was a good girl. She wasn't tough. She wasn't cut out for the life Smoke had led. Few people were. Lola was comfortable with the idea that he was a kindly older man who had made a lot of money in engineering and now built toys for retarded children.

Even that. He laughed at the word. 'Retarded.' She hated it when he used it.

'Why can't you say "special"?' she said. 'Or even "developmentally disabled"?'

He didn't know why. He just couldn't. He loved the children, God knew, but he hated the way people danced around what things were, describing them with words that didn't explain anything. 'Hearing impaired' for deaf. 'Vision impaired' for blind.

Fuck it.

Since the tourist, Smoke had started setting the traps again. And the traps had brought the dead children back to him. He saw the dark ocean water with flames riding on the surface, the bodies floating like dolls, the sharks gathering in the deep. The adults, OK that was bad. But the children . . . He saw their big vacant eyes most of all, the life gone from them.

'Shit,' he said, and rolled over.

He was fully awake now, itching to call her. Every minute she didn't call was another minute they had gotten her. He would call her, but that didn't conform to the rules. The rules were she was a big girl, she had grown up in the Chicago housing projects long before she met him, and she could take care of herself. She would call when she got in.

'Some tough girl,' he said. 'Can't even say the word "retarded".'

The phone rang, too loud in the close darkness.

'Hello?'

'Smoke?' It was her.

He smiled. He put the sound of sleep in his voice.

'Yeah, babe. Thought you forgot.'

'Did I wake you?' she said.

'Not really. How'd the audition go?'

'It didn't . . . it didn't go well. I don't think I'm going to get the job. I don't think they liked me very much.'

'Well, that's OK. You'll get 'em next time.'

'Sure.'

'We having dinner tomorrow night?' he said. 'You, me and Pamela?'

'We sure are.'

He thought he heard her voice shake just a little bit.

'Hey,' he said. 'Is everything all right?'

'I'm just tired. It's been a long day. I'm on my way to bed.'

'Well, I love you,' he said.

There was a pause. Sometimes he feared he said it too much, put too much pressure on her. Damn. She was half his age.

'You don't have to say it,' he said.

'I love you too, silly.'

When they hung up, Smoke picked up his wine glass. Somewhere in the room, the cats still played.

Smoke saw the flames again. He saw the dead eyes of the children.

He pictured two massive hands, grasping in the dark. They were groping for him, trying to find him. Hands that would seize him and crush him.

Searching, searching.

2

Denny Cruz had murderer's eyes.

That's why the waiter never looked at him. It wasn't the four-inch scar that came down the side of his face like a jagged stretch of highway – the scar that he left there against all the best advice of well-meaning people.

'Hey, Cruz, you got the money, why don't you get rid of that scar?' someone would say to him.

'Because I want to remember,' he would answer in a voice that rose just barely above a whisper. In Cruz's experience, you didn't need to talk loud to get people's attention.

'Yeah, but one day a witness is gonna see that thing and you're gonna go down.'

'I don't leave witnesses.'

It wasn't the scar. And it wasn't his slim, razor-sharp body. No. It was the eyes. Even now, after all these years, some mornings Cruz was startled to see those eyes looking back at him in the mirror. He had seen the same eyes in newspaper pictures from Rwanda. Men who had hacked thousands of innocent women and children apart with machetes, men who lived forty deep in small, unlit cells, waiting to go on trial for genocide.

Killers.

In newspaper photographs, these men had the eyes.

Cruz sat in the open-air restaurant just off the lush court-yard and in-ground pool of the elegant Hotel St. Therese in New Orleans. He had just finished his breakfast, and his appetite had been good. He had polished off a plate of Eggs Bayou Lafourche, two golden beignets piled with snowy sugar, a glass of juice, and two cups of real New Orleans French Roast with chicory. It would be nice to light up a cigarette right about now. Of course, it was *verboten* to smoke indoors. Smokers like himself had been hounded and persecuted by the good clean pink-lunged people of the world for going on ten years. Soon, the smokers would probably be packed off to camps in the countryside. For their own good, you see.

No matter. Cruz felt good — well laid, well rested, well fed.

Today was the day.

He took a pleasant moment to survey his surroundings. The courtyard was green with the dense tropical plants grown there to give the place ambience. A few people sprawled about in white chaise longues near the pool, chatting and sunning themselves. The air was heavy, the sun was bright and hot, and the sounds of conversation were muted. No children ran around, laughing and shouting. This was a place for adults.

The St. Therese was a stately old place that had been a whore-house before the turn of the century. It sat at the edge of the French Quarter, on busy North Rampart Street, across from Louis Armstrong Park, but no sound came in from the street.

It was fitting, Cruz noted, that he was sitting in an old whorehouse, and right across from him at the table, enjoying her breakfast in the splendid late morning sunshine, was a high-priced whore. She was Brazilian, this sexy girl, and had deep bronze skin and blonde hair. The combination turned Cruz on no end. That, and the red mini dress she wore that barely covered her succulent ass. He was going to have to take her back up to the room again before the morning was over, that much was clear.

He liked the girl, mostly. It was her looks that did it for him. He was trying to see past the other thing.

The other thing was her brain.

He had never met such a highly educated whore in his life. It didn't seem to flow, this being a whore and, at the same time, knowing so much.

She spoke four languages. Portuguese, Spanish, English and French. English was her weakest language, beyond doubt. As a teenager, she told him, she had gone on study exchange programs to both Paris and Caracas, Venezuela. After studying in Paris, she had taken three months and bummed around Europe, traveling as far to the east as Istanbul.

Where did the whoring come in? That's what he was wondering. What role did that play in this whole thing? She couldn't be very much older than twenty. What did she do?

Come back from Europe and decide the best thing to do was become a whore?

She had studied art and architecture. They were practically one and the same, she told him. She expounded on the architectural style of the hotel they were in, all the while scarfing down her Eggs Benedict with Canadian bacon. She told him about the paintings hanging on the walls of his suite. One was a bad knock-off of Van Gogh's style. One was a bad knock-off of Andrew Wyeth's style.

'You know a lot,' he said, as the waiter poured him more coffee. The waiter did not look at him or make any gesture or sign. 'Such a beautiful girl, and smart too.'

She smiled at him. 'How you talk.'

Her smile lit up her beauty like a thousand-watt lamp. Cruz sighed at the majesty and mystery of the world. Things were never what they seemed. He glanced at his watch again. It would be just another minute.

'Will you excuse me just one moment?' he said. 'I have to take a call.'

The girl shrugged. She would. She wouldn't. She indicated as much.

Cruz glided to the bank of old-fashioned phone booths at the back of the restaurant. Real phone booths, with real doors and real privacy. He slid into the middle one, the one with the sign on it that said 'Out of Order'.

He perched on the wooden seat that folded out from the wall.

The phone rang and Cruz grabbed it.

'Yeah?'

A man's voice came on. 'We checked the paper today. Still nothing.'

It was a deep, gravelly voice. The voice didn't introduce itself, but in his mind Cruz could see the man it belonged to right away. Crag-faced, like that cartoon hero from the *Fantastic Four* way back when – the one made of stone. Big Vito, a man who would never say his own name.

Cruz knew what he was talking about. They were monitoring the internet version of the *New Orleans Times-Picayune*. They had read it the past four days, waiting for word. His employers were not patient men, and sometimes that grated on him.

'It took me a couple of days to set it up. I had to check everything out first. But I'm happy to say it's all ready to go. It's gonna happen tonight.'

'Tonight?'

'That's right.'

'Good. We need you back here as soon as possible. We got a little something for you to take care of up north.'

'North?' Cruz said.

'Yeah, like New England.'

'Great. You gonna fly me straight up there?'

'No. We need you back here first.'

'All right. It's your dime.'

'So everything will be done by tonight?'

'Tonight,' Cruz agreed.

'Good enough.' There was a pause. 'Listen, how's the girl?'

Across the restaurant, Cruz could see her, still at the table.

She was examining something along the hem of her skirt. It gave him a flash of panty.

'She's great. Very smart.'

'Smart?'

'Smart.'

'Uh, OK. How's the suite?'

'Couldn't be better. Richly appointed furnishings. Views of the French Quarter. Twenty-four-hour concierge.'

'All right, then. We got a new service and I just wanted to make sure everything worked out.'

'It's great,' Cruz said.

'Then get it done, will ya? We'll see you soon.'

Cruz returned to the table. It was shaping up to be a hot and sticky day. The girl was finishing her fruit cocktail. For the life of him, he couldn't remember her name. Did it matter?

'What do you say?' he said. 'Let's go to the room, eh? I got a busy day today and I want to fuck you some more before I send you home.'

She slurped a cherry down, then licked the glass cup with her tongue.

'Good,' she said. 'More money for me.'

They went upstairs.

'That bitch,' Darren Pelletier said.

His voice had taken on a nasal pitch because of the cotton wadding stuffed up his nose. A white plaster splint made an A-shape across its bridge. Both his eyes were black, and the whole package together made him look somewhat like a raccoon.

'You know I'm gonna make her pay, right?'

Hal Morgan didn't say a word. He just sat in the living room of his ramshackle three-bedroom house in Auburn, Maine, thirty miles north of Portland. He let his friend ramble on. Hal's hair hung loose and he pushed it out of his eyes. Mr Shaggy, he often called himself when the young ladies asked. He held his first beer of the morning, a can of Budweiser. It was ice cold and felt good in his hand. He sipped it quietly while reviewing his menu of options.

They didn't look good.

He gazed out the front picture window. He lived just down the road from the Lost Valley ski resort. In fact, he could see the small mountain – little more than a hill, really – from right here on the sofa. He watched that mountain now, the bald ski runs bathed in morning sunlight, reds and oranges of fall mixed in with the evergreens along the edges of the trails.

Soon, another six weeks at most, the hill would be covered in snow. From his living room, he could watch the skiers glide down. Then, before he knew it, the scene would change yet again. The seasons passed faster and faster as he grew older. He was almost forty years old now, and it seemed like on Monday he would glance up that hill in green and sunny summertime, and on Tuesday a howling wind would blow powdery snow from the top of it.

Closer to home, his neighborhood sprawled out in what he liked to think of as the mountain's shadow. It was a quiet neighborhood of small saltbox- and ranch-style houses, not quite suburban, not quite rural. The neighborhood itself looked like it was leaning toward suburban – what with the houses just ten or twenty yards apart. But the pickup trucks with the gun racks and the sagging condition of some of the homes said the people were leaning toward rural.

Hal sipped his beer and watched Darren.

Darren sat sprawled in an easy chair. His shirt was off, revealing his well-muscled upper body. His sandy blond hair was slicked back. He was drinking a beer, smoking a cigarette, sulking, touching the plaster the emergency room doctor had put across his nose, cursing to himself, and looking over his various bruises all at the same time.

Mr Blue Eyes.

The moniker fit him perfectly. Nobody had eyes that were bluer than Mr Blue Eyes's. He had eyes of pale blue – like the sky, like a Caribbean lagoon. You could fall into his eyes, they were so blue. In fact, Hal knew that Darren wore contact lenses to give his eyes that color. There was nothing wrong with his eyes that needed correction – except their color: they were actually brown.

Darren had slept in the spare bedroom because he didn't want to go home to his wife after the beating he took. Darren often slept in the spare bedroom. Sometimes he slept in there with the girls from photo shoots they did – a lot of the girls weren't nearly as resistant as Lola to modeling with Darren. Sometimes he slept in there alone. Beating or no, Darren rarely wanted to go home to his wife.

'Gonna eat that bitch alive next time,' he said, almost to himself. He took a deep drag from his cigarette. 'Yessir, next time I surely am gonna do it to her.'

Hal smiled. 'We'll have to put a paper bag over your head, but OK.'

Darren's handsome face winced as he gingerly rubbed a large purplish blot on the side of his thick neck. He smiled around the cigarette. 'Man, she got me good right here.' The bruise looked like an octopus imbedded in his neck, trying to push its way out through the skin. It looked like somebody had hit him there with a baseball bat.

'Oh, yeah, that's the worst of it,' Hal said. 'What'd she do there?'

'Kicked me as I was falling.' Darren took a big slurp of his beer. 'Or maybe it was after I was down.' The two men glanced at each other for a moment, and burst out laughing. It was funny, if you looked at it the right way. Last night had been the worst screw-up they had experienced in their new careers. A couple of girls had almost escaped, at times, and one had even pulled a gun, which they talked her into dropping. But none so far had busted out with this Bruce Lee shit. That was the one thing they hadn't expected.

Hal took a sip of his Budweiser as the laughter subsided. 'Kid, we got our asses kicked by a little girl.'

'We sure did, partner.'

They lapsed into silence, and Hal looked around the room.

He had inherited this house from his mother years before, and there was no doubt he had let the place go to hell. It was in need of a woman's touch, maybe. The furniture was old, the window blinds were moving toward ratty, the rugs were threadbare and were bordered by scuffed wooden floors that had long since needed resurfacing. The kitchen cabinets were old – they had probably been put in during the 1940s. Ditto the stove, although it still worked well. The refrigerator was only two years old, but that was because the last one had broken. Outside, the lawn did whatever the hell it wanted. Right now, in mid-October, it was long and going toward brown, slowly dying. Bits of paper and other assorted flying garbage had embedded itself here and there on the grass. Beneath the grass, especially near the rickety front porch, were empty beer cans that Hal and Darren had chucked while sitting on the porch and bullshitting.

If the house looked bad, Hal could take comfort in the fact that it looked no worse than any of the other houses in the area. A lot of people in that neighborhood were struggling. Hal could also take some comfort in the fact that he was not struggling. In fact, with the free house and the little bit of money he had squirreled away over the years, and the new business he and Darren had been working these past eleven months, Hal felt like he was doing just fine, thank you.

Right out of high school, Hal had gone in the military. For four years, he had seen his chunk of the world. He went to Louisiana, to the Philippines, to South Korea, to Germany. On leave he checked out Southeast Asia and lots of Europe. What did he learn from all that traveling? Apart from the eye-opening food choices, he learned there are whores wherever you go. Some are a little more expensive than others, but in general, they're all pretty cheap if you get the right ones. Sometimes it's out of the goodness of your heart that you pay them at all — he learned that one too.

But these photo-shoot girls were the best.

Hal had a guy down in Florida who could sell anything Hal could shoot. In fact, the guy wanted more all the time. Especially these modeling agency interview shoots. People went nuts for it, and the girls lined right up to participate. Hal put up these ads, these flyers, looking for women *and* men. When men called, he ignored them. He didn't want men. He wanted girls.

Saying he wanted men made the girls think he really was planning on a calendar shoot, or a catalog shoot. When they found out otherwise, they didn't usually complain. Instead, they went limp. They obeyed. It was like, 'You want me to take my clothes off? Uh, OK. You want me to put that in my mouth? Uh, OK.' Girls were passive. It was in their nature.

Hell, maybe they even liked it.

After each shoot, he'd send them out with a 'We'll call you if we need you', or 'We'll send you a check'. He hadn't sent anyone a check yet, and nobody had complained. What were they going to say? Some of the girls really did seem to enjoy themselves. He figured the rest of them just tried to put it out of their minds.

In case of any future trouble, Hal took precautions. He moved the office around all the time, taking short leases. He had changed the name of the business three times so far. When he transferred the video from the Mini-DV tape to the computer, he always edited his own and Darren's faces out of the movie.

Then he would upload it to a secure web site the guy in Florida kept for submissions. Like magic, the guy would send

35

back money. It was fun, and they were starting to make a very decent living. But this whole episode with Lola, it could jeopardize everything.

'I don't know if you're just talking trash or not,' Hal said. 'But we do have to go back down there and talk to Ms Lola.'

'Yeah? Why's that?'

'She took the digital tapes, kid. We're on there. A brawl like that – you can hardly say she was begging for it, then changed her mind later. She decides to go to the cops, how much more evidence are they gonna need? We need to get those tapes back.'

Darren shrugged. He blew a smoke ring. 'I got no problem with seeing her again. I'll look forward to it. You know how to find her?'

'Well, she filled out that release with her address. I still have it.'

Now Darren smiled. His lumpy raccoon eyes glittered. He flexed his chest and his shoulder muscles. 'Like I said, I'm gonna put a hurtin' on that girl. I'm gonna split her wide open. And you know what? She's gonna like it.'

They're coming to get you.

The thought came to Smoke Dugan unbidden. It interrupted every quiet moment, ruining even the best of times. The more he tried to ignore it, the more he sent it back to where it came from, the more forcefully it resurfaced the next time. It was paranoid. It was stupid. But there it was – some part of him was convinced that they had found him.

He sat in his favorite outdoor chair, trying and failing to

enjoy the early afternoon sun and the slight autumn chill in the air. The chair was a metal patio chair set before an ornate iron table in his backyard. The chair had three brothers, although rarely did anyone join him at the table.

Normally, he would have no problem enjoying the day.

The setting was perfect. It was fall and all around the neighborhood, the trees were turning. He wore a pair of baggy workpants and a bright blue Carraig Don wool sweater. He had just clipped, and now held in his gnarled hands a small Romeo y Julieta cigar. It came from the Dominican Republic, not Havana. In his present circumstances, Havana cigars were not easy to come by. That was all right. In the meantime, these Dominicans did a good job. He held the stogie to his nose and inhaled. It smelled sweet.

He had a bottle of Concha y Toro in front of him, a heart-healthy and tasty Cabernet Sauvignon from Chile. Here in Maine, the vagaries – some might call it the corruption – of the wine industry meant he couldn't get the New York Long Island wines he had once favored. So now he experimented with the stuff from abroad, and much of it was to his liking. He had a bit of the red wine in his sparkling glass, which itself was imported Waterford crystal. Lola always cringed when she saw him using the crystal – how could he drink his everyday wine from such an expensive glass?

'Quality,' he would say, 'makes it taste better.'

Nearby, Lorena Hidalgo was working in her garden. The whole backyard, except for the stone patio where Smoke now sat, the small grave plot with the tiny headstone that said,

'Butch – One Smart Dog', and the work shed in the very back, was Lorena's garden. It was some fantastic garden. Smoke sometimes sat back there and marveled at it. It had tomatoes, cucumbers, green beans, hot peppers and herbs. It had all the easy stuff. It also had carrots and cabbage and, sure enough, she was growing a few pumpkins as well.

'Hey, Lorena,' Smoke said. 'Do me a favor and don't go in the shed, OK? I'm working on something in there.'

Lorena looked up and made a face. 'You know I never go in there. That is your place.' She went back to her gardening.

Lorena was a miracle and a menace rolled into one. She was an older lady from Guatemala. They had met a few months after Smoke had moved into the basement apartment of this house. He was sitting in the backyard at this same table, which had come with the apartment, skimming through a text on generating wind power. The backyard was a mess, and although he had toyed with the idea of clearing it, he hadn't made any move yet. At first, he hadn't trusted his new surroundings and was ready to leave at a moment's notice. But after a while – for instance, after he buried that smart dog Butch – Smoke began to settle in. By the time Lorena called to him over the fence, he had decided to forget about the backyard and focus on making himself a little workshop in the old disused shed way at the back of the yard.

He closed his eyes and imagined the yard the day she had first shown up, in late March some three and a half years before. It was overgrown in places by high grasses and thick brush. In other places it was shallow mud from melting snow.

Snow that hadn't melted sat in clumps here and there. A ripped plastic bag from Shaw's supermarket hung like a flag at the top of a bramble. Three cases of empty Pabst Blue Ribbon bottles crouched by the door – reminders of the previous tenant. A rusty shovel and hoe leaned against the fence – the very tools Smoke had used to lay ol' Butch to rest.

It was cool that day, but Smoke was in his shirtsleeves.

'Excuse me, mister sir!' someone called.

Smoke had a cigar that day as well, and he seemed to remember it was a dollar cigar he had bought at a highway rest stop. A man running for his life wasn't always picky about cigars. His new name was James Dugan, and although he himself had created the name years before, he wasn't comfortable with the first name. It seemed too bland to him. James. Everybody was named James.

He looked up from his reading and across the fence at the woman who was about to change his name for him. She was a small woman, round, impossible to tell her age, with gray and black hair, and Mayan or mestizo features that seemed to have traveled through time to arrive at his fence. Indeed, she wore a kerchief on her head and from the neck up she could have just as easily lived in 1399 as 1999. But that's where the illusion ended. She also wore a big bubbly winter parka. It was bright red and had the words 'TRIPLE GOOSE DOWN' stenciled in white on one of the sleeves.

'Accuse me, mister smoke,' she said, and outside of signing documents or paying bills, the name James went out the window.

He raised an eyebrow at her. 'Mister smoke?'

She smiled. She was just tall enough to clear the fence. 'Mister smoke, yes. Can I help you?'

'Can you help me?'

'Yes. Of course I can.'

Talk about turning the tables. The woman's smile was infectious. 'How can you do that? Help me, I mean?'

'I can clean your house for you.'

He frowned. 'Oh, that's OK. I don't need any house cleaning, thanks. I just moved in, and I don't have very many things. In any case, I only have the basement.'

She went away, but the next day she was back.

'Mister smoke!'

'Yes,' Smoke Dugan said. 'I am Mister Smoke.'

'I am thinking last night. It is a terrible shame about this garden. It is such a wonderful place.'

Smoke looked around at the murky jungle that surrounded him.

'I can help you with that,' the lady went on. 'I propose a deal.'

'Oh, I'm not thinking about doing any gardening.'

'That is the beauty of it. You don't do any gardening. You don't pay me. I do the gardening. I pay you rent in the food I grow.'

'Well . . .' he said.

'You will eat only the freshest foods. No bad chemicals on them. I only grow them natural. Please? I have such a small garden at my home. This will be much better. It will be the wonder of the whole town.'

And so it began. Against his better judgement, Smoke had keys made for Lorena. He had to have keys made because there was no entrance to the yard. The only ways to get in were either by climbing the fence (quite out of the question for a woman 'of a certain age' who just about cleared five feet tall), or by coming through the basement apartment. Lorena came there early in the mornings, tiptoeing through the efficiency apartment, past a sleeping Smoke Dugan. In the afternoon she came back, stopping for some small talk with Smoke if he sat at the back table, or leaving him alone if he was in his work shed. Smoke would sit at his table, absorbed in the problem of this or that, and gradually his awareness would begin to include sounds. The sound of clippers cutting, or the grunts of an old woman as she pulled weeds, or the squeak of the ancient wheelbarrow she had arrived with one afternoon.

And the place took shape. She cleared half the big yard that first year, the half that ran the length of the concrete wall. There was cabbage that year, tomatoes and green beans. The cucumbers were a disappointment, and the peppers were so hot that Smoke couldn't put them on anything. But all in all, he had to agree with Lorena that the backyard was better for the garden.

Now the garden was an oasis. She had put in flagstones to mark the path to his patio, and then on to his workshop. There were giant sunflowers. There were all manner of vegetables and herbs. There were flowers. She kept the mosquitoes under control through a variety of natural means, and in any event, mosquitoes tended to stay away from Smoke's cigars. All summer long he would get some vegetables here and there when their time came. But every year at harvest time, she presented him with a bounty of food, her part of the bargain for his allowing this garden to happen.

'Smoke,' she said now, placing three giant cucumbers and a pile of green beans in front of him, next to a paper sack filled with ripening tomatoes. 'It is a beautiful, beautiful day, no?'

'It sure is,' he said.

'On a day like this, I feel like there is nothing in the whole world to worry about.'

He grunted at this, hoping his grunt sounded like agreement.

'Hmm?' Lorena Hidalgo said. 'You say something, Smoke?'

'It's a great day,' he said.

Open on the table was a large book of the drawings of Leonardo da Vinci – anatomical studies, studies on the nature of water, drawings of the Deluge, and of various machines and other half-completed projects. Smoke loved Leo, less for his art than for his mind and for how he had pushed the envelope of human knowledge. Leo and his zany, high-speed dissections of the fresh corpses of criminals – there was no way to preserve the dead in the 1500s – had bridged the gap between the medieval understanding of the human body and the modern. Smoke could picture Leo, up to his elbows in wet gore, carefully describing and illustrating the relationships between the organs, the skeleton, the nerves and the muscle systems. But anatomy was just part of it – the sheer range of topics that came under his investigation was amazing: zoology, botany, geology, optics, aerodynamics and hydrodynamics among others. Long before these things came into being, Leo had imagined and drawn the bicycle, the automobile, the submarine and the helicopter.

Today Smoke had hoped to study the plans for Leo's proposed bridge across the Gulf of Istanbul, connecting the Golden Horn and the Bosporus. The bridge plan was squelched by the engineers of the time, who cringed when they found out how big it was supposed to be. Somewhere, Leo had gotten the last laugh, however, because modern engineers determined that the bridge would have been completely sound, even with the materials and methods of the 1500s.

But Smoke couldn't focus on Leo. Instead, he kept thinking about simple booby-traps. Ones you could make easily and that were practically guaranteed to seriously maim, or even kill. Wasn't that funny? There was a long road between Smoke Dugan and Leonardo da Vinci.

The particular death trap Smoke was fixated on at this moment was a light-bulb trap. He had made one earlier in the day. So simple, a child could do it. He had taken a medical syringe and filled it with gasoline. Then he had injected the gasoline into the top of a hundred-watt incandescent bulb. It had taken some doing to poke a hole through the top of the bulb, but once he had, it was nothing to inject the gasoline. In fact he injected several syringes full.

Then he had screwed the bulb into the overhead light fixture of the small corrugated shed that crouched in the back of his yard. The shed served as his workshop. *Voilà!* The bulb hung naked, and was turned off and on by a small chain that hung down beside it. If someone were to pull that chain, the bulb would come on and the filament would ignite the gasoline. Instantly. The bulb would shatter, spraying liquid fire all over anyone standing below. Breathing the flames would roast a person's cilia, the tiny hairs in the esophagus that protect lungs from harmful pollutants. Should be enough to kill anybody.

Maybe the person would even catch fire.

Now that would be something.

Smoke didn't like heights.

That's how he thought of it: he didn't like heights. He didn't consider that he was afraid of heights. He rarely talked about it, and when he did, he didn't describe the breathlessness, the shaking, the heart palpitations and the fear – nay, terror – of dying that seemed to come over him when confronted with a high place. Even in the reaches of his own mind, he seldom admitted the sense of things spinning out of control that heights brought on, or the waves of unreality that seemed to wash over him.

He didn't like heights, that was all. He didn't like them a lot.

On the drive over to Lola's apartment, Smoke got caught on the Casco Bay Bridge. He watched with dismay as the red lights began to flash, the safety arms – so like the safety arms at railroad crossings – came down, and the traffic ahead of his little Toyota Tercel slowed to a stop. The span that crossed the high end of Portland harbor, where it met the Fore River, was a drawbridge. He put the car in park and sullenly stared ahead as the giant steel grates of the bridge began to inch toward the sky.

He was ten cars back from the front of the line. He was way up there, six and a half stories above the high-water mark. And it seemed like more than that.

Smoke knew how high he was because he had studied the schematics in the public library. He crossed the bridge damn near every day – he figured he ought to know something about it. It was a new bridge, opened only in late 1997, and had won awards for design and for aesthetics. It had replaced the old, deteriorating and outmoded Million Dollar Bridge that had stood there before it. It was a vast improvement over the old bridge, which had cleared the water line by a scant two and a half stories.

Portland was a busy oil port, one of the busiest on the East Coast. It was also low to the water. To make any bridge tall enough for the tankers would have meant an impossible angle shooting straight up in the air and straight back down again. So they made these goddamn drawbridges instead.

Which was fine with Smoke except when he got stuck with the bridge up. Driving across the bridge itself – he was OK with that. Although it was nearly a mile long, all that meant was about a minute, maybe two minutes on the span. And most of the bridge wasn't all that high. There were maybe two hundred yards at the very top of the bridge that were a good six or seven stories above the harbor. Even this section was OK if Smoke kept his eyes on the road or on the car in front of him, and thought of other things, and drove smoothly along until he reached the stoplight at the far end of the span. He made it across the bridge many times in just this manner.

But today he got caught at the draw, and to make matters worse, he got caught at the very top. As he sat behind the wheel he felt beads of sweat breaking out on his back. Then they broke out on his brow, and his hands began to tremble oh so slightly.

Look at you, you're ridiculous, he thought, a grown man acting like this. And not just any grown man, he realized. A criminal. A bank robber.

A murderer.

He was a man who had sunk his own boat – his Boston Whaler – in a terrible storm off the eastern end of Long Island, and lived, not to tell about it, but lived nonetheless. He had been through real dangers and had escaped death. Yet this simple act of sitting on a bridge put him in his place. Just ahead, the steel cage towered high above him, still rising. It filled his windshield.

So don't look out at the water, he told himself. Which was silly, of course. It was like telling somebody not to think of the color red. Then of course all they can think about is the color red. Red barns and red apples and red fire trucks and red stop signs and bright red cherries. Don't look out at that view – the one some people raved about, how it took in the vast blue sky, and the sweep of the city's skyline along the harbor, green islands and white sailboats in the distance.

Smoke looked.

He was high above the water. Way down below, he saw

the tanker pulling through the bridge and into port. The deck of the tanker was about to pass through the opening. If Smoke were to somehow fall from that height, he imagined, he would smash like a tomato against the solid decking of that tanker. It would be a sickening five-second fall, followed by a wet thud as the liquid insides of his body splashed in different directions, much to the chagrin of a few startled Chinese sailors.

They'd probably laugh about it later.

Remember the suicide, he thought. Remember the suicide. Three years before, just after Smoke had settled here, a distraught mother of five had walked out onto the bridge. She had been put off welfare some time before, and had ground out a slow struggle on a work program. But she hadn't cut the mustard. Work just wasn't for her, not at the age of thirty, not after twelve years, her entire adult life, on the dole. Her electricity had been cut off, so she and her children were now sitting in the dark with no money, no prospects and, most of all, no lights.

She walked out on that bridge, and without so much as a scream or a speech or a final telephone call, she climbed the very low fence at the top. It was little more than waist high. Smoke had noticed it several times. To his mind, it was so low a person could practically fall over it, never mind climb over.

As traffic screeched to a halt all around her and people came running to stop her, she leaped to what she thought was a certain death. A crowd of people gasped as she fell away and, seconds later, hit the water far below.

And lived.

Without so much as a broken bone, or even a sprained ankle.

In fact, a young carpenter on his way to work acted without thinking, and jumped off the bridge in a desperate bid to save her life. And lived. Without a scratch. When the Coast Guard fished the two of them out of the water, the young man told the waiting reporters that the jump was the most fun he had ever had.

None of which made sitting there any easier on Smoke. He knew it intellectually. A person could live after falling from that bridge. But his body knew different. A fall from that bridge and he would be fish bait. And curiously, he felt drawn, compelled even, to the edge of it. The worst of his dislike of heights was the madness that gripped him – it made him want to jump.

Smoke's grip had tightened around the wheel and he heard his breath coming in shallow gasps. He was mouth-breathing, never a good sign. He tried to loosen up and relax, but gripped the wheel harder than ever. A bead of sweat rolled down to the end of his nose. It wasn't even hot out. His heart skipped a beat. His stomach lurched and did a lazy barrel roll.

He saw himself hit the deck of that tanker again.

'Shit,' he said through clenched teeth. 'Shit on this.'

It had happened more than forty years earlier, back in Hell's Kitchen.

He could see those days like they were yesterday. The five-story walk-ups they all lived in – tenements, the newspapers used to call them. All along Ninth Avenue, clothes were hung out to dry on the fire escapes. There was a constant buzz of sound, day and night, punctuated by the odd shouts or screams.

The Irish, the Italians, all poor, all cramped together, and now the Puerto Ricans coming in. Smoke couldn't remember a time when there weren't Puerto Ricans, but his mother – all the grown-ups – talked like the spicks had never existed just a few years before.

Smoke was still Wally O'Malley then, and he was already running with the wrong crowd. In Hell's Kitchen there was no other crowd.

Born with a bum leg, there was a lot little O'Malley couldn't do. He couldn't play stickball. He couldn't fight – in a fist fight, his leg would give out from under him.

But there was one thing he could do . . .

It was a hot spring day. The boys stood out on the corner of Fifty-Third and Ninth, laughing and joking. O'Malley was with them. They leaned against the lamppost or the wall, cigarettes hanging from twelve-year-old mouths, wearing stovepipe jeans, sports shirts with collars turned up. The teacher would wring your neck for a turned-up collar in school, but there were no teachers on the street. They patted down their slicked-back hair, every strand in place. Very carefully, very precisely cool. Squinting and watching the cars cruise the Avenue. Talking, talking, talking that good bullshit.

'You seen the tits on Maggie Lefferts?'

'Maggie Lefferts? Shit.'

'You seen the ass on that spick girl in class? Jesus. Now *that's* a nice ass. What's her name?'

'Yeah, but whaddya gonna do? Fuck a spick girl? You know

49

what I'm saying? Who gives a shit what it looks like if you can't get at it?'

Artie Mulligan came walking up the block. O'Malley could see from half a block away that something was wrong. He was walking . . . wrong. Then he saw the blood streaming down Artie's face. Artie Mulligan – twelve years old and already tougher than leather, a born leader of men, shot dead in a tangle with FBI agents eleven years later – Artie had gotten a beat down.

He stood among them now, his eyes on fire.

'Motherfuckers.'

He leaned on a car and lit a smoke. His hands were shaking. His whole body was shaking. O'Malley noticed, not for the first time, how skinny Artie was, how small. Size didn't mean shit.

'Who did it, Artie?'

'Ace McCoy, Phil Evans, some of those.'

The boys looked at him and nobody said a thing. Ace McCoy was sixteen years old. His whole crew were fifteen, sixteen, just about to cross the threshold into manhood. In a year or two they would go to work on the docks, or join the Army, or get on board as street muscle in man-sized rackets – in a few years they'd be doing man-sized prison terms. If they weren't men yet, they were about to be.

Artie stared right at O'Malley. Wally O'Malley was high up in Artie's brain trust. More than that – O'Malley *was* Artie's brain trust.

'What can we do?'

O'Malley shrugged. Then he smiled. 'I have an idea.'

The older boys had a clubhouse they kept in a vacant lot between two buildings. The clubhouse was made of wooden pallets stolen from the docks on the river. The pallets were tied together with rope. The roof was a slab of sheet metal placed on top of the pallets, and the furniture was discarded rubber tires. The clubhouse slumped in the back of that vacant lot, hidden by the weeds, but all the neighborhood kids knew it was there. They also knew not to mess with it, or go there at all.

'I need gasoline,' O'Malley said. 'And motor oil.'

A pint of gas, a pint of motor oil, that was all. The boys could siphon. The boys could steal. They had it in an hour. Then they gathered some rags together and two empty Coke bottles. O'Malley showed them how to make firebombs, two to be exact, with the gas and oil mixed together, the gas-soaked rags stuffed into the bottles, a long piece of rag blocking the neck and poking out as the wick for each bomb.

'Why the oil?' Artie said.

O'Malley smiled. 'It makes the gas sticky.'

He wasn't there when they bombed the clubhouse. He couldn't run away if it came to that, so he waited at home for the news. He sat on the Murphy bed in the tiny railroad apartment, watching a cockroach move along the wall. From where he sat the pungent odor of burning tires came through the open window and reached his nose.

'Yeah,' he said. 'We showed 'em.'

Artie Mulligan would be pleased.

A few days later, O'Malley was on the roof of the building. Up here, there was light and space. Up here, he could escape from the dark and cramped apartment, from the narrow hallways and stairs, from the crush of people on the street. The roof was his sanctuary. He moved across the gravel and gazed out at the endless vista of clotheslines and TV antennas. Three buildings away, a one-minute walk stepping over air shafts, old Mr Principato stood waving a white flag on a long pole, putting a flock of pigeons through their paces.

O'Malley sat along the low wall and gazed down at Forty-Ninth Street, five stories below. The street was a hive of activity, the people moving to and fro, and he watched it all as if he were stationed on some faraway planet.

A shadow moved behind him.

He turned and four teenaged boys stood there. They were slim and tall and well-muscled in their tight white T-shirts. True to form, one of the boys had a pack of cigarettes rolled up in his sleeve, showing off one bulging and tattooed bicep. Greaseballs. They loomed over him like dinosaurs above a scrap of hamburger. He became aware of how small he was – and not small like Artie. Small small. Small in his mind. Small in his presence. Small in his very being, somehow. He became conscious most of all of his right leg and of how useless it was.

He knew a few of their names. Ace McCoy was right out in front with the cigarettes and the tattoo. O'Malley had seen Ace and his crew around, and what was bad about the situation was they had evidently seen him as well.

'Hey there, Gimp,' Ace said.

'Hi,' O'Malley said.

'Hi, that's rich,' Ace said. He put a big fake smile on and waved like an idiot. 'Hi!'

The other three laughed — a merciless sort of laugh. A tall blond one said, 'You know why we're here, right?'

O'Malley tried to give them nothing, but already he could feel his body shaking. Already he could feel his heart pumping in his chest. 'N-no.'

'Nuh-nuh-no. I knew you were a gimp. I didn't know you were also a stutter.'

'I'm n-n-not.'

All of them laughed now.

Ace squatted down to Smoke's level where he sat on the wall. 'Our clubhouse got burned up the other day, Mr Gimp. You wouldn't happen to know anything about that, would you? You wouldn't know any smart guys who like to make firebombs, right?'

Smoke shook his head, moved to say something, if only he could get his lips unstuck one from the other.

'Now wait a minute, before you say anything you need to know something about us. What you need to know is, we like stand-up guys who tell the truth. Guys who lie, we don't like them. Bad things happen to guys who lie.'

O'Malley found his voice. 'I don't know anything about it.' Once it was out there, he found he had surprised himself with the statement. It came out strong and firm, like he meant it. 'The bombs, I mean. I don't know anything about that at all.'

'You don't, huh?'

'Nope.'

'Then how did you know there was more than one bomb?'

'You just said it yourself. You said it was bombs.'

'Did I say that, boys?'

'I didn't hear you say bombs, Ace. I heard you say bomb.'

'No, you didn't,' O'Malley said. 'You said bombs.'

Ace stood up. 'OK, if that's what you say, I guess we gotta deal with that. You say I said bombs. You say you don't know about it.'

'That's exactly right.'

Ace took a long drag on his cigarette, regarded the short butt remaining, then flicked it into O'Malley's face.

'Fuckin' liar.'

Three of them grabbed him. He tried to kick and punch them, but they were too strong. Within a couple of seconds, they had him under control.

Ace gestured at the open air on the other side of the wall, the five-story drop to the pavement below.

'Liars take the dive. OK, boys, let's see what he says to that.'

O'Malley fought them, but it did no good. They lifted him into the air and turned him upside down. Then they held him out over the edge by the legs. O'Malley's arms dangled down helplessly. His hair dangled down. His shirt came untucked and fell down almost to his nipples. He felt the pressure of the blood rushing to his head. He saw the activity down below, all of it oblivious to his plight up here.

It went on for a long time. They were saying things to him now, and he could hear their voices, but the sounds had melted together into a slow-motion, unintelligible mush. All there was out there was that upside-down view of the street, so far away. He felt their hands slipping on his legs. They grabbed him harder and higher, the split second as they abandoned their old grip for a new one stretching out sickeningly. They laughed because they had almost dropped him. The world spun.

He felt his bladder go.

The piss went with gravity as all things will do. Instead of running down his legs, it soaked through the fabric of his pants, it cascaded between his belt and his waist, and streamed down his torso and chest. Droplets made the journey past his shirt and rolled down his neck to his chin. His tasted urine on his lips. And still more came. He had never pissed so much in his life.

'Look! He's pissing on his own face!'

He heard that much clearly.

He didn't care that he was pissing on his own face. He didn't care if he ended up shitting on his own face, if that was even possible. What he cared about was these kids were going to drop him, either because they would lose their grip on him, or because they were sadistic bastards and they didn't care if they killed him. They were going to drop him and he was going to take an incredible dive to the pavement, one that would seem long but would be too short. One that would end with him splattered on concrete like an overripe gourd.

'I didn't do it!' he screamed. 'I didn't do it!'

The car behind him honked its horn, really leaning on it. Smoke looked up and noticed for the first time that the draw-bridge was down and he was free to go. He'd been free to go for a while, by the looks of things. Traffic was streaming by him on the left. To the right, that drop to the water still beckoned. The driver behind him honked again.

Glad as ever to be getting down from there, Smoke put the car in gear and cruised toward the end of the bridge.

'Are you going to tell him?' said Pamela Gray.

Pamela was Lola's roommate of two years – and in many ways Lola's opposite. She was pretty in an understated way, and dressed conservatively compared to Lola's sometimes sexy, sometimes outrageous sense of style. She had grown up in a quiet New Hampshire suburb with a typical nuclear family. She was bookish – she devoured romance novels, for instance. At the same time, she had an edgy side to her – Lola had picked up one or two of Pamela's romance novels. The books she read were the steamy kind – adventure tales of pirates on the high seas, of wild untamed women and dark men with powerful thighs and raging, uncircumsized members. Bodice-rippers, she sometimes called them, historical rape novels.

Pamela was shy about men, OK, but there was more to her than met the eye. When you got her going, she had a tongue that was plenty sharp. And she was not afraid to speak her mind.

'Am I going to tell what to whom?' Lola said.

Lola and Pamela were cooking dinner. As they talked, they bustled about the kitchen. Tonight was smoked salmon with cream cheese, lightly sauteed Digby scallops and shrimps, and garden salad made from Lorena's bounty. Pamela had made a chocolate mousse for dessert. They had already opened up the first bottle of wine. Smoke was coming, and the two women sometimes cooked together for him as though he belonged to both of them. They would share him, his conversation, his sense of humor, the warm smell of his cigar, right up until the time came for Smoke and Lola to go to bed.

'Are you going to tell Smoke about what happened?'

'Why? So I can upset him? So he can decide to be chivalrous and go off looking for them and maybe get himself killed? There's nothing anybody can do, and besides, no harm done. I fought them off. I won.'

Pamela didn't smile. 'But what about the next one? Will she win? What if it was me? Would I have won?'

Lola was silent.

'I'll have to think about it.'

'I think you should tell Smoke and then you should go to the police.'

Lola began to think she should have gone to Smoke's for dinner. If Pamela was going to be so adamant about this, what slip of her tongue might be loosed during conversation after a few glasses of wine?

But then, going to Smoke's would be too strange. Lola rarely went to Smoke's apartment at all, and never went there to stay the night. She liked many things about Smoke. She liked that he worked with his hands, and that his hands were the thick, rough and strong hands of a working man. She liked the smell of his evening cigar, especially when they were on the deck together, looking out over the water, and the sweet smoke would pass for a second before the breeze lifted it and took it away on the air. She liked his smile, and the fact that he chose to do his work for children. She liked that he was so smart. It seemed he could make anything.

But she didn't like his apartment. He lived in a dingy basement efficiency with bad light. He kept books and papers piled up on the kitchen table at all times. He kept six cats, who had the run of the place, with all the unpleasantness that suggested. Their litter boxes were in the bathroom, and Smoke wasn't the most fastidious man on earth about cleaning the boxes. Smoke often brought greasy and dirty pieces of machinery into the apartment from his shed out in the garden, and left these either on the kitchen table or on the floor. Finally, the place smelled like smoke. It wasn't the wisp of cigar smoke blowing on the wind, but the built-up smell of dozens of cigars trapped in the apartment during the three-year period he had lived there.

No, sir. Lola did not want to spend the night in such a place. She had done it a few times, waking up each time with a cat nestled on her head and the smell of cigars in her clothes. They had come to an agreement. If Smoke wanted to spend the night with her, then he had to spend it at her place.

They lived on the top floor of a three-story brick building at the top of Munjoy Hill. It was a large two-bedroom apartment. The back deck gave out on a view across the backyard to the Eastern Promenade, and a splendid view of the harbor and sailboats out there.

The apartment below them was empty. When the previous tenants had moved out, the landlord had decided to renovate, and so workmen were there during the day on weekdays, and in the evenings no one was down there. On the very bottom was an old man who had come to Portland to play with the Portland Symphony Orchestra. Pamela had a crush on him.

Which brought Lola to the crux of the Pamela conundrum – she was attractive, smart, and well-read. She kept herself fit by jogging and working out with weights, and made good money as a librarian at the Portland Public Library. Yet in two years together, Lola hadn't seen Pamela go out on a single date with a man.

Oh, Pamela.

'I just think,' she would say, 'you know, you've got an old man and it seems to be working out, so maybe I should go for one myself.'

'Pamela,' Lola said, 'Smoke is almost sixty. OK, he's a lot older than I am. But Mr Lindstrom must be seventy-five at least. That's old. I mean, who can say if he even gets it up anymore, or even wants to?'

'Is that all that matters?'

Lola shook her head. 'Obviously, that's not all that matters. But it's one of the things that matters, at least to me. Men are good for some things. Other things, they're not so good for. That happens to be one of the things they are good for.'

Pamela smiled. 'Oh, I bet he does get it up. He's fit for his age. He's a musician. He's vital and creative. I bet he does everything, wants everything. He wants to experience every-thing right up to that last moment. He wants to be fully alive.'

Lola held her tongue. She wasn't sure, but she guessed the library might not be the greatest place to meet men.

Not that it mattered. Lola thought a woman could go about her business and have a full life without a man in it. She had spent plenty of time without a man in her own life. But for Pamela, men seemed an obsession. She wanted to be with a man, but then seemed to repel them as though they were invaders. If any young attractive man approached her, she went stone cold. Then she developed elaborate fantasies about people like Mr Lindstrom, a man she had hardly ever spoken to. She didn't know anything about him except he was a musician and played for the Symphony. Sometimes the two of them heard the strains coming from his violin as they entered the building. Lindstrom was practically a hermit, yet Pamela had given him this rich life as a vital genius musician. Who really knew what he was doing in there?

Lola, on the other hand, had never suffered a lack of male attention. In fact, she had always received too much of it. She knew she was sexually attractive from the time she was twelve. She was long and leggy. She had wild curly hair and deep brown eyes. She was high-yellow black, with a taste of American Indian blood in her that gave her an exotic look. The family legend had it that her great-great-grandfather was a Sioux who had fought at Little Big Horn alongside Crazy Horse. Lola often felt she had the blood of that long-lost Indian brave singing in her soul. It was like she could feel him there, approving when she took the bold and courageous road in life, quietly disapproving when she was not brave.

What would be the brave thing to do here? To go to the police? To tell Smoke?

She thought warmly of Smoke – her old man. He had a way about him, a quiet confidence, that made her want to be with him. He was handsome, for sure, and the best lover she had ever had. She remembered the first day she had seen him at the school where she had started working as a teacher's assistant. All the women there were enthralled with him. He came to the school because he made toys for the special children, especially the ones who came from poor families. They were wonderful toys with lights and sounds and big colorful buttons. The children would laugh and laugh, delighted each time they pressed a button. And Smoke made the toys for free – the story went that he was a retired engineer and inventor who had made a lot of money and who was now giving of himself. His eyes had a glint to them as he played with the children, a sparkle that made her think of a slim and wiry Santa Claus. When her eyes met his, it was there between them the very first time.

'Young lady,' he said, 'if we've met before, and I don't recall the exact day and time, then I must be growing old indeed.'

But he was no fighter. He had a bum leg and could barely walk without his cane. And there was nothing in his personality that was violent or even aggressive. In fact, despite his strong hands, and the forearms of a sailor, Smoke was about the gentlest man she had ever met.

No, she wouldn't tell Smoke about what had happened. She didn't want to drag him into some kind of showdown he wasn't built for. If there was any more to what had happened, she could and would handle it herself.

They were just about done putting the dinner together. Pamela poured a little more wine in both their glasses.

'So what are you going to do?' she said.

'I'm going to wait and see,' Lola said. 'OK?'

Lola stared at Pamela, waiting for an answer. At last, Pamela raised her hands as if she were under arrest. 'OK. I'm not going to say anything.'

Just then, a key turned in the lock, the door to the apartment opened, and the object of their attention walked in. Smoke Dugan appeared in the flesh, a dapper grin on his face, his cane in one hand, a paper bag with a loaf of long French bread cradled in the other.

Again Lola realized how happy she was to have him. Some would say that Lola could have any man she wanted – and that was probably true, as far as it went. She could have any man for a night or two, any muscle-bound young man who wanted her for only one thing. Smoke wanted that thing too. And that was great. But he wanted more, and he wanted to give more. The past year, she reflected, had been the fullest, and the happiest year of her life.

'Ladies,' he said. 'Fantazize no more. The man of your dreams has arrived.'

Night in the French Quarter.

The crowds swirled down the narrow streets. Above them, the lacy ironwork of the Spanish-style balconies were like tropical gardens teeming with ivy, begonias, ferns and young women flashing their breasts to passers-by. Shouts and laughter, and strings of Mardi Gras beads came from the streets below. Camera flashbulbs popped.

Disneyland for drunks, Cruz had heard it called.

He leaned against an ornate light post on Decatur Street, watching the people move along. He wore khaki pants and a large colorful Hawaiian shirt that hung down below his waistband. He slowly sipped from a plastic bottle of lime seltzer.

A young guy in gym shorts and a T-shirt peeled off from a group of college kids, boys and girls, all-Americans. The guy wore a baseball cap backwards. His shirt – pulled tight to a chest inflated by many hours in the gym – said 'DON'T MESS WITH TEXAS'. He had a big plastic tumbler of a fruity drink. He came toward Cruz, stumbling just a bit and grinning. He was four or five inches taller than Cruz, and probably outweighed him by seventy pounds. It looked like a lifetime of mild success at sports had convinced the kid he was immortal. He reminded Cruz of one of those kids he had seen on TV, the ones that threw the cheerleaders in the air at college basketball games.

'Hey, Scarface,' the kid said. 'How ya doing?'

He stuck his hand out. Cruz ignored it.

'The girls over there? They think you're cute. They want you to come out with us.'

Cruz glanced over at the gaggle of college kids across the street. The group looked over at him. A couple of the girls laughed. He turned back to the kid.

'I'm busy.'

The kid poked Cruz's shoulder.

'Didn't you hear me? They think you're cute. The way you got your hair all greased up. It's cute.' He poked Cruz again. It was more of a push the second time.

'I want you to do something,' Cruz said. He hadn't moved from the post.

'Yeah? What's that?' the kid smirked.

'I want you to look right here, into my eyes, and listen to what I tell you. OK? Look right here.'

The kid did so, and already the wild light was dying from his own eyes. In an instant, he saw something there, something Cruz well knew. It was the reason Cruz rarely looked directly into the eyes of the straight world. It did him no good to go around scaring grocery cashiers and rent-a-car clerks.

'You're a good kid, right? Grew up in a nice house? Gonna have a nice life, sell stocks or some shit. Right?'

The kid nodded. He looked down at his sneakers.

'No, don't look away. I want you to look right here.'

With some effort, the kid lifted his gaze again. Cruz spoke quietly, his voice raised just above a whisper – but loud enough for the kid to hear.

'Good. That's good. Now I'm only gonna tell you this once, but I think once will be enough. I said I was busy, and I meant it. You stay here any longer and I'm gonna cut you up and feed you to my dogs. You understand, right?'

The kid looked down again, nodded.

'OK. Now get lost.'

An hour passed.

It was after midnight. The streets were still jammed. Cruz

had hardly moved since the kid had left. No one had spoken to him since then. He watched the door of the hotel across the street, trying not to grow annoyed.

He had called upstairs a few minutes ago. Carmine was still up there in his room. When Carmine had answered, Cruz had affected an accent, looking for Pablo, and Carmine told him to go fuck himself, he had the wrong number. Rather, he had slurred it. Carmine was drunk again.

Carmine Giobbi. Carmine the Nose.

Carmine had money problems. He had borrowed so much that he had no way to pay it back. It was OK when he owed it somewhere else. But once you started burning your own people for money, the game was over. Carmine couldn't even pay the juice anymore. Half a mil, the dossier said he owed.

Half a mil? Cruz suspected it was more than that.

Carmine had already been gone a month with no contact. That was way too long.

Now it looked like he had no plans of coming back. It looked like he was going to stay down here and drink. Cruz had watched him two full nights so far, and by the end of them, Carmine had been so drunk the whores he picked up could hardly keep him standing. Carmine was a big heavy man. He had a goddamn big nose too.

They couldn't have Carmine down here, drinking every night with strangers. The time had come to send him home.

Here came the big lug now. He stepped out onto the street from the hotel and started down the block. No surprise, he looked just like an enforcer on vacation. White silk shirt, top three buttons open, showing his hairy chest and his gold crucifix, hanging loose at the bottom as if to cover a piece in his waistband. There was no piece, at least, not the night before. Cruz had crept close enough to Carmine the night before to thoroughly examine the area at the bottom of his shirt. Carmine might be loaded with weapons in his hotel room, but he went out at night unarmed. Khaki pants and alligator shoes rounded out Carmine's clothing ensemble.

His gold watch sparkled. Of course it was a Rolex. Cruz had gotten an up-close look at it in a bar the night before. It was a wonder nobody had rolled Carmine for it yet, for the watch and that fat billfold he kept whipping out.

What was wrong with this guy?

He was drunk already. Sure. He had probably been knocking them back in his room since whatever time he woke up. Sitting on the balcony, drinking, watching the day pass into evening, watching the evening pass into night, the crowds gathering, the streets glowing with excitement.

Cruz pushed himself away from the light post and started walking.

Up ahead, Carmine weaved through the crowded streets. His big shoulders bumped a couple of people out of his way. Carmine was a handful, all right.

Cruz kept a safe distance. He watched as the Nose entered an open-air bar, grabbed a woman's ass, then got in a shoving match with the woman's boyfriend. He nearly shoved the guy through the wall. The bouncers, three of them, walked him out of there, consoling him with pats on the back. Big guys were all the same, and they liked to see those pushy, big-guy traits in each other. A guy Cruz's size pulled that kind of shit in that bar? Those bouncers would take him outside and tap dance on his skull.

Carmine stumbled on. He went into another bar and grabbed another woman's ass. This ass grabbing, this was something new.

After an hour, Cruz had had enough.

The streets were still crowded, but the tone had changed. People were very drunk now. Women screamed for no reason at all. A man leaned over and puked into the gutter. A small crowd gathered around a young man who had fallen down and lay sprawled on the concrete, unable to stand. Carmine staggered along through it all like Frankenstein's monster. Then he stopped, looked around and turned down an alley.

Shrewd Carmine, making sure the coast was clear.

Cruz surveyed the scene from across the street. No cops anywhere. Lots of people milling about, going this way and that. A darkened alley between buildings. And Carmine down there, probably taking a piss.

Cruz crossed the street and walked toward the mouth of the alley. As he did so, he took two thin leather gloves out, one from each of his front pockets, and slid them onto his hands, like a doctor preparing for surgery.

Down the alley, just twenty yards down, big Carmine leaned up against the wall, bracing himself with a hairy arm. The other hand had worked his whanger out of his pants. A steady stream emanated from it, soaking the wall and splashing back on Carmine's pants and shoes.

Jesus, the guy was a mess.

'Carmine.'

'Yeah, just a minute here. Gotta water the flowers.' Carmine's lower lip hung down.

Cruz worked the stunted black Glock pocket pistol – the .40 caliber M-27 – from the back of his pants. Cruz always demanded the M-27. It was smaller than the standard Glock, it was light, it was concealable, even with a longer, threaded barrel attached so it could take a silencer. Nine rounds was more than enough for Cruz, .40 cal was excellent stopping power, and the gun itself always worked – rain, heat, cold, snow, it didn't matter. The Glock worked.

He quickly attached the silencer, a Gemtech SOS-40, a nice one. They always gave him nice toys on these jobs, anything he wanted. And he was a creature of habit – what had worked in the past would work in the future. He held the gun so his back was blocking it from the sight of any pedestrians on the street. He glanced out there. Nobody was looking. He stepped closer to his quarry.

'You know me, Carmine?'

Carmine looked up, his eyes half-closed and bloodshot. He squinted at Cruz.

'No.'

Cruz approached and put an arm around Carmine's massive shoulders. Cruz felt nothing out of the ordinary. His heart wasn't beating hard. He wasn't sweating more than the humid southern night warranted. If anything, he felt a pang of mild embarrassment, what with Carmine's Italian sausage hanging there.

'No, you're right. You don't know me. We've never met before. But I know you.'

Carmine peered down at his fancy alligator shoes, wet now with urine.

'I think I'm gonna puke.'

'Carmine. I know you, you understand? It's important you understand this.'

Carmine looked at Cruz again. Something like a dull light ignited behind his eyes. 'They sent you? From New York?'

'That's right.'

The big man nodded. 'OK.'

'You get it?' Cruz said.

'Yeah. I get it.'

Cruz clapped him on the back. 'Good man. You got anything you wanna say?'

'Yeah. Tell 'em to go fuck themself.'

Cruz brought the Glock around with his left hand and placed the silenced muzzle against Carmine's meaty chest. Carmine looked down at the gun. Cruz looked at it. All it took was a few ounces of pressure and he would send Carmine off to the next world.

The seconds passed.

And for some reason, the finger didn't pull the trigger.

Shit, it was happening again.

Then the gravity of the situation penetrated Carmine's pickled brain. His eyes opened wide and he came awake.

'Hey, get that fucking thing away from me.'

His reflexes, now activated, were fast. He grabbed the gun with both hands. He forced Cruz to point it heavenward, pushed Cruz back against the brickwork, then came up with a savage knee to Cruz's gut.

Cruz felt his wind go out of him in a long hiss. He felt the gun yanked out of his hand. He sank, knees to the hard pavement, trying to catch his breath. He ripped the buttons of his shirt away and reached inside.

Carmine tottered over him, huge, towering. Gun in one giant hand.

He brought it down to point at Cruz. Cruz stared down the black maw, death just seconds away. He felt nothing, thought nothing.

'Hey, dickhead,' the Nose said.

Cruz pulled the surgical tape away from his chest. He grabbed the four-inch Buck Woodsman knife he kept strapped there.

'Tell 'em I ain't that easy, see?'

Cruz lunged, just as Carmine fired. He stabbed, fast and crazy, in and out, four times, five times.

The gun made a near silent 'phut, phut, phut'.

A breeze went past Cruz's head. Bullets whined off the brick wall and ricocheted down the alley.

Cruz looked up at Carmine, who stared down with something like surprise. Cruz had plunged the knife up to its handle. It was buried in Carmine's lower abdomen. Cruz renewed his grip. Then he ripped upward, all the way to Carmine's ribcage.

Carmine's face went slack again. Blood flowed from his mouth.

Gently, Cruz took the gun from Carmine's hand.

He stood and put the gun to the big man's heart. Again. Again he hesitated. Carmine was weaving. His eyes had gone blank. Blood flowed from him. Either it was the booze or his own brute strength and stupidity that kept him standing.

Well, he was going to die anyway.

Cruz pulled the trigger. He fired three times into Carmine's heart, then lowered him to the ground.

Back out on the street, gloves off. The crowds were still there. People staggered to and fro. A woman with a big floppy sun hat fell down, laughing. Cruz began to stagger just a little, as if he himself were drunk. His flowery shirt was splashed with some of Carmine's blood. Worse, Carmine's smell was on him. The sharp scent of booze mingled with the coppery stench of blood.

It made him sick. It made him shake.

Cruz walked around the block. Knots of people laughed, stumbled, screamed. More beads flew through the air. Cruz turned a street corner, quickly wiped the knife handle for any possible prints and dropped the knife down a sewer hole. He would break down the gun and get rid of it later – a piece here, a piece there, the further apart the better.

He came past the alley again. From the street, there seemed to be nothing down there. Just a big drunk sleeping off a bender.

A beam of cold moonlight stabbed into the room.

Smoke sat up in bed, sipping his last glass of wine. It had

been a lovely evening, sitting on the deck with two lovely ladies, eating a fine meal, watching the ships pass as the sun set behind the building. They had chatted and laughed with Pamela until it was full dark and too cold to sit outside anymore. Then they had made an assembly line and washed all the dishes.

Some coffee, a little more wine and laughter in the living room, then Lola and he had come in here for a long, slow bout of lovemaking. They began, but the spark wasn't there. His hands had felt like lead.

It started, it stopped. It fizzled out.

'You seem distant,' he said after they gave it up for good.

'Not distant,' she said. 'Just thoughtful.'

'OK. Thoughtful.'

Now, Lola's warm and sleeping form pushed up against his. Her arm was around his waist. Across the room, the digital clock read 2.35. There was no sound anywhere. That was the thing about this city — when night came, the sidewalks rolled up and it was almost as if no one lived there.

Her voice came, quiet and thick with sleep. 'Smoke?'

'Yeah, babe.'

'Do you love me?'

'You know I do.'

'That's good, Smoke. Real good.'

A few moments passed, and her breathing deepened and became rhythmic. She was gone again and he was here, awake and on the case. Her protector.

He was going to have to tell her something soon. He just didn't know what that something would be.

3

Cruz slumped in the back of the black Mercedes S-500, sunk deep into the plush leather, his eyes closed behind reflector sunglasses. The earphones of his Sony Discman hung slightly askew, just enough that he could hear everything being said up front, but not so much as to arouse suspicion. At the same time, he could listen to his music. The compact disc was *Dance Party Hits of the 70s*, the soundtrack of his youth.

The song was 'Le Freak', by something called Chic.

He remembered it. He saw himself at a Manhattan dance club, brooding, holding up the bar, watching the young girls flaunt themselves out on the dance floor as the lights strobed crazily, streaks of technicolor electricity flying through the air. Again, he felt the rage, the yearning and the frustration. Nearly thirty years had passed since those days, and in all that time he had only managed to slap a few thin coats of whitewash over the real Cruz. His personality was like a slice of linoleum pasted over a dark abyss – if you dropped through, there was no bottom.

He had done this kind of work since the age of eighteen. That year, he had been cut loose from the youth home with two hundred dollars, plus cab fare to his aunt's house in Corona, Queens, and an appointment to see a job counselor out there a week later. They had let him go with a kiss on the cheek and a kick in the ass.

He never made it to Queens.

His aunt didn't want him, and why should she? He had lived with her at the age of ten, then again at fourteen. He was bad news, the product of her sister the drug addict's wasted life. His face carried a deep knife scar from one of her sister's many boyfriends, a maniac who one night decided to cut the little boy's eyes out. Luckily, the maniac had been too drunk to see what he was doing or hold onto the boy – Cruz – for long, who ran screaming out of the squalid apartment. But the scar on his face was only an emblem of the deeper scars he carried. Cruz was trouble, and he knew it. No, his aunt would not have him, and on some level, he didn't blame her. She wasn't yet thirty years old herself, struggling with three young kids of her own. Cruz was enough to sink them all.

She had called him the day before he was set to leave the home. He stood at the payphone in the concrete stairwell. A couple of younger kids were talking and laughing down at the other end of the narrow hall.

He looked at them. Gradually, they sensed his stare. Then they left.

'Chuco, do me a favor, ah?' his aunt said.

'Yeah,' he said, already knowing what was coming.

'Don't come over here. I got enough to worry about with the kids and the rent and all the rest. You know? I like you, Chuco. You was good when you was a kid. But now . . . you know? It'll be bad having you here. I don't got the room. I don't want the cops coming here. You understand, right?'

'Yeah. I do.'

'You'll do good, Chuco. You'll figure it out.'

'Yeah.'

'Just don't come here. You come here, I can't let you in. I'll call the cops myself, OK? I'll tell 'em you stole my money.'

Cruz hung up.

He rode the cab into Manhattan, stopped at a check-cashing place, cashed the two hundred, stuffed most of it in his sock, and checked into a twenty-dollar-a-week room at a Single Room Occupancy hotel on the west side, not far from the river. He paid for a week up front. Then he sat upstairs and cried for an hour. Cried for everything. He gave himself one hour to get the cry in, no more. He even timed it on the Timex watch one of the teachers at the youth home had given him. At the end of an hour, he stopped and looked around. The room was about twenty feet long and fifteen feet wide. There was a narrow bed and a sink. There was a cheap wooden dresser with a sticky blotter pasted on top of it. There was a closet with a couple of coat hangers. The old white paint was peeling crazily, showing a nasty green behind it – the walls, the ceiling, everywhere. A window looked out on to the fire escape. The street was three stories below. The bathroom was down the hall.

He'd never been here before, but instinctively he knew the game. There would be predators in the bathroom. They'd be looking for an easy mark on the shitter, an easy mark in the shower. People would break into his room while he wasn't home, looking for money. Junkies would drop dead from ODs. He'd be lucky if some junkie didn't burn the place down in the middle of the night with a cigarette or a hot plate left on. The management wouldn't do shit about any of it.

Anyway, it was a start.

He went out. If there was an answer to his problems, he wasn't going to find it staring at the four walls of his room. The answer was out there, on the streets. He resolved that he would find that answer, whether that meant he had to go to prison, or whether he died with his blood running in the gutter. The thought appealed to him. He would live, and thrive, and make it big, or he would die. No compromise.

He went to Times Square.

It was 1976. The Bicentennial. Two hundred years of flag waving and good times. *Rocky*. *Jaws*. And in a lighter vein, *18 & Horny* and *Guess Who's Coming*. Just outside the Theatre District, the Broadway of *A Chorus Line* and *The Wiz*, Times Square lay spread like the blighted whore she was. The lights dazzled Cruz. The pimps and hookers and drug dealers hanging out with beer cans in paper bags, the streams of runaway kids, the junkies, the scumbags, the pickpockets, the johns, the freaks who wanted to fuck children – a circle of lost souls. The blood banks, the liquor stores, the X-rated movie houses, the massage parlors, the greasy-spoon diners with deals going down in every booth – there was barely a legitimate business in the whole neighborhood. Times Square was an open sewer. In 1976, for someone with the right kind of eyes, it was also a glittering promise.

Cruz loved it.

He went to a live peep show and watched a big black guy tool a tiny oriental girl on a table. He bought a dollar in booth tokens, and every time the screen went down on this little act, he pumped in another token.

Then he went and bought himself two hot dogs, fries and a Coke at Nedick's. He stayed there a long time, watching the action out on the street. The sex, the freedom, the crazy sparkling madness of the place – it was a revelation.

'Hey, kid,' a fat little bald man said one night a week later. 'I seen you hanging around here a lot. Wanna make some money?'

'What do I have to do?'

'You look like a sharp kid. Ever hurt anybody before?'

Cruz smiled. 'Sure.'

Now, a much older man, he smiled again at the memory.

He opened his eyes and glanced around. He liked this Mercedes. It was a comfortable car, damn near the top of the line, and probably three years old. Cruz hated new cars. The new car smell made him sick to his stomach. This car was perfect. It didn't smell like anything and had that kind of smooth ride where the bumps in the road were like a rumor you had heard years ago. You couldn't hear the outside at all.

Quiet as a tomb.

The car was cruising the highways somewhere in New England. It didn't matter where right now. They had passed Hartford a little while back. The kids up front were supposed to wake him up when they entered Maine. From behind his shades, he noticed the color on the trees along the highway — reds, yellows, orange.

Cruz was tired. He had flown in from New Orleans on about two hours' sleep. At La Guardia, he bought a small tin of Vivarin caffeine pills, crushed two up, and snorted them for breakfast. The limo — a big Lincoln Town Car — snatched him at the airport and whisked him straight into the city. The driver — an old Polack or Russian — gave him his next gun, his next Glock. It came in a handsome padded traveling case that Cruz threw into a garbage can before they even left the airport. Cruz didn't care about presentation — he planned to carry the gun, loaded, ready to pop.

The driver also gave him the dossier for this job, sealed for Cruz's eyes only. The same dossier was now at Cruz's feet. He read it while the limo took him across the Triborough Bridge into Manhattan, then down the FDR Drive. He would read it again before they got to Portland. Gave him everything he needed to know about this guy Smoke Dugan.

The meeting in Manhattan had been short and sweet. It was at a coffee shop on Fifth Avenue in Greenwich Village, just up from the park. They moved around all the time, staying one step ahead of the bugs. Big Vito and Mr C.

Mr C never spoke. Just in case the bugs were already in place. After a lifetime on the outside, he was not going to die in prison. He sat there wrapped in a long wool coat, his thin hair slicked back, his face old and lined and unshaven, his eyes bright, sharp and aware. At all times, he held an unlit Havana in his liver-spotted and palsied hand. The world had changed and now cigars were bad for you. Mr C would regard that cigar at the end of his fingers and sigh. Sometimes he nodded at something that was said. Sometimes he managed a ghost of a smile.

'You gonna eat?' Big Vito said. In person, his voice sounded like gravel pouring from the back of a dump truck. His nose was wide and flat. It had been broken so many times, it looked like a lump of mashed potatoes. Above it, his eyes were like twin lasers. His eyebrows were gray. His hair was gray shot through with white.

Fantastic Four, getting old himself. Cruz imagined those big stone hands choking the life out of someone. The legend was that's how Big Vito used to do it to you. Strangle you with his bare hands.

'I don't know. How's the food?'

'Would we be here if it was bad? Come on, Cruz. You gotta eat. Keep up your strength.' He looked to Mr C for confirmation. Mr C nodded his agreement.

'All right, I'll eat.'

Vito waved over the skirt.

Cruz looked at the menu. He spoke in a quiet voice. 'Three eggs, scrambled. With Swiss cheese. Sausage. Corned beef hash. Black coffee.'

'That's what you're gonna eat?'

'What'd you think, a fruit cup?'

'Nah, it's just, you know. They got healthier items. Look. Egg whites. Turkey bacon. Anything you want.'

Cruz put the menu down. 'I think I'll stick with what I said.'

The girl went away.

'We read the paper today,' Vito went on without preamble. 'You know, got the box scores. Checked everything out.'

'Yeah? What do you think?'

'Good. We're happy the home team won.'

Mr C nodded, licked his lips, gave his cigar a long look.

'Very pleased,' Vito said.

'Good,' Cruz said. 'I want everybody to be happy.'

'Everybody is.'

There was a pause. 'You looked at what we left you? The driver gave it to you?'

'Yeah. Not sure I get it, but . . .'

'What's to get? It's in plain English, right?'

'Oh, yeah, that's not it. It just seems like, maybe a little lightweight. Retrieval isn't my thing. I'm usually in – how do you want to call it? – disposal.'

'It ain't lightweight. You let us worry about the thinking end of it. You just make it happen.' Vito wrote something on a napkin and passed it across to Cruz: '63 and Lex. Black Mercedes. Massachusetts plates.'

'I'll make it happen,' Cruz said.

The girl was coming with the food. The two men got up to leave. 'Enjoy your breakfast.'

'You guys ain't gonna stay?'

'You know, we got business. Never ends.'

Cruz looked at the breakfast. It made his stomach turn. Mr C eyed him closely.

'Hey, Cruz,' Vito said. 'How ya feeling?'

'All right.'

'You know, because you look like shit. We worry about you. Maybe you need some time away, like down in the islands. Maybe when things slow down a little.'

'Yeah,' Cruz said. 'That sounds good.' He dug into the food.

Now, in the Mercedes, he watched the two young men up front with some interest.

The dossier at his feet included information about both these two kids. The driver was a big muscle guy, wore a leather cap and black sunglasses. The other one was skinny and missing three fingers on his right hand. Jesus, who were they hiring nowadays? Cruz was wary of the whole thing. He had worked on his own for years, and now they gave him this babysitting job, with these kids to drive him. He didn't like it.

The one in the passenger seat was Ray 'Fingers' Pachonka. He had lost those fingers playing with explosives. Lucky to be alive after a fuck-up like that.

The driver was Roland Moss. Late twentysomething.

Former bouncer, former legbreaker. Barely two years in the murder business, and he had been in on a dozen hits.

'Roland is strong as an ox. He likes to hurt people. Likes to make them talk.' That's what the dossier said.

Cruz watched them carefully, mostly because he didn't trust them. Cruz had learned early on that it was best not to trust anybody, especially young men who believed themselves to be on the rise. He had learned this from himself.

He listened in to their conversation for a moment.

'So they sent us to do this jigaboo one time,' the skinny one, Fingers, said. He spoke rapid fire, like a machine gun, or the heartbeat of a rabbit. Bippity, bippity, bippity. 'The guy had ripped somebody off. I don't remember the details. Different job, same bullshit. Right?'

'Yeah,' said the big one, Roland Moss. The guy could be a pro wrestler, Cruz thought. His broad shoulders extended past the edges of his bucket seat. His neck was a trunk line, his head sitting perched on top like a pomegranate. The muscles in his neck stood out and flexed like cables.

'They sent us to Gary, fucking Indiana, just outside Chicago.' Fingers paused, seemingly for effect. 'I mean, we fucking drove out there. Me and Sticks. You know Sticks? Little guy, smokes a lot. Pissed off, always wants to cut somebody. Somebody doesn't signal in the car ahead of him, he wants to cut the guy. You know him, right?'

Moss nodded. He spoke slowly, like syrup pouring from a bottle. 'Yeah, I know him. Did a couple jobs with him. Saw him cut a man's eyes out once.' He sounded like he was giving it a taste of the South. The dossier said he was from New Jersey.

Fingers nodded. 'Yeah, that's him. Sticks. Crazy as a fucking loon. So we drive out there, me and him. And Gary, Indiana is like nothing you ever seen before. Everybody is gone, except some jigs that couldn't make it in Shy-town. All the buildings are empty. Or just plain gone. A wasteland. So we find the jig, drive him around for a while. He's all acting cool, like his life is worth something. Like he thinks we drove all this way just to, I don't know, shoot the shit or something. He has this gym bag with him. He has a fucking Tec-9 in there.'

'Piece of shit,' Moss drawled.

'All right, a Tec-9. It's a piece of shit. But, I mean, this jig has it in the gym bag, and he has a forty-round clip in it, and then he has this custom twelve dozen round drum magazine, you should've seen the fucking thing. Like something out of the movies. He says he has the thing modified for full auto, and this big drum to attach to it. Can you imagine this guy running around, spraying bullets everywhere? No wonder all these little kids get shot in these jig neighborhoods. You got these guys running around, think they're fucking Rambo. Am I right?'

'I never saw a gun like that,' Moss said.

'You wouldn't see one. Only a crazy person would have one. So anyway, we bring him to this abandoned building, right? We take him upstairs. Now he's not as cool, he's starting to get the message. We bust him up a little. Then, you know Sticks, he starts to cut the guy up. It's all right, but it's a lot of blood and shit now. The jig is crying and all this, half his face coming off. Sticks cut the jig's lips off, you know what I mean? The guy's teeth are like *out to here*.'

Fingers held his hand out about a foot in front of his face. He laughed, an uncertain sound. 'I don't know about Sticks, man. He should've been a butcher or some shit. He gives me the fucking creeps, to be honest.'

'And the guy never pulled the gun?' Moss said.

'Yeah. He never pulled it. He never got anywhere near it. A hundred and forty-four rounds. A lot of good it did him, right? So finally, I take over from Sticks and I'm just like, let's do this shit and get out of here. So I take the jig and I tell him, you know, that's it, man. You're done. He's grateful by then. He just wants the whole thing over with. They got these floor-to-ceiling windows and they're all busted out. So I send him out the window. We're about six stories up, right? By now, it's full on dark. And I send him down into a vacant lot down there. I mean, the whole city's a vacant lot. The guy didn't scream or anything. He just sailed down there in total silence.

'So here's my point. We go downstairs to the street, and it's like, let's check it out, let's make sure this guy is dead. We go around back and here's the jig. He's laying there and the whole top of his head is broken off. You know what I mean? I mean, he hit the pavement and the top of his head broke off — right above the eyes. He was like a stewpot with the lid off. His eyes were open and I thought for a second he was looking right at me — I thought he was gonna say something. And his brain had come out and was sitting there on the ground. So I'm just standing there looking at this brain, and the jig with his eyes open is laying there like he's awake. And the brain – it was like a bowl of Jello. You know, when you turn the Jello upside down and it comes out all in one piece? It was like that. Like a toy. It was fucking perfect.

'So what does Sticks say? He's like, let's take the brain.'

'He wants to take the brain,' Moss said. He laughed, a short, deep bark. 'That sounds about right for Sticks.'

Fingers nodded. 'Yeah, he wants the brain. I'm like, you got to be fucking kidding me. Is this a joke? He wants to take it for a souvenir. Thinks he'll put it in his refrigerator or maybe pickle it. And he starts getting adamant about it. I'm like, man, I am not driving twelve fucking hours to New York with a brain in the car. You want the brain, call a cab.'

Cruz had had enough of their conversation.

He slipped the music back on his ears and picked the dossier off the floor. He started to read about Smoke Dugan again, but then changed his mind. Instead, he gazed out the window and watched the passing trees.

Pamela jogged the Back Cove trail.

It was three and a half miles of dirt track around the Cove. On a cool fall day like today, the trail was packed with joggers, walkers – some with baby strollers – and bicyclists. It was high tide and the Cove shimmered blue with the skyline of the city in the distance. Out on the water, two wind surfers raced back and forth.

Pamela was an avid jogger. She jogged here often, stealing glances at the men who passed. The Back Cove trail was a veritable smorgasbord of fit people out getting their exercise. She noticed the women too. The women in their tight Spandex shorts and halter tops. The sexy women with whom she could never compete.

She in her sweat pants and layered T-shirts.

God, what was wrong with her? As long as she could remember, she had always been this way. Shy, retiring, tongue-tied with people she did not know. But she was good-looking. At least she thought she was, and Lola always told her she was. But she was twenty-nine years old, and for more than three years she had been alone. She thought of her last boyfriend – Thomas – bookish, thin, with glasses. He was smart and had an offbeat, self-deprecating sense of humor. He was a student at the University of Maine Law School, and when he graduated, he asked her to marry him.

She said no.

Things were good with Thomas, and she thought long and hard about becoming his wife. But in the end, he wasn't her type. At least, he wasn't the type she imagined was hers. And she was not the quiet suburban wife of Thomas the corporate lawyer. She recalled the last time they had made love, right before he left town for Providence, Rhode Island. He had cried, and so had she, and they had stopped halfway through. It made her think of the old joke – if I'd known the last time was really going to be *the last time* . . .

Why could she never seem to find a man?

SMOKED

She was bookish, certainly, just like Thomas. From the earliest age, she had been more interested in reading books and watching movies than in dealing with people. Life seemed so boring sometimes, and the lives lived in books, well, they seemed so exciting. She had grown up in Newmarket, New Hampshire, a town where the big excitement was the freight trains passing through town — so close to her family's backyard that Pamela often thought of jumping aboard as the open cars passed — and summers on the nearby Seacoast beaches. In the evenings, she and her brother would often play Scrabble or Monopoly with her mom and dad. It was a normal, stable life. And for Pamela, from the time she was a little girl, the real excitement — and maybe the only deep enjoyment — came from escaping into the stories. The *Nancy Drew* mysteries. *Encyclopedia Brown*. A little later, *The Lord of the Rings*. And of course, the movies: *Star Wars*, *Indiana Jones*, and *The Neverending Story*.

She envied Lola. She loved her like a sister, but there was also the sting of envy. Could you imagine? Lola had grown up in a Chicago housing project — a slum where drug deals went down on street corners, where gunfire sounded at night, where men murdered each other in the hallways. Just last week, two men tried to rape her, she beat them both at once, and now she acted like it had never happened. Pamela could never do that, would never want something similar to happen to her, and yet, there was something about it that enticed her.

She remembered how, as a girl, she would imagine herself as a pirate. Not as a woman who hung around with pirates,

87

but as an actual pirate herself, sailing the high seas, attacking and plundering other ships, making people walk the plank.

She would give anything to live a life of swashbuckling adventure. She should have become a cop, or a spy, or an ambulance driver – not a librarian who half the time felt afraid to meet the eyes of library patrons.

Face it, her life was boring. It was an endless string of days, each fading into the next, her youth passing away fruitlessly. The lives of the library patrons were boring too. She watched them. She saw the emptiness in their eyes, the longing for escape, the unfulfilled wishing for something, anything, to happen. Even the homeless people – she had once held a romantic notion that the life of a homeless person might be exciting. But they came into the library by the dozens during the cold weather. They slumped in chairs and dozed. They leafed through magazines for hours on end. Some of them simply sat and stared into space. The homeless people led boring lives.

Adventure. That's what she longed for, what she had always longed for. To be in danger. To survive on the edge. And to take a lover, a dark and handsome stranger – yes, just like in the books – a desperate man with rippling muscles, yes, and long hair and a fire in his belly. A savage, passionate man. Yes.

She finished her run at the parking lot. She was sweaty, out of breath, and felt exhilarated as always. It was a nice day, and it was good to get these negative thoughts out of her system. She consoled herself as she stretched on the grass near her peppy little car, a Volkswagen Golf.

Someday, she thought, it will happen. I will be like Lola. And I'll lead a life of adventure just like the one she has led.

Empty hand, empty mind.

Lola sat cross-legged on a wool blanket. She had placed the blanket on the gently sloping hill of the city's Eastern Promenade. Eastern Prom was the extremity of the peninsula that made up downtown Portland. A long avenue of stately Victorian mansions giving way to early twentieth-century tenement buildings on one side of the street, and a grassy park and pedestrian walkway overlooking the islands of Casco Bay on the other side, the Prom was just around the corner from her apartment. Indeed, Lola could see this same bay from her back deck, if she chose. As on any Sunday in the fall, the bay was dotted with white sails driven by the wind — there was a sailboat rental concession on the waterfront not a half-mile away from where she sat.

Lola came here to meditate.

Empty hand was karate. She learned to fight with no weapon but herself — and she believed now, for the first time, that she needed no other. Empty mind was Zen, a path that had been married to karate almost since the beginning. It was a term one of her teachers had given her. The karate practitioner — the *karateka* — sought to train herself to develop a clear conscience, an empty mind. This would enable her to face the world truthfully. An empty mind was tranquil — because to see the truth meant no fear of death, no fear of pain, no fear of anything. An empty mind lived in the present, the essential time, the only time that was available. The past was irretrievably lost and the future was forever unattainable. There was no time but now.

She sat, eyes closed, facing the water. Her hands were upturned and resting lightly, one on each folded knee. She wore jeans and a light jacket. Her feet were bare, her sandals kicked off in front of her. The cold breeze blew across her, each gust with the bite of the coming winter embedded deep within it. She took deep breaths, each one coming from the belly, and with each breath she tried – she tried too hard – to let go. It was no use. The memories flooded back. They always did.

She thought of the time when the bad thing happened.

She was living with her grandmother, an old woman who had seen more than her share of heartbreak. They lived together in a two-bedroom unit at the Robert Taylor Houses, at that time the largest public housing complex in the world. Lola hated it there. She hated the grim towers that dominated the landscape, and she hated the fenced-in outdoor walkway that made their apartment seem like some kind of motel room. She hated the drug dealers who plied their trade, bottle by bottle, in broad daylight. She hated the police who circled like vultures. She hated the pimps and the crack whores and the crack heads. She hated the couples who fucked – there was no other word for it – in the stairwells, and the muggers and the molesters who lurked in the shadows, and the thieves and the murderers and the corpses that sometimes turned up on the sidewalks in the very early mornings.

She hated them all.

She kept her hate inside herself, clutched it tightly to her like she clutched her schoolbooks. She didn't show her hate to them. Instead, she went about her business and dreamed of the day when she would be away from here. She knew from the television that there was another life outside of this one, a life where people weren't afraid all the time, where you could go outside after dark, where it was OK to show weakness, where people smiled and said 'thank you' and 'please'.

But for now, this was where they lived, and since Lola's mother had died, there was nowhere else for her to go. And Lola's relationship with her grandmother was great. They talked and laughed together easily, as though there weren't fifty years between them. Her grandmother had even scraped the money together to send Lola for modern dance instruction. By sixteen, it was clear that Lola wasn't going to Broadway, but she still enjoyed it and it kept her fit.

But dancing for fun ended that early spring afternoon.

Months before, she had discovered a short cut, a path that cut across a vacant lot about a quarter of a mile down from where the project started. She would walk home from the bus station, and spy that path cut through the weeds, and think that it would probably save her five minutes' walking time. At first, she wouldn't walk that path. But then one day, she got up the guts to do it. It was a weedy jungle back there, ripped clothes hanging from the bushes, broken glass littering the packed-down earth. Her heart was beating something terrible, but she made it through.

Afterward, she realized that if she stuck to the path, there was only a moment, perhaps thirty seconds of walking, perhaps a full minute, where she lost sight of both the street behind her and the one ahead of her. Surely nothing could happen during those short seconds. She started taking the path regularly, and nothing happened except she reached home five minutes earlier.

But there was a boy named Kendrick who said he liked her and kept nagging her when she walked the streets. She didn't like him. He had been tall, a big dumb boy, always playing basketball in junior high school and early on in high school. He was gonna go pro one day, right? He was still tall, but now he was selling drugs and he didn't go to school anymore. With his vacant stare, and his bloodshot eyes, he looked like he was high most of the time.

Kendrick was a loser.

He was never going to get out of the neighborhood and, by that age, Lola realized that the only hope a person had was to get out of the neighborhood. In any event, she could tell the look in his eyes. He only wanted her for sex. She wanted no part of that – no part of a boy who thought of himself as a desperado, and would soon go the same way as the rest of the desperadoes. Jail. Addiction. Death. One of those, and maybe all three.

But Kendrick the loser was insistent.

'Oh, you're gonna be with me,' he told her with a smile. 'You think you're too good for everybody. I tell you, little sister, you ain't gonna be uppity like that for long.'

On the fateful day, she debated with herself as she always did. Should I take the short cut? Should I go the long way around? Once again, she took the short cut. As soon as she reached that point where neither street was visible, a voice spoke behind her.

'Little Miss Uppity Nigger. Girl, why you always cutting through this back way? You looking for somebody back in here?'

There was laughter. She turned.

Maybe twenty feet behind her was Kendrick, and he wasn't alone. He was accompanied by two other boys, Tyrone and Abel. Lola knew all three of them. Tyrone and Abel were a year behind her at school. They were following Kendrick down the sewer. They grinned at her.

The facts came to her in one second flat – pierced her awareness like a bullet to the brain. The boys were here for a reason, and it was all business. They had been watching her, and they knew she took this short cut.

She dropped her books, turned and ran.

Just ahead on the path were two more boys. They were brothers. Michael and Ishmael. Coming this way. For a moment she thought she was saved. Two people on the path. Witnesses. Then she saw the grins – the boys hadn't come to rescue her. They had looped around the block on Kendrick's orders.

They went for her. She tried to bolt past them with her big legs and her speed. But then their strong young hands were on her. One hand grabbed her by the hair and yanked her head backwards.

'Bitch, where you think you going?'

Bitch. The word stung like a slap. It was a strong word, a hateful word, and she felt paralyzed against its force.

They took her deeper into the lot, behind some bushes. There was an old mattress back there, and some old and tattered pornographic magazines. She could hear the traffic out on Dan Ryan Freeway, but she didn't cry out. Then they stuffed a dirty sweat sock in her mouth and she couldn't cry out.

They did their dirty business, one at a time, while the others looked on and critiqued the action. She didn't remember much except the sharp and terrible pain in the beginning, and then the sun in her eyes as it sank behind the buildings, bringing an end to another gray day in Chicago. That and the sound of their whispering voices as they talked about her as if she weren't human, as if, except for her body, she wasn't even there.

'Damn. I didn't know she was a virgin.'

'Nigger, how you gonna know something like that?'

'Learn something new every day.'

'She ain't one no more.'

They giggled like the children they had been only recently.

Then she was alone. No, there was one person left. It was Kendrick, more than six feet tall, towering over her as she lay on the mattress. He spit on her, and the saliva landed on her breasts and stomach.

'You ain't so uppity now. Am I right?'

Then he too was gone.

It was almost dark. There were sounds of rustling in the weeds: the rats that lived at the edge of human society. Thousands of them were all around the Robert Taylor houses, maybe millions of them, feeding off the garbage of more than twenty thousand people. She didn't want to stay there a moment longer. She didn't want to see the rats, of course. But at night, back in that horrible lot, there were worse things than rats. Anybody might come along. Somebody worse than those boys, even.

Her clothes were all around her, on the mattress and on the ground. They at least had the decency to leave her something to wear home. She got dressed, went back to the trail, gathered up her books, and went on home.

Smoke lay in bed, enjoying the bright play of light, and the cool breeze coming through the open window. Both Lola and Pamela were out somewhere.

Sunday was the day Smoke most loved to sleep in. It had little or nothing to do with it being a day of rest after a week of labor. Smoke's schedule was his own. No, it was a sense of nostalgia, of romance.

And football.

It was already noon. In an hour, the Patriots would come on TV. Smoke had adopted them since he had been here in Maine. He would spend the day with them, sipping his wine, and perhaps enjoying a cigar on the deck during half-time. He might watch the second game, he might not — but for three hours, the New England Patriots would command his complete attention.

He lay there and relished this thought.

Then he remembered sitting in the darkened living room.

It was a sunken living room in another life, when he wasn't yet Smoke. It was the kind of living room in the kind of house that middle-class housewives looked at and salivated over in glossy magazines. Black leather furniture converged in the center of the room. At the far end, there was a fireplace that was as clean as a hospital floor – split logs were piled inside it, but it probably hadn't been lit in years. Floor-to-ceiling windows looked out across the patio and the sloping lawn to the Long Island Sound. To the left of the patio, blue and red lights beamed up from the floor of the in-ground swimming pool. Behind the sofa Smoke sat on, there was a huge canvas – a giant orange dot on a white background.

Modern art. The fat man was a collector.

Presently the fat man came out of the nearby bedroom wrapped in a thick terry-cloth robe. He wore slippers and walked through the shadows of the living room, headed toward the kitchen. Must've heard something in his sleep, Smoke mused. Decided to eat something. Smoke noted that his hair was greased, even now.

Smoke reached inside his jacket and fingered the Taser pistol strapped there. Before he came he had popped eight new Energizer AA batteries in it. It was ready to fry.

The fat man waddled along like he wasn't going to stop.

'Roselli,' Smoke said.

The fat man stopped, did a double take, looked again at

Smoke sitting there on his couch, legs folded, cane in hand.

Give Roselli credit. He was half asleep, no reason to expect anyone, no way anyone could get in, the whole house alarmed, yet he didn't look frightened or even all that surprised. The fat fuck never lost his composure — if he had, Smoke had never seen it. Roselli was like all the rest. When it came right down to it, it was hard to scare these guys. The only emotion you could get from them was anger.

'O'Malley? What the fuck are you doing in my living room? At . . .' he looked at the clock on the opposite wall, 'three-thirty in the morning?'

'I came to talk. Why don't you sit down?' Smoke gestured at one of the leather chairs.

'Sit down, shit. How the fuck did you get in here?'

Smoke offered the chair again.

Something in Smoke's eyes registered with Roselli. The fat man walked over and eased his weight down into the chair. He pulled the robe tight around his belly. He ran a beefy hand through his hair, making sure it was slicked back. He stared at Smoke across the short distance between them. He squinted.

'O'Malley? I wanna say something to you right now. I known you a good long time. You were always a good kid. This ain't right, you being in my house like this. People eat shit for this kind of thing. Less than this. What if my wife was here? My kids? It don't look right.'

'Your wife and kids live in Florida, Roselli.'

Roselli stabbed the air with a finger. His face turned red. 'Don't fuck with me, O'Malley. You know that's not my point. You want me to come over there and wring your neck? Is that why you're here? You're in my fucking house, you fuck. And you got exactly three seconds to explain what you're doing here.'

Smoke took a deep breath. 'Flight 1311,' he said. 'New York to Helsinki with ninety-seven people on board.'

Roselli stopped. He shrugged. His hands floated upward in the air, palms toward the ceiling. They lingered there, and a long moment passed.

'Well, I'll tell you what,' Roselli said. 'You wanna talk about that, I got no problem. But now ain't the time. And this ain't the place. You got a work-related problem, you need to call me and set up a meet. Go home, O'Malley. Call Angela on Monday, she'll set you up with a time. Then we can talk.'

Smoke didn't move. 'In 1978, I torched twenty-one buildings up in the Bronx. Remember? That was 1978 alone. We did buildings starting in '74, and I did my last one in '80. It was a brisk business there for a while. You know how many people died in all those buildings I did? You know how many?'

Roselli waved his meaty hand. 'O'Malley,' he said, 'I'm telling you. You go on out the way you came in. If you disappear right now, I'm gonna forget this ever happened. You call Angela on Monday, and we'll set up a time and place. We'll talk all you want.'

'None,' Smoke said. 'That's how many. We spread the word, cleared everybody out, and nobody died. We even cleared the bums and the junkies out of the real shitholes, didn't we? Even gave them a chance to live, right?'

Roselli cleared his throat. 'That's right, we did.'

Smoke reached inside his jacket again. 'So what changed? What changed so much that you're willing to blow planes out of the sky, with women and children and goddamn fucking exchange school students on board? What happened, you fat piece of shit?'

Roselli was silent for a time.

'Times changed, O'Malley. And money changes things. You know that. It was the Russians. You know how those mother-fuckers are. There was a guy on that plane, a Moscow guy on his way home. They couldn't get near him on the ground, so . . . Listen, O'Malley. Somebody tells you the biggest score out there is you bring down a plane. They're gonna pay you, maybe you owe them a favor and this is a way to get out of it. Maybe there's even more to it than that. I don't give a shit who you are. You do it.'

'You told me it was a bank job. You told me you needed some C4, a timer, and a blasting cap, something to detonate with. Did I have the stuff? Could I put it together? You said you had some guys who needed to bring down a cinderblock wall.'

Roselli stood from his chair. He sighed, and then managed a small smile. He seemed to like the smile, so he tried on a bigger one. It worked for him. He showed his teeth.

'I didn't think you'd do it if you knew what it was for.'

Despite the grin, his eyes flashed malice. They said he would never forget this intrusion, that as far as he was concerned, O'Malley had signed his own death warrant.

Smoke stood, rising on his cane. 'I wouldn't have.'

They faced each other. Abruptly, Roselli's grin disappeared. 'Is that what you came to tell me? That you're better than I am? Got more principles? If so, it could've waited. It can wait for ever, actually.' He pursed his lips. 'You want more money? That I'll consider. Call the office, like I said.'

Roselli turned to go.

'Now get the fuck out.'

Smoke pulled the Taser out of his jacket.

'Roselli, one thing before I leave.'

The fat man spun around. His robe flapped open again, exposing the hairy expanse of his chest. 'Yeah?'

Smoke stepped forward and let Roselli have it. The twin probes of the Taser flew out and caught Roselli just below the neck. Fifty thousand volts of electricity coursed into Roselli's body. His nervous system overwhelmed, Roselli jittered and jived, the rolls of fat on his neck jiggling, his teeth clicking together. Five seconds was a long time. He danced a bit more then went down, all three hundred pounds dropping like a lead weight. His eyes rolled back in his head. Drool formed at the corners of his mouth.

Smoke looked down at him.

'Roselli?'

The fat man's eyes fluttered, then opened. After a moment, they focused on Smoke again. When Roselli spoke, his voice was a rasp. 'You know Ice Pick Tony? Maybe you never had the pleasure. Well, now you're gonna. I give you my word. Tony's gonna take you to his place in Queens, hang you upside down in the shower, and bleed you like the fucking pig that you are.'

The probes spent, Smoke used the Taser's touch-stun feature to give him another jolt.

Roselli blanked out. He woke up one more time before the end.

'You ain't shit, O'Malley. You never were more than hired help. Ask anybody.'

Then he rode the juice again.

Smoke was three miles away when the place blew. He parked on a hillside, looking back west toward the city. Over the far horizon, he could see the glow from millions of lights against the darkened sky. New York City, where the lights never went out.

Much closer, a fireball went up suddenly, literally a ball of fire, on a straight vertical line like a rocket ship headed for orbit. A long rolling boom came across the land a few seconds later. An after-burst went up, a smaller one, and then another boom.

Moments of silence passed, orange and red flames flickering in the night. It was so quiet that Smoke could hear them licking and crackling across the miles.

Then the sirens began.

Smoke got back in the car and started it up. Roselli was dead. Soon, O'Malley would join him, going down with his boat in heavy seas off Orient Point.

And somewhere out there, a new life was waiting for James Dugan.

The children were all the same.

Big Roland Moss was going to fuck with him now, test him a little.

'Hey, Cruz,' he said from behind the wheel. 'How come me and Fingers here can't stay in your hotel?'

His eyes met Cruz's in the rearview mirror. A razor-sharp, predator confidence showed there. Cruz knew from that look that Moss was one of those guys who never felt fear. Unlike Cruz, Moss had been born without the capacity. No fear. No empathy. Moss was the ice-cold center of his own barren universe. He had probably tortured kittens as a little boy.

'You know, it makes us feel a little left out. You get to live it up in some swank place, and we get the Holiday Inn. It don't seem right somehow.'

His comments elicited an embarrassed giggle from Fingers.

Cruz glanced out the window. The sleek Mercedes nosed its way through Portland's end-of-season throngs. The narrow streets of the Old Port – the newly glittering waterfront district – teemed with well-heeled tourists peeking in shop windows or laughing as they stumbled out of the public houses.

'Hey, Cruz, I'm talking to you, son.'

Cruz regarded Moss again. Thick neck. Wide brow.

'You ever kill a man by mistake?' Cruz said. He spoke just above a whisper. They could hear him all right up front.

Moss smirked. 'Me? I don't make mistakes.'

Cruz smiled. 'I do. Sometimes I get a big guy around me, kind of a pushy type, you know? And I end up misreading his intentions. Maybe he startles me. Better he goes down than I do, right? Can't be too careful these days. So they put me somewhere by myself. It cuts down on the mistakes I make.'

Moss pulled the car into the cobblestone circular driveway of the Portland Arms Hotel. A man in top hat and tails, white gloves, the whole silly get-up, hovered by the door. He eyed the car, ready to pounce.

'I guess I'll need to remember that,' Moss said.

Cruz stepped out, dossier in hand. He hadn't been out of the car in nearly six hours. The first thing he noticed was the temperature change – it was colder here than in New York. And New Orleans? Forget about it. He had only just left there this morning, but already it seemed like weeks ago.

Hopefully, they'd be out of here in two days or less. Maybe even by tomorrow night. Otherwise, Cruz was going to have to buy some new clothes.

'Call me if you get anywhere,' he said to Moss and Fingers. He waved off the doorman, and carried his own bag up the steps. The Mercedes pulled out just as he entered the hotel.

Inside, the lobby was all carpeting and polished chrome. The help tiptoed around and spoke in hushed tones. Ageing yuppies in lime-green cardigan sweaters and sunflower-yellow pullovers lounged in overstuffed chairs by the fire. Their cheeks were rosy with the brisk chill of the Old Port, not to mention the flames of the fireplace, and the sherry and port wine in their glasses.

Check-in was effortless and Cruz went straight to his suite.

Once in his suite, Cruz double-locked the door. He was on the third floor, so there was no chance of them coming in that way. The only way in was through that thick, solid door. That pleased him. The kids weren't staying in the same hotel as Cruz for one reason: Cruz had no intention of letting his guard down so some young stud could move up the ladder by putting him in a box.

Cruz poured himself a seltzer from the mini-bar and took off his light jacket. Jesus. It had been a long day. He went in the bathroom and was pleasantly surprised by the two-person Jacuzzi tub built right into the floor. He took the Glock out of his waistband, and laid it on the sink. He removed the rest of his clothes, checked the windows and doors again, then went out to his kit bag. He brought the bag into the bathroom. He locked the bathroom door. He turned on the jets of the tub, as well as the underwater lights. He brought the bathroom phone within reach of the tub. He killed the overhead lights, moved the Glock to the edge of the tub, then settled into the hot bubbling water.

He picked up the gun and chambered a round. He grunted to himself and laid the gun, ready to fire, along the tub basin just above his head and well within his reach. Nine shots if trouble found him here relaxing with his pants down.

He went back into his kit bag. Inside was a six-inch straight razor. He opened the blade, gazed at it for a moment, then brought it into the tub and under the water. He placed it on the bottom next to him.

A gun, and if that somehow failed, a blade. Anybody who tried him while he was in the tub was in for a nasty surprise.

Now he could relax. Facing the locked door, he reached back and put his hands behind him, forming a cradle for his head. The Jacuzzi jets pounded water against his back and his legs, working out on the stiff muscles in his body. He closed his eyes.

Fucking kids.

They weren't going to get him. Not like he had gotten Oskar.

How many had Cruz killed?

He wasn't sure. He had done quite a few in his time. Beginning with those first messy jobs in and around Times Square — the blitzkrieg knife attacks, the shoot-'em-ups in welfare hotels, the guy he had gut-shot six times but who had still managed to run screaming into the street — Cruz had moved onward and upward.

And being apprenticed to Oskar? Well, that was part of what had made Cruz a pro. Oskar was the very definition of the professional — smooth, calm, utterly devastating. Oskar's was the first death that rattled Cruz, and made him wonder about this life. All these years later, and he was still wondering.

They were doing a job out in Short Hills, New Jersey and they both knew that the time of Cruz's apprenticeship was coming to an end. For one, Oskar had asked for, and received, permission to retire. For another, Cruz had become a polished and effective killer in their four years of working together. He had always been ruthless. But now he had verve and style. Now he could kill without emotion. He could appear, disappear, and cover his tracks with the best.

Oskar was sixty-three years old. Cruz was twenty-four. Cruz had never counted his own kills. Oskar had his own kills memorized. One hundred and ninety-nine. They had two to do in New Jersey. Oskar had suggested they each take one, and then he would finish with an even two hundred. Cruz thought that a fine idea.

They cruised along a narrow road of estate homes set back in the woods. They were driving a nearly new 1980 Alfa-Romeo Spider. It was small, fireapple red, with a black convertible roof and classic sports car looks. Although it was a sunny day, they had the roof up. The car had been a gift to a girlfriend by one of the men in the house, Mr Eli Sharon. Eli was an Israeli who had come to the United States to enlarge his fortunes. He was fifty-eight years old and ran penny stock scams. His business partner was an American, forty-four-year-old Howard Brennan.

The girlfriend was young and beautiful. She was from India. That morning, she had left the house in Short Hills to go shopping. In a parking lot, she had been abducted and taken by van to a house in Brooklyn. The transfer had gone without a hitch. When the girl, shaken and tearful but not hurt, had climbed into the van, Cruz and Oskar had climbed out with her car keys.

The way Cruz understood it, she would not be harmed. Indeed, one of Cruz's jobs today was to retrieve her passport from the top drawer of her armoire. Very soon, she would book a Tower Air flight from JFK to Delhi. She would settle in back home, maybe find a nice boyfriend her own age. That was the plan, and when they explained it to her, she agreed that it was time for a change.

They pulled up to the gate of the sprawling mansion. It was a wrought-iron gate with electric cattle wire strung along the top, which would issue a non-lethal charge to anyone who tried to climb it. It was a low-level type of security installed by a man who either felt he had few dangerous enemies, or who was confident in his ability to deal with them.

The Alfa-Romeo had an electronic device on the dashboard that sent a signal to an electronic lock box on the gate. Once the lock box recognized the device on the dashboard, the gate slid slowly open. There was no guard around of any kind.

So much for security.

Cruz was driving. It was a nice car, a little tight with Oskar's big shoulders there next to him, but nice none the less. He was thinking about buying one. Just from driving it around that day.

'What do you think of this car?' he said.

Oskar sat upright and alert in the passenger seat. He wore thick, round glasses. As always, he wore a suit and tie – today, a suit of light summer linen. His face was lined like that of an old, old man. Oskar wore black gloves, and had a MAC-10 submachine gun cradled on his knees. It had a huge Sionics specialty silencer installed at the end of the barrel. Oskar used to laugh about the MAC. People would get a load of it and all the fight would go out of them. They'd become like jellyfish, ready to do anything and everything he said. Oskar carried the MAC for show — he did his actual kills with the Ruger he kept strapped inside his jacket.

Cruz smiled. Oskar was a man ready for action. Even on his last assignment. Cruz respected that and always would.

'This car?' Oskar mused. 'It'll break down all the time.'

'How do you figure that?'

'It's Italian. That's a bad sign. Italians don't make good cars. You want a good car, then spend the extra money and get a German car. The Germans, God help us, do everything well.'

'Even if you say so yourself.'

Oskar shrugged. 'I don't say it because my parents were from Germany. I say it because it's true.' He laughed, and Cruz laughed with him.

They drove up along the tree-lined and curving avenue that passed for a driveway. If all was correct, the servants had been given the day off today. All was correct, Cruz knew. All was always correct.

He drove the car up the driveway, which ended at a circle in front of the grand entrance to the house. Next to, and attached to the house, was a four-car garage. Eli was rich — there must have been good money in manipulating stock prices — but he was no Rockefeller. Cruz felt a stab of pity for him.

An Italian sports car, a nice-looking exotic girlfriend, a four-car garage and a big house in Short Hills. The guy probably saw himself as a new-age sultan. Untouchable.

He was about to find out how wrong he was.

Their garage door was the second from the left. The smoked windows of the car, combined with the glare of the sun, would probably thwart anyone from inside the house seeing into the car and alarming themselves. The device on the dashboard opened the garage door as well, much as the girl said it would.

Everything was normal. The girl had arrived home from shopping and had just slid into her normal position in the garage. The power garage door slid shut behind them. As it did so, the automatic overhead light came on in the garage.

Cruz checked his guns one last time. Beside him, Oskar did the same. Cruz favored a big .44 Magnum in those days. Its silencer was huge as well. Howard was to die first, with a blast from the Magnum. This would intimidate Eli and get him to open the safe. There was a diamond in the safe that was on its way to Los Angeles tomorrow. Besides that, any easy cash lying around, Cruz could have it. This was a loot-for-cash job. Nothing else was to be touched except for the passport. And after all was said and done, Oskar could end his career with a bullet to Eli's head.

'Ready?' Cruz said to Oskar.

Oskar had checked and rechecked the MAC and the Ruger. 'Of course.'

They exited the car. The door to the house was locked, but

there was a key on the girl's ring. Cruz opened the door and it gave upon a large kitchen with an island in the middle and several workstations. Huge pots hung down from the overhead rack.

They passed through the kitchen, walking quickly.

'There you are, my dear, we're in the sitting room,' a voice called. 'We have some wine for you.'

They turned a corner and here was the sitting room. Two men sat in easy chairs. Eli was the one on the left, the one with a large mole on his cheek. Cruz knew both of them from the dossier. They were fat men, and Cruz felt another pang of embarrassment for Eli. He was the fatter of the two, a corrupt middle-aged man with a lot of money. He thought he had the love of a beautiful young woman. Maybe he thought he had swept her away with his abilities as a lover, yes? Cruz wouldn't put it past him. Rich men on the verge of violent death were prone to making such miscalculations. The girl had given them everything they needed to reach this man. She had done it in a heartbeat, to save her own life.

Eli and Howard gazed at Cruz and Oskar. Oskar held up the MAC as if it needed amplification, and Eli nodded.

'I have money,' Eli said.

'So do we,' said Oskar.

Cruz couldn't resist. 'The girl was with you for your money,' he said. 'There was nothing else.'

'No, it was love,' Eli said.

Oskar said nothing.

Cruz paced into the room. 'She went home to India today,'

he lied. 'Next week she'll have a new lover. Probably a young man with a hard body who drives a Porsche and will inherit his father's fortune.'

'Still, I know her. It was love.'

Cruz shrugged. Leave it at that, then. It was love. He took a step forward and shot Howard in the forehead with the Magnum. In the second before Cruz pulled the trigger, Howard squinted and cringed, but made no other move. The shot made very little sound, but the man's head came apart with an audible crack. Brains and bone flew. A mirror against the wall twenty feet behind him smashed into a dozen large pieces.

Eli's eyes went very wide.

'It's in your interest to tell us some things,' Oskar said.

Eli talked a lot. It seemed he had a lot to say. One thing he described was the safe's location and the combination. Then he opened it for them. At the end of it all, Oskar finished him with a gently laid bullet to the forehead. It was almost a blessed relief, by the look on Eli's face.

Oskar went about pulling some things from the safe. First, he laid his gun down. He opened a pouch and placed the diamond inside it. It was quite a thing to behold, that diamond. Then it disappeared into the bag.

Cruz stood behind and about ten feet away from his teacher.

They had each gotten their own dossiers for this operation. Oskar's had included descriptions of Eli, Howard, the girl-friend, and the diamond, as well as the layout of the house. Cruz's dossier had included all these things and one more: a description of Oskar and his upcoming retirement.

'Oskar,' Cruz called.

'Yes, yes, one moment.'

'Oskar, you need to turn around.'

Something in Cruz's voice made Oskar stop what he was doing. He stood very still for a moment, no longer looking at whatever paperwork he held in his gloved hand. Then his back slumped. It had to be a disappointment for things to end in this way.

'It's like that then, is it?'

'It is.' Cruz felt something well up in his eye. He brushed it away, whatever it was or might be.

Oskar turned around slowly. He gazed wistfully at his Ruger, just out of reach on the table. He made no move toward it.

'You got your two hundred,' Cruz said.

'Yes, I did. Somehow, it no longer tastes very sweet.'

'You were the best,' Cruz said.

'A cold comfort, I'm afraid.'

The two friends stared at each other for a long moment. 'A final lesson, if you haven't moved beyond learning,' Oskar said.

Cruz shook his head. Of course there was time for one last word from the teacher. If only time could stop in this moment. 'I haven't.'

'Avoid the mistakes I've made. For one, never try to retire. I gather now that it cannot be done. For two, never flatter yourself into believing you are not expendable. You are. And three, never turn your back on a young man in your charge.

Especially one with great potential. Especially one that you loved like a son.'

Cruz nodded.

'End of lesson,' Oskar said.

Cruz shot him four times. The first bullet entered his brain and killed him. Without pain, Cruz hoped. The next three were insurance.

Years before, the first lesson, delivered in Oskar's clipped no-nonsense tone, had gone as follows: when you kill a man, make sure he is dead.

They didn't call him Fingers just because he was missing some.

One of the things he prided himself on was being able to steal just about any American-made, late model sedan in less than two minutes.

They were in a small seafood restaurant along the waterfront. Nets and lobster traps hung from the ceiling. A huge old steering wheel was mounted on one wall. An ancient anchor stood upright, mounted on a pedestal near the front door. Fingers had already finished a platter of fried fish, French fries and coleslaw, and Moss was still demolishing the bread bowl that some New England clam chowder had come in.

In a little while, they would head out to the airport and Fingers would pick up a work car out of the long-term parking lot. The Mercedes wasn't for work – it was for maximum comfort while driving up here. For work, they needed something nondescript, with local plates, maybe five years old but with a good solid engine. Something with a little bit of go power. The body had to be good, no rust, but the paint a little faded, a real middle-class blubber boat. Left there by some hard-working citizen who had parked his car and flown out to see his sister in Ohio for two weeks.

Fingers looked forward to it. In fact, he could hardly sit still. He loved these missions, and no doubt he liked to whack people. But one of his favorite things, although he would never tell a guy like Moss, was stealing cars. Moss would probably relegate grabbing a car to the scrap head of STUFF THAT HAD TO GET DONE, like reading your dossier, like ditching evidence, like getting to the fucking airport on time. Not Fingers. He loved it when he had to take a car – it was what he had come up doing as a kid – and he liked to show his stuff. At one time, he had practically lived for it. That feeling of moving low and fast, his sneakers barely touching the concrete, his eyes darting, sizing up the cars on the fly. This one? A blue 1995 Oldsmobile Achieva?

Nah.

This one? Yeah, that's the one. A green 1999 Chevy Impala. Yeah.

After he snatched them a car, he and Moss would see about this wetback who cleaned Dugan's apartment. Put her through her paces. For now, however, it was dinner time. And dinner time was downtime.

'I tell you what,' Roland Moss said in a long, lazy drawl.

Fingers sat across the table from Moss and waited for the rest of his statement. It could be a while before the big man decided to finish it.

Moss did everything slow. It wasn't that he couldn't move fast – he could. Fingers had seen him move with sudden lightning speed. It was almost as if Moss did everything slow on purpose, to allow people to let down their guard.

Fingers watched him destroy the bread bowl, slowly, deliberately tearing its remains apart, and putting them in his mouth. Here was a big lumbering creature of a man. Everything about him said 'SLOW'. He even talked slow – sometimes pausing for what seemed like a very long time between words and even syllables. He claimed that he talked slow so that everyone – even the simplest of simpletons – would understand.

And his sheer size and the crazy mayhem in his eyes meant that his patience was rarely tested. Clerks were terrified of him. His two monstrous hands on the counter, the epic bulk of his shoulders and upper body leaning forward, his body relaxed but the brow of his forehead creased with mild annoyance . . .

'Son,' he might drawl, letting that word linger, the time stretching out between himself and the startled mouse of a desk clerk below him, 'I hope you're gonna go on and do what I ask.'

This was enough. This was more than enough.

Fingers had seen it happen. Times when he, Fingers, would practically have to throw a tantrum to get what he wanted – and he was a hired killer, for Christ's sake – Moss merely had to clench his jaw in disapproval.

Six months ago, Fingers had watched Moss break a man's neck with the same bland expression on his face that he wore right now while eating his dinner. It was a mixture of boredom and detached concentration.

Moss chewed the bread with near infinite care. 'The thing is,' he said, his impassive eyes roaming the restaurant, soaking in the other early dinner patrons, 'I'm not sure I like that boy.' He nodded, as if in agreement with himself. 'It's his attitude. Rubs me the wrong way.'

'Cruz?' Fingers said, to make sure they were on the same page.

Moss raised his eyebrows, as if to say, 'Who else?'

'That's probably why he works alone, right?' Fingers said.

Moss motioned to the waitress. 'Well, he ain't working alone on this job. If he's gonna act this way, he might need a talking to.' He cracked his mighty knuckles for emphasis. The waitress, a blonde with a young, firm body, and a face and voice that were middle-aged from years of smoking, came over.

'Darling,' Moss said, 'may I have a cup of coffee and a dessert menu? Any time you get a moment.'

Over his apple pie with whipped cream on top, and two cups of coffee, Moss half listened as the little monkey chattered away. Hell, let the boy talk. He was just working out his nerves before the job.

'You know what it is?' Fingers said, talking low and fast, glancing around between every statement to see who was looking. 'It's this: I *like* killing people. That's why I feel like I got the best job in the world, you know? I go out on a mission, and I know we're gonna do somebody, I'm like right there, man. I'm ready. I look forward to it.'

That's how the monkey sometimes talked. He called them 'missions'.

'Look at this fucking hand,' Fingers said. He held up the hand with the three missing fingers. He touched his pinky to his thumb, rapidly, three times, like a crab with its pincers. The hand was permanently discolored, an angry lobster red.

'I *like* this hand. You know why? Because it's a war wound. I ever tell you how I fucked up this hand?'

Of course he had. Probably three times. But here it came again.

'I blew it up, see? I had a fucking bomb in my hand. And it blew up.' He pointed at Moss with the angry red pinky. 'But that's the kind of life I lead. Action. Everybody should lead such a life. I like to go out on missions where I know there's gonna be some action.'

'What do you think of this job?' Moss said.

Fingers shrugged. 'Retrieval duty. Whatever. I don't really like it, but I don't criticize. It looks like a boring one. But you know, maybe we'll see some action. Who knows? You know, I do what I'm told — I steal a car, whatever — and I shut up about it.'

The fingers of his good hand drummed on the table.

Moss sipped his coffee. Retrieval duty. He didn't mind it. Money was money. No fuss, no muss. Pick up the old man, find out what he did with the money, and get it back if possible.

Then bring the old boy down to New York, with the money or not.

The money.

The money, the money, the money.

The dossier said the old boy had killed Roselli and made off with $2.5 mil from the fat man's safe. Moss mused on this for a moment. He had met Roselli a few times when Moss was bouncing at the club on Bell Boulevard in Queens, knocking around the college boys when they got out of hand. The fat man used to come in there, sometimes alone, sometimes with a couple of guys from his crew, sometimes with a fake-tit platinum blonde on each arm.

He had wagged a fat finger at Moss one time. 'When I talk, you listen. Understand? When I say jump, you jump.'

He had said this to Moss. To Moss! Didn't he realize Moss could snap his neck with one hand?

Moss snorted. Roselli was a fat, bossy fuck with a big mouth. Sooner or later, he might have killed the man himself.

In any case, this trip wasn't about Roselli. Nobody missed Roselli. This trip was about don't fuck around, and give us back the money you took. The money was the reason there were three of them on this job. One man, on his own, might stumble upon all that money – it was just too tempting.

Moss waved it away. He made plenty of money. The way he saw it, he exchanged his time and his peculiar talents for a high standard of living. He lived alone in a big three-bedroom condo in Rockaway Beach, a place he hadn't been back to in the past month. He had ten suits and fifteen pairs of shoes.

He owned a big damn Hummer H2, which he almost never had the opportunity to drive. He had silk shirts and silk sheets. He was busy and that suited him fine. On rare days when there was no work, all he did was he sat on the beach and watched the waves crash. At night, he went to the clubs, sucked down the booze, and threw money away on the whores. He spent big money, and you know what? He could live this life for ever.

He wasn't about to risk all for a one-time grab at the brass ring. Not even thirty yet, and he had already put too many dumb fuckers out of their misery for trying exactly that. He knew, he *knew*: it was a dumb play. You don't get away with it. It was a lesson the old boy was about to learn in spades.

And Cruz?

Moss didn't like that fucker. He didn't like that pocked-up face or those beady little eyes. He didn't like the way he talked down to you, like he was above it all somehow. Cruz was getting old himself. To Moss, he seemed like a guy about to take a fall.

And that was good.

'What do you think, slim?' Moss said to Fingers. 'Is it time to get ourselves some wheels or what?'

'Travis, you get down off that goddamn tree!'

From his perch on a white plastic chair on the back porch of Darren's single-wide three-bedroom trailer, Hal had an ample view of the wreckage of his friend's life. The trailer sat on cinderblocks, surrounded by thirty similar trailers in a house park optimistically named Metro Gardens.

Hal mused on the name. There was nothing metropolitan about this place, and there were no gardens in evidence. The lot was hard-packed earth, with thick bushes along the edges of the property, and the Androscoggin River just past them, close enough to bring the mosquitoes in the spring and summer. The bushes served to obscure the river and the ancient, decaying factory on the other side.

The property was fenced along the river, so the kids from the trailer park wouldn't be tempted to ford their way across and break into the abandoned factory. Nothing but trouble over there. Nine-year-olds smoking pot. Thirteen-year-olds having sex. Rejects, maniacs and predators of all kinds would haunt a spot like that. Nobody in this trailer park would want their kids going over there. But it did no good. Hal could see two gaping holes in the fence right from here.

He took a slug of beer and chased it with a sip of Jack Daniel's. He shrugged his big shoulders. In any case, on a cool October day like today, the skeeters were all gone, and it was still just warm enough to sit out and barbecue back here. Darren had gone inside to replenish the little six-pack cooler from whence they took their beers.

While Hal waited, the sun went down across the open trailer park from him. In the fading light, he watched Darren's three kids, ages nine, eight and four, and Darren's wife, Lynn. Lynn, never particularly attractive, had reached her mid-thirties, and was becoming fatter, more sallow, and ever more disagreeable by the day. Come to think of it, that last child, the four-year-old, was probably a trap set by Lynn – she hadn't worked since the first one was born, and one more child had put the final nail in the coffin of Darren's dream that she might ever get another job.

The kids raced around the lot with all the other trailer-trash children, shouting and screaming. Travis, the eldest, was the offending tree climber. Lynn stood by a circular clothes hanger, smoking cigarettes and talking with two other mommies going to seed. Now and then, she would turn her attention to the kids and unleash instructions or abuse, depending on what the situation warranted.

Living in a trailer with three kids and Lynn. Man. Not for the first time, Hal reflected that his friend Darren was like a flashlight without a battery. He had worked low-paying, back-breaking shit jobs his entire life. This is where he had ended up. Without Hal's influence, Lynn would probably be the extent of Darren's sex life, and he wouldn't have an extra dime to put in his pocket.

Darren was being sucked under. Lynn spent what she could, and Hal knew, was constantly critical – where they lived, what the kids wore, where they shopped, what they drove. None of it was ever good enough. In Hal's estimation, Darren needed to leave this bitch and get out of this rat's nest of a living arrangement. It seemed strange that a big boy like Darren allowed himself to get pushed around and used up like this.

It wasn't right.

Darren came back on the porch. He smiled with that big jaw of his. Atta boy. His eyes were still blacked, his nose plugged and taped, and that bruise on the side of his neck was coming along good. They had skated by on the damage by telling Lynn they'd been down to Old Orchard Beach drinking in a bar, and got in a scrape with some black boys. Lynn hated those blackies in Old Orchard.

'Only got four beers left,' Darren said. 'Guess we'll need to head out for some.'

Hal smiled too. The sun was just about gone. Twilight was coming in, and with it, the night's chill. 'Wanna show you something before we do.'

'Yeah, what's that?'

Hal's grin grew even broader. He was feeling good. Despite everything, or maybe because of it, he was feeling real good. He looked forward to a challenge, after all. And getting even? Boy, was there anything quite like it? Even being around Lynn today couldn't bring him down.

'Out in the car,' he said.

The two men sauntered, beers in hand, the flask of Jack in Hal's back pocket, through the gathering gloom and over to the parking lot. They reached Hal's big Caddy Eldorado. He pressed a button on his key chain and the trunk popped open a few inches, the light coming on inside.

There was no one around.

Back over by the bushes — the woods is what they called them — the kids were still running and screaming. They had flashlights now.

Lynn's voice floated across the lot. 'OK, come on, you kids. Get in the house. Now, I said.'

'Whatcha got?' Darren said.

Hal opened the trunk. Lying there, amidst the jack, the tire iron, some recyclable beer bottles, and a few assorted sundries, was the gun case.

'Oooooh,' Darren said.

'You know that Mossberg 20-gauge I had my eye on down to Kittery Trading Post? The single barrel with the pump action?'

'I guess I do.'

Hal unzipped the case and yanked out the shotgun. 'Went down and bought her last week. I forgot to mention it in all the recent excitement.'

Darren giggled like a boy. 'Are you thinking what I'm thinking?'

Just like Darren to be a step behind. Why else would it be in the car? 'Sure am, kid. Thought I'd bring it with us down to Portland tomorrow night, see what Little Miss Lola does with her prize pussy when she gets a look-see at that big barrel.'

Hal took another slug of his beer. His smile was wider than ever.

After Lorena finished in the garden, she lingered for some time in Smoke's apartment itself. It was a tiny place, a bachelor's home in every way, with a double bed in one supposed room, then through a wide open double doorway to the kitchen and dining area, then out the door to the back. The cats had a little doorway they could squeeze through in the lower panel of the back door itself. Oddly, Smoke kept triple locks on both doors, and sometimes at night he placed a T-bar against the bottom, secured with a bolt, which he had mounted into the floor.

She teased him sometimes about this. 'Who are you afraid of, Smoke? Will the secret police come to get you? I am like the janitor – I have so many keys on my chain. They are all to get into your home.'

Smoke didn't keep the place very clean, and sometimes Lorena cleaned up after him. She didn't clean too often, though, because Smoke had a woman who should take care of that for him. Lorena was well past the age of competing for a man.

She sighed, not realizing she had done so, then stood and left Smoke Dugan's apartment. Once outside, she walked the half-mile to the Shaw's Supermarket near the bridge and purchased some milk and eggs, and a very few other items she needed at her own small apartment.

She walked along the darkened street toward her own home, not far from that of Smoke Dugan. It was quiet and chilly, and dead leaves rustled as they blew along the ground in the breeze. Lorena could just see her own breath.

A man came toward her. He was a tall man, a young man who looked strong. She imagined that if she were not a mixed race old woman from Central America, this young man would offer to carry her bags home to her apartment. Instead, because things were as they were, he would ignore her. She did not believe he would do this out of spite, but out of fear. People were afraid of one another, of reaching out and being together.

This she knew about people. The boy would probably fear that if he offered assistance, she would answer him in Spanish and he would not be able to respond.

The young man passed her without so much as a glance in her direction.

There was something unusual about him, but she wasn't sure what it was. Only after he passed did she realize that his right hand was missing nearly all of its fingers. He seemed to have a pinky and a thumb, and that was it.

She continued to walk, allowing the weight in her hands to settle deeper, pulling down harder on her shoulders. *La Mula*, she called herself. The Mule. She was as strong as one, and could be just as stubborn. She was a fool for engaging in these fantasies about people and their nature. The boy hadn't given her a thought.

Here came another man up this same deserted street. Also a young man. What is he thinking, Mula? Will he help you with your bags?

The man approached slowly, but this man was very definitely looking right at her. She thought she didn't like the look in his eyes. He was a big man. She stopped and studied him carefully. He was very big. Violent crime was almost unheard of in this city, but this one had the dark, hard and wild light in his eyes – that light she remembered from so many murderers in her homeland. There was hard laughter in his eyes, but no real mirth or warmth. Nothing was funny.

She thought of the man who had just passed. Perhaps she

could run to him. She turned, and he was right behind her.

A hand clamped on her hair from behind and pulled her backwards. She dropped her groceries. She felt rather than heard the eggs smash. She tried to turn, to struggle, but to no avail. The big man had her in a powerful grip and was dragging her along by her hair, keeping her off balance.

The smaller man approached her quickly. He smiled and punched her in the eye. It hurt, it was horrible, it was shocking. Then he hit her again. Things were moving too quickly. Her heart beat rapidly.

She fell to the ground.

They pulled at her, yanking her along the sidewalk. *Dios mio!* What did they want? Her bag, she realized. They were pulling her along the ground by her handbag. She felt her dress, then her skin tearing as she bumped along the gravel. They wanted her money, her little bit of money.

Well, they could have it.

She let go of the bag. At last, she thought. They would be gone.

But no. Now one stood over her and kicked her. It was the small one. He delivered swift, sharp punishing kicks to every part of her body. He kicked her in the head. She grew dizzy. The world went dark, then swam back into focus. Then went dark again. She saw the big one, standing nearby watching the little one kick her to her death.

As she faded from consciousness, she realized the madman was still kicking her.

* * *

Sirens howled somewhere close by.

Cruz heard them approaching as he sat slumped and bleeding to death in the front passenger seat of a black car. He was shot, he didn't know how many times. He looked over at Carmine the Nose, who had just crawled into the driver's seat. The Nose was a bloody mess. His intestines hung out into his lap where Cruz had gutted him. His big hands caressed the steering wheel.

'Where to, old buddy?' the Nose said.

Cruz opened his eyes.

He stared up at the ceiling of the bathroom in his suite at the Portland Arms. His head rested on the marble apron of the tub. The water was hot. The jets were still going. Steam rose all around him.

The bathroom phone was ringing near his head. It echoed against the tiled walls and the marble floor. He reached back, brushed the gun to make sure it was still there, and picked up the phone.

'Yeah?' he said.

'Cruz.'

'Yeah.'

'You awake? It's Moss.' Moss, the clown who didn't like staying at the Holiday Inn. He wasn't supposed to disturb Cruz tonight, not unless he got to the Guatemalan.

'Yeah, Moss.'

'Listen, son, we got the wetback.'

Cruz stifled a yawn and sat up in the tub. 'Tell me.'

There was a long pause over the line. 'We got her.'

'What else did you get?'

Cruz could practically hear Moss's lazy grin cracking ear to ear over the phone.

'We got all the keys to Dugan's place.'

4

Smoke left Lola's apartment around eleven the next morning. Both Lola and Pam had gone to their day jobs, so Smoke lounged around for a bit before heading back to his own place. He was in no hurry, and it was a nice day.

He came down the stairs into his apartment, still with lingering thoughts of Lola and her body from the night before. Last night had been better, thank you. It was almost noon and she should be on a break soon.

Yessir, he was a lucky man.

A large pile of fur was heaped on the linoleum floor of his tiny kitchen. At first, he thought one of the cats was merely sprawled out there. It was Bubbles, a big lazy yellow tabby. Sprawling out on the floor was nothing new for Bubbles. In fact, Smoke barely looked at the cat.

Then he did.

There was something abnormal about the way Bubbles lay there. Smoke's heart raced off in a wild tattoo. Rat-a-tat-tat. The cat looked almost like it had been broken, or even smashed. Smoke approached Bubbles cautiously.

His heart pounded in his chest.

Run, you idiot.

The cat was demolished. It was humped and bloodied, like it had been tortured and killed by a cruel and sinister child. A streak of blood stained the linoleum beneath its carcass.

RUN. *RUN*.

He turned and a man stood behind him. The man had just emerged from the bathroom hallway. The man was short and dark, in jeans and a white T-shirt, covered by a light autumn jacket. His face was pock-marked and scarred along the side. He looked to Smoke like a man in his mid-forties, maybe a little older. Behind him stood a much taller, much broader young man. The kid was huge. He wore a leather cap on his head. Greasy brown hair strung down from it. He had a cowlick on the front of his hairline and a wild light in his eyes.

Smoke had seen the look before. It was the look of a crazy kid who should have been locked up someplace, but instead was hired as muscle. It was the look of those guys who went on bank jobs, then suddenly started spraying civilians with gunfire. It was a bad, bad look. It was the look of murder for hire.

Smoke turned to bolt out the back door, but another young man stood there. This one was slim, clean-cut, not as crazy-looking, nor nearly as big as the other one. This kid's eyes said he had seen a few jobs, and did exactly what the bosses told him. This was the survivor type. The survivor type with a Colt .380 in his hand.

The backyard was blocked, and the way to the stairs was blocked. Smoke couldn't outrun these guys. He had his cane, but he couldn't outfight them. He couldn't do anything.

Damn! So stupid to wait and wait and wait. Now it was too late.

He had had a bad feeling, and here it was in the flesh. The bad feeling personified.

'Can I help you fellows?' he said.

The small, dark man lit a cigarette.

'That's OK, go ahead and smoke. I don't mind.'

The man shrugged. 'James Dugan, right? That's what you call yourself these days?'

'Who wants to know?'

The kid ambled out from behind the small man. He was even bigger than at first glance. Smoke watched him approach. It was like watching a dark and terrible storm move in across a valley. He angled toward Smoke across the dingy linoleum, taking his time, not hurrying at all.

'Son,' he said, 'the man asked you a question. It ain't polite to answer him with a question.' He cracked his knuckles.

'You guys are in my home. Ever think of that? That puts me in charge of asking questions.'

The big man feinted with his left hand, then delivered a hard right cross to Smoke's jaw. Smoke stumbled backwards, crashed into the kitchen table and went right over it. Two cats scattered as he rolled over and fell to the floor.

The kid came, and smiling, stood over him. His huge hands, like the mechanical claws that sift through scrap metal at the junkyard, reached down and picked Smoke up by the shirt. The kid backed up and swung him around in a large circle, then let him go. Smoke felt himself crossing the room as if he were flying, his feet barely scraping the ground. He hit the far wall, plowed into it, then bounced off and stumbled backwards. He turned, pinwheeling for balance. He spilled and slid across the floor.

Then the small man was standing over him. Smoke looked up at that hard face. The scar stood out in sharp relief. Smoke thought of the old dueling societies in Germany, where the guys would wear the scars as badges of honor. The guy took a drag on his cigarette.

'Friend,' the guy said. His voice barely rose above a whisper, 'I want to talk to you. And I want you to look at me when I do. Right here, in the eyes.'

Smoke did. The eyes. Somehow, this guy had eyes that were worse than the madness of the kid's eyes. It was almost like there were flames behind those eyes, and the guy was burning in there, burning in a hell you would have to live through to appreciate. Smoke had also seen this look before, but maybe never this strong.

The eyes held him. 'Do we understand each other?'

Smoke nodded.

More whispers from the little man. 'OK. Here's the rules. I'm going to ask you some questions, and you're going to answer them. You're not in a position to act funny. You're not in a position to ask me any questions. Do you still understand?'

Smoke nodded again.

'What? I didn't hear you.'

'I understand.'

The scarred face smiled. 'Good. Now, I want to show you something.'

He stepped aside and again the giant psychotic kid appeared. This time he was holding one of the cats. Melon was the cat's name, so called because it was orange and as fat as a melon. Smoke's heart sank at the sight of the kid with Melon. The kid stroked Melon's fur, and even from the floor Smoke could hear the cat purring.

'That's a good kitty,' the big boy said.

Jesus, after just watching this kid knock the piss out of me. Talk about betrayal.

Then the kid stopped stroking the cat and instead grabbed it roughly by the head. He turned the cat's head to the left with a sudden and vicious snap. The cat went limp and the kid dropped its carcass to the floor. Two cats dead. It was a fucking cat holocaust.

The kid would pay for the cats, Smoke decided. In blood.

The scarred face appeared again.

'James Dugan, also known as Walter O'Malley?'

Smoke spit at the face. 'Fuck you.' These guys were worse than the cops.

The karate works.

Lola sailed through the morning on that thought alone.

Two big men had tried to take advantage of her – face it, they had tried to rape her – and she had kicked ass, just like the tattoo on her back said. It had been scary, sure, but now that it was over and gone, she wanted to do it again. This time, she wanted to go in knowing she would fight, and just get in there and, and, and . . .

KICK ASS.

God, the feeling. She had put their lights out in seconds flat. She could have really hurt them both. By the end there, they were both completely under her power. Even now, she felt a tingle of electric excitement up her spine at the thought of it.

Smoke hadn't been ready for her last night. That feeling of power, well, it had translated into everything. Friday night had churned up a lot of memories for her, had made it hard, but now it was clear, after last night, that it was for the good.

She felt great, that was the simple matter of fact.

She had lunch monitor duty today so she couldn't call Smoke. Now she could barely wait until her afternoon break so she could check in with him.

It was a long day.

Smoke opened his eyes and was surprised to find himself on the floor again. For a while, they had put him in the chair.

He looked at the floor around his head. The linoleum was tacky with blood.

The skinny kid, the one who was missing the fingers, stood

over him again. Good for a laugh – they even called the kid 'Fingers'. Smoke knew all their names now. They had introduced themselves. Fingers, Moss, and Cruz. It was a bad sign – worse than bad. *He knew their names. He knew what they looked like.*

It meant he was dead.

'Well, look who's awake,' Fingers said. 'Your girlfriend called a while ago. She left a message on the machine. She knows you're out in the shop working. She just wanted to tell you that she loves you.'

The kid's eyes showed rising good humor. He had a sheet of paper in his lobster-claw hand. He referred to it, then looked up with a smile. 'That would be Lola Bell, right? Twenty-five years old, African-American, resides at 210 Joye Street in Portland? Top-floor apartment?'

Jesus, Lola. He had to keep her out of it at all costs. It didn't matter what they did to him. Lola was not part of this. She knew nothing about this. He wouldn't take the bait. He wouldn't say anything about her. If he let the comment die, perhaps they would forget about her. If he could get a message to her somehow, tell her to run . . .

Moss placed another dead cat on Smoke's chest. He took a moment to get it positioned just so. Then he stood up. Smoke pushed the cat off. This time it was Minefield, so named because he was the three-legged cat in the bunch. Three down and three to go. He looked around. The others appeared to have scrammed. Good for them.

Moss settled into the chair. He pulled out an emery board

and began filing his nails. 'Smoke, she called you. Is that some kind of nickname?'

'What does it sound like?'

The kid smiled. He rolled his eyes slowly. 'Son, you're gonna learn to appreciate how patient I been with you thus far. Like that cat of yours . . .' he gestured at the crumpled remains of Minefield. 'I took all that time to get it just so. It was a piece of art how I had it. Then you knock it away. What you think of that, Fingers?'

Fingers flashed a silly grin. 'I think it's rude.'

'Rude. That's exactly the word I would have picked.'

The dark man, Cruz, came out of the bathroom. He was not smiling. Another lit cigarette dangled from his mouth.

'O'Malley. I see you're awake. Anything you'd like to tell us about your life up until now? Like, for instance, what you did with about two and a half million dollars you took from Roselli when you killed him.'

Smoke lay back on the linoleum and sighed. 'I'm telling you. You have the wrong man. My name is James Dugan. I'm retired. I used to be an engineer for Sikorsky down in Connecticut. Now I make toys and adaptive devices for retarded children.'

Cruz nodded at Moss.

'Roland?'

Slowly, the big man moved his bulk out of the chair. He flexed his triceps as he did so. He cracked his knuckles. He smiled.

'Friend, I'm starting to get bored, you see what I mean?'

136

Then the pain came again. And when the pain came, Roselli was dead and Smoke was holed up in a motel all the way out in Greenport, Long Island, waiting for the bad weather to come in, with all that money stashed in a satchel under the bed. The urge was there, to take that cold, hard cash and spread it out all over the bed and just lay in it and roll around in it, but he fought off the urge. When the storm came, he finally made the call, yeah, Walter O'Malley making reservations on Block Island, halfway between the North Fork and Rhode Island. Yeah, I'm coming in on my own boat, is that OK? The weather? Oh, it'll be a wet one, but I've been in worse than this. Sure, I'll see you tonight.

Then he was out on the Boston Whaler, in the dark and the rain and the wind. Whitecaps topped the waves, the foam tearing off and blowing in his face. He went inside and set the charges in the cabin. He set them against the hull, one on each side. Wet hair dripping in his eyes, Smoke working feverishly as the boat rocked and listed. He lowered the red fiberglass dinghy, no ordinary dinghy, a sturdy survival boat that would rock and roll. He loaded up and powered out of there. The Whaler was on its own.

He heard the muffled blasts moments later, and then the Whaler was gone. And O'Malley was gone. And bedraggled Dugan raced across heavy seas toward New London, where his car was waiting like a trusty dog, man's best friend. He could take that car and run anywhere, anywhere at all, and wherever he went it would never be far enough. So when he found a place he liked, he stopped. He stopped way too soon.

Sometime later, Smoke opened his eyes.

His wrists were cuffed together, and they were attached to a rope slung over one of the exposed pipes that ran along the ceiling. The whole thing was pulled just tight enough that his toes barely touched the ground. He looked up at his hands. They had turned purple while he was passed out. He knew he had lost some teeth. In fact, he had seen them come out. It was possible that he had some bruised ribs as well. At least bruised. Maybe broken.

A new and terrible thought had occurred to him. 'How'd you get in here?' he gasped to nobody in particular.

The one they called Fingers floated in front of his face. He grinned. His face looked like a carved-up jack-o'-lantern. In his own way, he was as bad as the other two.

'We talked to the housekeeper.'

Shit. Lorena. She had been swept up in this too.

'Where is she now?' Smoke said. He felt his Adam's apple bob. He was afraid of the answer, afraid of everything now, afraid of what he had wrought with his goddamned stupid laziness. He had played a role, he had pretended to be a normal person, and then he had come to believe in the role himself. He had lied, and then he had bought the lie.

Stupid.

'She's sleeping, brother,' Fingers said. He raised his eyebrows.

Smoke went numb.

Time passed as he hung there. He noticed the shadows were growing long outside. The light was starting to fade from the sky, and from the room. Death would be a relief of sorts. It was the money, of course. That was why they were here, and it was the only thing keeping him alive. They wanted to know where the money was.

It seemed like an effort even to blink.

There was pain everywhere in his body, and now that he thought about it, that was probably a good thing. They hadn't severed his spinal cord, for instance. If ever he got away from these guys, he'd still be able to walk.

The beginning of a plan began to form.

Cruz stood in front of him. 'You're a trooper, O'Malley. I'll give you that much. You can take a beating. We're getting tired of it, actually. You see, we don't like beatings. They're slow. They don't work on old-school tough guys like you. But our orders were not to hurt you too bad. You see, we had to keep you presentable in case that money was in the bank somewhere and we needed you to go in and get it.'

He shrugged, as if to himself. 'But I guess it didn't work. So when it gets dark out, we're all going to take a little ride down to New York. You're going to talk to some people down there about what you've been up to these past three years. Then you're going to officially retire.'

'Well, that's nice to know,' Smoke said. 'I've been looking forward to retirement.'

Cruz nodded to the other two. They untied the rope from the ceiling and Smoke collapsed in a heap. The back of his head hit the worn floor hard, but it was just another pain to add to the list. Still, he faded in and out for a few seconds.

Cruz hunkered down next to him. He stood in a squat like a farmer, like he might run his hands through the deep rich soil. Smoke figured he couldn't stand like Cruz was doing now even on his best days.

Cruz's voice took on a conspiratorial tone. 'They're going to kill you. You know that already. What you don't know, and what you're probably wondering, is why they're bothering to bring you down to New York when we could do it just as easily here. I'm going to tell you, you know why? Because I don't like to see anybody suffer needlessly, and you seem like a pretty good guy.'

'Thanks,' Smoke said. He made an effort to swallow.

Cruz went on, 'You worry them, you understand? Here's a guy who's involved in big jobs over the years, suddenly up and disappears. Kills a guy. Steals a lot of money. Sinks his boat in a storm. You didn't think anybody bought that lost-at-sea bullshit, did you?' He smiled. 'No, nobody bought it. They've been looking for you the whole time. You're an important man.'

Cruz paused, as if in reflection. 'There was something you did that had to be kept real quiet, am I right? Yeah, I am right. So they want to know who you talked to about this thing during three long years away. Did you talk to girlfriends? Did you talk to a shrink? To a priest?'

'I didn't talk to anybody,' Smoke said, giving up the charade that he wasn't the man they wanted. 'I kept it to myself.'

Cruz turned to look at the two men standing behind him. Then he turned back to Smoke. 'And the money?'

'Safe deposit boxes. Six different banks. Four here in town. One in Boston. One up in Quebec City. In case I had to run.'

Cruz nodded solemnly. 'I believe you. But they're not going to. They're going to torture you, you understand? They're going to cut your teeth out, one by one. They're going to crush your balls. They're going to break your fingers and toes. They're going to impale you through the ass on a stick. They're going to cut your eyes out. They're going to do whatever they want. If you talked to anybody, they're going to find out, and it's going to be a slow process. The way you can beat that, and die quickly, is to tell them everything up front, right away.'

Smoke started to shake. 'Look,' he said. His words tumbled out in a torrent, a flood of chatter. 'You win, all right? You win. Am I keeping my mouth shut? No, I'm not. I told you where the money is. We can get most of it tomorrow, if you want. And I didn't tell anybody. I can prove it, too. For the first couple of years I kept a diary. I wrote in loose-leaf notebooks almost every day. I kept stacks of them. I couldn't keep it in my head, but I was afraid to tell anybody. For just this reason – I didn't want to get anybody in the soup with me when you guys eventually showed up. I probably even wrote about stashing the money in the banks. I don't remember now. But you can look at them. We got all night, right? The banks are closed by now. If we hadn't spent all day with this . . .' He gestured at the floor around himself, the dead cats, the blood, his own crumpled form, and somewhere out there, his dead friend Lorena, who only wanted to have a garden,

'. . . with this bullshit, you could've gotten the money . . .' Abruptly, he started crying, and that surprised even him. But it hurt. It hurt so bad, and they had hardly even fucking started yet. New York was going to be worse. He knew that. He knew how bad it was going to be. His body was racked by sobs.

'You can have the fucking money. Read the notebooks. It's all in there.'

Cruz smiled. 'OK, notebooks. That'll be a start. It won't be proof that you didn't talk to anybody, but it might make things easier on you. Where are the notebooks?'

'I keep them out in the workshop.'

Cruz looked at the two men standing by the doorway, watching the sun go down. 'Moss, go check out those notebooks.'

The big man smiled, apparently at the thought of this little man giving him a direct command. 'You heard the man, Fingers. Go on and get those notebooks out of the shed. We can see what our friend's been up to all this time.'

Smoke shook his head, the tears still flowing. 'The kid will never find them by himself. They're in there under about a million different things. He'll never be able to figure out all my junk.'

An amused, mocking light came into Cruz's eyes.

'You know, if you try anything funny, I am personally going to cut your left eye out. You realize that, right? You can't get away from us, so don't let something in your mind convince you otherwise. It'll make your life, what little is left of it, a lot harder.'

Smoke shook his head. 'I know all that. I'm just trying to help. The kid won't find the stuff. It'll take him half an hour. I'm not even sure where they are myself. But I'll do a better job of finding them than he will.'

Cruz gestured at Smoke, and Smoke lay there until the two young men came over to help him. They grabbed him under the arms, and lifted. Smoke let his head loll backwards as they raised him.

Then he was standing. 'I need my cane,' he said.

Cruz was right in front of him.

'Never mind your cane. Fingers here will help you walk.'

Smoke allowed Fingers to support him as he and the kid passed through the garden backyard and approached the work-shop. Cruz followed behind them. They passed the little grave marker for Butch.

'You used to have a dog, Dugan?'

'Not me. The dog was buried there when I got here. I never felt like digging it up.'

Fingers leaned Smoke up against the wall of the shed, and handed him the key chain they had taken away from him earlier. Smoke worked the key in the lock and pushed the heavy door. It creaked as it opened. The shadows were long inside the workshop.

The kid shoved Smoke through the door and Smoke bounced across the room, then fell to the dusty floor. He was lying below the window that led to the back alley, and from there, the street. That back alley was overgrown with weeds that came right up to the window. He locked that window whenever he was away from the shed. But he kept the lock well oiled and ready to open. It got hot in there, some days.

Fingers laughed at him. 'You know what, old man? You're pathetic. This is the easiest job I been on in my life. You know what I mean? I mean, we didn't even hurt you. Not really.'

Smoke reached up and used the window to claw himself into an upright position. He leaned on the window sill. He reached up to the top of the window and clamped his hand on the lock. Motes seemed to float in front of his eyes. He was going to pass out again, and soon.

'The stuff is over here somewhere,' he said. 'Look, can you turn that overhead light on? I can't see, I need some light if I'm gonna see over here.'

'Do it yourself,' Fingers said.

Obnoxious kid. 'Can't you just do it? You guys come here, beat the shit out of me, and tell me I'm gonna be killed. Then you push me down onto the floor of my shop. I can't even fucking walk, you know that? Shit. Fuck it, I'll turn the light on myself.'

He made a move like he would turn around and pull the chain on the light, the simple hanging bulb. If only it was right there behind him. If only he could move a little better. If only he wasn't so sore from the beating he had taken. He turned around wearily, creakily, gazing upward at the bulb. It was dark out, getting darker.

'What's taking so long?' Cruz called from somewhere outside. It sounded like he had drifted back toward the house.

'Jesus fucking Christ,' Fingers said. 'I'll turn on the fucking light, you gimp.'

Smoke braced himself as the kid moved into the room behind him. It was too bad it was just he and the kid in here. He wished it could have been everybody. OK, this would have to do. His hand quietly turned the lock on the window. He imagined himself yanking it open then leaping through, blasting headfirst through the bug screen, propelled by both his legs and arms. It would take everything he had.

Fingers played with the chain. 'I can't seem to get this thing to . . .'

Come on, kid. Light it up.

'You gotta do this fucking thing, you gimp.'

'Why? You can't turn on a fucking light?'

COME ON.

'All right,' Fingers said. 'I got it.'

Whooooosh.

Smoke saw the flash of light played out against the wall. He heard the tiny pop of the light bulb going and then he felt the sudden heat on his back. An instant later he heard the kid start to scream.

It was loud, like a siren.

Smoke wrenched the window open and sailed through, his back in flames, the fire eating away at the hair on top of his head. He fell to the ground in the alley behind the shop, rolling to put out the flames on his back, patting out the flames on top of his head.

The inside of the shop was already on fire. With the paints

he kept in there, the thing was going to blow sky-high. He saw a shadow stagger through the bright orange and yellow of the flames. It was the kid, lit up like a torch. He screamed for only a second longer, then went silent, and keeled over. Smoke pictured the kid inhaling fire. His larynx ruptured, the scream had died almost before it began.

The kid was a goner, but the other two weren't. Smoke dragged himself up the footpath between yards in the gathering dark. Behind him, the shadows leaped and danced in red and amber.

Precious seconds passed.

Smoke turned right on the quiet street. No one was coming. No one was running. Soon, though, they would all come soon enough.

Paint cans. Gunpowder. Blasting caps. These were just a few of the things he stored in that shed.

He thought of the two ladies, old biddies, sisters, who owned the house. They could have been twins, but after so many decades, who could tell? Neither one stood five feet tall. They both had their white hair pulled back into buns. Neither one could hear worth a damn. They were eighty if they were a day. He rented his apartment from them, and they lived upstairs. How far was that shed from the house? Thirty yards? Less?

The neighbors, the firemen, *someone* would come and get them long before the house was threatened — he felt sure of it.

He lost his balance and fell into his neighbor's dense bushes.

His vision swam and darkened. He crawled deeper into the hedge.

He heard the explosion just before he lost consciousness again. The sound was deep, like faraway thunder. It made an impression in the air, like a wave on the ocean. The wave passed over Smoke Dugan as he lay in the bushes. His face was lit with the firelight as the flames burst toward the heavens.

At the very end, a thought occurred to him. They knew about Lola.

His eyes rolled back in his head and he slept.

Cruz ran up the street, Moss loping along beside him.

In his mind, Cruz saw Fingers go up in flames again and again. The image was imprinted on his mind. He had stared at Fingers for several seconds too long.

Then the whole shed had blown, and he and Moss were over the fence and running together up the block of tidy suburban homes. No signal, no teamwork, just BOOM, and they were gone.

They reached the work car. It was a green Ford Taurus, a couple years old, nondescript, a real piece of shit. It had twenty thousand miles on it. At least it would run for a while. They jumped in. Moss took the wheel and Cruz slid into the passenger seat. Moss started it up. Fingers had removed the lock mechanism. He had left four license plates in the trunk for them, in case they had to switch later. Fingers had done his job. Now he was dead.

Moss was laughing.

'OK, what's funny?' Cruz said. He didn't see much humor in it. The whole job, *everything*, slipping away in the two minutes it took for Dugan and Fingers to go out to the shed.

Moss cruised past the house with the backyard on fire – ice cold, Moss – burning embers flying everywhere, black smoke funneling into the sky against the red and orange glow. The house was in danger of going up next.

Moss turned slowly onto the main thoroughfare – Broadway, it was called – still cruising slowly. His head did a slow swivel, looking for possible tails. None. Only now did he turn on the headlights. Cruz watched him check the rearview.

Now he sped up into traffic.

'You,' Moss said. 'You're funny. You tried to send me in that shed with the old man. If you had your way, it woulda been me going up in flames. That was the biggest fuck-up I ever seen. Only way it could have been bigger was if it had been me.'

Cruz sat back. 'I didn't see you warning him off.'

Moss only shrugged. 'You're the boss, big man. That's what the dossier says, anyway.'

At this moment, Cruz would love to know exactly what else Moss's dossier said.

Moss went on: 'And you know what? I didn't mind Fingers. Had a sort of way about him. You didn't know him, seeing as how you work alone and all, but I did. He was a good kid. Didn't get scared. Did what he was told, didn't complain too much.'

Moss nodded at the truth of this eulogy.

Cruz figured it would amount to about the kindest tribute Fingers would get now. If he had a mother somewhere in the world, God knew she would have been expecting her boy to go down in flames for years – except without the actual flames.

Sirens began to wail in the distance. As of yet, Cruz didn't know from what direction they were coming. Moss stopped at a traffic light. Three or four cars were ahead of them. No one was looking or acting strangely.

'Do you suppose the old man got out?' Moss said.

Cruz regarded the question. He didn't answer right away. It was his job, they had sent Fingers along with him, God knew what for, and now the kid had been deep fried. Toasted. In his mind, Cruz saw the kid go up in flames again. His insides felt scraped raw. Shit. *He cared*. He had to get out. He was tired of seeing them die, even guys like Fingers, who had probably lived on borrowed time since he was ten years old, and had deserved his fate ten times over.

We all deserve it, Cruz thought. All of us.

These maniacs had killed the fucking Guatemalan cleaning woman or whatever she was. Why? No loose ends. That was the excuse, anyway. That was always the excuse. The real reason was they had killed her because they felt like it. They had tied her to some cinderblocks and dumped her off of the pilings near one of the lighthouses. It was about twenty feet deep, they thought, and murky down there. Oh, somebody would find her sooner or later, sure, but they'd be gone by then. When they had told Cruz about it, he had nearly cried.

But he kept on the face. Impassive. A mask. Hell, he had seen it all before.

A thought surfaced like a shark from the depths of his mind. Dugan's money was out there, enough money to drop out of sight and get away from all this bullshit. Six safe deposit boxes, four here in town, one in Boston, and one up in Canada. Could it be true? Cruz found himself clinging to the idea that it was true, that most of the money was right here somewhere, and all he had to do was make Dugan go in the banks and get it for him. Tricky, but after seeing what Dugan was capable of, Cruz would be more careful next time. And Moss? Cruz could handle Moss if necessary.

'Yeah,' Cruz said. 'I suppose he did. That's what it was all about, wasn't it? Getting out? He had the place booby-trapped.'

He scanned the streets, looking for what he knew he wouldn't see – Smoke Dugan, bloodied and battered, his lungs half seared, limping along with the secret to more than two million unmarked dollars tucked away in his head. No, Dugan was back there somewhere, back near the flames.

Damn! Cruz had done exactly the wrong thing. If he had wanted Dugan, he would have had to risk the cops and the good people of South Portland and wait around back at that house. Instead he had run.

Getting old, Cruz. Getting weak.

'What's your big plan now?' Moss drawled.

Cruz had one ready. 'We go forward,' he said. 'Back across the bridge and into the city. We go see the girlfriend. If Dugan,

O'Malley, whatever he wants to call himself, lived through that, he's going to run to her next. Either to warn her, or collect her before he leaves town, but he's going to get her. And when he does, we'll already have her.'

'What if he don't?' Moss said. 'What if he just gets the money and leaves?'

'He won't,' Cruz said. 'An old guy like that, he's going to run for the girl.'

Moss smiled. 'All right, I'll buy it. The girl I saw in the pictures, I'd like to run to her too. Can't wait to meet her, in fact.'

Moss hit the gas and the stolen Taurus took off across the long, winding bridge toward the city.

Hal had a bad feeling.

He and Darren were parked in the Cadillac, the bucket seats lowered way back, watching the action on the dark, quiet street around Lola's building. The way they were sitting, Hal could just about scan the area over the top of the dashboard. A moment ago, they had watched two men pull up in a Ford Taurus, park it up the street, and climb out. One of them was fucking HUGE. To Hal, it seemed like his massive arms hung down almost to his knees. He was like a gorilla, only taller. In fact, the big guy had captured his attention so completely that it was only after a moment he noticed the other one – a little guy, thin, dark, wearing a light spring jacket, no doubt with a gun inside there somewhere.

His first thought: cops.

Sure, he had made these guys as the real thing in no time. Lola had called the cops and these guys, plainclothes detectives, were working the case. They were probably doing some follow-up with the victim — cop talk for 'let's go back and ogle that sexy chick some more'.

Shit.

All these thoughts had passed through Hal's mind in the first seconds after spotting them. Then they had come down the block, moving fast, and gone into Lola's little walk-up building. Here's where it got squirrelly. The building was old. It fronted the street with a red wooden door, right on the sidewalk. The door was locked — Hal had checked it half an hour ago. The big boy had jimmied the lock on the door and had it open in about ten seconds flat. Of course. These locks were to make the straight world feel safer. They were there to keep honest people on the narrow path. They didn't mean shit to somebody who knew how to take them down.

But why would two cops break into the building?

Easy answer: they're not cops.

He glanced over at Darren, who was smoking a joint to calm his nerves. The lumpy skin around Darren's eyes was slowly turning a sickly yellow. Darren smiled and offered the joint. It was clear from the beatific look on his face that Darren had taken the edge all the way off.

'No, thanks. Look, do me a favor, OK? Go up the block and break the right taillight on that Taurus those guys popped out of, will you?'

'Why?'

Hal shrugged. 'No reason. Just looks to me like something's going on, that's all. Boyfriends, maybe, but I doubt it. Boyfriends usually have a key to the front door. A broken taillight ain't really any harm if I'm wrong, is it?'

'Suppose not.'

Darren climbed out and moved up the block in the darkness.

Simple Darren. The two guys – bad guys, trouble – go in our building. A building we already cased. There's three apartments in there. The first floor opens on the street, and we already saw a creaking old man enter there just as the sun went down, straw hair swooped back over his head like a cartoon version of a symphony conductor. Then there's a second-floor apartment, currently empty. Then there's a third-floor apartment, belonging to Lola Bell / Pamela Gray, according to the mailbox. Roommates, apparently. These guys break in there, and Darren's wondering why I might want their taillight broken. So I can tail them, you silly fuck.

He loved Darren like a brother, but this is how Darren got to the trailer park. He didn't think. He couldn't think.

Hal heard the sound of a breaking taillight. At least Darren got that part right. Here he came now, floating back up the sidewalk like a ghost.

He slid into the passenger seat. 'No problem,' he said. The grin seemed permanently locked onto his face.

Hal glanced at the building again. He imagined reaching up and hitting that carved granite face he had seen go in there a moment ago. Just the thought of it made his arms tired. Another woman, a young white woman, her hair pulled straight back, came along the street and entered with what looked like a bag of groceries. She didn't even stop and notice the door was already open. She just went right inside.

'Well, it looks like we got ourselves a party now,' Hal said.

The pain was like a rotten tooth lodged in Smoke's skull.

'Shit,' he said. 'Motherfucker.'

He stood at the public phone in the parking lot of the Gas-N-Go. Traffic flowed by, the people oblivious to the life and death struggles going on all around them. Lola's telephone was a loud, obnoxious and constant busy signal. The girl was in her twenties, supposedly of the new modern generation, and she seemed like the only person left in America who didn't have call waiting.

He slammed the receiver down.

'Shit!' He walked around in a tight little circle.

Only moments ago, Smoke had awakened and crawled through the hedges next to his home. When he reached the end of the hedge, he had lingered in the alley a moment, staring out at the parked cars. Behind him, huge orange shadows had danced on the sides of houses. Every few seconds, his vision had grown dark at the edges and he thought he would pass out again.

The fire department had already come, hosing down the backyard and the shed, which burned intensely. Crowds of people had gathered. Smoke came out and began walking along the street, eyes downcast, his head spinning, limping along at just under double speed. Bad enough just to walk. But worse if people noticed him and saw how badly he had been beaten the same night that his workshop exploded. Either way, he had no choice – he had to get moving.

Now, he stepped a few yards away from the phone. He could still see the red-orange glow on the horizon. Cruz was out there now, rolling around like a loose ball bearing. No telling what he was going to do next. Then Smoke realized why Lola's phone was busy. Cruz was already there. He had taken the phone off the hook – maybe ripped it out of the wall. Maybe Moss had wrapped the phone cord between his hands and . . .

Shit, Lola. A searing pain ripped through Smoke. It had nothing to do with the beating he had endured. It was the pain of separation, the impotent fear for her safety. His mind raced. He couldn't breathe. He drifted back to the phone.

Call the cops. Call the fucking cops. Smoke had never called the cops in his life. Call the cops. Call them NOW.

A woman stood there next to him. She was blonde and slim, that kind of early-forties suburban mom who chauffeurs her children in a late model minivan from school to soccer practice to music lessons.

'Sir, do you need that telephone? My cellphone died.' She smiled, but the smile died when she saw his bloodied face.

'I'm using it,' he snapped.

'Are you all right? Do you need an ambulance?'

155

'I'm fine.'

He punched in Lola's number again. This time it rang. Thank God.

It rang and rang.

Finally, she picked it up. Her voice came, upbeat and musical as ever.

'Hello?'

Cruz and Moss paced through the second-floor apartment.

It stood to reason it would have a similar layout to Lola's place upstairs. Two bedrooms, a narrow bathroom, a living room, and a combined kitchen and dining room by the front door. This apartment was stripped – no furnishings, half painted – paint cans, ladders and canvas tarps piled in a corner of the living room. It had that stale, musty smell – that stench of paint and sawdust trapped inside for too long. Cruz looked around. All the windows were closed. The smell was giving him a headache.

It was crazy roundabout bullshit to do it this way. If they had the girl Dugan would have to give himself up. Or would he? Some men would ditch, Cruz knew. It all depended on what the old boy felt for this hot little black girl he had seen in the dossier, and that remained to be seen. If she was just a piece of ass to him, he would leave her behind and run.

That simple.

And then Cruz would have blown the job and would have one more person to kill, an innocent. Two innocents, including the old lady. Not to mention Moss. He'd have to kill Moss too, wouldn't he? Sure. If he blew this job, there was no going home again. Man, this shit was wearing on him.

'It ain't lightweight,' Vito had said. 'You let us worry about the thinking end of it.'

Well, it wasn't lightweight so far.

Someone was coming up the stairs. Moss pulled his gun and stepped lightly to the door and watched through the eyehole. Cruz heard the person reach the top of the first flight of stairs. Footsteps moved along the hallway.

'It's a girl,' Moss whispered. 'Going upstairs. Must be the roommate.'

Shit, another one. Another innocent in the way of this bullshit job. Cruz flashed to the cleaning woman weighted down in twenty feet of seawater, being picked clean by the crabs and the elements. When they pulled her out of there, they'd have to check the dental records just to know who she was.

Cruz didn't want to go up there, not with Moss. Moss could turn this thing into a bloodbath. Unless . . .

He felt the sudden urge and let it carry him for a moment. What would it take? Pull the Glock right now and put three slugs in the back of Moss's neck. Finish him with one to the brain. Walk out of this building then get in the car and drive.

Without the money.

No. It was too soon. Either do the job all the way through, bring Dugan back to New York, or wait around and get the money. Don't do neither. The realization came to Cruz like something that had always been there, submerged at the bottom of a deep pool but slowly working its way to the surface over long years. The way you retire, he grasped now, is you don't announce it beforehand.

Moss turned back to him. 'Ready?'

Cruz couldn't let Moss know just how far he had drifted in the past hour. At least, he couldn't let him know yet. 'Let's do it,' he said.

'You've gotta get out of there!' Smoke shouted. 'You gotta get out of there right this minute.' It made no sense.

Lola stood with the phone to her ear. She was distracted momentarily as Pamela came in from work. She had just this moment walked in the door with a bag of groceries from Micucci's Italian Market at the bottom of Munjoy Hill. She was in her neat work attire, slacks, a blouse, and a sports jacket. It was neat, but hardly sparkling. She wore sneakers for the long walk up the hill.

'Hey, babe,' Pamela said. 'You left the door open downstairs again.' She began to put the food away.

'I'm pretty sure I locked it,' Lola said.

'Listen to me! Will you listen to me?' Smoke was babbling, almost incoherent. Something about she had to get out of the house. He was insistent, he was raging, he was out of his mind. She had never heard him like this before.

'Wait a minute,' she said. 'Wait a minute. What are you saying?'

'I don't have time to explain,' came his voice. He sounded like he was outside somewhere, next to a highway. Cars were going past him in the background. 'Some men attacked me today.'

'What? Some men attacked you? Are you all right?' She thought of Mr Shaggy and Mr Blue Eyes. Had they attacked Smoke? Why would they attack Smoke? They could have been following her, seen Smoke, and decided to take out their revenge on him because they knew they couldn't harm her. Jesus!

'Who were the men? What did they look like?'

'Lola, shut up and listen to me!'

She stopped. She hated that. She hated when any man thought he could end the conversation just by being louder, or by putting on his man-authority voice. If he had been attacked, he needed to tell her about it. But he didn't have to tell her to shut up. She wouldn't stand for that. He knew as much too.

She heard her voice go cold. 'I'm listening, but it had better be good, and it had better come with a box of chocolates and some roses.'

He didn't take the hint, or even stop to comment on it. That, more than anything, made the skin on her back tighten into gooseflesh. He spoke slowly, as if to an imbecile or a child. There was something in his voice . . .

'Lola, I need you to trust me. Can you do that?'

'Yes.'

'OK, there's a lot I can't get into right now. I've been meaning to tell you, but I never did, and now you just have to do what I say. Some very dangerous men are in town. They want money from me. I got away from them, but I'm worried they're coming to get you. You have to get out of there.'

'Smoke, come on. What is this, a game?'

'Go out the back way. Right now. GO!'

Pamela came out of the bathroom, in stocking feet with her shirt unbuttoned halfway down from the collar. She headed back into the kitchen.

A knock came on the door. Lola looked at it. So what? Somebody was knocking. But how did they get in the building? Pamela changed directions and headed for the door. She reached out for the lock and the knob simultaneously. She wasn't even going to glance through the peephole.

Suddenly, Lola was afraid.

'Lola, you've got to get out of there right now. If Pamela is there, you have to take her with you. It's not safe.'

Pamela's hand was on the knob.

'Don't open it!' Lola screamed.

Too late.

Pamela turned to look at Lola, her eyes puzzled by the sudden outburst. She had unlocked the door, but hadn't opened it. The door burst open, knocking her backwards. Lola watched Pamela take two stagger steps backwards and fall to the floor.

A man came in. He walked with a swagger. He was huge, with impossibly muscular arms. The hand at the end of one of those arms held a gun. The gun had a large silencer attached to the end of it. He looked down at Pamela sprawled on the worn carpet near the door. Then he looked up at Lola.

He smiled.

Lola dropped the phone.

Cruz followed Moss up the narrow stairway. Moss's bulk barely fit between the walls. His head nearly scraped the low ceiling.

Moss burst through the door and Cruz padded in behind him, moving fast, moving quietly. Moss backed the black girl, Lola, into the living room with the gun. The other girl, a slim, bookish white girl, was lying on the floor in a daze. Cruz pulled the door shut and locked it.

The girl on the floor stared up at him. Pretty girl, gone numb.

'If you do anything, I'll kill you,' he said to her. He held up his gun for her to see it better. 'It has big bullets. It'll put big holes in your body. Understand?'

She nodded. Her eyes were wide and hollow like those of a Japanese cartoon.

'Is anyone else here?'

She gazed at him and didn't answer. Couldn't answer.

Cruz did a quick sweep of the apartment. He already had one extra witness. He hoped nobody else was in here. God, the bodies were piling up. He didn't want to think about it. He went into a room. It was a bedroom with a double bed, the headboard against the wall. There was a poster of a black girl in tennis whites on the wall. Black girls played tennis? So much Cruz didn't know. He picked around in the closet. Nothing here, except some clothes, skirts and such. The room was clean. He went back outside.

He paused in the doorway and glanced over at Moss, who had Lola at gunpoint. She wore a pair of black tights and a belly shirt. Her body seemed to defy gravity. Her hair hung down in wild curls. She was something.

Moss looked at Cruz.

He grinned, and gestured at her with the gun. 'Whaddya think?' he said.

Just then, Lola kicked out.

Amazingly, she knocked Moss's gun right up into the air. Her kick finished high, nearly as tall as Moss's head, and the gun flew back up and over his head, into the room Cruz was standing in. It slid across the floor. Moss watched it go. The girl followed up with a punch at Moss's throat. Moss stepped back just before getting the brunt of it.

He laughed.

'Girl, I never saw anyone kick that high. Not in real life.'

Then she came for him.

Her movements were a blur. Moss blocked her first two punches. He was still laughing, the embarrassed laughter of a ten-year-old boy being attacked by a little girl in his class. Then Cruz saw her knee go into his groin. Moss grunted. A fist connected with his face. He barely moved. It was almost as if he was watching it happen to him. He couldn't get his engine going. His eyes said that this sort of thing just didn't happen. She hooked his leg, whirled and elbow-smashed him in the face.

He lost his balance, stepping backwards and sideways. She kept coming.

162

A punch, a kick and down he went. Moss went down.

MOSS . . . WENT . . . DOWN.

It was like watching a building fall. Cruz felt the floor shake. Incredible.

'Pamela!' Lola shouted. 'Pamela, get the gun.'

The girl Pamela looked up from her stupor. Her eyes brightened as she became aware of the situation. She was four feet from the gun. Cruz was halfway across the room from her. Ridiculous. Imagine if that little girl actually picked up the gun and began shooting it? She probably wouldn't hit anything, but then again she might. In any event, a lot of shooting wasn't the answer in this small apartment building in this residential neighborhood.

She crawled across the floor and reached for Moss's gun.

Despite everything, Cruz felt calm. Very cool. He had seen worse than this. A lot worse. He had seen worse this very afternoon.

He held up his gun again. 'Pamela,' he said.

She looked up at him. He pointed the gun at her and drew a bead down the barrel. He didn't want to kill her. That was the last thing he wanted. Her face was perfectly centered in his iron sights.

There was no way he could pull this trigger.

'Pamela, if you pick up that gun I'm going to kill you. What I want you to do is crawl right back to where you were.'

Long seconds passed.

She backed away from the gun.

'That's a good girl.'

As Pamela crawled away, Cruz moved in and picked up the gun. Then he backed into his doorway again, where he could get a better view of the whole apartment. He looked back over at Lola and Moss. Moss was up, circling in. He was still laughing, but he didn't sound as enthusiastic as before. Lola circled away from him.

'Yessir,' he said, almost to himself. 'I never seen anything like it.'

She swung and he blocked it with his thick arm, but an instant later her other hand came around and caught him on the side of the head. Then a foot shot up and kicked him in the balls. She danced away, just out of his reach.

'Lola!' Cruz called.

She cast an eye at him, all the while minding Moss.

'I want you to stop now,' Cruz said. 'If you don't, then I'm going to have to kill Pamela. Do you hear me? We're here to see you. Pamela is worth nothing to us. If you don't stop I promise I will kill her. If you do stop, I promise I'll let her live. How does that sound to you?'

Lola faced Moss again.

'Lola, I'm going to kill her right now. Do you understand?'

Sure, she understood. She must have because she hesitated for a moment, then let her arms go slack by her sides. She was winded, and she had a fine sheen of sweat on her face. Cruz pictured her dancing at a nightclub with a similar sheen on her. For an instant, he pictured her moving in bed, her body glistening.

'All right,' she said. 'You win.'

Moss walked over to her.

'My friend's going to give you some handcuffs to put on,' Cruz said.

Instead, Moss smacked her hard across the face, an open hand slap. She fell backwards onto the couch.

'The bitch kicked me in the balls,' Moss said. He wiped his mouth with his hand.

Cruz watched as Moss took out the cuffs and slapped them on.

Cruz looked at Pamela. What to do about her?

Moss came over and stuck out his hand. It seemed a foot wide. He didn't look Cruz in the eye. He doesn't like that, Cruz thought. Tangling with a little girl, and being rescued by me. He doesn't like *me*. Cruz had known this since yesterday, but it was the first time he actually thought the words. Moss didn't like him. Moss might look for a reason to kill him.

'Gun, please.'

Cruz handed Moss his gun back.

Moss looked down at Pamela on the floor. He toyed with his gun a moment, as if he were thinking everything over.

'You serious?' he said. 'You plan on keeping this one?' He pointed at Pamela with the gun. It would take nothing, a few ounces of pressure, a mistake, and he would shoot her in the face.

'I gave my word, didn't I?'

Moss shook his head. 'Son, this is the most fucked-up job ever.'

* * *

Hal and Darren sat slumped way down below the dashboard of Hal's Eldorado. They watched as, down the block, the two men came out with Lola and the other girl. The smaller guy seemed to be leading Lola along by her elbow. Oh, they weren't cops, these two. Something deeper was going on.

Hal felt that old tickle of curiosity. This was even better than what they came for, maybe. 'Her hands seem to be cuffed to you?' he said to Darren. 'You catch a glint of metal there or anything? Both the girls, they got handcuffs on?'

Darren was watching. 'I dunno. Can't tell. What did you think?'

Hal shrugged. 'I think I saw something.'

He kept watching. Now he really saw something. Up ahead, the two men opened the trunk of the Taurus and helped the girls inside. What the fuck? They put the girls in the trunk! And the girls went right on in there!

Unbelievable!

'Did you see that?' Darren said.

'I saw it.'

'What do you want to do? Call the cops?'

Hal's wheels were turning like mad. 'I don't know. And say what? This girl we were trying to put into porno just got abducted by two other guys? First off, I don't like to let two guys just walk off with my girl. Second off, I don't want to just hand this over to the cops. Could be something big here. Could be money involved. Could be Lola needs to be rescued, and we're the ones who need to do it. What do you say? You want to follow these guys? I mean, if we let them go, what else are we doing tonight? Aren't you the least bit curious about what's going on?'

Darren heaved a heavy sigh. 'Did you see the size of that guy?'

'I saw him. Don't worry, partner. I saw him, and we'll steer clear of him until we're good and ready.'

'Do I have any other choice?' Darren said.

Hal smiled. 'Nope. It's either this or crawl back to Auburn with your tail between your legs.'

He waited until the Taurus had turned left at the next corner onto Congress Street. Up at this end of town, the top of Munjoy Hill, Congress dead-ended into a quiet street of walk-up apartment buildings and storefronts. Down at the bottom of the hill, it became the main artery for downtown Portland.

Hal pulled out onto the street and cruised to the corner of Congress. The car was up ahead, driving down Munjoy Hill into the lights of downtown.

'We should've used handcuffs the other night,' Darren said. 'On Lola, I mean. Keep her pacified.'

'Maybe we will,' Hal said. 'Maybe we'll make handcuffs a regular part of the act.'

Hal made a left, and he and Darren followed the Taurus downhill. The naked bulb shone bright white, while the rest of the taillights shone red and yellow. Darren had done a good job. Hal was going to be able to read that thing from a hundred yards back.

Hal knew how to tail.

For a long time, Hal had drifted from place to place and

job to job. For a while he worked as a security guard, and that job led to undercover store security, and finally to a gig working with a private detective agency. He spent five years as a detective, then started his own firm and went belly-up in a matter of months. But he was good at surveillance, he knew that much.

In truth, Hal figured that he excelled at almost everything he did. Amazing really, since he had just about graduated high school, after all. Now, he had spent more than twenty years finding out how good he could be at things.

Tailing with one car, though – this was going to be work.

'You're letting 'em get too far ahead,' Darren said.

'I got 'em,' Hal said.

'Yeah, but—'

'Brother, you got to keep it shut and let me do this, OK?' He said it forcefully, in a way that would pre-empt any more conversation. He needed all the concentration he could muster, and he couldn't afford a smoked-up Darren butting in every couple of minutes. Darren was not the brains of this operation.

The Taurus was three blocks in front already. Ahead and far below was the skyline of the city, lit up at night. Hal let them put on a nice lead, and kept his eye on that broken taillight. It disappeared for a second behind another car, then came back. He didn't worry. It took an instinct, and he had it. You had to know where that car was going to be. Here was his guess: they would turn right on Washington Avenue and head for the highway – 295 North – or they would head straight downtown.

'No problem, no problem,' he said to the Taurus. 'Do what you need to do.'

When Hal did detective work, on important jobs, two tail cars was the minimum. Three cars were better, if the client would pay for that sort of thing. The more cars the better. One car would be on the tail awhile, then drop back and another one would pick it up. The extra cars would be on the radio, following along on parallel streets. On the highway, they'd drop waaaaay back, or they'd speed up and get out ahead. Whatever. Keep dropping in and out of the tail, give them different looks, that way the target wouldn't catch on. Leapfrogging, they used to call it.

But one car. That was an art. You had to play it real cool. You had to lose touch sometimes. You couldn't give them any reason to suspect you. If they did, if they made you, then they'd bolt. They'd blow red lights. They'd drive the wrong way on one-way streets. They'd make U-turns at police speed traps on the highway. They made a move like that, then you were lost. You blew it. You couldn't follow.

Hal had a hunch here. It buzzed in his head like electricity. These guys weren't going to blow any red lights. They weren't going to try to shake a tail. There was something happening, and they couldn't risk getting busted by a traffic cop – not with a couple of prisoners in the trunk.

In the trunk! He couldn't fucking believe it. Man, this beat everything. This was like the movies. This was better. This was real. Totally awesome. Goddamn! They had walked right into some kind of full-blown hostage drama.

Hostages. Sure. These bastards had taken the girls hostage.

In some sense, hadn't he and Darren done the same from time to time?

'Make a right,' Cruz said. 'Right here, take this right.'

Moss took a long looping right past a fried chicken takeout and onto a main drag, Washington Avenue. It was long, nearly deserted, a big old warehouse or factory passing by on their right. The highway entrance was at the end of this strip.

Cruz found himself sulking as they drove along. It hadn't gone as he intended. Nothing on this whole trip had gone as he intended. That fucking taillight. He didn't like that at all. Trouble was, he wasn't sure that it hadn't been broken in the first place. Fingers would know, but Fingers was dead.

Why would Fingers steal a car with a broken taillight?

He wouldn't, that's why.

'Now! Make this left!'

Moss veered in front of an oncoming car and made the left. They cruised down a steep hill, a side street with run-down houses climbing the hill. At the bottom, there were low-slung garden-apartment-style housing projects. From an unlit basketball court, dark black faces peered at them as they passed.

'I'm telling you, son. I've been in this game a little while now. There ain't nobody back there. It was a kid that broke the taillight.'

'Why ours?'

'Why the fuck not? You paranoid, Cruz? That the problem?'

Cruz didn't like it. The variables were piling up. Two girls in a trunk. A broken taillight. It was supposed to be a quick snatch, and then a return drive to New York. Goodbye, Smoke Dugan O'Malley, you worry about your problems, I'll worry about mine. Instead, two people were already dead, and this Lola girl would have to go when all was said and done. She would have to go just as surely as the skinny girl, her roommate, would have to go.

And all the while, Cruz was thinking about getting out. Face it. He was no good for this business anymore.

Moss cruised the side streets, moving slow, making random rights and lefts, stopping at all stop signs. They passed a parked police car. The cop was inside, writing something in his book. He didn't look up.

'We done out here? You mind if I get back and get on the highway now? That's all we need, a porky little pig pulling us over for a broken light,' Moss said.

'That'd be one dead pig,' Cruz said absently. He meant it. No matter what trouble he himself was having, he knew Moss would drop a cop without giving it much thought.

He checked in back of them one last time. No one back there. Just dead, deserted streets.

'Yeah, go for it,' he said. 'Make a left here.'

Moss made a left and climbed back up toward Washington Avenue.

'I think you're losing your focus, son. We got the girl, like we said we were gonna do. OK. The man'll either give it up or he won't. If he don't, then we got problems. But in the meantime, we got this extra girl back there. And that's a problem right now. She's baggage back there. I can't have that and neither can you. It's bad for business.'

'I see what you mean,' Cruz said. To Moss, his decision to spare the roommate must have looked like weakness. To Moss, this entire job must have looked like weakness.

'I hope you do,' Moss said.

They were back on Washington Avenue, right near the chicken takeout again. A group of dark-skinned men sat out on plastic lawn chairs in front of another eatery, this one with no sign on it at all. The whole long strip of the avenue was darkened and nearly deserted. As they headed down the street, a few people loitered here and there in the gloom, standing around in ones and twos.

'Let me see your phone,' Cruz said.

'Son, you need to stop giving orders. Your big-shot orders got my little buddy killed earlier today.'

Cruz and Moss crossed eyes like swords. Now was not the time for the showdown with Moss. Or was it? Cruz pictured whipping out his gun and blowing Moss away right here in the car. It was one measure of how far he had fallen that Moss would say these things to him. The deeper measure, however, was that Moss was still alive. He couldn't fight the man – Moss was too big, too strong. In the old days, Cruz would have just killed him instead.

'Lend me your cellphone, will you?' he said. 'I want to call Dugan so that we can save this job before it goes all the way down the shithole.'

'That's better,' Moss said. 'I thought you didn't use cell-phones.'

'In an emergency, I'll make an exception.'

Moss handed him the phone, a small black number with a lot of meaningless features. Cruz scrutinized it for what he needed, the green SEND button, for one. He fished in his pocket for the girl's home number, straight from the dossier.

'What's the story with this phone?' he said. He hated cellphones. He didn't even like to look at them. Cops could snatch these conversations right out of the air. Cops could trace back these phone calls. Somebody dies, and then what? The cops check the phone records, right? And here's this cellphone number. Hell, maybe it's right there on the caller ID. Shit, he hated these things. Lazy people used cellphones.

Moss shrugged. 'It's clean.'

'How clean?'

'It's PCS. Completely digital. Encryption codes make it almost impossible to intercept the call.'

To Cruz, it sounded like so much mumbo-jumbo. 'What about trace-backs?'

'The phone belongs to a gentleman from Fresno, California. He paid the whole contract, a whole year, up front. He likes to travel a lot, this gentleman. He's got coverage everywhere in the great forty-eight. Anybody traces back a call, they'll find out this gentleman made that call.'

'Who is he?'

Moss smiled, showing the gap in his front teeth. 'Someone who don't exist anymore.'

Hal leaned up against a telephone pole in the dim light along Washington Avenue.

Thirty yards away, the Cadillac was parked in the lot of the old bread factory. Now it was an office building, a low-rent warren filled with the offices of low-budget social service organizations. Hal glanced at the Caddy. Darren was hunched down low, probably wondering what the hell he was doing out here.

'Come on,' Hal said under his breath. 'Come to me, baby.'

All the same, he was starting to worry. He had seen them make that sudden turn down the side street. But he knew those streets. He knew there was nothing down there for them. He *knew* it. There was nothing down there but machine shops, auto shops, and housing projects filled with refugees from African wars. Imagine, the wretched of the earth, refugees from Somalia and the Sudan, the desert, the baking heat, the sand storms, being relocated to Maine. It was like a cruel joke. Don't like all the warfare, you desert nomads? Here, try snow and ice six months out of the year.

A car was coming along the avenue.

Hal looked at his shoes.

It passed, and he looked up. A green Ford Taurus. The broken taillight shone bright and white as it receded in the distance. They were heading for the highway.

'Ha! I knew you couldn't leave me!'

He stepped into the shadows and ran for the Caddy.

It was cramped and dark in the trunk.

At times, little beams of light stabbed in through some crack above their heads. It was hard to breathe. They were on their sides, hands cuffed in front of them, facing each other. For a while, Pamela had hyperventilated. Now, as Lola watched her, Pamela simply lay there, eyes wide like saucers, tears streaming down her face, her lower lip quivering.

'Listen!' Lola hissed. 'Pamela! Listen to me.' Pamela was beyond listening.

The car hit some kind of dip in the road. They went down and then up. It was like riding a roller coaster. Lola nearly fell over on her face. The car accelerated, and she guessed they were on the highway now.

'It's going to be OK,' she said, not sure if she was saying it to Pamela or to herself.

She thought of the moment the two men burst into the apartment. Smoke was on the phone, shouting something into her ear. Then that massive man with the stringy hair was there. He seemed to fill the entire room. And she had fought him. Kicked him. Punched him. Knocked the gun out of his hand. Knocked him down.

When he had slapped her, it was like a car crash, the force of it. He was that strong. She had been stunned. No one had ever hit her that hard before. And she knew he hadn't hit her nearly as hard as he could.

But he wasn't unbeatable. None of them was. They could be beaten, and she could do it. Maybe if Pamela . . . no, Pamela was a goner. Well, you could hardly blame her. Two strange men storm the apartment, handcuff them, and whisk them off.

To where?

Where are we going? Who are these men? The questions piled up. She had never seen either of them before in her life. She pieced it together. They were the ones who had attacked Smoke. Did they know Mr Shaggy and Mr Blue Eyes? Maybe not. Smoke had said it had something to do with him – they wanted money from him. Why did they want money from Smoke?

She sighed heavily.

All these men.

She had defined her life in relation to them. If she could, she thought she would thank those boys that raped her now, if she ever saw them again. Unfortunately that in itself would be hard to do. But she would if she could because the boys had awakened her. They had created the Lola that existed now.

At first, she had crumpled up and died inside.

After she was raped, she had dropped out of school, she had quit dancing lessons, she didn't go anywhere. She didn't see her friends anymore. She stopped taking an interest in anything. She stayed in her room and watched soap operas on television most of the day. She didn't even read.

One day when she woke up, there was a thin, paperback

book on the table next to her bed. Her grandmother had gone out to run her errands, but that book was there. It was called *Sandinista Woman*. It had a photo of a woman on the cover, a Hispanic woman in a green camouflage military outfit.

Lola didn't pick it up at first. First she watched TV. But later in the day she grew bored with the television, and she picked up the book. It was the story of exactly that, a woman who had fought with the Sandinista revolution in Nicaragua. The woman had been captured by the fascist forces of the Nicaraguan government, and raped by dozens of soldiers. It was a source of terrible shame for the woman, until she met other women who were fighters for the cause. They came to realize there was nothing to be ashamed of in their suffering, that indeed it was a badge of honor. Gradually, all of the women came to realize this, as did the men who fought alongside them.

Lola read the book in two days, stopping only to eat and use the bathroom.

Still, she didn't buy it right away.

The next day, a flyer slid through the crack under her bedroom door. It showed an Asian man flying through the air, kicking and shattering a brick that must have been suspended ten feet from the ground.

'DEFEND YOURSELF!' the flyer read. 'Learn devastating self-defense techniques from a master.' At the bottom of the flyer it said, 'Special Women-Only Classes Available.'

Below that, her grandmother had scrawled in pencil: 'Interested?'

So Lola joined. What else was she going to do? She couldn't stay in that room for ever. At first it seemed like a joke. The basic techniques she was learning, she didn't think they'd work on anybody. But times passed, and months later she wasn't so sure.

She started to come alive again.

And as part of being alive, she began to think of revenge. They had stolen her old life from her, but now she had this new life. She was increasing in confidence, and with that newfound confidence came a new question. Could she get back at them somehow?

If so, how?

She began to keep alert for news of them. Five boys, one older than her by a year, a couple her age, one a year younger and one a year younger than that. Kendrick. Tyrone. Abel. Michael. Ishmael.

A whole year went by and she was still musing on this subject. She had changed – she was astounded by the things her body was capable of. It still didn't mean she could take her revenge with that body, though.

Michael died in a drive-by shooting. A week later, Tyrone and Abel were arrested for the crime. A year after that, Ishmael was shot in the groin and then in the back by an unknown assailant or assailants. He lived, but he was paralyzed from the waist down. The rumor went that not only was he impotent, but that his member was actually obliterated. That left only Kendrick alive and on the streets. And he had disappeared.

Five years ago, it came to pass on a chilly evening in March that she climbed off the bus three blocks from her apartment and her dying grandmother, and began to walk home. It had been raining all day, and had just stopped recently. The ground was wet, the air was wet, and she could see her breath as she moved along. Just in front of her, a big man shuffled along in a long and ratty trench coat. From behind him, all she could see was the slope of his back, the shake, rattle and roll of his legs, and the fluffy crown of unkempt nappy hair piled on top. She moved along behind him, walking slow, watching the tall man weave.

The back was familiar, but she almost couldn't believe it was him.

On this strip, nobody was around. Two young crack dealers lolled on a bench to their right. One said something to the other and they both laughed. Tall and skinny, they looked to be about twelve years old. They both wore big bubble TROOP jackets, their legs sticking out the bottom like pipe cleaners. They looked like some new kind of dinner bird, fattening up for Christmas.

Lola watched the big man approach them. He said something, but they shook their heads. 'Ken, you used up all your credit already. Go on back to Gary, you want credit.'

The big man shuffled on.

The kid called him Ken. Her heart did a lazy barrel roll. It had been years since she had seen him.

She let him get another ten yards past the prepubescent dealers. Then she moved in. 'Kendrick?' At first her voice came out as a croak and the man heard nothing. He just shambled along, bopping to some music only he could hear.

'Kendrick!' And this time it was a shout.

The two dealers sat up and took notice. Perhaps here came some of the family strife that was such a constant backdrop to the ghetto. This was entertainment. For two young men on the fast track to oblivion, this would be better than the lame, watered-down fare on television. This was real-life, messy, often action-packed and bloody, and without any commercials.

The man turned around, his body moving as slowly as the glaciers.

He was tall, a full head taller than Lola. That was the first thing that sank in. The next thing that sank in was how horribly wasted he had become. His shoulders were broad, and so had seemed to give some shape to the trench coat as it hung down. But beneath that coat he wore a Milwaukee Brewers T-shirt and red sweat pants. Both were ratty and had holes in them. And he was skinny. The T-shirt, which must have been a small or a medium, clung to a frame that had once worn extra large. His navel showed at the bottom of it. The clothes had probably come from a mission somewhere that gave out such clothes. Summer clothes in the winter, winter clothes in the summer. He wore old Air Jordan sneakers with no socks.

Sure, wearing somebody's cast-off sneakers.

He peered at her and she came closer. Closer, she began to get the smell of him, the funk of days without a bath, of nights on benches in train and bus stations. In the light of the streetlamp she saw his rheumy bloodshot eyes and that he trembled just slightly. An old scar ran under his chin.

It was Kendrick. Times had caught up with him.

'Lola?' he said, squinting just a bit now. His voice was hardly more than a whisper. 'Lola.' The second time he said it with a nod to himself, as if the sudden appearance of Lola now confirmed everything, as if this was the final rung of his downfall. He smiled a grim smile and showed the black spaces where some of his teeth once were.

'We got you good, girl. Stopped going to school and everything. That's what they told me. Never saw you on the street no more. Yessir, we got to you good.'

She dropped her bag, much like she had dropped her books four years before. She stepped up, hands protecting her face, and gave him a front kick to the groin. She didn't try to kick hard, she just concentrated and moved her body properly. This generated more than enough force, coming out in a line from her torso, her buttocks and finally the big leg muscles above the knee.

Kendrick melted to his hands and knees on the wet ground. He coughed hard as if to clear his throat.

Only a second had passed, maybe two. Lola resumed her stance, then fired a roundhouse kick that caught the side of Kendrick's head. He fell over sideways and sprawled half on the sidewalk, half on the muddy weeds and dog shit that bordered the sidewalk.

Behind Lola, one of the drug dealers whooped and hollered.

'You go, girl! Bruce Lee, motherfucker. She fucked that ass up!'

The two boys laughed.

And like that, the anger evaporated. It was replaced by a calm and almost bitter disappointment. She immediately understood that it was a feeling from which she would spend a long time reconciling, maybe the rest of her life. For four years she had hated this bastard. No, she had more than hated him. He had become almost everything to her. She had trained for the day when they would meet again and she would be ready for him. She carried a carving knife in her bag in anticipation. She imagined he would be the strong and arrogant and evil Kendrick that he was at eighteen, not this pitiful character, already the walking dead at twenty-two. She imagined theirs would be an epic battle that would take all her energy to fight, and might take both their lives. Her identity, her life had become defined in relation to this man and what he had done. Her revenge had become her obsession.

And here she was, standing over him. But the victory was far from sweet. The ghetto had taken revenge long before she ever got there. If she wanted to kill Kendrick, she would have to spend six months cleaning him up first, feeding him, keeping him off drugs, building up his wasted muscles. Otherwise it wouldn't mean anything.

Kendrick's breaths came in rasps. He was down and out, as far down as most people get without being dead. Drug-addicted, weak, cold, and now lying in the mud after a swift beat down from a woman wronged. It was a long walk back, and Lola knew that when someone had come this far, they didn't even try to make that walk. It was too damned far.

'Bitch,' Kendrick said in that same hoarse voice. 'Bitch.' Lola looked closer and saw he was crying. She thought about spitting on him, for old times' sake, but she couldn't even bring herself to do that. Everything had once again been stolen from her. She picked up her bag and continued on her way.

When she was half a block away, she turned around to see if Kendrick had managed to get up yet. He hadn't. He was on all fours on the wide, glistening sidewalk. Like circling vultures, the two boys had moved in after she was gone. When a man was down, a man was down. The law of the jungle prevailed. They took turns kicking him and jumping up and down on his carcass.

From where she stood, their laughter was carried to her on the breeze. It was the laughter of childhood. In another time and place, two boys might laugh like that on their way down to the creek to go fishing.

It was time to go home.

Smoke arrived at the apartment knowing how late he was.

It was full dark. He parked his little Toyota half a block down from the apartment. He killed the headlights, then waited and watched. No one was moving on the street. TV lights flickered from homes on his left and his right. His sense of dread was so complete that he felt he might vomit. All along, he had made mistakes, and now it had probably cost Lola and Pamela their lives. He should have told Lola long ago about his life before now. Scratch that — he shouldn't have become involved with Lola, or anyone.

A breeze kicked up and the trees along the street creaked and swayed. Shadows moved. A young couple, bundled up and leaning on each other, laughed together as they walked along the sidewalk.

He had killed the kid without thinking of the fallout. It had been an instinct. Kill the kid. Kill them all. Get away. But of course he hadn't been able to kill them all. That big guy, Moss, it would be hard to kill a guy like that.

He should have let them take him in — maybe he could've escaped some other way. Lola's death was a horrible price to pay for his own life.

He had been unable to go back to the apartment — the neighborhood was crawling with cops and firemen. His car was around the corner, so he had simply climbed in and driven off. He didn't know when he would go back there. So the long and the short of it was he couldn't pick up his guns. They were trapped in the apartment. In the old days, he had loathed guns, but over time he had made a certain peace with them. Since he had been on the run, he had kept three of them: two, fully loaded, safeties off, hidden in the apartment, and one small two-shot Derringer here in the car, tucked away under the driver's seat.

At least he had the Derringer — the Bond Arms Cowboy Defender. He held it in his big hand. Five inches long in total, with three-inch, over-under barrels. It was so small that it looked almost like a toy cigarette lighter. But it packed a wallop. It fired two .45 rounds, and was fully loaded. The barrel was so short that the gun was useless except for the most up-close fighting. That's why he kept it in the car. You couldn't hit the side of a barn with it if the barn was more than ten yards away, but if somebody was sitting in the car with you, or standing right in front of you, you might just kill them. He thought of Moss again. He looked at the tiny Derringer in his hand.

Jesus.

He climbed out of the car and moved slowly toward the building, limping, gun palmed in his hand. He could palm the fucking thing, like they used to do to hide their cigarettes from adults when he was nine years old. Despite the chill of autumn in the air, beads of sweat ran down the back of his neck. He had incinerated their friend, so God only knew what they had done to his friends.

Unless, of course, they were still up there, lying in wait for him. He had called the apartment again, and had gotten only a busy signal, but that didn't mean anything. They could be sitting there in the living room, waiting for him to walk in. Or lurking in the stairwell along the empty second floor.

Well, fuck it. If he was going down, he was going down shooting.

He reached the building. The old man was home downstairs, playing his violin. The haunting beauty of the music seemed to come from a world other than the one Smoke inhabited. Looking around, up and down the street, he entered the building.

Nobody was in the bottom hallway.

The overhead light was on. He reached up and smashed it out with the gun. The small crash of the bulb breaking didn't disturb the violinist in the least. Smoke ventured up the narrow stairs into the gloom of the second floor. He tried not to let the ancient wood creak. It was ridiculous. If they came now, he would be doomed. Then again, better they come for him than kill Lola. He stopped trying to hide himself.

He reached the second-floor landing, and hobbled along until he reached the bottom of the stairs to the third floor. He peered up. The door was closed. There was no sound up there. He climbed the stairs.

The door was unlocked. He walked in.

Nobody here.

He could feel the apartment's emptiness. The light in the bathroom was on, throwing shadows through the living room. The coffee table in there had collapsed, as though someone had fallen on top of it. That was the only sign of struggle he could see.

He stood for a moment, holding his breath, looking and listening.

No sound, except from below. Far away, the strains of the violin.

He settled onto one of the dining-room chairs. His breath came out in a long, low groan. OK. He had come this far. Now he would take a moment, gather his emotions, and then search the rest of the apartment. If anyone was here, they were dead.

I'm so sorry, Lola.

The phone was on the floor. He stood, picked up the receiver, and placed it back in the cradle hanging on the kitchen wall.

It started ringing.

Smoke jumped so high he nearly banged his head against the low ceiling.

Two rings. Three rings. He stood and watched it ring. He picked it up just before the answering machine.

'Hello?'

'Dugan?' the voice said. It was Cruz. It had to be.

'Yes.'

'Are you alone?'

'Yes.'

'Good. I was wondering when you were going to finally get there. That was some job you pulled with the kid. It's not going to make this any easier on anybody.'

Smoke swallowed. 'I understand that.'

The voice went on, 'Your friend is here with us. OK? Other than that, we don't have much to talk about.'

'There's no reason for her to be involved.'

'Well, sure, I agree with that. But you involved her. OK?'

'OK.'

The little man went on, 'The other one too. The roommate.'

'Was she here?'

'Oh, yeah.'

Smoke nearly choked. 'Where is she now?'

Cruz said nothing. He didn't even answer. Smoke had dealt

with men like this for most of his life. They were fucking animals. They had no reason to keep Pamela alive. No reason at all.

'Where is she?' Smoke repeated.

'See if you can find her.'

Fuck.

'So it seems like the thing for you to do is to get moving. That place is going to get pretty hot by tomorrow, if not later tonight. I don't think your friend here wants you to see that kind of heat, you know?'

Smoke knew. Sooner or later, the explosion at his apartment, combined with the death of the kid and Smoke's disappearance, would lead the cops here to Lola's place. In fact, sooner or later the cops were going to find out that there was no Smoke Dugan. Probably sooner rather than later. They were going to take some prints in that apartment and find out that Smoke Dugan was actually Walter O'Malley, convicted felon from thirty years ago. Shit. He needed some time before the police came down on him. The last thing he needed was to get picked up by the cops. Getting picked up by the cops was worse than getting picked up by Cruz. They'd kill Lola and then get him in jail.

Cruz went on. 'Do me a favor, all right? We need a place to meet, a public-type place, a crowded restaurant, say. We're there, you walk in, sit down at our table, your friend gets up and walks out. And we need to know where you'll be staying tonight, a place we can reach you. Got any ideas? We're open to ideas right now. Ways we can make this happen without too much pain.'

'There's a Best Western in South Portland,' Smoke heard himself say. 'It's a motel right by an exit off the highway. There's a big restaurant there, Governor's, a lot of people go there for breakfast.'

'Yeah? How's the food?'

'You eat eggs? Bacon? It's a buffet.'

'OK, that sounds good. Best Western, South Portland. Governor's Restaurant.' There was a pause as Smoke imagined Cruz writing this down on a napkin or an envelope. 'Your friend know how to get there?'

'Sure.'

'OK, then. Take a room at the Best Western. We'll contact you there tomorrow, or maybe later tonight. You won't know. If you're not there when we call, I guess you know what happens. The deal will be off. The trade won't happen. Do you know what I mean?'

'I do.' The trade was Smoke for Lola. That's what they were offering. 'Is the trade for both of them?'

'Sure, if you like.'

It didn't sound right. He didn't know whether to believe them or not. Lola and Pamela could both be dead already.

'Put her on the phone.'

'Who's that?'

'You know.'

'Tomorrow.'

Smoke shook his head, as though Cruz could see that. 'Not tomorrow, now.'

'OK, that's enough chat. Never know who's listening

nowadays. Do me that little favor I mentioned, will you? Wouldn't want anything to get in the way.'

Smoke was about to say something else.

The line went dead.

He stood there with the phone in his hand for several minutes. Out the back window, and far away, a boat went by on the dark water. He couldn't see the boat at all. He could tell it was there by the red running light at its stern.

The phone started buzzing violently. 'If you'd like to make a call,' a robot woman said, 'please hang up and try again. If you'd like to make a call . . .'

Smoke hung up.

Shit.

He walked through the rooms absently, checking out the rest of the apartment. Shadows loomed all around him. No one was here. Pamela wasn't here. Whatever they had done with her, they hadn't left her behind.

He went into Lola's room and the life-size poster of the black tennis player startled him. It hung there over the bed, accusing him. You murdered her. You did it. There was nothing he could say in his defense.

He kept an extra cane here at the apartment. He rooted around in the closet and found it at the back, behind a pile of clothes. That, at least, was something.

He went back into the dining area and sat down again.

Smoke looked at the cane in his hands. It was knobby wood, more of a walking stick than a cane. Along its shaft was a button, camouflaged to look like a part of the cane itself. You'd have to look closely even to notice it.

Hell, you'd have to know it was there.

He pressed the button and the bottom twelve inches of the cane detached and fell off. A sharp stiletto spike six inches long protruded from the end of the shaft that he held. A solid jab with that would pierce anyone's heart, even big, bad Moss.

Smoke looked at his large workman's hands.

He had the strength. He could do it.

'You see, I don't often hit girls,' Moss was saying. 'I don't like doing it.'

They were driving north along Interstate 95, Moss's big hands gripping the wheel. All around them, the darkness had closed in. Cruz marveled at how the city simply ended and the country began. There was nothing to see out here but trees. It was like driving off a cliff into complete darkness.

Well, they'd let all that smoke clear back there, and hide the girls somewhere Dugan couldn't try to get at them. In the morning, they could go and collect Dugan, provided the cops hadn't already done so. Or they could make Dugan wait a little while. Fear him up that they were going to kill his girls.

In fact, Cruz wasn't sure what to do next.

He thought of the money again.

How many times? How many times had he put down someone who thought they could run? Too many. No amount of money was enough. Certainly not a couple mil.

He glanced sidelong at Moss. That thick, solid skull. It wouldn't stop a bullet.

Would it?

'So,' Moss said. 'You know, the girl is kicking me and hitting me, and I'm not fighting back.' He shrugged. 'You know?'

Cruz lit a cigarette. 'I know. But you think we ought to shoot this other one?'

Moss looked at him. 'Don't you?'

It was Cruz's turn to shrug.

'Anyway, it's one thing to hit a girl,' Moss said. 'It's another thing to shoot somebody. Shooting's easier.'

'Very true.'

A half-hour passed, each lost in his own thoughts. They got off the highway and cruised slowly down the dark and quiet exit ramp and along a feeder road. There was not another car on the road. They turned at an intersection, empty except for a hanging streetlight that blinked red in all four directions. The area was deserted this late in the tourist season. The road ahead was a winding, two-lane blacktop. Moss drove along between dense stands of forest. Cruz wasn't sure what he was looking for — he figured he'd know it when he saw it.

And see it he did.

'There,' he said. 'Stop in there.'

A sign said: 'COUNTRY HOME MOTEL & COTTAGES — Open Through Thanksgiving'.

A long winding driveway led up from the road to the motel compound.

'Let's go up there and see if it's quiet.'

5

It was indeed quiet.

One car was parked in front of the low-slung motel office, a slab of concrete with a flickering fluorescent sign mounted on top: 'Country Home' – besides that, the place was deserted. There wasn't a single other car. A series of about twenty small, rustic cabins surrounded the office in a rough semi-circle. The semicircle served as the dirt parking lot. Just outside the circle was an in-ground swimming pool behind a green fence, long closed this time of year.

Moss pulled up and Cruz climbed out into the brisk, chilly air. He walked into the sparsely furnished office. An old man, tall and gaunt, watched television behind the counter. With his hair swooped back and his pale skin, he looked like a vampire. He glanced up at Cruz without much interest. 'Hmm,' he said. 'You got lucky. I was just about to close the place up and head on home.'

Cruz avoided eye contact, pretending to examine the paperwork on the counter. 'Kind of quiet, huh?'

The old man sighed. 'Well, the season's over, you know. The local kids come in because they want some place to fuck, but I won't rent to 'em. I just keep her going because I don't head down to Florida myself until December first. We get a couple real customers in now and again. People like yourself, wandering around like peas at the bottom of a can.'

'Well, that's fine,' Cruz said. 'I'm traveling with a friend, so I'll take two separate cottages, if you don't mind.'

'I don't mind at all. We got units B and D all ready. Both of them have kitchenettes, and both have their own space heater.'

'Well, that should be cozy.'

The old man raised a bony finger in warning. 'They're electric space heaters and they get very hot, so I caution you not to leave them on overnight, or let them get too close to the bed.'

'Wouldn't want to burn down one of your cottages,' Cruz said.

'Oh, you can burn it down if you want. I'm insured. I'm more worried that you'll burn it down with yourself asleep inside of it.'

Cruz didn't answer. He was already tired of the old man.

'And do me a favor, eh? If you have to smoke, step outside the cabin before you do. There's no smoking in these cabins.'

Cruz nodded and went back to where Moss waited by the

car. He handed Moss his key and Moss moved the car across the lot to the front doors of the cabins. They were going to make a show of going to their separate cottages and loading a few things inside. They had to open the trunk to do so. There were a couple of duffel bags in there left over from the car's previous owner — they would make decent props for the luggage transfer. 'Ready?' Cruz said, inserting the key in the trunk lock.

The trunk was pointed away from the motel office, about fifty yards across the compound from there. Moss stood by the trunk, gun in hand but pointed down, waiting.

Cruz took his own gun out, not to show the girls, but in case Moss did anything. You never knew. You just never knew. Even this staying in the same motel compound together, Cruz didn't like it. It meant a restless night of half-sleep, waiting for Moss to come in the window.

Cruz opened the trunk.

As soon as the lid opened, Moss pointed the gun into the face of the girl inside. Lola's face, not the other girl's. Lola was still bound, but her eyes said she was calm. They didn't have the bugged-out look, like the eyes of so many other people who had ended up locked inside of car trunks over the years. Like the eyes of the other girl.

'You move a muscle, you try to scream or make any noise, I will kill you right away,' Moss said quietly. The calm eyes watched him. 'And if I kill you, then I'm gonna have to kill that old man in the office. You don't want me to that, do you?'

Cruz registered no emotion there. They would have to keep a watchful eye on her.

'I think I'm going to have to throw a scare into the little lady,' Moss said. 'Maybe later, she and I will do a little dance together.'

'How are you going to do that,' Cruz said, 'after she beat your ass?' He was tired of Moss too. He was tired of the whole fucking business. Just then, he was thinking how nice it might be to snuff Moss, take the girls, and make a run for Canada. Leave Smoke Dugan, or whatever the hell he wanted to call himself, right where he was. Maybe the girls would like Cruz, and if so, he would take them across the border. If not, he would just kick them out of the car twenty or thirty miles from the nearest town in the middle of the night. He wouldn't even kill them. Cruz just didn't seem to have much stomach for killing anymore. Moss, he could kill. But the girls? For what?

For the money? Please. It had never been for the money, not for years and years. Maybe at the beginning, sure, but not any longer. Whatever it had been for, it seemed to be over now.

But it could never be over, it seemed.

'I think I'll find a way,' Moss said.

Cruz could feel Moss's eyes boring into him as he reached in and pulled the suitcases out of the car. He dropped them on the ground, slammed the trunk lid, then looked up at Moss. How much emotion could a man like Moss actually experience?

'Come on, man. It was only a joke.'

Moss wanted the girl. Cruz knew this – had seen it in his eyes back in the apartment. He also knew that the more Moss entertained himself with the girl, the less likely he would be to come creeping into Cruz's shack in the middle of the night. Cruz briefly considered giving the girl over to him, just to get a good night's sleep.

Fuck it, that wasn't going to happen either.

'I think you two will be very happy together,' Cruz said, then picked up his bag and, one eye still on Moss, walked sideways toward his cottage.

An hour more passed before the old man finally went home. He stopped by Cruz's cottage before he did. He was wearing a crumpled fedora, with a feather in the hat band. He was a dapper old vampire, if nothing else.

'Well, I'm gonna get on home to the wife,' he said. 'She's got arthritis something terrible, so I like to get home to her as soon as I can. You fellows are going to be on your own out here. There's a problem with the payphone here in the court, but I assume you have a cellphone.'

'We do,' Cruz said. This dad act the old man did had worn thin before it began.

'Good. One last thing. The office has an alarm that goes right to the State Police barracks down the road. There's nothing of value in the office anyway, so there's no sense in trying to bust in there. The troopers would arrive two minutes later, if you see what I mean.'

Cruz nodded. 'That would be bad.'

'Bad indeed. The soda machine by the office still has a few cans in there. I'll be back at six thirty in the morning. I trust you won't need anything more before then.'

'I trust we won't.'

'Good night, then,' the old man said, and tipped his hat.

'Good night,' Cruz said.

When the old man had gone, and his taillights had disappeared down the road, Cruz and Moss converged out by the car. They had both been watching and thinking the same thing. They opened the trunk again, same way as before.

The girls were still awake, still watchful. The two men reached in, Cruz getting Lola's arms, Moss wrapping his arms around the bottom of her legs. They lifted her out and placed her on her feet. Then they walked her into Cruz's cottage. Cruz held her lightly, so she could maintain her balance, but she didn't seem to need his help.

They tied her to the bed.

She lay on her back, tied as though she were nailed to a cross. Her arms reached out on either side of her, the wrists firmly secured to the bedposts. Her legs were still tied together, and reached down to the bottom of the bed, where ropes secured her ankles to the bottom bedposts. So her legs were at once tied together and immobilized from moving. They gagged her mouth with a strip of rag.

What was intriguing to Moss, the girl, who had been so tough earlier in the evening, had made no attempt at resisting them.

When they were done tying her, he and Cruz looked down at the work they had done. Moss noticed Cruz still held that big gun in his hand. He was still waiting for Moss to make some kind of move on him. Dumb fuck. It was a bad sign.

The two of them stepped out of the cottage and into the parking lot.

'All right,' Cruz said. 'I've gotta go check in with New York.'

'Why don't you just use my cellphone?' Moss said, as if he didn't know.

'Cut the shit, Moss. You know I can't. I've already burned it on this operation by calling Dugan's girlfriend's place. Anyway, you don't call Big Vito on a cellphone. Especially when there's a problem. I gotta go use a payphone. You use a payphone in this situation.'

'Well, good luck finding one,' Moss said. Cruz was playing with fire, talking like that. When this job was over, Moss was gonna ask around, see how connected this little fucker was. If he wasn't connected well enough, Moss was gonna drop his narrow ass into the East River.

Cruz stopped. He looked into Moss eyes. Now he was trying to play that mean killer look with Moss. The eyes. Sure, there was something to it, but Moss wasn't buying it. It was all he could do to keep from slapping the guy's face.

'Look, Moss. Do me a favor, all right? When I'm gone,' he gestured into the cottage, 'don't fuck with the program, all right?'

Moss grinned. 'What's that supposed to mean?'

'I mean, we're giving her back tomorrow, right? So don't fuck with her. You upset her, and it fucks up the trade in the morning. If it fucks up the deal, you're going to have to answer to me.'

'Who we giving her back to?'

'Herself. We're giving her back to herself.'

'So whaddya want me to do, boss? Keep an eye on her?'

'Yeah. That'll work. I'll be gone fifteen minutes. You think you can last that long?'

'And what about the skinny one?'

'I'm gonna take her with me.'

'Yeah? Why's that?'

Cruz shrugged. 'We don't really need her, right? If I leave her here, something might happen to her.'

'And you wouldn't want that, would you?'

'No.'

Moss watched as Cruz pulled the second girl out of the trunk, helped her into the passenger seat, then got in the car, started it, and drove slowly out of the compound. As soon as the taillights disappeared, Moss got out his own cellphone and went into the cabin. He dialed a number in New York. Fuck it, the phone was dirty. They changed these phone numbers in New York like every week. He wasn't going to sweat it.

While the phone rang, he looked down at the girl on the bed. She wasn't going anywhere. He went back outside into the darkness of the compound.

A voice answered the call. It was that gravelly voice. Big Vito, the guy who ran the show. 'Yeah?'

Moss kept his voice low. Not that it mattered. The girl would be dead tomorrow, and the nearest other person was probably ten miles away. Cruz was fucking crazy. Giving her back to herself. They were going to have to kill both these girls. If Cruz didn't know that, Moss couldn't understand how he had survived in this business all this time.

'Jacobs calling,' he said. 'I been homesick for years.'

'Go ahead, kid.'

Moss thought for a second. How could he best sum up the operation he had witnessed, had been a part of for the past thirty-six hours?

'Well?' the voice said.

'It's a gigantic fuck-up. It's the biggest fuck-up I ever saw.'

'Tell me.'

'Right now?'

'It's clean. Tell me.'

So Moss told him.

After ten minutes of listening, Vito signed off. The phone went dead. Moss looked at its glowing number pad in the darkness of the fall night, forest shimmering with fog all around him. It was a big mess. It was a big mess that Cruz had made. Moss turned the phone off and went back inside.

Hal and Darren had parked the Cadillac among some junked-out heaps in a used car lot a little way down the road. From where they were parked, they had a perfect view of the bottom of the road out of the compound.

Twenty minutes before, they had watched the old man cruise out of the compound, turn left and head sedately back toward the highway, his big boat of a Lincoln, a new one, a rival for the Cadillac.

Just now, they had seen the Taurus come down as well. It

cruised past, headed in the same direction as the Lincoln. Hal and Darren hunkered down behind the dashboard and watched the car go past. It was easy to see that there were two people in the car, and neither one was the football linebacker they had seen earlier. The little man was driving, and sitting in the passenger seat was the other girl, not Lola.

'What the hell is going on?' Hal whispered.

'What do you think?' Darren said. It was a standard part of their strategizing. Darren would ask Hal what he thought, and Hal would sum up the situation for him.

'I think he left the big guy in there with Lola. Now he's gone out to get something, whether it's food or whatever, I don't know. But it probably means we don't have much time.'

'So what do we do?'

Hal smiled. 'We cruise up there, nice and quiet, halfway up the hill, say. Then we walk the rest of the way, take care of business with whoever's left, and then we get what we came for.'

'You sure you want to go for all that?' Darren said.

'Kid, this is the kind of thing I live for. You stick with me. It's going to come off smooth as glass, I promise you that.'

Dead inside, Smoke Dugan went to the land of the dead.

He went shopping.

He drove his Tercel slowly through the city, thinking about what he would need, and where he might find these items after five o'clock in Portland, Maine. The fact was, he wouldn't find them in Portland. When the workers left the downtown buildings, the city closed up shop.

But the city was ringed with suburbs, and these suburbs were choked with megastores. Indeed, according to maps he had found at the library, and by all accounts he had heard from locals old enough to know, the furthest reaches of South Portland had been rolling pasture for cattle farms not thirty years before. Now, the approach to the airport on Western Avenue was packed with strip malls, all-you-can-eat buffets, big box stores, and the Maine Mall, one million square feet of department stores, electronics stores, toy stores, jewelry stores, fast-food restaurants, fat people and teenage girls in tight pants.

That's where he headed.

You can buy anything you want in America, if you know what you're looking for. Smoke's shopping list included, among other things: Cellophane, laundry soap, a bag of clothespins, a bag of plastic eyedroppers, some copper wire, a cigarette lighter, a soldering iron, two dry-cell batteries, two electrical igniters, two bags of ice, a hot tub thermometer, an electric hot plate, an eyeglass repair kit, wire cutters, four glass beakers, nitric acid, sulfuric acid, glycerin, a numeric pager – the kind people used before cellphones appeared everywhere – and a cellphone. He purchased service accounts for both the pager and the cellphone. He bought all of these things in a kind of a daze, moving from store to store, driving from monster indoor mall to strip mall to megastore. He traveled from Radio Shack to a small hobby shop, to the Home Depot to Wal-Mart to an independent hardware store that had survived by specializing in stocking those things you just couldn't get anywhere else. He stopped in at a store where parents oohed and ahhhed over all the science toys they could buy for their little future Nobel prize winners. He finished up at a store that cashed checks, sold phone cards, issued auto loans and auto insurance, even served as a travel agent and sold concert tickets. The overhead lights in this store were much too bright. The walls were orange. There were three upright video games at the back of the store, like in a video arcade, each of them contributing its own electronic cacophony. It was a harsh environment in which to do any kind of business. Here he bought the cellphone and the pager.

The kid behind the counter had slicked hair and acne all over his face. He had a prominent Adam's apple that bobbed when he spoke. He explained the cellphone plan to Smoke in extravagant detail – how many minutes, at what times, to where, and for how much money every month.

Smoke glazed over.

It didn't matter. None of it mattered. He wouldn't need the phone after tomorrow.

'Name,' the kid said.

Smoke looked at him. He raised an eyebrow, not sure if it was a question or an answer.

'Your name?' the kid repeated.

'Oh. Fillmore. Barry Fillmore.'

Barry Fillmore was Smoke's third and last available identity. Fillmore lived with James Dugan. He had a social security number, two credit cards and a driver's license issued in New Hampshire. Every month, Smoke purchased one or two items in Fillmore's name, just to keep the accounts current. If he lived, Smoke knew he would be shopping for new identities soon.

When he finished his shopping, Smoke drove the Tercel back into the city, looking for a Catholic church that was open. It was only a little after nine o'clock, but they were all closed, the doors locked against him. Every single church he pulled up to. He didn't know when that had happened. When he was a kid, even when he was a young man, one of the things the churches prided themselves on was that they stayed open around the clock. It could be two in the morning – if you suddenly decided you needed to pray to God, you could walk up to any church and let yourself right in. You could settle into any pew in the deep silence and darkness of a church at night, you could dig all those stained-glass windows and the flickering candles up at the front, and you could let ol' God know exactly what was on your mind. You could tell Him all about the department store job you had pulled an hour ago. And you could explain how you would give some of that money – ten percent, say – to the poor and starving in Appalachia or Bangladesh or Africa, to the widows, to the orphans, if only He let you off the Almighty hook and kept the lawmen off your trail.

And it would work. Time and time again, those little after-hour church house bargaining sessions would work out just fine.

Well, not anymore. Nowadays, it seemed God closed up shop at night.

It was just as well.

A long time had passed since Smoke and God were on speaking terms.

Cruz drove through the darkened lanes of Maine in autumn,

looking for a payphone. It took him about ten minutes of driving around to find one.

'Who are you?' Cruz said quietly to the girl. She had come around a little bit, was no longer in shock, but was still sobbing a little.

'My name is Pamela Gray. I work at the Portland Public Library.'

'You're Lola's roommate?'

She nodded.

'OK, Pamela. Do you go by Pam or Pamela?'

'Pamela. Most people call me Pamela.'

Sure, Pamela, Cruz could see that. This seemed like a formal kind of chick. Probably had a mom and dad who she pecked on the cheek when she saw them at Christmas. He glanced at her. She wasn't bad-looking, if a little plain. A little make-up, a new hairdo, yeah, he could see it. Get rid of that hair-pulled-back-against-her-scalp thing. She could be cute. Her clothes were a little baggy. Hard to say what it was all like underneath there – could be anything.

'OK, Pamela, here's the deal. I'm going to tell you a lot of things I shouldn't tell you, and wouldn't normally tell you. That's because I want you to help me. And what I need help with is keeping you and Lola alive. Understand?'

She nodded, the tears flowing again.

'OK, I can't always look at you for the answer. First thing I need you to do is to speak. So let's try that again. Do you understand?'

'Y-yes.'

'Good. Now, as you probably guessed, we're not interested in you, right? We're not even interested in Lola, to be honest. What we are interested in is Lola's boyfriend.'

'Smoke?' The girl's eyes did something funny now. Cruz noted it, but didn't even try to decipher it.

'That's right, Smoke. You may not know this, but Smoke is bad news. He killed a friend of ours a few years ago, and he stole some money. A lot of money. Earlier today, we tried to stop in and talk to him, and he killed another friend of ours.'

'Smoke did this? Today?'

'Yeah. He did. So we came over to your place and grabbed you and Lola as sort of bargaining chips in our, eh, our negotiations with Smoke. You see?'

She shook her head now, her eyes wide again. Cruz was afraid she was going to go away again, retreat from this place where nothing made sense to that other place, where nothing had to make sense.

'I think you have the wrong man. Smoke's not a killer. He makes toys. He's like, I don't know, Santa Claus, or like an elf. He's like an elf that makes toys. Don't you see?'

Cruz checked the road. He was in the center of a town, and he pulled up in front of a general store.

The sign in the window read 'CLOSED FOR THE SEASON. SEE YOU NEXT YEAR!' There was no one around. Everything closed up when the tourists went home.

'He makes toys.'

Cruz looked at her and gave her a gentle shake. 'Pamela,

I don't have the wrong man. You do. OK? Now, I want to tell you something else. The people I work for want to kill him. They want their money back and then they want to kill him. If they knew I was telling you all this, they would want to kill me too. And generally speaking, people like you and Lola, who get caught up in things like this, well, you'd be killed too. But I don't want to play it that way, OK? I want to see you live through this, OK? And I want you to help me do that.'

The girl looked at him with big blank eyes. Deer-in-the-headlight eyes.

'Listen, I need to make a call. I want you to wait right here, OK?'

She nodded, again with those big eyes.

Cruz got out of the car. There was a chill in the air, and crackly multicolored leaves moved along the ground pushed by the breeze. There was not another car in the parking lot. There was not another sound except the wind rustling the tops of the trees.

The phone worked. Well, at least something worked for a change.

He dialed a number.

A woman answered on the first ring. She sounded like a gentle and kindly older woman. Cruz had spoken to her before.

'Maple Enterprises,' she said. Maple Enterprises, that was a new one. It was always something with these people. Not for the first time, Cruz wondered what the old woman thought she did for a living. Did she have any inkling she was speaking to a man who had killed more than a hundred people in his life? Could she keep that sunshiny disposition if she did know?

Cruz thought not.

'I'm calling for Mr Franklin,' Cruz said. 'Is he available? This is Mr Jones.'

'Oh, I'm sorry,' she said. 'Mr Franklin is no longer at this number. I can give you the new number for him, and you can reach him there. Will that be OK?'

'That will be fine.'

The woman gave Cruz the new number. The numbers were always new. Everything always changed, that was the rule.

'I'm sure Mr Franklin is eager to hear from you,' the woman finished.

Cruz hung up. What was he supposed to say? 'Thanks so much. Have a nice evening,' was probably something a person would say. Cruz wasn't in that business.

Mr Franklin was probably very eager to hear from him. The spies were everywhere, and word of the fire and the corpse inside of it had probably gotten back to New York. After all, it was a cop who had originally called this thing in, wasn't it?

Cruz swallowed hard. This was going to be tough to explain. That Canadian border was looking better and better.

He dialed the number and listened to the phone ring in New York.

Lola lay on her back, finding that inner calm.

Nine years of study had taught her to look for the stillness during stressful times. Much to her amazement, she sometimes found it. She had never tried to explain it to anyone, because she didn't much understand it herself. But there seemed to be something going on beneath the surface of the world, or rather, something not going on. It was as if the world she knew, and in which people ran around and worried themselves sick about things, was a Hollywood stage set, and behind it was something else. At times, it was almost as if she could pull the world she knew down like so much wallpaper to reveal the real world hiding behind it.

What would this real world look like? A stillness, she thought. A quiet, calm knowing, beyond care and worry, and beyond reasons to care or worry. Beyond death, even. When she accessed it, even death didn't seem like that big a concern. Perhaps it was what people were talking about when they talked about God. Maybe it was deeper and quieter and more knowing even than God.

She was looking for that stillness now.

And again to her amazement, it was there waiting for her.

So she thought about the stillness, her arms tied to either bedpost, her legs tied together and immobilized. She thought about the stillness even as the big man, the one with long brown hair who they called Moss, removed his pants and his flannel shirt. She watched him quietly, thinking about stillness.

Now here was a sight to remember: a huge man in nothing but a New York Rangers T-shirt and a pair of red bikini briefs. He picked his gun up off the table, then came over to the bed. Inside those briefs, he was already erect. He surged against them. He climbed onto the bed and crawled across her arms until he was straddling her.

'Tomorrow,' he said, 'we're going to trade you for your boyfriend. You see? We're going to take you back to South Portland, to a place called Governor's. You know it? Yeah, you know it. You're going to help us find it. And when we go inside there, Smoke Dugan is going to come in and sit with us at our table. Then you're going to leave, and you and I will never see each other again. That only leaves us tonight, so tonight we're going to be real good friends.'

She thought about the stillness, and on the heels of that thought came the idea of how absurd this situation must look. She looked into his eyes.

In the stillness, she realized once again that it was OK to make people pay for the stupid or just plain evil things they did. It was more than OK. It was necessary and right. It was part of the natural order of things, and so therefore became a person's responsibility. She must do whatever was necessary, without doubt, without remorse, without fear. Without judgment. Like the lion in the hunt for her prey.

'What I'm going to do,' Moss said, 'is remove that bandanna from your mouth. You'd probably like that, right? Your jaw is probably awful strained by now. That's a bitch, I know. Unfortunately, I've been there once or twice myself. Anyway, when I take that gag off, if you scream, I'm going to kill you. So I need you to be nice and quiet. Do you understand?'

Lola nodded. It was a lie he was telling her, but she nodded anyway. She wasn't going to scream, but not because she thought he'd kill her. She knew they were after Smoke, and she also knew they thought she was some kind of bargaining chip to get at him. So they had to keep her alive at all costs. The reason why she wasn't going to scream was because it would do her no good. The glimpse she had gotten of this place said they were in the middle of nowhere out here. No one would hear her scream, and then this idiot would probably beat her senseless to get her to shut up. She couldn't afford to be beaten senseless right now. She was going to need her senses. At some point, somewhere along the line, these two were going to make a mistake, and when they did, Lola would be ready.

'So then after I take off that gag, I'm going to give you a minute to get that feeling back in your jaw. That's the favor I'm going to do for you. Then there's going to be a favor I want you to do for me. It's tit for tat around here, honey. So let's begin, OK?'

He placed the gun on the bed next to her head. Then he reached with his hand and gradually worked the gag loose. He got it untied, then pulled it free.

Lola worked her jaw around. It was stiff, even from just the past fifteen minutes. It was sore. It was great to be able to open her mouth again. She imagined the feeling would be ten times stronger once she got her arms free.

'Yeah, get that feeling back in there,' Moss said. He reached down and touched his erection. 'Then I'm gonna put this bad boy in there for a little while. What do you say to that? We're friends, right? Don't you want to be my friend?'

Moss smiled. He rubbed it inside his briefs. It looked like he was rubbing a big wooden soup spoon in there. Then Lola began to shake. She had no control over it.

'Don't worry,' he said. 'This'll probably only take a couple of minutes. I've been working non-stop, and haven't had time for fun in a while.'

He climbed closer to her, straddling her shoulders now. Lola began to shake so hard she thought she would never be able to stop. It took a force of will to keep herself from crying. The stillness had held for a few moments, but it was almost gone now. She hoped and prayed she could keep it just a little while longer.

'Man, I guess I been stressed out. This is gonna be good.'

'Yeah, it sounds like a real big fuck-up,' Big Vito said into Cruz's ear. 'We're not happy, Cruz, you know what I mean?'

'I know.'

'I mean, whatta we got to be happy about? You're not making us happy.'

'I know,' Cruz said. 'It's a fuck-up. But I'm gonna handle it.'

'I don't even like to talk on the phone. My wife calls, I don't even take the fucking call. Now here I am in the middle of the night, what am I doing? I'm talking on the phone about all this bullshit, all these problems. You know who could be listening? Anybody, that's who.'

Cruz scanned the deserted parking lot, leaves blowing around in small tornadoes. A car went by on the road. It was the first one he had seen in a while. In the deep darkness, its headlights cast strange shadows on the surrounding trees. The shadows looked like tall, thin people, grasping and writhing in agony.

'Look, I'm sending somebody up there.'

Wait a minute, another person. That was the last thing he needed, to deal with yet another person. Things were already too crowded. 'Who are you sending up?'

'You don't know them.'

'Them?'

Jesus.

'You got a pen?' Vito said.

'Look,' Cruz said, 'give us another day. This thing is just about wrapped up.'

Cruz heard a car door slam. He felt in his jacket pocket for a pen. No, he didn't have a pen.

He looked up. Shit, the girl!

She ran across the parking lot toward the road. At first, all Cruz noticed was her big white running sneakers, incongruous at the bottom of those brown office casual dress pants. Her hands were still cuffed together in front of her, so her two arms moved together in jerking motions, swinging side to side like a pendulum. He and Moss had cuffed the girls in front because it would be easier for them to walk out of the apartment like that – less chance they would fall down or need help balancing as they walked down the street to the car. Cruz had seen people cuffed in back fall down for no reason at all. It did something to your equilibrium.

'I guess you can see I'm not lying,' she said. She even managed a smile.

He could do it. He could blow her brains out right here. It wouldn't even make a sound. Then what? What would he tell Cruz? Fuck Cruz. What would he tell Vito? I killed her before we got Dugan because . . .

Because . . .

No fucking reason. There was no reason that would wash.

He climbed off her, put his pants back on, and then threw his gun across the room. It bounced off the wall and landed on the floor. He noticed her flinch when he did that. It gave him a mean little satisfaction. If she were a man, he would have already killed her. Back at the apartment, when she knocked him down, he would have gotten up and killed her. If she were a man, it would never even have gotten that far.

He looked at her and she watched him.

'Tantrums aren't going to solve anything,' she said.

Moss stormed out of the cottage.

In another minute, he would kill her anyway.

The screen door slammed behind him. He stalked across the dirt compound toward the beckoning light of the Coke machine. It sat like a fat, squat space alien outside the door of the motel office. The cold air felt good. The trees swayed at the edge of the parking lot. The scene brought him back to himself for a moment.

The girl had called his bluff. He shouldn't have lied about killing her. What he should have done was smack her around a little.

'OK, I can do that,' he said to no one.

That's what he would do when he got back. She wanted to be uncooperative? That was fine. He would just get himself a soda here, maybe drink it standing right there by the soda machine, take a few deep breaths, then go on back and get to work on that girl. She'd see things his way before long. He felt certain of that.

Cruz didn't like it? He could go fuck himself.

The soda machine took dollars. He fed a crisp one-dollar bill into the slot. The can of Coke ka-thunked into the little tray at the bottom.

Moss reached down to pull his cold soda out.

Hal timed it perfectly.

He stepped around the machine and brought the barrel of the shotgun down hard on the back of the big man's head. The man collapsed to the ground, landing on all fours. Hal hit him again, raising the gun way in the air, and bringing it down with all his might.

Darren came around the other side of the machine and kicked the man in the side. That knocked him over. Hal brought the gun down on the guy's back. Darren kicked the guy in the head. They worked him over pretty good for about half a minute.

The guy was lying still.

Hal held up his arm to Darren. Darren stopped kicking.

'Check him,' Hal said.

Darren kneeled and patted the man down.

Hal watched the guy. There was a lot to watch. His arms were like a normal person's legs. His legs were like redwood trees. The big boy was still breathing, but not moving, and probably good and fucked up. He wouldn't cause them any more trouble. Now if only his friend would stay away for a while longer . . . Hal peered in the direction of the gravel driveway to the main road.

'Nothing,' Darren said.

'We better hurry,' Hal said. 'Before this other guy gets back. Go get the car and I'll go grab Lola.'

Darren gestured at the slot at the bottom of the soda machine. 'You want that Coke he bought?'

Hal shook his head. 'You go for it.'

As he turned to walk off toward the cottage, Hal saw Darren reach down to grab himself a free can of soda. Simple pleasures for simple minds. And why the hell not? Hal figured. Why the hell not?

Moss faded in and out of consciousness.

He sprawled face down in the dirt, cataloguing the pain. His head was the worst of it. It throbbed behind his eyes with each beating of his heart. Some moments, it would get so bad that he would drift away with it, and then both he and the pain would be gone. Then he would return and the pain would return with him, if possible, worse than before.

THUD. THUD. THUD.

He wasn't sure how long ago they had attacked him. It might have been hours, but he felt like it was only a few minutes. He didn't know who they were, or why they jumped him. The only thing he could think of was it was Dugan and somebody he had enlisted to help him save the girl.

As soon as they clobbered him, Moss had gone limp. If you went limp, there was a chance they'd think they had finished you, and then they'd leave you alone. The whole strategy was geared toward conserving energy and not getting mangled too bad. You wanted to be able to come back and fight some more.

Moss thought maybe he could do just that.

He opened his eyes. The hard-packed dirt filled his vision. The light from the soda machine glimmered behind him. He hurt so bad he thought he might vomit. He could move his head, and this he did, affording him a better view of the way he had come. Moving his head sent a wave of nausea from the pit of his stomach up to his throat.

A long car pulled into the lot. It wasn't the Taurus he and Cruz had. It was a bigger car, looked like a Cadillac. It pulled around the compound slowly, tires crunching gravel, and eased up to the door of the cottage. A man got out, and entered the lighted cottage. Sure, they were rescuing the girl.

Not if Moss could help it.

He did a push-up, and forced himself to a kneeling position. Blood was caked to the ground where his head had lain. He felt the dirt from the ground stuck to his head and his face. He reached back under the hem of his right pants leg, inside his boot, and ripped out the knife he kept taped to his calf.

The fucker who had patted him down must have learned from watching TV.

The knife gleamed in the light of the Coke machine. It was a folding knife, a big hunting job with one side razor sharp, and the other side razor sharp and serrated. You could clean a deer with that knife. You could clean a man with it too.

Slowly, awkwardly, as if he had never balanced himself on two legs before, he worked his way up to a standing position. He began the long walk across the compound.

From the start, he weaved and staggered like a drunken man. Try as he might, he could not keep his balance. His vision faded, then came in sharper than ever. He thought about a time when he was a kid. The school, or somebody, some program — who the fuck could remember these things now? — some program had taken them horseback riding. It had been a sunny day, and as the ride went on, it got hotter and hotter. He started to get dizzy way up there on that horse. He began to slide off. But even then, at that young age, Moss was tough. He wasn't going to tell his teacher he was sliding off the horse. His face was close to the horse's neck. And he was sliding down. He was sliding down off that horse and the ground was far below him.

He had sunk to his knees again. Now he was on gravel, and the tiny sharp stones dug through his pants and made themselves known to his knees. He looked up, and there was the cottage with the car parked in front, not too far away. It seemed to shimmer and vibrate. Light came through the open door.

OK, they had jumped him and done him in pretty good. But that didn't mean he couldn't do some damage back. He could do anything he wanted.

ANYTHING HE WANTED.

He staggered to his feet again.

He made no attempt to hide himself. He just stumbled toward the cottage, keeping himself as steady as possible.

They weren't going to take the girl. It was just that simple.

The two men came out of the cottage dragging the girl along with them. Her arms were tied together, but her legs were free. They opened the back door of the big Cadillac on the side away from Moss. They stuffed her in there, then slammed the door.

Moss ran for the car, a shuffling shambling wreck of a run.

Neither one of these was Dugan. That registered on Moss for a second, then went away. It didn't matter who they were or weren't. The fat guy climbed in behind the wheel. He had a shotgun in one hand. The other guy came running around the back of the car, his head down.

Moss crashed right into him.

He plunged the hunting knife into the man's stomach, then ripped upward with the serrated edge. The man's eyes went wide. Moss collapsed on top of him, still stabbing, gutting him like crazy. The man fell over backwards with Moss on top of him.

Moss lost consciousness, for how long he didn't know. Everything was confused, hazy, remote. He rolled over onto his knees.

He had lost the knife. It was still in the man's gut.

The man lay on his back, convulsing. He clawed at the ground. His eyes were wide open. There was a look of shock mixed with pain mixed with terror in those eyes. He stared at the sky. His mouth fell open into a horrified O. Blood drooled down his neck. Dark blood. The man reached up for something only he could see.

'Aah . . .' he said. 'Aaaah.'

It wasn't Dugan. Who the hell was it? Some guy, a much younger guy.

'Darren! What the fuck are you doing?' yelled the fat guy.

Darren said nothing.

Moss thought about that shotgun. It was coming into play any second. Fuck the girl, he decided. It was time to bail out.

He dragged himself to his feet and ran for the cottage. There were two doors, three doors. The cottage went sideways.

A scream came from inside that car.

Moss made the shack and crashed into the wall. He reached for the door, found it and tore through it. He dove for the floor of the shack. The gun. He had thrown the gun on the floor somewhere.

A shotgun blast ripped open the night.

Chunks of the door and the wall flew through the air. Another came and the door broke in half. The top part went flying off its hinges.

Another blast came.

Another.

Here was the gun, under the bed. Moss slithered like a worm, his whole body propelling him in a whipsaw motion. He snatched the gun and crawled out the other side.

He turned and braced the gun on the bed.

The fat man was in the doorway, shotgun in hand. He racked the slide, chambering a round, an evil sound.

There were two of him. There were three of him.

Moss aimed for the middle one. He fired the big .44 Mag. And missed. The shot took a chunk out of the wall. There was no sound. He fired again. And again. And again. He kept firing. He was gonna use up every round he had.

Another clip. Did he have another clip?

Shit.

The big man had disappeared.

A few seconds later, he heard the Cadillac tearing ass out of the compound, sliding on the loose gravel, gaining traction, and barreling down the driveway toward the main road. It screeched as it hit the blacktop. The engine roared off into the distance.

Moss held his position. How many shots had he fired? He had no idea. Time passed, and soon there was no sound but the wind. Moss held out a moment longer, gun still pointing at the door.

It was no good. He could not keep his arm steady. He could not keep his eyes open. He gripped the gun even harder.

When he collapsed, he wasn't even aware it had happened.

Sometime later, he opened his eyes. The pain was intense, the light in the room stabbing into his mind. He was lying on the floor and looking up. The gun was gone. A pair of leather shoes scraped the floorboards and then a figure stood over him. He gazed up into the eyes of the man who had just walked through the door.

'Hang in there!' Hal screamed.

His hands gripped the wheel like twin vises. His foot mashed the accelerator to the floor. The needle pinned at 120 and stayed there.

He tore along a blackened country road, following the double yellow. The line writhed like a snake. The trees were so dense it was like being in a tunnel. He came out of the trees and a small area of stores zipped by, all closed. Darren lolled in the seat next to him like a big dummy, his face bled white, his mouth gone slack, his throat and his shirt stained with blood.

Hal had no idea where he was heading, no idea where the nearest doctor might be.

It didn't matter. If he had to go to prison so that Darren might live, so be it. The first cops he saw, he would crash right into them. Hell, at these speeds, the cops should find him first. He was gonna find somebody. He was gonna find anybody.

'Just hang in for a few minutes longer. We're gonna get you a doctor.' He put a hand on Darren's knee.

'Uh,' Darren said. 'Uhn.'

'Shit, oh shit. Motherfuck.'

Hal kept driving. He was all over the blacktop, going so fast he could barely follow the curves. There wasn't a single cop on these goddamn roads. There wasn't a single cop anywhere. Hadn't they heard all that shooting back there?

He turned to look at Darren again.

Darren was slumped all the way back against the seat now. His head rolled to the left. His eyes were wide open and staring.

'Darren!'

Hal slammed on the brakes. The tires shredded on pavement and Darren's lifeless form leaped off the seat, his chest hitting the dashboard, his head smashing against the windshield. He bounced back into the chair, flopping like a fish. He made no sound, his eyes still gazing at some point far in the distance – gazing at nothing.

Behind him, Hal was dimly aware that the girl had rolled off the seat and onto the floor with a thud. He had a girl back there, a sexy girl in handcuffs. That was going to be part of the act, remember?

The car skidded to a halt, straddling the double-yellow line.

Darren, what had been Darren, slid halfway into the space between the bucket seat and the glove compartment. He had fallen in sideways, his head, his eyes, still facing Hal. It was obscene, the way he was stuffed down there.

'Aw shit,' Hal said. 'Fucking shit.'

Hal sat for a long time, his head on the steering wheel, his friend's lifeless body slumped next to him. He didn't think. He didn't feel. There was a great big tidal wave of a thought out there, literally a tsunami of a realization, but at this moment he managed to keep it at bay by going blank. Somewhere deep inside, he knew what the thought would be when finally it came.

His plan had killed his best friend in the entire world, the best friend he had ever had. In essence, when all the bullshit was boiled away, he, Hal, had killed Darren. But there would be time for that — time during the deep darkness of years and years to think that one over. To chew on it, as it were.

He had killed Darren.

Yes, yes. In some way that was true. But in a more immediate way, in the way that really mattered, that big fucker back there had done it.

And that called for revenge.

Revenge. It was something he could focus on. It was something that could carry him through the difficult tasks that lay just ahead. It could become everything to him, blotting all this out until some future time he could not imagine now.

Yes. Revenge.

The car had stalled. He started it again and pulled away, driving slowly this time. No sense getting pulled over with a corpse in the front seat. As he drove, he gradually became aware that he was weeping.

After a time, perhaps twenty minutes, he pulled down an old dirt road. The road was rutted and pitted, and there were no lights. Trees hemmed in close on either side. He stopped the car, killed the headlights, and sat there. He let himself cry until all of it was out of him. It was over. He would never have a better friend than Darren.

When he was ready, Hal put on his leather work gloves and dragged the body of his best friend deep into the woods. It was tough going in the thick underbrush with nothing to guide him but the headlamp-style flashlight he wore. In death, Darren seemed a hundred pounds heavier than in life. Hal tried not to think about how this heavy object trailing behind him was Darren. He tried not to think how the best plan he could come up with was to leave ol' Darren in the forest for the crows and foxes and the flies and the worms, and whoever else might want a piece of his action later tonight and tomorrow. He tried not to think about it, but there wasn't much else to think about.

'I'm gonna come back for you,' he said. 'Tomorrow or the next day, when I get this thing worked out with these assholes, I'm gonna come back with a shovel and give you a decent burial.'

In the darkness, Hal began to imagine all sorts of things. First, Darren was nearby, watching him drag the corpse along. Then the forest was filled with eyes, all watching in disapproval as he abandoned his friend. There were ghosts here. There were ghouls in these October woods, waiting to feast on Darren's rotting flesh.

In the end, he dropped the body in a ditch and kicked leaves and dead brush over it. Then he hastened back to the car.

He stood, scanning the darkness in either direction. There were no lights and no sound anywhere nearby. There was nothing to mark this place by.

It didn't matter. He would come back and find Darren again, regardless of what it took. He wouldn't leave his friend to rot and be eaten by animals.

He leaned against the car and tried to piece together how everything had gone so wrong. It had seemed funny, hadn't it? They tried to snatch a little black girl, and she fought them off. They tried to snatch her again, a little pissed off and serious this time, and found that somebody else had snatched her first. So they decided to snatch her from the men who had snatched her.

I decided.

Not Darren. Darren had gone along for the ride, as always. And now this. Darren was dead. Darren was worm bait lying in a ditch in some woods.

It had looked easy. They had gone easy on the big man. They gave him a couple of bops on the head, maybe a few kicks to the body. But the big man hadn't gone easy in return. He had come back at them with deadly force. These were serious customers, this big man and his partner, and they needed to die. They were going to die, in fact, if Hal had his way. And it was all because they wanted the girl.

The girl. Lola.

Hal turned around and looked inside the Cadillac. She was still back there, slumped in the rear seat, staring straight ahead.

He walked back around and climbed into the front. The car shifted to accommodate his weight. He took the shotgun and pointed it at her head. He could just as easily kill her right now and worry about these other guys later. He didn't want to, she was his only link to them, but if she gave him any lip at all he knew he would kill her.

'Just who the fuck are you?' he said.

It took some time for Lola to register the shotgun.

At first, she just noticed the details. She stared down the gun's gaping maw. It was big and dark, just inches from her face. She mused that it could be a cave where a bear lived. She noticed that Mr Shaggy's hands trembled just slightly as he worked to hold the gun in her face. Behind and above his hands, his eyes were wild and angry.

She remembered how he had just dumped Mr Blue Eyes in the woods about a hundred yards from the road. She had watched him drag the body away, and had seen his light – the one he wore on his head like a coal miner – blundering around out there in the dark. Then he had returned.

During all his time away, it had never occurred to her to do anything but sit here and wait for him. Now he was pointing a gun at her.

Did he blame her for Mr Blue Eyes's death? That seemed wrong. It was the big one, that horrible Moss, who had killed Mr Blue Eyes. She thought of Moss, how he wanted her to suck him, and how she had refused – and of the terrible fear that had gripped her after he left the cabin. She thought of how Mr Shaggy and Mr Blue Eyes had appeared out of nowhere, smiling and laughing while they untied her. It was almost like they were old friends of hers, these professional rapists. Then she almost thought of the killing, but stopped herself. It was too much. She had never seen anyone murdered before. She never wanted to see it again.

Mr Shaggy poked the gun at her.

This is what it's like with soldiers, she thought, the ones who go crazy in the war.

'Who are you?' Shaggy said again.

'My name is Lola Bell.'

'I know your name. And what, you do modeling? Acting? Are you some kind of cop, or some kind of spy?'

'No, I work with learning disabled children during the week.'

He waggled the shotgun some more. 'Don't fuck with me, bitch, because I'll blow your fucking head off right here.'

'I'm not fucking with you! I work as a teaching assistant. That's it. That's all there is to it. Those men grabbed me because of my boyfriend. He's some kind of criminal or something, and he ran away. Now they're after him.'

Shaggy lowered the shotgun.

'Where is your boyfriend now?'

Lola looked up. 'He's on the run. They told him to meet them at Governor's in South Portland. They were going to exchange my roommate Pamela and me for him. I don't know what they're going to do now that they don't have me anymore. I don't know what they'll do with Pamela.'

The fact of that, the cold hard reality of it, hit and stopped her cold. They still had Pamela. Lola began to cry. Her body shook with the force of her sobs. She was quiet about it, and half-buried her face in her hands, which were still tied together.

'I'm going to kill those two guys,' Hal said. 'You with me on that?'

A long moment passed.

When she finally answered, Lola did not recognize her own voice. 'Yes,' came the voice, sounding small and very far away.

'I've got a plan,' he said as he worked on the knots that bound her wrists. 'But I'm going to need your help.'

Lola tried her voice again. 'I'm with you,' she told the pornographer, the man who had almost raped her.

This time it sounded like she meant it.

'Pamela, give me a hand with this guy, will you?'

They stood over the massive figure of the man who had burst through her front door earlier that night. He lay on the floor, facing the ceiling. His head and face were streaked with blood. His stringy hair was tacky with it. His shirt and his pants were splotched with it. His eyes were open and staring. He was the biggest man Pamela had ever seen, and something terrible had happened to him.

'Is he dead?' she said.

Cruz toed him in the side. 'Moss, you alive?'

The big man groaned. His eyelids fluttered closed.

'Oh, I think he's plenty alive. You should see what the other guy must look like. Right, Moss?'

Pamela stared down at the bloodied man. She had come alert running along that road, almost as if she had gone to sleep when these men had burst into the apartment, then awakened on a two-lane blacktop in the dark night, running, running, searching for any sign of life, anyone she could run to. Then Cruz had caught her, and falling into his arms had been almost . . . No, it hadn't been anything. Cruz had stuffed her into the trunk of a car, and now he wanted to act like they were friends. He could act that way, but Pamela was awake now and looking for a way out.

Cruz kneeled down beside the one called Moss and checked under his eyelids. He checked Moss's pulse at the neck.

'He's fine, but it looks like he lost Lola on us.'

He gave Moss a slap across the face. It made a sharp sound in the quiet of the cabin. 'Hey, Moss. Come on, work with me here. Was it Dugan? Did Dugan come here?'

Slowly, Moss shook his head. It moved like it was attached to his massive neck with a rusty hinge. 'Not Dugan.'

Pamela looked around at the room. The door had been smashed apart. The wall in the back of the cabin had a huge hole ripped in it. And the big man, the monster, had been laid low. Then it came to her. Lola had done all this! She had beaten him like she had beaten the two rapists. Then she had run away, and now she was out there calling the police. Any minute they would hear the sirens and these two scum would be on their way to jail.

'Pamela, I need you to help me lift him. We've got to get him out to the car and he weighs a ton.'

'Why should I help you?' she said, emboldened by Lola's success.

Cruz looked up at her. He pulled back his shirt, revealing the gun. 'Because I'm being a nice guy and not killing you, that's why. Now come on and grab the other side there. We don't have all night.'

It took several minutes just to drag the man upright and flop him onto the bed. Cruz seemed to do OK with his side, but Pamela could barely move Moss at all. He was immense. The weight of his arm alone was enough to scare her. When they dropped him on the bed, he grunted and his eyes came open.

'Come on, Moss,' Cruz said. 'You gotta help us. We can't stay here anymore.'

When Moss spoke, his voice was low. 'I can walk.'

'Show me.'

Moss rose on his own power and stumble-stepped out the door to the car. Cruz directed him to the back seat. Moss sprawled out back there and the car groaned under his weight. He promptly passed out again.

Cruz looked at Pamela. 'You drive.'

Brian Knox sat on the couch nursing a beer.

His modest suburban home was dark. The only light was the glow from the TV set in front of him. He had the sound all the way down. Upstairs, in the bedroom, his wife was sleeping. She had to work in the morning.

He was watching *Full Metal Jacket*. Knox must have seen this movie half a dozen times. It was the scene where the squad of American soldiers was under attack by a mysterious Vietnamese sniper during the battle for the imperial city of Huê. Every time an American would dash out into the deserted street to save one of his buddies, he too would be gunned down. It was a frustrating scene, all the more so because in a few minutes, when they finally managed to shoot the sniper, they were going to find out it was a teenage girl. But Knox barely noticed.

The truth was he often sat up like this at night, drinking beer with the TV set on, staring into space and absently scratching the long, snake-like scar that wound its way around his torso. Gut-stabbed, he had been. Ripped open from ass to tea kettle. He was on permanent disability now, and he realized he might never work again.

He had been a cop down in Boston once, but those days were gone. They were gone since the night he was sliced up by a guy who was supposed to be easy to kill. It was a hit, and he was the hitter. *OFF DUTY COP KILLS DRUG DEALER*. That's how it was supposed to read. And it did, except for the four pints of blood he lost before the meat wagon even got there. He had died, they told him, and then come back.

He remembered none of it. No warm, beckoning light at the end of a tunnel, no feeling of wellbeing and love washing over him, no St Peter telling him he still had work left to do on earth. Nothing.

He didn't even remember the hit. The last thing he could picture was lunch that afternoon at an old railway car diner all the way out in Worcester, a guy wearing a floppy hat telling him about the job. Then, three weeks later, waking up in a hospital bed, in pain, the overhead lights too bright, an old black aide scowling down at him.

'You're a very lucky man,' she said, flashing a mouth low on teeth.

'Lucky,' he said now, sitting in the glow of the televised carnage, not even aware he was speaking. 'Yeah.'

Physically, he was OK. The doctors had put everything back where it belonged. He could probably work some sort of desk job. He could drive a truck, or maybe he could become one of those guys on roadside construction sites who stands there with the SLOW sign so that commuters know to slow down. Yeah, his body was fine.

It was his mind – *his mind* – that was fucked.

He saw a therapist twice a week. She asked him how things made him feel.

How did it make him feel to be ripped apart like that, to know that he had been sprawled in a pool of his own blood in a convenience store parking lot? How did it feel to know he had killed the man who had stabbed him? How did it feel to fill his empty days with television shows and drives in the countryside? She thought it made him depressed. He denied it. She tried to push some drugs on him. So far, he had resisted. He wasn't the kind of guy who needed drugs.

The phone rang.

Knox looked at the receiver. It was rare that anyone called at night. He picked it up on the second ring.

'Yeah?'

The gravelly voice came over the line. 'Kid? How ya doing?'

'Why are you calling me at home?'

'It's an emergency.'

The scar across Knox's belly itched more than ever. 'OK,' he said.

6

The first rule in making nitroglycerin: don't blow yourself up.

Smoke wouldn't normally risk fucking with nitro — it was too easy to die in the process. C4 plastic was his explosive of choice. C4 packed a wallop, and was so stable American soldiers had used bricks of it as firewood in Vietnam. But Smoke couldn't get C4, not in his current circumstances. He couldn't get C4, but he could make nitro.

He was lying on his bed, fully dressed, the Derringer on the pillow by his head. He was in Walter O'Malley's ground-floor room at the Best Western, gazing at the supplies laid out on the desk. To the items he bought at the store, he had added a blasting cap, one of several he kept in the trunk of the car. The Best Western was across the massive parking lot from Governor's Restaurant. If Smoke wanted, he could pull the

237

wide curtain back from his window and look out at the eatery where he was supposed to surrender himself tomorrow.

He didn't want to do that.

He didn't want to get started on the nitroglycerin either. The remote detonator he planned to make from the numeric pager? That was simple and not dangerous. He could make that in his sleep. A kid could make it. The clothespin detonator wired to the blasting cap, and tripped by someone opening the door from outside? That was trickier, but still not dangerous. He could do it, even now, even after the day he had lived through.

The nitro, the very thing both detonators would be wired to set off? That was the trouble. It was a highly explosive concoction, and very unstable. If he let it get too hot, it would blow up in his face. If he did anything too fast, it would blow up in his face. If he jiggled it too hard, it would blow up in his face. Any little mistake at all, and Smoke would die right here in the hotel room, his head blown off by his own hand.

He was too damned tired to face the nitro.

Before coming here, he had made two reservations by telephone. The first was this room, under the name O'Malley. Certainly, it was the name of a dead man, but Best Western wasn't going to know that. Also, O'Malley's workshop hadn't burned down today with a man inside it.

Soon, probably within twenty-four hours, the police were going to know about Walter O'Malley, but as of yet, Smoke reckoned, they couldn't know. Smoke Dugan, on the other hand, was probably wanted for questioning RIGHT NOW.

They were looking for him. So the other person who made a reservation at Best Western was a man named Barry Fillmore.

When he checked in as O'Malley, he made a point of asking the young woman working as the desk clerk when she would go off shift. He did it by asking her if she wanted to go for a drink afterward. With him? Bruised face, missing teeth, dark bags of exhaustion under his eyes. Of course she didn't. But she did tell him that she would be off shift at eleven. At precisely one in the morning, Smoke planned to walk in again and check in as Barry Fillmore with a new desk clerk.

Cruz and Moss had no reason to suspect anyone named Barry Fillmore. They didn't even know such a man existed. Nobody did, and that included Lola.

The items on the desk began to fade from view. First they became fuzzy and insubstantial, then the world went black and they were gone. He was drifting off, not a good thing, but his body was weary, more tired than he had been at any time since he had first escaped New York three years before.

The phone rang.

He picked it up on the second ring. He looked out through the partially drawn curtains.

'Yeah?'

'O'Malley you're calling yourself now? I thought you didn't like that name.'

He recognized Cruz's voice. Cruz was on a cellphone, fading in and out with the movement of the car.

'I'm sorry, I don't know who this is.'

'Dugan, let's cut the bullshit. We want to make the trade. You know the one I'm talking about?'

Smoke took a moment to respond. 'Of course.'

'Tomorrow morning at nine, you walk into that restaurant and look for us.'

Smoke interrupted. 'Let me speak to Lola.'

'Tomorrow you can speak to her. We'll have a table for four, and there'll be four of us sitting there, including Lola and her friend Pamela. You sit down with us and we'll all have a nice breakfast. You can talk all you want. After we eat, the girls get up and walk out of the restaurant, just like that. No big farewells, they just get up, walk out, and run as far and as fast as they can. They go to the cops, you know we'll get them. If they go away, maybe we never find them again. Maybe we never even try. If you want to hand Lola a big pile of cash under the table, so much the better her chances, and so much the better you'll feel. As you know, we don't want her.' Cruz's voice paused for just a moment. 'After the girls have been gone a few minutes, we all three of us get up and walk out to the car. Then we take a nice long ride to New York. You'll have time to make peace with everything while we drive. I'll even let you listen to my CD player if you want.'

Smoke listened. He said nothing right away. Of course, something about it sounded wrong. Everything about it sounded wrong. Lola getting away seemed the longest of possible long shots. Smoke getting away was no longer an issue at all.

'Dugan?'

'How do I know you won't have somebody waiting outside the restaurant to grab her as soon as she leaves? Then you've got us both.'

Cruz laughed. 'I guess you don't know your girlfriend very well. There's not many who could just grab her, as you say. And if somebody shoots her, how far are they gonna get in a crowded parking lot on a weekday morning? Come on, Dugan. We'll let her run. Don't worry about that.'

Smoke gave it a moment's thought. 'OK,' he said. 'I'll walk in there at exactly nine.'

'That's what I like to hear. See you then. And, Dugan? No funny bullshit this time, OK? That's how innocent people get killed.'

The line went dead.

After Smoke hung up, he lay there, thinking.

Lola was either already dead, or would be just as soon as they had hold of Smoke. There was no way they were going to let her go. The thought of Lola already being dead stabbed him in the heart.

That was tit for tat, but more than just that. They didn't leave witnesses behind. He knew the mentality. In his early years, when he still went on bank jobs, he had seen people killed simply because they might have seen something, might have known something.

But put that away. Assume for the moment that Lola was alive. They had no plans to allow her to remain that way.

And that meant this meeting at the restaurant tomorrow was bullshit. Either they would hold her and have the meeting, letting her go just long enough so that somebody else could grab her outside the restaurant, or something else would happen. If someone was to grab her outside the restaurant, that meant they needed another person, who was either on the way or already here. That person couldn't be known to Lola, because then she would avoid such a person in the parking lot.

The whole parking lot thing was tricky. If she walked out of that restaurant, she could throw herself on the mercy of the first person she saw. It could be an old couple. It could be a team of construction workers. It could be a Mexican dishwasher outside on his break for a smoke. Or cops could be pulling into the parking lot at exactly that moment. Cops could be eating in the restaurant. All of it meant collateral damage trying to get her back, high-visibility collateral damage in a very public place during busy daylight hours. Lola could suddenly decide to run into the kitchen area and throw herself on the mercy of the people back there – causing a scene and screaming about the murderers there at that table, holding her boyfriend hostage.

No fucking way.

Which meant they couldn't let her go at all. At the same time, they had to know Smoke would come in with a gun, or a bomb, or more than one bomb, or something rigged to explode out in the parking lot bringing cops and firefighters and rescue vehicles. They also had to know he would use these things if they didn't let her go.

So the restaurant meeting was just an out-and-out sham. They had no control of the variables in such a meeting, and so simply couldn't allow it to happen. They were going to try to get him before he ever got inside the restaurant. So now there were two other variables to consider. Either they were going to try to grab him again, and bring him to New York, or after everything that had happened, they had abandoned that idea, and were just going to pop him as he stepped out his door to walk across to the restaurant.

Smoke stopped to consider this deeply. His mind became very still. Minutes slowly passed, and he still couldn't decide. It was an important distinction. If they just wanted to kill him, that left very little wiggle room. If they had started with that plan, he would already be dead.

After a long time, Smoke climbed off the bed, splashed some water on his face in the bathroom, and sat down at the desk to work.

'Good girl,' Cruz said. 'That's a good girl.'

He had his left arm draped around Pamela as they hustled through the hushed corridors of the Portland Arms Hotel. His right hand was in his jacket pocket, holding the silenced Glock in there, pointed across his body right at her. They had dropped Moss off at the Holiday Inn just minutes before. The big man, who had washed up at a highway rest area, walked into the hotel under his own power.

Now, Cruz cooed to Pamela as they moved down the hallway toward his door. There was no one around. He kept that arm on her tight as he released the gun and fished the door card out of his pants pocket. He slid the card into its slot and guided Pamela inside.

Right now he might kill for a cigarette, and he had a non-smoking suite.

Non-smoking suite? Now why had he done that? He couldn't remember asking for one – but he knew he sometimes did to keep his habit under control. He glanced around the place. They had mounted smoke detectors above the bed, above the toilet in the bathroom, and out in the middle of the room. The only out they gave you was you could sit right by the open window and blow the smoke into the street.

There was an old radiator in a corner of the bedroom, probably there more for style than for actual heat. Cruz hand-cuffed Pamela to the radiator, then tied one of his T-shirts around her mouth as a gag. She had started crying again while they drove back into town. For a while, Cruz had been concerned that he would have to take the wheel, but she had hung on. Now, she was no longer crying. She must have cried herself out. Instead, she was lying there morosely on the floor, staring into space, her head resting on the pillow he had given her. No, he wasn't expecting any more trouble from Pamela.

Cruz lay down on top of the bed, an unlit cigarette between his fingers. He took a deep breath, and popped on the TV. In front of him, a late night talk show host yukked it up with two celebrity guests. One of the guests was a young Hispanic woman in a slinky gown who was stunningly, achingly beautiful. Cruz kept the sound on mute. Instead of listening, he watched the faces contort in mindless laughter. Occasionally, the camera panned the studio audience, who laughed right along.

Impossible fuck-up piled on top of impossible fuck-up.

Now they didn't even have Lola. They still had Pamela, and at least that was something. But Cruz had had a hunch, and so had called Dugan at the Best Western. Good enough, he had gotten him there. Even better, Dugan seemed to have no idea that Lola had escaped.

Not only were the two guys who attacked Moss not Dugan, they had nothing to do with Dugan. Which made things very strange.

Cruz didn't even bother to call it in to New York.

It was so far gone now it seemed better not to talk about it.

Moss had taken an entire handful of Advil he had fished out of somewhere. With any luck, those wallops he had taken had put him right to sleep. Cruz didn't relish the idea of Moss awake, thinking and moving around just ten blocks away.

'Mmmmmm,' Pamela said from the floor. 'Mmmmm.'

Cruz looked at her. She rolled her eyes. 'Mmmmmmmmm.'

Cruz sighed and climbed off the bed. He was bone tired. He couldn't believe how tired he was. It was an effort just to stand up.

'Pamela, I'm too tired to tell you what I'm going to do if you scream.'

He pulled the shirt down just a bit from her mouth.

'Do you mind if I get in the other bed? I can't see the TV from down here.'

'The TV?'

She smiled. It was a nice, bright smile. Strange in these circumstances. She had damn-near perfect teeth. White like in the toothpaste commercials. Someone had paid for that smile when she was a child. Sure, Cruz thought. Middle-class America. They all have those teeth.

'I like this show,' she said.

Cruz glanced at the flickering box. As killers went, now he knew he was all washed up, that he was even considering this. In the old days, Pamela would be lying in a swamp somewhere. He thought back to half-dead Moss, incredulous, uncomprehending, all kinds of long words, that Cruz was bringing this girl back to his hotel room. After the beating he had taken, Moss had apparently decided that the time had come to get rid of Pamela.

And Cruz could see it in his eyes as he climbed out of the car: Moss had decided that Cruz was weak.

Yeah, his career was over. Any more kills he had left in him were in self-defense. Or maybe to get his hands on that money and get away.

'Sure,' he said. 'You can watch it.' He looked into her eyes. 'Just don't give me any problems, OK?'

He set about moving Pamela up to the bed.

Moss paced the floor of his room.

The TV was on, some bullshit Hollywood stars talking their bullshit.

He had gone down the hall and gotten some ice out of the machine. Then he had wrapped the ice in a motel towel. He held the cold, wet towel to his head as he paced. The pain had subsided somewhat with all the Advil he had taken, but not enough to erase the anger that was bubbling over. Not nearly enough. Nobody had ever cold-cocked him like that. Ever. In his life. He had gutted that one bastard, and that was good. But he hadn't gotten the other guy.

He yearned – no, he ached – to see that fat fuck again.

Now Cruz, who had lectured him about not fucking with the hostages, was down there at that fancy hotel with the skinny chick. Moss had noticed. Oh yeah, he had noticed. The skinny one looked good. Under that whole schoolteacher front she put on, she looked good. She wasn't Lola, hell no, but few chicks were. But she looked good.

And Cruz had her over there. Cruz, who had left him behind at the cabins without explaining himself. Cruz, who had been gone when the shit went down. Cruz, who was in no pain, and who was probably going to dip his wick tonight.

Moss had been pushed too far.

Moss was ready to kill.

Man, if Big Vito ever decided Cruz's number was up, Moss hoped they picked him to do the job. With pleasure.

He imagined a scenario. In it, he waited until the morning. Cruz and the chick came to pick him up, then he just walked up and popped the chick right in front of Cruz. No warning, no mention of it, no debate, just . . .

BANG.

Yeah. Moss liked that.

'Collateral damage, son,' he might say, and keep a round ready for Cruz in case he got uppity.

* * *

The show was over.

Cruz lay back, staring at the ceiling. His gun – fully loaded, round chambered – lay on the bed right at his fingertips.

He yearned for a smoke.

It was possible, Cruz realized, that Moss was lurking outside right now, hoping to kill him in the dead of night rather than broad daylight.

'Why do you keep your gun on the bed with you?'

Pamela. Lying on her side, hands cuffed together and through the bed frame, watching him with those big deer eyes. He hadn't bothered to put the gag back in her mouth. It was uncomfortable and she wasn't going to scream anyway. For a while there, it had looked like she was going to fall asleep.

She looked pretty. He imagined that she spent a lot of her time living in Lola's shadow. It was one thing to be a quiet, pretty girl. It was another to be a sexy knockout.

'What?'

'Your gun.' She gestured with her head. 'You have it there by your hand. Are you afraid somebody's going to break in and kill you while you're sleeping?'

'Am I afraid?'

She nodded with seeming eagerness.

What an odd way to put it. But of course. Pamela came from that world where people were afraid all the time. Cruz only skimmed the surface of that world from time to time, dipping in and trying not to get noticed – occasionally scaring the herd into a blind panic. In Cruz's world, nobody was afraid. Of anything.

Try to explain that to her.

'No, I'm not afraid.'

'Then why do you have it?'

Cruz smiled. 'In case somebody breaks in and tries to kill me while I'm sleeping.'

She smiled with him. 'Is there much chance of that happening?'

He shrugged. 'Tonight? I'd say about one chance in two.'

'That big guy?' she said. 'Moss. You're afraid he might try to kill you.' It wasn't a question.

'I'm not afraid.'

'OK, not afraid. You never get afraid, right? Now that you mention it, I read that fact somewhere, that violent criminals, uh, people like you, action-oriented people, don't feel emotions like fear. At least, not in the same way. You don't register pain the same way as normal, uh, most people, either. You're wired differently.'

Cruz listened to her analysis without comment.

She lapsed into a moment of silence.

'But you do think he wants to kill you.'

'Kill me, or kill you,' Cruz said.

Her eyes widened at that, but she kept her mouth closed. 'Do you mind if he kills me?' she said at last.

He looked at her now. She was probing him, and it was a strange position to be in. Strange because this woman should have been dead hours ago. Strange because he never talked about himself – he never let anyone get close enough to ask him anything. On those occasions that he did talk about himself he invented some other person with a different life and talked about that person. But this questioning was strange most of all because he found he was kind of enjoying it. He had lived a long time on a dangerous edge, and he realized now that there was a wealth of stories to tell.

What would he say to her, this . . . what?

'I'm tired of killing,' he said.

'Have you, have you . . .' he could almost hear her gulp before she spoke again, '. . . have you done it a lot?'

He turned to look at her across the three-foot gap between the two beds. Their eyes met, and he stared deeply into hers. He showed her what was there, not to scare her, not get his way, but for once, just to show somebody. Within seconds, three seconds maybe, she looked away. After a time, she brought her eyes back to his. But then she looked away again.

'Yeah,' she said, staring at the bed in front of her bound hands. 'I guess you have.'

The pause between them spun out into eternity.

'You work for the Mafia, am I right?'

Cruz smiled again. 'Pamela, you watch too much TV. I work for businessmen.'

She seemed to chew on that for a little while.

'Pamela, what did you say you do for a living? You're a . . .'

'I'm a librarian at the public library in Portland.'

'What kind of job is that?'

She looked puzzled. 'What kind?'

'Yeah, like is it a good job? Would people want a job like that?'

She seemed to think it over. After a time, she came to some sort of conclusion. 'It's an excellent job. I love books, I like people, and I do a good job. I'm highly skilled and qualified. I went to graduate school to get a degree in Library Science.'

'You went to graduate school?'

'Yeah, to get my master's degree.'

'You mean, you have to have a master's degree to be a librarian? All those people running around in libraries went to graduate school?'

Cruz didn't know why this idea impressed him.

'No, it's not like that. The thing is, most people who work in libraries are actually clerks. You can't really tell who the librarians are unless you're behind the scenes.'

'Librarians get paid more?'

'That's right.'

'Do you think you help people? In your job, I mean?'

She didn't hesitate. 'I know I do.'

Cruz smiled. 'So why wouldn't I mind?' he said. 'If Moss killed you, why wouldn't I mind? See, we don't really help people, Moss and me. I think maybe we don't. But that's OK because the people we, uh, hurt, they don't usually help people either. But this, hurting people, who help people, that's not OK anymore. It was never OK, but it's really not OK now.'

'Did something happen to make it not OK?' she said.

Cruz had no answer for that one.

Lola hung up the telephone.

'There's no one named James Dugan registered at the Best

Western in South Portland, or at any of the hotels in town,' she said.

Hal looked up from where he was slumped on the living-room sofa of his ramshackle home in Auburn. After he had dumped the body, they had driven up here. They had come here more because neither one of them could think of what else to do than for any other reason. Hal had said this place would be safe, and that made sense to Lola. No one knew he was involved. And Lola figured that after all that had happened, she didn't have much to fear anymore from Mr Shaggy. Further, there was no reason to believe Lola's apartment would be safe.

Hal's eyes were swollen from when he had wept. He had a bottle of beer in his hand. 'He wouldn't register under his own name. Not if he had the use of an alias.'

'It worries me to be here,' Lola said.

Hal shook his head. 'I'm not going to hurt you. I'm sorry that it ever happened.'

'That's not what worries me. I'm worried because Smoke is out there with those killers, and I don't know where he is. I'm worried because they still have Pamela. I'm worried that something terrible is going to happen, and I'm all the way up here in Auburn, and I can't do anything about it.'

Hal sipped his beer. 'I wouldn't worry. We'll go down there in the morning in time for the exchange. That's all we can do.'

Lola paced into the living room and sat down in the chair across from Hal.

'What are you going to tell his wife?'

'You mean if I live through tomorrow morning?' He

shrugged. He poured the last of his beer down his throat. That was the third bottle of beer he had polished off since they came into the house not fifteen minutes before. His eyes watered. 'I'll tell her that I'm sorry.'

He stood on unsteady legs and walked off toward the kitchen, probably to get another beer. The floorboards of the old house creaked under his weight.

There was a photo album sitting on the coffee table. Lola sat up in her chair and opened it. Maybe in the back of her mind she thought the album would give her some insight into Hal's life. Maybe in the back of her mind she thought nothing.

She was beyond tired.

In any case, she began to thumb idly through the book.

It was pornography, all of it. Photos of Hal and Darren – mostly well-endowed Darren – with a variety of women and teenaged girls in different settings. Some were fake beach and mountain scenes. Mostly, the settings were sparsely furnished offices, very much like the one where Lola first met them.

It took Lola more than a minute to realize that this was going to be the whole book: cheap, exploitative porno. It was a portfolio of sorts, and Hal must have stopped to look it over proudly during happier times. She closed the cover.

He was standing in the doorway with another beer.

'You know?' she said. 'You've been a really bad man.'

She didn't say, 'And now both you and your friend Darren are paying for it.' She hoped that much was understood. By the look in his eyes, she believed it was.

* * *

In Barry Fillmore's room, Smoke watched the sky brighten.

It had been a long night, but he felt satisfied as he lay there. It had taken him most of the night, but he had made the nitro, and he had successfully wired a door bomb that could blow in two different ways. He could blow it with a call from the cellphone to the pager, or someone could blow it by opening the door from the outside.

He had caught himself whistling while he worked, as he often did when his mind was clear and he was happy. By focusing on his work, he had found he could keep a lid on his boiling emotions. He felt, right up front, like he had been ripped in half. The pain of separation, forced separation, was almost too much to bear. Although he had told her many times since that first instance over a year ago, he realized now, perhaps for the first time, that he loved Lola. It took a circumstance like death or the threat of death to get Smoke to recognize or think about love. That alone bothered him.

But there was much more at play here.

Lola was in terrible danger, and so was Pamela. And he had put them there through his negligence, through his sheer carelessness. The anxiety he felt for their safety, the *fear*, was like a tumor growing on his brain.

He had to save them if it was even possible anymore, and at whatever cost to himself.

Maybe there would still be that possibility.

Soon, he would have to get up. He had to get outside and get in position. He had to be ready to control the action.

While shopping the night before, he had picked up a slim

jim – a long, thin and flat piece of metal he could use to pop open the door to just about any car more than five years old. There were plenty in the parking lot to choose from. The least of his worries was the owner of the car finding him there. When he stationed himself in the parking lot, he had no choice. He couldn't use his own car, just in case they had forced Lola to tell them what it looked like. Of course, she wouldn't want to tell them, but . . .

In the end, they could make just about anybody talk.

The thought of them making Lola talk sent a spasm of guilt and horror along his spine. He had to shut out all thought if this was going to come out OK. If he saw her, and she was hurt – bruised, beaten, raped, any of these were possible – he was going to have to shut that out too. He was going to have to function while wading through a mud bog of horror. And he was going to have to take these guys out, both of them, so that Lola and Pamela might live.

He steeled himself for the effort.

There was a coffee maker in this room. He stood, and limped his way over to the desk. He was still in pain from the beating he had taken, and he had stiffened up during the night. He felt like a very old man, and he imagined he must look like a scarecrow.

Maybe this would be his last day alive.

The thought held no terror for him.

7

It was 7 a.m.

'Hey, kid, wanna make twenty bucks?' Cruz said.

The kid was about eighteen, sitting on the curb outside Governor's Restaurant, having a smoke. He wore a stained kitchen smock. He had long hair, and looked for all the world like one of those kids who would spend the best years of their lives sweating in the back rooms of restaurants.

Cruz didn't look directly at the kid. He stood above him, smoking a cigarette himself.

'What do I gotta do?' the kid said.

Cruz nodded in the direction of the giant motel across the parking lot. There were dozens of cars out there, glinting in the early morning sun. Dugan was out there among those cars. Maybe. Or maybe he was still in his room. Cruz could just make out the door from here.

'I got a friend staying in the hotel there, Room 108. He's got a girl in there with him, and I want to play a little joke. He put the Do Not Disturb sign on his door for the maid. All you gotta do is run over there and take down the sign.'

'That's it?'

'That's it,' Cruz said. 'The easiest twenty you ever made.'

The kid was back in three minutes. He brought the door hanger with him. Cruz slapped his palm with the money.

'No sweat,' the kid said. 'Have fun.'

Smoke slumped in the passenger seat of a Ford Crown Victoria. It was an old person's car. Blue on the outside, gray interior. It was, to Smoke's mind, an absolute blubber boat. He chose it because it was across the lot about fifty yards from Room 108, facing the door. He also chose it because he figured if the person who owned it came out of their room, he could spot them approaching, get out of the car, and get away. A young person's car might not afford such a luxury.

He watched and waited. His eyes watered. His vision became unfocused. Wired on fear as he was, his eyes were trying to shut. He blinked them rapidly, trying to keep them open. He began to think thoughts and remember people from long ago. The past was intruding on the present, his dreams were intruding on reality.

He remembered a time when a guy was telling him about the safe in the jewelry store where he worked. When was that, 1969? Smoke saw the cars, a little sports coupé, a big muscle car. He was driving a red Dodge Challenger in those days.

The kids were on the TV, dying in the jungles of Vietnam. The girls pranced with their long straight hair and their miniskirts. College kids. Smoke saw them more on TV than anywhere near his own life. This punk kid was talking – he still wore that slicked-back hair that had been out of style for years – some bullshit about going in and getting some of the display case stuff. They were in a coffee shop near Grand Central Station, smoking cigarettes and drinking coffee. Every time this kid put out a cigarette, he lit another one. He was wired wrong, this kid. Talking fast, trying to pull down his finder's fee.

'Brooklyn, O'Malley,' the kid said. 'Brooklyn. Out by Grand Army Plaza. You won't believe this shit, man. You won't fucking believe it.'

'OK,' Smoke said. 'OK, we go in and get the display case stuff, get pinched, and go upstate for what? A bunch of trinkets and shit, right?'

'You don't get it,' the kid said. He took a long, crazy suck on his smoke. This kid could smoke the whole cigarette in one drag. 'Yeah, you get the display case stuff, but only because it's there. Why the fuck not? But the gig – the *gig* – is the safe. That's why you take the risk.'

From how the kid described it, Smoke knew he couldn't break it. But then the kid described its location – it was built into the back wall of the office, right up into the bricks. Dumb. Smoke put a crew together. They went in through the store right next to it. It was a dry goods place. The kid drew a map and they went right to the place where the back of the safe should be. Smoke put down a small charge, baffled it – it sounded loud to him, but in the papers an upstairs tenant said he thought he heard someone sneeze – and then they yanked the bricks out of there with their bare hands. They were in. Shit, they grabbed a lot of money from that one. It was 1969 and Smoke had $30,000 in cash sitting up in his apartment. You could buy a real nice house for that, no mortgage, and Smoke had it in cash. He was twenty-seven years old. Those were good times.

He snapped awake.

Still in the car, the Crown Victoria. The weight of the years sank into him in a second flat. The weight of the current circumstances made him feel even heavier.

Maybe he was wrong. Maybe Cruz wouldn't come for him this way.

Well, if they didn't come, then at 10 a.m., he would disable the charges behind his room door, then he would walk into Governor's and see what was what. He had his little gun, and that was it. He had no other plan, and right now he was too tired to think up another one. He hadn't slept a wink.

A long minute passed. He spotted a young woman under the awning, walking along the sidewalk toward his door. She wore a blue smock and pushed along a cleaning cart.

She walked right to his door and knocked. That didn't make sense. He had placed a sign on the doorknob. Do Not Disturb. Didn't that mean anything?

Her back was to him. She had long, sleek black hair. The chambermaid. She was going to open the door.

Holy shit.

He scanned the area, looking for them. Nothing.

Now the maid rooted around on her key chain. She brought out the key she wanted.

Smoke pushed open the heavy door of the car and jumped out.

'Hey!' he shouted. 'Hey, you! Maid! No!'

He was running almost before he said it. It was a horrible, shuffling gait. He had left the cane in the car. In his haste, he had taken the Derringer and the cellphone, and left the cane.

He was twenty yards away.

He shouted again. 'Hey! Don't open that door!'

She looked up, the key in the lock. For a moment, he thought it was Lorena. Then her face resolved into that of a young woman. It was a mask of confusion.

Smoke pointed the gun at her. 'Don't you dare open that fucking door.'

Hal snorted another line off the mirror he had placed on the dashboard. He snorted with a rolled-up hundred-dollar bill. He saved the coke for special occasions – this was a special occasion if ever there was one.

His nostrils burned, all the way back into his throat. Oh yeah. He had been sagging until about ten minutes ago, despite three cups of coffee. Now he felt huge, and he was growing bigger by the minute.

Here came the surge.

'Oh my God,' Lola said.

She burst out of the pickup truck. Hal had the Mossberg across his lap, and at first he just watched her go. He didn't know these people out on the sidewalk, but now he gathered she did. They had been hunkered down low in the front seat of his old black Ford pickup, parked way in the back of the lot, away from Governor's Restaurant, away from everything.

Now Lola was running across the tarmac, no weapon, straight toward the man and woman out in front of that motel room.

Swelling confidence buzzed in Hal's head. Let her run. It was exciting. Everything seemed crystal clear out there.

He stepped out of the truck with the shotgun.

He stood tall.

In his pocket, he had another gun, a .25 caliber pocket pistol for up-close fighting.

He saw two men moving in the same direction, coming in from the left. They were all converging on the scene in front of the motel room door. One of them was that big bastard that Hal had sworn to kill. He moved like an ape, long gangling arms hanging practically to the ground.

'Run, monkey,' Hal said.

He raised the shotgun and sighted along the tops of the cars.

Cruz and Moss were fast walking across the parking lot and toward the door. Cruz drank it all in. There was the chambermaid. There was Smoke Dugan, just past her, leaning against the building.

He seemed to have a gun. Jesus, was that a gun? It might have been a cigarette lighter. Cruz watched as Smoke swiped at the cleaning cart and knocked it over. He nearly went over with it.

Ridiculous.

'Dugan,' Moss said. It wasn't a shout, but was loud enough to be heard. 'Dugan. Hey, son, just one moment now.'

This wasn't bad. There was nobody here right at this moment, no citizens. They could snag Dugan, bring him straight away to New York. He could let Pamela go, though she interested him now. She was . . . intriguing. He figured he would have to run roughshod over Moss to ensure Pamela's safety, but he could do it. He'd never see any of Dugan's money, and that retirement he was toying with would have to wait, but you know? That was better. Who was he fooling? They don't let you retire. And these, these fuck-ups yesterday, they were bad, but probably not career-ending. Cruz was going to live through this, and come out on top after all.

Mission accomplished.

All this went through his mind in less than five seconds.

Then Lola appeared.

'Smoke!' She sprinted across the blacktop. She screamed it again. 'SMOKE!'

Cruz pulled his gun. Beside him, Moss did the same.

'Uh-oh, son, here comes the family reunion,' Moss said. His words drawled out like molasses. 'I hate that bitch.'

Then came the explosion.

* * *

'RUN!' Smoke screamed at the maid as she shrank back against the door. Her hand jiggled the doorknob. Smoke jabbed with the Derringer.

'Run, you bitch, will you run?'

He knocked the cart over for emphasis and almost lost his balance.

Shit. Shit on this.

Behind her, Cruz and Moss were coming. Moss loomed larger and larger as they approached. He looked like a dinosaur. He looked like a tidal wave.

'Dugan,' Moss said. 'Dugan. Hey, son, just one moment now.'

The maid glanced back. The sight of Moss decided her. She threw her hands in the air and ran straight out into the parking lot, away from everyone.

Smoke heard his name called.

He turned and Lola was running across the lot toward them.

Shit.

Smoke backed away from the door. He slid along the wall of the motel. All the way back, get all the way back. The fake stucco of the building clung to his jacket. Moss and Cruz were almost here. They drew their guns. He raised the tiny pistol at them.

Here they came.

Moss smiled. His face was bruised, like he had taken a beating.

Smoke glanced down at the phone. He had the pager on speed dial.

He pressed the SEND button.

Nothing happened.

He looked at the phone again.

SEND, right? You were supposed to press SEND.

Dugan was *right there*.

Then the back windshield of a parked car shattered, ten yards away. Cruz and Moss moved as one, crouched behind separate cars. A second later, a long, rolling BOOM sounded across the whole parking lot. Someone screamed back near the restaurant. A fat man with long hair and a beard walked across the lot toward them, shotgun raised. He fired the gun again.

Dugan disappeared between two parked cars.

The second blast demolished the rear windshield of the car Cruz was hiding behind. That was two windshields down, two huge shotgun blasts on a normal straight world morning. This was the last thing they needed.

Now the fat man was just across a lane of cars. He ducked down.

'Who is that?' Cruz said to Moss. Moss rested his gun on the car he was crouched behind, aiming across the parking lot. His eye was cast down in a squint.

'He's the fat fuck who clubbed me.'

'You see him?'

'Not right this second. But I know where he went under. When he comes back up, I'm gonna take him.'

Cruz looked for Smoke. He looked for Lola. He didn't see either one.

The cops were going to be here any minute.

Five seconds had passed since the fat man ducked under.

Then the fat man stood up, two cars over from where he had gone under. He started firing again. Moss and Cruz started firing. Cruz fired randomly, across the parking lot, away from the fat man, away from anybody. Could Moss see this?

Windows shattered. Bullets whined off pavement.

Moss's line caught the fat man. The fat man did a strange jitterbug as Moss hit him three or four times.

'Bingo!' Moss shouted. 'Dance, fat boy!'

The fat man went down like a wall of bricks.

Just then an explosion ripped the air just behind Cruz and to his left. A rush of hot air blew over him. The explosion had no sound. It was too big for sound. He was lifted into the air. He flew over the top of the car he had hidden behind. His arms pinwheeled madly, and Cruz thought for sure he was dead.

Hal couldn't feel his legs.

He lay on his back on the blacktop. He had barely registered the explosion – he had more important things on his mind. He could feel the burning in his gut where he had been shot. He swallowed, then lifted his head and stared down at his feet. Everything was still down there and still attached – he just couldn't feel any of it.

The bullets severed my spine.

No thought had ever caused him such horror. Darren's death paled in comparison. Valuable seconds passed as he watched an image of himself in a wheelchair roll slowly across his mind.

He shook his head. There was no time for that. There was only time for action. The shotgun was above his head and behind him somewhere. He reached back there – it hurt just to raise his arms like that – but he couldn't find it. He started crawling backwards, dragging his useless legs after him.

Something caught his eye. He looked up and here came that big motherfucker, swaggering toward him. The bastard's face was swollen, but he was grinning.

As he approached he raised his gun. He pointed it at Hal.

'Hey, fat boy,' he said.

Hal fell back and threw his hands up in front of his face.

I'm sorry, Darren. I'm sorry.

'Smile,' the big man said.

Just then, Hal remembered the pistol, the small .25, still in his jacket pocket. He felt its reassuring weight there. He reached for it, hoping that somehow, by some miracle, he wouldn't be too late.

Cruz hit the tarmac, surprised but still alive.

He glanced back at where he had been.

Jesus.

The door had blown out from the hotel room. Its fragments had sprayed all over the parking lot. The doorway was on fire. The cars near the door were on fire. The car Cruz had hidden behind was on fire.

There was no sign of anyone.

Then he saw Moss, up and pacing across the lot. He stopped about three cars away. He stood over something, looking down at it.

'Hey fat boy,' Moss said. Cruz heard him clearly through the smoke and early morning air. Gawkers were going to gather soon. Gawkers always did. They had to get away before then.

Cruz struggled to his feet.

There was Moss, pointing his gun at the figure on the ground. There was the fat man, hands raised to ward off the blow. Cruz walked toward them.

'Smile,' Moss told the fat man.

'Moss,' Cruz said.

Moss fired three times.

Brain salad sprayed onto the blacktop in a fan shape.

Moss looked at Cruz. 'What?'

It must have been a faulty connection.

Smoke thought about this while he lay sprawled between two parked cars. Now was not the time, but all the same, he thought about it. The nitro had worked. Good. The phone had worked. Good. The connection from the pager to the detonator? Well, he probably could have wired it better.

He wondered if anybody had died.

Then Lola was there next to him.

'Smoke!' she said. 'Smoke!' She said it over and over. She cradled his head in her arms. She was alive. She was free. He didn't even question it.

'Are you hurt?' she said.

He shrugged. 'Me? I'm fine.'

She helped him up and he leaned on her as they picked their way between parked cars. He tried to stay low. They crossed the lot, and ducked through the bushes into the next lot. Here was the Tercel, parked away from the action.

Back behind them, an engine raced, and a car screamed out of the parking lot, tires squealing. Then the buzz of people, the shouts, the sobs, the commotion began.

Smoke put the key in the ignition.

He looked at Lola. She looked at him.

'I love you,' they said in tandem.

They stopped and laughed.

'Hon, we gotta go,' Smoke said.

'Fuck, man,' Moss said. 'Fuck!'

He was back behind the wheel of the Taurus.

They moved in heavy traffic down Route 1, the major thoroughfare in South Portland. Cruz watched Moss drive. Moss worried him. His outlook had taken a sudden U-turn. From the temporary elation of bagging the fat man, to a treacherous and burning rage. That was not good.

It also nagged at Cruz that they were still in this Taurus. They'd had it too long; it had seen too much action. They had changed the plates, sure. But they needed another car, and Fingers was the car thief of the bunch.

Who had witnessed all that? A lot of people. Cruz had seen eyes looking out from doorways in the motel, from the windows of the restaurant. An old couple were sitting in a car outside Governor's as Cruz and Moss ran past. Cruz had glanced in their window and seen the look in their eyes. The shooting had kept them in the car. But they were seeing every-thing.

Including this car.

He glanced back at Pamela, handcuffed to the hand grip above her seat. Had anybody witnessed that?

'We gotta do something about this car,' he said.

'I hate this fucking job, Cruz. You know that? I hate this fucking job and I hate you. How you think they're gonna feel about this down in New York? In broad daylight all this shit happened. You know what? If we go down for this shit – and I never thought I'd say this, I never thought I'd go down for anything – if I do any time for this, until my dying breath I swear I'm gonna take you out.'

Cruz had never heard Moss talk so fast. 'The car, Moss. We gotta do something about it.'

'I'm working on it.'

He turned right, signaling, driving perfectly normally. He had turned at a sign with a harness racing figure on it that said 'Scarborough Downs Raceway'. They cruised along a deserted feeder road, with hedges and a fence on either side. Up ahead, the raceway itself loomed in the distance. They crossed a vast, empty parking lot, with just a few cars stationed near the entrance to the raceway. Weeds grew in cracks in the tarmac.

'No races today,' Pamela said from the back seat. Her eyes

had gone large again. Cruz knew the look. The shootout had blown her mind.

'You know what?' Moss said. 'I've had it with you too. You should've been dead yesterday.' With his right hand, he whipped his gun out of his jacket. He kept his left hand on the wheel, and turned nearly all the way around. He put the gun to Pamela's head. Pamela gasped, a long hissing moan of air going out of her tires. The car rolled along slowly.

'We're gonna ditch this car anyway,' Moss said. 'I don't mind a little mess.'

Cruz pulled his own gun. He put the barrel against Moss's temple.

'Pull that trigger and it's the last thing you do,' he said.

Cruz felt calm.

'Cruz, what the fuck's the matter with you? Why you keeping this bitch alive? The job's over, son. That was it, don't you get it? Dugan got away, with Lola this time. He's halfway to fucking Timbuktu by now. The job's a total loss, and we gotta get out of here.' He gestured at Pamela with his head. 'We can't bring her with us.'

'I disagree. I think Dugan's coming back for her. I think we still have a trade.'

'Cruz, are you fucking crazy? All those people saw us back there. You don't think we can stay here, do you?'

Cruz ignored the question. 'Moss, I'm about to kill you. You understand?'

Moss cast an eye at Cruz. The look said he understood well enough.

'Now drop the gun in the back seat. You hear me? Drop the gun.'

Moss hesitated, then smiled, and did as he was told. The gun made a heavy bonk as it hit the floor in the back. Moss turned back around to the wheel. Cruz kept the gun against his head.

'You're dead. You know that, Cruz? Ain't no way they gonna let you off now.'

'Pull up over there by the hedge.'

'I mean, I hope I'm there to see it when they get you. Gonna fucking bleed you, probably. You know? Do it real slow.'

He pulled over to the hedge and stopped.

'Now get out of the fucking car.'

Moss opened the door and climbed out. He was grinning so broadly the top of his head might slide off. He was standing practically in the hedges. Cruz pointed the gun up at him. Cruz didn't like this position with the door open like this, but it was what he had at the moment.

'Drop your cellphone on the ground,' he said. 'Do it slow.'

'Bleed you, motherfucker. Like a fucking cow.'

'Drop the cellphone, Moss, or I'll kill you right here.'

Moss took the cellphone off his pants. He glanced at Cruz like he might consider throwing the phone, then he dropped the phone to the blacktop.

'Now start walking toward those cars over by the building. Don't turn around until you get there. Got me? I got no reason to keep you alive except out of the goodness of my heart.'

'That's why you're gonna die so badly,' Moss said. Then he started walking.

When Moss was thirty yards away, Cruz got out of the car. He walked around to the driver's side. He picked up the cellphone and smashed it against the pavement. He glanced at Moss, still walking slowly toward the raceway. Then he looked in on Pamela.

'We have to do something about this car,' he said.

'I have a car,' Pamela said.

Smoke drove the old Tercel slowly through side streets extending out behind Route 1. They drove along in silence for a time. The silence spun out and became awkward. At some point, they came back out onto Route 1 and Smoke turned south toward Scarborough and Old Orchard Beach. They were moving in heavy traffic. There was no pursuit. Nothing unusual was happening at all.

'Smoke,' Lola said. 'What's going on?'

He shrugged. 'I don't even know where to begin.'

'Why don't you start at the beginning? Who are you?'

For a moment, he pondered how to answer this. His mind raced along, looking for loopholes and escape routes. The safe-cracker, the arsonist, Walter O'Malley, looked for a way out. But then Smoke Dugan took over, and he realized there was no way out. More than that, he realized that Lola deserved the truth. She deserved the truth because he had put her life in jeopardy. She deserved the truth because Pamela's life was still in jeopardy. She deserved the truth because Smoke loved her, and when you loved someone you told them the truth. It was that simple.

So he told her.

Everything.

It took a long time, and before he was done they had driven out to Old Orchard Beach. Old Orchard was just about dead this time of year. The big amusement park, Palace Playland, was closed. A backdrop there, ancient, fifty years old, showed minarets and scenes from the Middle East. 'Asalam Aleikum' said a huge sign over the ride. To Smoke it was odd – a hint of the exotic as people thought of it when he was young.

All of the amusements, the bathing suit stores, the T-shirt and poster stores, and the small boardwalk – open every year since 1898, said the sign – were closed. The pizza joints were still open, and so were the fried dough places along the strip. But few people still wandered around Old Orchard in October, especially on a Tuesday. The sun was shining but the breeze off the water was cold. They picked up a pizza to eat in the room.

Smoke could hardly believe it was Tuesday. He couldn't tell whether the past day had gone by in the blink of an eye or over the period of several lifetimes. All he knew: if this ever ended, and if he was still alive, he would sleep the sleep of the dead.

They decided to take a beachfront efficiency apartment. The motel where they stayed was nearly empty. Smoke interrupted his story so they could deal with the desk clerk in the threadbare office. The clerk was a girl about eighteen, and she was bored. She looked away from the soap operas on TV just long enough to check them in.

'The news came on before,' she said, her voice flat. 'Came

on right in the middle of my show. Said there was a big shootout right at the Best Western out on Route 1. Somebody got killed. Ain't that something?'

'We heard all about it,' Smoke said. 'That is something.'

They reached the safety of the room. Smoke looked at Lola and she at him. Their clothes came off as if of their own accord, as if by magic, as if by acclamation. Then they were on the bed, moving as if tossed about by a stormy sea.

Only afterward, lying there, did Smoke begin to take note of his surroundings.

The room was threadbare but serviceable. A large bed, a desk, two chairs in the main room, with a sliding glass door looking out on a small deck. The deck was three stories above the beach. The ocean shimmered out there, endless, eternal, unaware.

'Wouldn't it be nice,' Smoke said, 'if none of this had happened and we were just here, looking out at all that water, having a nice little getaway?'

'It would,' Lola said.

She hesitated. 'They said you killed people, Smoke.' She didn't look at him.

He looked at her.

She was sitting up on the bed eating a slice of pizza. It was just after noon. Behind her, the water was a deep, dark bluish-green. Two tears rolled down her cheeks, one on each cheek. She looked beautiful. He wanted to freeze this moment, because he was going to say something now, and after he said it, everything might be different for ever.

'It's true. I killed people. I killed a lot of people.'
She looked up. 'Oh, Smoke.'

Pamela sat in the passenger seat of the green Ford Taurus as Cruz drove through the narrow streets of the Old Port. Her hands were free. In fact, her hands were so free that they played with the radio dial, looking for a good song.

She felt . . . like she had never felt before.

On the drive back up here from the raceway, it had occurred to her that she had missed work today and not even called in sick. In a past life – yesterday – this fact would have turned a knife of worry in her stomach. She would have been so nervous she might have felt like vomiting. She certainly would have had an upset stomach.

Today? Nothing. No feelings for the job. If anything, she had a sense that she wouldn't be going back to work anytime soon. She had lived through a home invasion, a kidnapping, a shootout in a parking lot, and an attempted murder. All of this in less than twenty-four hours. She had barely slept and was damn near exhausted. She had nearly died, yesterday and today.

And she felt good.

She felt better than good.

'Turn here,' she said to Cruz, pointing to the right. Cruz was her ally now. Cruz had saved her life. Why? Because he wanted to trade her for Smoke Dugan? She no longer thought so.

'We can ditch this car in the parking lot at the Ferry

Terminal. We can buy a month and just leave it there.'

She was *thinking*. She was planning. She was part of this. This was a Pamela she had never known before, but had always suspected was there.

The terminal, with its three-story garage, loomed up ahead. People milled about in the little courtyard along the dock. A couple of dreadlocked teenage skateboarders jumped their boards down a small flight of stairs. Cruz pulled into the gloom of the parking garage and found a space.

'I'll go into the office and pay for the spot,' Pamela said.

Cruz pulled out a stack of bills. 'Pay cash if you can. And, Pamela? I'm trusting you. No funny stuff, OK?'

She smiled. 'Furthest thing from my mind.'

In the office, the woman at the desk didn't look twice at her. Paying in cash was OK. She gave her own name and her own license plate number. Would this woman ever check? Pamela doubted it. Pamela realized that she was digging some sort of hole for herself – at some point, they would find the car – the police probably – and her name would be associated with it. A stolen car, stolen plates, a shootout in a parking lot.

Yes, she was digging a hole, but as fast as she dug, her mind dug her right out again. She was good at this. If it came to it, she would show them all tears and tell them how the men forced her to park the stolen car in her name. How they threatened to kill her if she didn't, and how the smaller one, the dark assassin named Cruz, took her to a hotel room, threw her down on the bed and . . .

Well, that was a story for another time.

When she came out onto the street, Cruz was standing in the shadows of the big parking garage. She could tell he was trying to make himself invisible.

'I have to lose these clothes,' he said to her as he surveyed the scene. 'I need to put on something a tourist would wear.'

'Cruz, with a face like that, you're never going to look like a tourist.'

'I have no choice,' he said.

'OK,' Pamela told him. 'I have an idea.'

'Jesus fucking Christ, you guys are too much. You know that?'

'It ain't me,' Moss said into the mouthpiece of the public telephone at the McDonald's on Route 1 in Scarborough. 'It's that fuck Cruz.'

'Look, let's not talk about names, all right? But Jesus fucking Christ, you know what I'm saying?'

'Yeah. I know.'

When Cruz had disappeared with the car, Moss had walked back here – more than half a mile, he figured it had to be. Now he was listening to Big Vito bemoan the cascading fuck-ups Moss himself had witnessed since yesterday. Vito's voice was especially harsh and gravelly today. Moss wondered if the big guy had caught cancer. Wouldn't bother Moss much if he did.

'I'm hung out to dry up here,' Moss said.

'How bad?'

'Not sure. I think I can get back to the hotel. But I don't

278

want to spend too much time outside, you know what I mean?'

'Here's the deal then. Get back to the hotel and keep out of sight. I'm sending up another team.'

The thought of being replaced on a job was about as foreign to Moss as darkest Africa. In fact, until this moment the thought had never even occurred to him. It still hadn't, not in so many words. It floated out there, unformed, unarticulated, a shadow that made him profoundly uneasy.

'Look . . .' Moss said, not sure what would come out next, only knowing that he had to fill the empty space in the conversation before Vito did.

Vito cut him off. 'Don't say another fucking word, all right? It's done. I had these guys all ready to go last night, put 'em like on standby. Now I'm calling them in. They'll be up there in what, like five or six hours? All right? They'll meet you at your room. When they get there, you'll know where your orders come from.'

'Hey, look,' Moss said again.

'Yeah?'

Moss wasn't sure quite how to play it. This wasn't his fuck-up, that was for sure. This was all Cruz. He didn't plan on taking the fall for Cruz in any way. If they wanted to punish him somehow, maybe dock him for this job, OK. But if they planned on hitting him for this, he wanted Vito to know he should expect more bodies.

'We ain't gonna have any problems when they get up here, right? I mean, I'm still me, you know what I'm saying? I don't go down easy.'

There was a long pause in New York.

A sound came over the phone like an old motorcycle revving up. It took a moment for Moss to figure out what the sound was. It was Big Vito laughing. Moss smiled. He wasn't sure, but he couldn't remember a time when Big Vito had laughed before.

After a while, the big man settled down and his voice came back on the line.

'That what you think? I'm gonna waste my time hitting you when I got all this other bullshit going on? You got nothing to worry about. Now, for once and for all, let's stop all this fucking around, get the job done, and get everybody where they need to go. All right? Keep your chin up. You got that?'

'I got it.'

Vito rumbled again, a deep liquid sound. 'I'll let you in on a little secret. It's Sticks that's coming up. You know Sticks? He's your buddy, right?'

'Yeah. He's my buddy.'

'Well, that's good. You boys get it done this time.'

The line went dead.

Moss hung up, then picked up the phone again and dialed for a cab.

Pamela took a taxi the five-minute ride up Munjoy Hill. It was something she hadn't done before. Normally, she walked up the hill from work, a half-hour trek up Portland's answer to a San Francisco hill. But today was a special day, and she didn't want to run into anyone she knew.

Deeper than that: if anything suspicious was happening at the building, she could tell the cabbie to keep going. She glanced at the cabbie. Typical Portland cab driver: lined face, bloodshot eyes, unlit cigar in his mouth, jabbering at and about the other cars. Would he remember her? Would the day come when the police asked him? She wondered.

Cruz had bought some tourist clothes – a bright green fleece pullover, some Dockers slacks, and a hat like a boat captain might wear – then had gone back to his suite at the Portland Arms. She could tell he was embarrassed by the clothes. She could tell he was embarrassed by having to trust her.

She thought about that. She could run now. She could get away. She could go straight to the police and tell them that a wanted fugitive, a murderer – and here a small shiver went down her spine and back up again – was holed up in Room 238 at the Portland Arms. When they came for him, he would have nowhere to run. He wouldn't consent to an arrest, she knew. He would go down in a desperate last stand, a blaze of battle between himself and the hated coppers.

She could bring all this down on him, on the man who had kidnapped her. But she wasn't going to. And what was even more interesting, even amazing: he knew she wasn't going to. He knew it body and soul. Otherwise he would never have let her go like this.

What else was amazing?

She had asked him, 'What about Moss? Doesn't he want to kill you? If he gets away, won't he go straight for your hotel room?' He had smiled. 'Moss? Nah, he won't go to my hotel. He can't kill me in or around the hotel in broad daylight. Not with the kind of fight we would have.'

And in his eyes, that wild light: he would enjoy such a fight to the death between he and Moss. He actually looked forward to it.

She sighed. Well, this was sure better than any book, wasn't it?

The cab passed the building and rolled on another half a block.

'Here,' she said. 'Right here.'

She glanced back the way they had just come. There were a couple of young moms across the street, dressed for the fall chill in jackets and tight jeans, pushing strollers down the block.

Pamela paid the cabbie and walked back down the street at a nonchalant pace. The car was right here on the street: the black Volkswagen Golf, five years old. It was a peppy little car, and she kept it well maintained, just the way her father had taught her. It had a few nicks and scratches and tiny nobs of surface rust – it hadn't escaped the salt air of the Maine coast – but other than that, she knew it was tip-top.

She walked by without glancing at it. First things first. She was going in the apartment. Maybe she would find Lola there. Maybe she would find someone else there. She didn't spend any time contemplating this last point. It seemed near impossible that Moss could beat her here.

Moss, the stuff of nightmares. From her perch in the Taurus, she had witnessed Moss walking up and killing that man in cold blood. It had been far enough away that she didn't really see the man's head come apart, but . . .

Yes, she had seen his head come apart. It was just that she hadn't seen the details.

She pushed the horror of it away, and turned to the problem at hand. If no one was up in the apartment, she would leave the note she had written for Lola.

She reached the door to the building. As she fiddled with her key, she noticed the curtain moving in the window of the first-floor apartment.

Not Mr Lindstrom. Not now.

Sure enough, the door to his apartment opened.

He appeared there, white hair slicked back to his head in a swoop. His body was slightly hunched, his hands were gnarled, but his eyes were bright and aware.

He seemed somewhat . . . diminished. This old man was the one she had felt something for just as recently as . . . yesterday?

'Pamela, hello,' he said.

'Hi, Mr Lindstrom. How are you?'

'I'm just fine, but there's been some trouble. The police have been here twice already since last night, looking for you or Lola. Have you been . . . OK?'

She shrugged and tried on a smile. It seemed pasted on and made of plastic. 'Oh, great. You know, I went out of town, uh, last night. And so I wasn't around.'

He smiled too. But his smile seemed even more fake and more pained than her own. 'The police officers thought it odd that the door to your apartment was left unlocked.'

'Hmm. Lola must have left it unlocked. She does that sometimes when she just runs out for a little while.' She read his look of alarm at this news. 'I know, I know, two young women living alone. We should always lock our doors.'

'Lola hasn't been back either,' he said. 'I've been watching for her, for both of you.' From his expression, this seemed to be the checkmate.

She shrugged. 'I don't know where Lola's been. Maybe she was over at Smoke's?'

'Well,' he said. 'That's just the thing. She couldn't be with him. I hate to be the one to tell you this, but there was an explosion at a workshop at his house yesterday. It appears that he's dead.'

Her smile floated there. 'Dead? Smoke?'

'Yes, it was on all the TV stations last night, and the radio. There's been a delay with, uh, with the dental records, but it would seem so. I'm so sorry.'

'I see,' she said. 'I see. Will you excuse me?'

He reached out and touched her arm. 'Pamela, are you all right?'

'Yes, it's just that . . . uh, well, it's such terrible news. I need to go upstairs.' His hand rested on her arm. It was time to break off this conversation. She didn't know how well her mock heartbreak, or shock, or whatever she was going for, was playing. She could picture him speaking to the police sometime in the future: 'Well, she acted quite strangely when I gave her the news.'

'Will you excuse me?' she said again.

284

'Of course.' He looked at his hand as if it was a naughty pet that had gotten away. He took it back. 'Of course. If you need anything, please don't hesitate. I'm always here.'

'I know,' she said. 'And thank you.'

She went upstairs.

The stairway was gloomy and narrow. She had never noticed it quite this way before. The stairs themselves tilted at crazy angles. It was something from a fun house, something slightly wacky and slightly menacing.

She reached the door. Sure enough, the cops had left the door unlocked. They had taped a sealed Portland Police Department envelope to the door. She took it down but didn't open it, and went on inside. Everything was just the same as they had left it. She walked through the rooms, remembering her life from the day before as if it had taken place a thousand years ago.

OK. It was time to leave the note. She took two sheets of computer printer paper and wrote identical notes on each one: 'Let's meet for dinner? 10 p.m.?'

Would the cops come back? Maybe, but they would have no idea what the notes meant. There were only two other people on earth who would know – Lola and Smoke Dugan. She could go to the dinner place every night at 10 p.m. for ever, she figured, if it took that long. If the cops saw the notes, they might even get the mistaken impression that all was well here.

She took one sign and taped it on the door in the stairwell. Then she came back through the apartment and out onto the deck. Here were the fire stairs, old wooden steps, firm and strong enough, that snaked down the outside of the building. She and Lola almost never used these stairs, except to go to the washing machine and dryer in the cellar of the building. The backyard was a postage stamp, accessible by only a narrow alley from the street. A high fence and thick hedge blocked the yard from the yard of the building that faced the next street. They never used the backyard itself.

If ever there was a time to use the backyard, Pamela figured this was it.

She posted her sign on the door leading into the kitchen.

Then she left to go see Mr Dennis Cruz in his hotel room.

Moss drove the big Mercedes away from the airport.

It felt like home to be back in this car. It wasn't a work car. It wasn't some bullshit nondescript sedan the straight world drove. This was a fucking automobile, and just riding in style made everything seem right again.

The Mercedes wasn't dirty the way the Taurus was.

Let's keep it that way.

He sank back into the leather seat. He toyed briefly with the idea of putting on the news, see if they had a description of him. After a moment, he rejected it out of hand. Why dwell on an obvious bummer? If they had his description, he would know soon enough. There was nowhere to hide, a guy like him, so there was no reason to try. Drive this bad-ass car, walk into his hotel big and bold, look everybody in the eye, and go to his room. Order up some room service, take a shower, and change out of these clothes. Do it all on his time, and in his way.

If they stormed the room, he figured he'd take a few out with him.

He drove sedately, and clicked on the radio. Some classical music came on. Yeah, he was feeling better. Sticks was coming too. Provided Vito was telling him the truth, and there was no plan to hit him, Moss felt he could swing with Sticks. He had worked with him before, and he was a sick motherfucker.

He remembered the time Sticks had cut the guy's eyes out. The thought of it sent a shiver along Moss's spine. Sticks had held the man's head steady with one hand gripping his hair. Then he had simply inserted his knife in and behind each eye.

Pop. Out came one.

Pop. Out came the other.

The man would have screamed but he was gagged. He would have struggled but he was bound hand and foot. Sticks displayed a bloody eye in the palm of each hand. To Moss, they looked gigantic.

'Lookee there, Moss. They came right on out just like I said they would.'

Then he dropped them on the floor and crushed them with his foot.

Sticks coming meant that the debate team bullshit was over. Sticks coming meant there was going to be pain.

Sticks. Holy shit, was there a worse one out there than Sticks? For a split second – and the feeling came and went almost before he was consciously aware of it – Moss imagined what it might be like to be on the receiving end of a service visit from Sticks. He shuddered. Moss needed to keep his eyes open from here on in. He needed to keep Sticks and his team at arm's length.

'I ride alone,' Moss said, trying it out. Sure, it sounded right. 'Hey, Sticks, son, I ride alone, you know what I'm saying?'

Moss drove to his hotel with a smile on his face. He pulled into the parking area. The kid came out for the car. Sure, big and bold. Let the kid park the car, and tip him good. Give the geek a thrill.

Parking cars. Moss smiled and shook his head at the thought of it.

He climbed out of the car and towered over the kid. He gave the skinny geek the keys with a twenty-dollar bill. The kid smiled. 'Thank you, sir.'

That's right. Sir. Should have said 'sire'.

Moss paced through the lobby to the elevators.

A little food. A shower and change of clothes. Some coffee and maybe a couple of drinks from the wet bar in his room. Then, if he was feeling motivated, maybe scoot up to Lola's place and scope the place out a bit before Sticks and them got here.

His mind roamed back to how he blew away that fat bastard in the parking lot just a couple of hours before. Inside the elevators, in the gleam of the polished chrome, he caught himself smiling a big, goofy grin.

'Yessir, it's been a hell of a day.'

* * *

Pamela stood in front of the door to Room 238.

It was a nice hotel.

It was a really nice hotel. She hadn't noticed how nice it was last night, what with the way they had come in, Cruz holding the gun on her.

She found that she was shaking just slightly. Why should she be nervous? Just stopping in to see Cruz in his hotel room. That was all. She reached toward the door with her fist as if to knock, but then hesitated. What was she doing? She should run as fast and as far away from here as she could. This was nuts.

She pulled her hand back. She raised it again.

The door opened. Cruz stood there, wearing the clothes he had bought. 'Geek clothes,' he had called them, but they fit him well and looked good on him. She saw him as if for the first time. He had a thin, sleek body, more like a triathlete than a body builder. His hair, after a shower, was combed back from his forehead. The scar ran down his right cheek, thick and long. He had been cut there, she realized, and wondered why she hadn't thought of that before. A knife had entered his face and cut through four inches of it. What had that felt like?

His arms were at his sides. His hands were small, and the backs were covered with dark hair. She thought of Smoke Dugan's hands doing the dishes in their apartment in earlier times. Smoke's hands were huge compared to Cruz's hands.

Cruz's work was different from Smoke's.

His eyes were deep and intense, watching her. Murderer's

eyes. The intensity of them took her breath away. There was a fire in there, an inferno. This man had seen things, had felt things that most men never had. She almost looked at her shoes, but didn't. She held his gaze instead.

He smiled, but his eyes never changed. 'I was wondering if you were going to knock or what,' he said.

'I was about to.'

The smile widened, still not reaching the eyes. He shrugged and moved away from the door to let her pass. 'Well, come on in then.'

She passed him. He held a glass in his hand. There was a thick yellow liquid in there with two ice cubes.

'What do you have there?' she said.

He held up the glass. 'This? Oh, nothing. Doctor's orders. A drink. Scotch and ice. You know, trying to take the edge off a little.'

'I didn't know you took the edge off.'

'Once in a while, I do.' He seemed to shake a thought away. 'Can I make you one?'

'What else do you have?'

He gestured at the little wet bar. 'Anything, really. How about a gin and tonic? Vodka tonic? A beer? Wine? It's all in there.'

'A gin and tonic sounds pretty good right about now.'

He opened the little bar and began to take out the ingredients. He seemed distracted, not at all himself. Pamela stood for a moment and watched him, then she came to a decision. She was the new Pamela. She was the bold Pamela. Pam? No one ever called her Pam, mostly because she preferred the more formal Pamela. Maybe she was Pam now? Maybe Pam was the adventurer.

She stepped up to Cruz and got close. He turned to face her, his drink in his hand. He was just a few inches taller than she was. That was fine. That was perfect. They were face to face. His face showed alarm, everywhere but the eyes. She took the drink from his hand and placed it on top of the bar. He watched it go.

'Why don't we save the drinks for later?' she said.

'OK. What would you rather do?'

Her lips rose to meet his. They hesitated for a moment, the two of them, and she thought: he's shy like me. He's shy around girls.

Then they met again, and the kiss was deeper, longer.

'That was nice,' she said.

He watched her. They met again. She closed her eyes. This was the longest and deepest yet. They pressed close.

'Thanks for saving my life,' she said, her mouth against his.

'Thanks for being there to be saved.'

She opened her eyes. She saw him and they both laughed.

And tumbled toward the bed.

Moss drove the black Mercedes right up to the apartment house. He pulled into an open space just across the street. It wasn't a work car – he felt a twinge of regret about burning it like this – but fuck it, he was in too good a mood to go creeping around.

He imagined Cruz out there — somewhere nearby, for sure — hiding like a rat in a hole. He had probably ditched the Taurus in favor of a goddamned Yugo or some shit.

Moss himself felt like new. He had eaten — two cheese steak sandwiches and fries, with a beer and a tiny two-shot bottle of Jack Daniel's from the wet bar. He had knocked back three cups of black coffee and a palmful of Advil. He figured he didn't need to eat again until tomorrow.

He had his long black Diesel leather jacket on. It was a beast, weathered and beaten half to death in all the right places. He had reflector sunglasses on against the bright glare of the day. His hair was pulled into a tight ponytail. He fancied he looked every ounce the killer. Indeed. He looked like a modern grim reaper.

And well he should. Back at the hotel room, he had re-upped the weapons he had spent and then some. He was strapped with two guns and another knife taped to his calf. He had handcuffs and brass knuckles. He was ready for the show.

He strolled — and that was the right word for it: *strolled* — across the street toward the building. From here, it looked like it was huddled away from him. It should huddle. He felt bigger than that fucking building.

As he approached, the door to the first-floor apartment opened.

An old man poked out, old beak nose way out ahead of his face like a dog off its leash, fine white hair brushed back in a swoop.

Moss fished inside his jacket for the badge.

'Hello there,' the old man said. He spoke in a mild tone.

Moss flashed the badge. No sense getting bogged down with this dink. He gave the old man the government-issue impassive face. 'Federal officer. Official business.'

'Oh, I thought you were the police coming here again. That's what made me wonder about that car. The police don't usually drive a car like that. Why is the Federal Government involved in this case?'

Moss shrugged, a gesture that said nothing. It was none of this old man's business if the Feds were in on this or not. All the same, he felt that twinge about the car again. Burned it. The minute he went upstairs, this old geek would run outside and jot down the license plate.

'In any case,' the old man went on, 'you just missed her.'

Moss put the badge away. 'Who did I miss?'

'Pamela Gray, one of the young women who lives upstairs. She stopped in here for a few moments, then left again. This happened not a half-hour ago.'

'She was here, eh?'

'That's what I said.'

'Well, I guess I'll go upstairs and have a look around. Thanks for the information. Do you have a key to this outside door?'

The old man hesitated. He hovered there, halfway in his door and halfway out. Moss loomed over him, put the old man entirely in his shadow, then took off the reflector shades. He looked hard at the old man, and the old man came outside

293

and juggled some keys out of his pocket. 'I have an arrangement with the landlord,' he said, by way of explaining why he had the key to the door. 'I keep an eye on the place, sort of like a property manager.' He opened the door and stepped aside. 'What branch of the government did you say you worked for?'

'I didn't say. But I'm not here to hide anything. I work for the DEA – the Drug Enforcement Agency.' Let the old man chew on that one for a while.

Moss climbed the stairs quickly. The door to the apartment was still unlocked – hell, the lock was probably fucked by their tumultuous entry the night before. Surprised that old bird downstairs hadn't been snooping around for that one.

But something had changed. There was a sign on the door now: 'Let's meet for dinner? 10 p.m.?'

That hadn't been there before. He toyed briefly with tearing it down, then left it there. It was a message from Pamela to the others. OK, better that the message gets sent than doesn't get sent, as long as we're here to intercept the recipients.

Moss went inside. He roamed the apartment for a few moments, grid searching it for other clues. There was nothing. In fact, the place was just about the same as it had been the night before.

Moss was mindful of the old man. That old boy wouldn't be able to sit still down there for too long without calling somebody.

Moss went out on the deck to catch a view of the bay from across the way. It was almost like the two buildings back there had been built with the idea of not obstructing this view. OK, it was a somewhat distant water view, but decent enough. Not like his, of course. He had the real deal. But still, it was OK. He imagined they sat out here and ate their meals in warm weather.

He glanced around the deck.

There was a sign on the door to the inside: 'Let's meet for dinner? 10 p.m.?'

Facing outside. As if somebody might come in this way. He turned around and looked at the deck again. Sure enough, there was a set of stairs leading down from here. You wouldn't see them unless you were looking for them. In fact, you had to open a gate to get to them, and the gate looked like a continuation of the railing. He stood at the top of the stairs and watched them wind their rickety way down to the overgrown backyard. He squinted down. There was an overgrown hedge back there, and a small chain-link fence buried in the hedge.

A man could come from the street over there, walk between those two buildings, then climb this fence and at the same time force his way through that hedge. Somebody fit. Not Smoke Dugan, for sure. The fuck could hardly walk.

Lola could do it.

So the message was for Lola.

Pamela figured Lola might come up these back stairs.

OK. Now we were getting somewhere.

Moss went back into the apartment, crossed through and went down the stairs. When he came onto the street, the old man was not around. Moss jumped in the Mercedes and headed back to the hotel. It was a nice day, with a stiff breeze, and as he drove down the steep hill on Congress Street, clouds skidded across bright blue skies above the office towers downtown.

It was a nice city. He could almost see why Dugan had stopped running here.

Back at the hotel, the kid hopped to it when he saw the Mercedes pull up. Moss gave him the keys and another five bucks. It was a gold rush day for the geek.

'I'm gonna need it again in a little while.'

'Yes, sir,' the kid said.

He got back into the room, and had barely fixed himself a whiskey and ice, and settled into a chair facing the door when the knock came. He sipped his drink. Calm. Roland Moss, if anything, was ice cold. He had his round glass in his left hand, and his big right hand rested on his knee, gripping his gun, a round chambered and ready to go.

The knock came again.

If they wanted to get him, they wouldn't knock.

'It's open.'

The door swung wide and three men stepped into the room. The first of the three was about average height, but thin almost to the point of pain. His body looked like a razor. His face looked like a weasel's face. He wore black leather – not a trench – and jeans. He hunched his shoulders when he walked. Like a fake tough guy, like a skinny guy who was trying too hard.

Only this guy wasn't trying at all.

Moss thought of the man with the eyes again. Or, should he say, the man without the eyes? And this guy had done it to him, smiling – not quite laughing – and humming to himself all the while.

This guy was Sticks, and Sticks was a maniac.

Sticks looked at Moss. He looked at the gun on Moss's knee.

A short burst of air escaped his mouth. It might have been the beginning of a laugh, were it someone else. He sucked his teeth for a moment.

'What's the matter, Moss? Your friends come in, you don't look happy to see us.'

'I'm always happy to see you, Sticks.'

'Then how come you don't offer me a drink?'

Cruz and Pamela walked hand in hand along a long, curving crescent of sand beach in Cape Elizabeth, about ten miles outside of the city. The waves made small, one-foot crests and crashed to shore, the sound of the crashing all out of proportion to the size of the waves. In the distance was a small cove where fishing boats bobbed. About a half mile out to sea was a large island. Even from here, Cruz could make out what looked like tall grasses, waving in the breeze.

The sun slowly settled behind some woods that came down almost to the beach. The horizon lit up in red and oranges. They had both taken off their shoes, and were walking barefoot in the cold white sand. The wind made Pamela's face bright red.

It was a day like none other.

To Cruz, this was what retirement might mean. A long walk at sunset along a beach with a pretty girl. Maybe this pretty girl.

His mind reviewed backward, thinking of all the girls – all the whores, essentially. His work had made it hard. No, it wasn't his work. It was him. It was him that made the work possible. He had distrusted women from his earliest days. He had feared them. And still, he had lusted for them. What was the easy way out of the dilemma? To hire them for a night or two, pay them, and never see them again.

What he had missed!

He had been with this, this girl now, and even though it was only once, only today, and he had known her since only yesterday, already it was different.

'What are you going to do?' he heard her say now.

He shrugged. 'Walk along here some more, go back to the hotel, have a nice dinner in the room, and then think about it.'

'OK.'

They had driven out here in Pamela's car, finding a very expensive hotel along the beach just a short walk from here. The Ocean House Hotel. So they had taken a suite. He couldn't trust what would happen at the other place in town once the dark came in. Eventually, Moss would come to check his room. A showdown with Moss – well, he didn't want Pamela to be anywhere near it when it happened.

It occurred to him that this might be his last night on earth.

No! Not now. Perhaps for the first time, Cruz felt himself

clinging to life and its possibilities. This was no way to be. This was what made people afraid.

He sighed. All he could do was put it out of his mind until tonight.

They sat on the beach near the bottom of a sandy path between high hedges. The path led back to the hotel. The suite was perfect. They had a balcony overlooking the dunes, the waving sea grass, and the water. You could hear the waves crashing from there, and Cruz imagined sleeping with that door open, the sound coming through all night long. Of course, it wouldn't happen, not tonight, maybe not ever. The balcony itself was a lapse in security, but no one knew they were here, and Cruz would go back to the city to fight his battles. Pamela could stay out here at the hotel and be no part of that.

The hotel had a fine dining room, but Cruz imagined they would order from room service instead. Maybe he would order a drink with dinner. A bottle of wine, perhaps? Sure. The thought came again: after all, this was his last night on earth.

Amazing to think that. For a long time, Cruz had gone into these situations with total confidence, total belief that he would come out alive and on top. But tonight? He didn't know. Moss was so big, so strong, so young, and took real delight in killing. Cruz had seen that when he shot the fat guy in the parking lot. Moss had been almost absurdly pleased. It could be that Moss was better suited for this, that Moss was the better man.

Cruz was getting old.

They could run. They could have dinner, make love again,

sleep for a few hours, then before first light get in her little car and run. But where would they go? Cruz had less than a thousand dollars in cash on him. He had money, sure, a few hundred thousand. But most of that money was spread out in safe deposit boxes – a few in New York, one in San Francisco, one in LA, one in Detroit, one in Miami. Did *they* know where he kept his money? He thought maybe they did. If he drove from here up to Canada, then crossed the continent, and slipped back in the country on the west coast, how could he be sure they wouldn't have someone waiting for him when he pulled up to his bank in San Francisco? He couldn't be sure.

He had credit cards, he had a checking account. But they left a paper trail. Anybody could find him like that. Pamela probably had a little money, but they knew her name by now. No, it was no good. Even if he was able to get all his money out of the bank, even if he could do that and disappear, the day would come when it ran out. Worse, the day would come when he came into his home and found Roland Moss waiting for him with a couple of other guys – and there were guys in this business who were worse than Roland Moss. Cruz knew. He used to be one of them.

No. He would go tonight to find Smoke Dugan. And he would try to convince Dugan to split the $2.5 mil he had taken. Moss would find them – of course he would. And Cruz and Moss would finish their business with each other.

He tried to imagine it the way he wanted it to go. No hesitation. No remorse. As soon as you see him, kill him. He couldn't really picture it somehow. Earlier, the fat man had been shooting at them, and still Cruz couldn't take him out. He was done killing, it seemed. It didn't bode well for the meeting with Moss.

It didn't bode well for any future meetings.

The last red rays of the sun were disappearing behind the trees.

'What do you say, Pamela? Do you want to head back to the room? Maybe order up some dinner?'

She smiled, but he could see the pain in it. 'Sure.'

'They said you stole a lot of money. Did you?'

'I took it as a payment.'

'Do you still have it?'

'In a manner of speaking, yes.' Smoke sat in the chair facing her. He had spent most of the afternoon telling her his story, the relevant parts, filling in gaps in his history that he had paved right over in the year they had been together. The sun had gone down outside their window on the re-telling of his story.

She had taken it in her stride. She didn't blame him for the deaths on that airplane – on the contrary, she sympathized with him. He had been used, she said. She even sympathized that he had killed Roselli. He had never murdered anyone like he had done to Roselli. If the airplane had never happened, then Smoke Dugan would never have murdered anyone.

Very surprising to Smoke, however, was her story of recent days. He knew she was a fit girl. He knew she had taken all this karate and had these black belts, but he had never put much credence in that sort of thing. It was a straight-world hobby, and to Smoke, a hobby was . . . well, a hobby. Kind of like roller-skating.

'So these men were . . . pornographers?'

'Yeah, and what they did was trick girls into being in these pictures.'

'Jesus, Lola.'

'So I made a mistake. It seems like a pretty common mistake.'

'And you could have been hurt.'

She smiled. 'And that's exactly my point. I wasn't hurt. Not at all. I kicked their tails. And when the time came, I kicked your big man Moss's ass, too.'

Smoke had some trouble swallowing that one.

'I'm like, I'm like a ninja, Smoke.'

Smoke raised an eyebrow.

'That's what I'm realizing about myself. Even when they had me tied down in the bed, before Hal rescued me and his friend was killed, I felt calm. I felt like I could handle anything that happened. Which is why I say it should be me who goes up to the apartment tonight.'

It was a bone of contention between them. Smoke was of a mind that Pamela was likely dead by now. Lola was of a mind that she was still alive. Smoke was willing to go along with that premise, and the premise that they should rescue her. But going to the police was out of the question – Smoke couldn't afford to be arrested because he wouldn't last long once his old friends knew he was in custody. And anyway, the presence of cops would mean that if they hadn't killed Pamela yet, they sure would now.

So it was up to them to save Pamela.

And Lola thought that meant it was up to her.

'Look, Smoke, it's got to be me. I'm younger than you are. I'm faster than you are. I'm stronger than you are. I kick high and hard. And I'm darker. At night, I'm going to blend in better. And they don't want me, anyway. They proved that already. When they had me, they just looked for a way to trade me in for you.'

'I should go with you,' he said.

She shook her head and the curls bounced. 'No. You'll only slow me down. I'll be up those stairs, in the apartment, and back out again in five minutes or less.'

He hated it. It terrified him. It made him feel weak.

But she was right. In every way, she was better suited for this sort of thing than he.

'And then what? What if there's no sign of her?'

Lola shook her head again. 'I don't know.'

They stared at each other for a long minute.

'I guess we wait another day,' she said, 'then go back again tomorrow night. If there's still nothing, I guess we take your money and run.'

They lay together on tangled sheets.

Cruz opened his eyes and only then became aware that he had slept. He glanced at Pamela, her eyes closed, her stomach rising softly. She wore only a white tank undershirt of his, which she must have pulled on while he was asleep.

The sliding glass door was still open, and Cruz could hear the waves pounding. He wanted to hear that sound for ever. The breeze coming through the screen had turned cold, and he pulled up the blanket to cover them both. Across the way, on the table lay the ruins of the meal they had ordered from room service, including the bottle of red wine they had finished.

His head was floating from the food, the wine and from Pamela's heat. This time had been different, wilder, more about physical needs. He thought about that and it made him hunger for her again.

The digital clock on the desk said 8.13.

Cruz sighed and reached across for his jacket, which hung on the chair. He searched the inside pocket, and found what he was looking for: a pair of stainless-steel, chain-link hand-cuffs. These were the very same cuffs Pamela had worn last night and earlier today. He opened one of the cuffs, gently took Pamela's wrist, and cuffed her to the bedpost. He made it tight enough that she couldn't slip out. She would find it uncomfortable, but probably not painful.

He stood, closed the glass door to the balcony, and pulled the curtain shut. The breeze on his naked skin had given him gooseflesh. Then he turned on the lamp on the desk. He turned it to its lowest setting.

Her eyes opened a moment later.

'Cruz?'

'Hi, Pamela.'

It took a few seconds before she noticed she was cuffed to the bed. She pulled on it but she was going nowhere. 'Cruz, hey! What are you doing?'

Cruz unplugged the telephone from the wall, and picked it up off the desk. He walked it over to the other side of the room and deposited it on the dresser.

'Pamela, I made a decision. It's too dangerous. You can't come tonight.'

'Cruz! Let me go!'

'Sorry, I can't do it. Moss is going to show up. Somehow, some way, he's going to show up. You know that. And when he does, he's going to shoot first and not bother with any questions. I can't have you there.'

He dug into her jacket pocket and took out the keys to her car. 'Listen, I'm going to borrow your car, OK? But I'm going to bring it back. If I hurt it, I'll pay for it.'

'Cruz! I'm gonna scream. I'm gonna scream for help.'

He smiled. 'Don't scream. If you try to scream, then I'm going to have to tie both your hands and put a gag in your mouth. You don't want me to do that, and I don't want to do it.'

He began walking around the room, getting dressed and ready while she watched him from the bed.

'But I can help you.'

'No you can't. You'll only get in the way, and I'll spend the whole time worrying that you're going to get killed. I won't be able to act naturally if you're around, and that'll get us both in hot water.'

He reached into his jacket pocket. Moss's gun was in there. He took it out and looked at it. He wouldn't need it. He never went in for that opinion some guys had, that you went on a job strapped to the gills. It was plain stupid how many guns some guys brought to the show. Cruz carried the one Glock, semiautomatic, well-maintained, nine shots in the clip, two extra clips in his inside pocket, plus a knife taped to his waist. If you couldn't get the job done with twenty-seven rounds and a knife, then you were in the wrong business.

Indeed. He only carried the extra clips out of long habit. He had never changed clips in the middle of a job.

So what to do with Moss's gun?

Simple. Give it to Pamela.

'Pamela?' he said. He walked over to where she lay on the bed, staring at her cuffed hand and sulking. He sat down next to her. 'I want to leave this with you. Have you ever fired a gun before?'

She looked at it like it was a poisonous snake. Cruz guessed that was exactly what it was. 'What do I need it for?' Pamela said.

He shrugged. 'You probably don't. Probably, nothing's going to happen. But I might be gone a long time, and you're going to be by yourself. It might make you feel better. Here, take it.'

She accepted it in her hand. She was uncertain, and the gun was big in her small hand.

'What do I do?'

Cruz pulled the slide back and chambered a round.

'OK, there's a bullet in the chamber. All you have to do is pull the trigger – the bullets will chamber automatically now. So, if you fire once, you can just keep firing, you see? Now, you see this lever? That's the safety. Right now, it's on, which means you can't pull the trigger. But if you push it here . . .' he did so, 'the safety is off and you can shoot.'

'How should I leave it?'

Cruz thought about that. If there were a reason to have gun in hand, Cruz would never risk having the safety on. The second it took to flick it off, even knowing exactly where it was, even having it as second nature, might be a second too long. But still, it was unlikely anybody was coming here. And she might hurt herself with the safety off.

'Will you remember about the safety?'

She thought about it. 'Yes, I'll remember.'

'Then you should leave the safety on. If you hear any suspicious noises, or you get scared, you can take the safety off. How's that sound?'

She sighted down the barrel, like she must have seen on TV and in the movies a thousand times or more. It looked sort of comical, what with the big gun that Moss had carried and the small hand that Pamela had.

'OK,' she said.

'OK, then there's the remote control if you want to watch some TV or whatever. If the morning comes around, and I haven't come back, then hide the gun under the mattress and start screaming. In a little while, somebody'll come along and let you out of here. Tell them that I forced you to do everything. If the cops have me, that's what I'm going to say.'

Cruz stood, and when he next looked at her, the barrel of the gun was pointed at his face. Her eyes were behind the barrel, squinting down at him.

'OK, Cruz, now come on over here and take these cuffs off me. Slowly. Right now.'

Cruz shook his head. He came over and kissed her on the cheek. 'Stop fooling around. I gotta go.'

As he walked across the room, the gun was still sighted on him.

'Cruz!'

'Wish me luck,' he said, and went out.

Brian Knox pulled up to the dairy bar on Route 77 in Cape Elizabeth. As Knox got out of the car, his stomach itched more than ever.

Every time, it seemed to Knox that it was he in some deserted place with all this fog rolling around. The dairy bar was closed for the season. There were no cars out here in the dirt parking lot. Through the windows, he could make out the vague shapes of picnic benches that sat out here in the parking lot all summer, piled up inside for the winter.

A car passed on the road, its headlights looming up out of the fog. It made a strangely flat sound as it passed, as if the fog damped the acoustics.

Knox walked to the payphone.

Everything was closed, there was nobody around, but at least the payphone still worked. That was the thing about

Maine – it was one of the last places in the country where you could still find a payphone that worked.

Knox shoveled some quarters in.

A woman's voice came on the line. 'The number you're calling has changed. Hang up and somebody will call you back in a little while.'

'How long?'

'I don't know, sir. A little while.'

Knox hung up. He stared out into the swirling mist. He thought about getting back in the car, maybe listening to the radio for a while. He thought about maybe moving to Florida, the west coast, anywhere really.

Somewhere nearby, a buoy clanged out on the water, its bell ringing as the waves knocked it around.

The phone rang.

Knox picked it up.

'Yeah?' the gravel voice said.

'I saw a friend of yours today. Saw him in Portland, then I saw him out here in Cape Elizabeth. He checked into the Ocean House Hotel. Nice place. Route 77, right on the water. He went there with a friend of his, a young woman named Pamela Gray. They checked in under her name. Room 215. Had some room service sent up.'

'He still there?'

'Nope. He just headed back into Portland, driving a Volkswagen. Black. Maine plates. He's alone.'

'Where's the girl?'

'Looks like he left her at the hotel.'

'Looks like?'

'He left her there.'

There was a pause. 'OK, kid. Good work. Do me a favor, eh? Keep your eyes open a little while longer. Look sharp. Drop me another line tomorrow. You're a good kid. We don't get too many good kids in this business anymore.'

The line went dead.

'Remember this boxer Mike Tyson?' Sticks said. He was standing in the middle of the living room in Moss's suite, holding court. He had a bottle of Budweiser in his hand. 'This guy used to go around saying he was the baddest man on the planet or some shit. Then he'd go out and beat up some geek in a parking lot. It's too bad he's such a chump now, because you know what I used to think about it? I used to think, man, I wish I could run into that fucker some night after hours. Just me and him. Jesus, what a pleasure that would be.'

The phone rang.

Moss picked it up, his eyes still on Sticks and his two buddies. They were having a nice little party here in the room. They had polished off just about everything in the wet bar, and had another six pack of beer sent up. Why not?

Moss himself was drinking slowly, in a measured way. This wasn't his thing, getting fucked up on a job. It also wasn't his thing to let his guard down, turn around and have Sticks putting knives in him all night long.

'Hello?' he said into the telephone.

Big Vito was on the line. 'Cruz is on the move, headed for you right now.'

'Yeah?'

'Yeah. He left the girl behind. You got a piece of paper?'

'I'll remember it.'

'Room 215, Ocean House Hotel. Route 77 in Cape Elizabeth. You finish up there in town, then you take care of everything. Got it?'

'Yeah.'

The line went dead.

He looked at the partygoers. They looked at him.

'Big Vito,' he said. 'Checking in. Told me not to fuck this up.'

Sticks smiled. 'You know what?' he said. 'When this is done, let's order up some whores. They got whores in this burg, right? The kid at the front desk will know. Me and the boys'll get some rooms here, then we can order up all the whores in the whole fucking town. They'll never know what hit 'em. Whaddya think, Moss?'

'Sounds like a capital idea.' But Moss didn't think it would play that way somehow. Oh, he was gonna walk away from this, and Sticks – God knows nothing would happen to Sticks. But these two other guys looked like clowns. They looked like the kind of guys that went down and stayed down. Dugan was slippery as an eel, and Cruz was an old-time killer. Moss would be surprised to see these same faces gathered in this room just a few hours from now.

Moss wondered if Big Vito knew this was how Sticks played

it these days. Getting fucked up with a bunch of clowns.

'I could use a good bang or two myself,' Moss said. 'You see this guy Dugan's girlfriend, you might wanna save her for yourself. They don't make 'em like that too much anymore. I plan on laying her one.'

Sticks shook his head.

'I don't know, Moss. Vito says nobody lives. That simple. You guys have fucked up so much we can't take chances on anybody still breathing.'

Moss shrugged. 'So I'll kill her first. Then fuck her.'

The clowns grinned and gaped at that one.

Lola walked along Eastern Promenade in the fog. She kept herself on the city side, closest to the houses and buildings. On a clear night, the view to her right would be of Casco Bay, perhaps four stories below her down the bluff, and stretching out toward the horizon. The running lights of boats would be out on the water, and the blinking lights of an electricity plant would be out in the distance, as a warning to low-flying planes.

But tonight there was nothing out there but this soup. No running lights, no power plant, just dense rolling fog. Even the streetlights were dampened, leaving the street in shadow.

Lola had to focus. There was a lot on her mind. Smoke's story had been a lot to digest. They had been together for more than a year, and he had never suggested that he had spent most of his life as a criminal. It had put Lola's life in danger, and Pamela's, and his. In the months ahead, if they lived that long, she knew she would shake with rage at the dishonesty of it. But she also knew she would let it slide. She had been less than honest about some aspects of her own life. The man had tried to recreate himself, as she herself had done. He had tried to make amends. He had hoped that the past would stay in the past. It just hadn't.

And let's be clear: Smoke hadn't killed Lorena, nor had he done anything to Lola and Pamela. These men had done that.

She was approaching the buildings. Her heart beat faster as she noticed them.

She glanced around. No one was out. There were a few parked cars on the street, but no one was in them. There were no cars coming.

She started to run.

She took a hard left and sprinted on the grass between the two buildings. She felt fast and loose. Her heart pounded against her chest. Her breathing was harsh and rapid.

The hedge was up ahead. In the windows of the two buildings, TV sets played.

She ran right at the hedge and dove into it. It was three feet of scratchy thickets to the fence. She pushed her way through, the branches clinging and swiping at her. She climbed the short fence, all the while branches pushing and poking, and forced her way through to the other side.

She stopped before entering the yard. There was less fog here – the fog was so thick it mostly stopped at the hedge. But it was dark back here – there was no moon. Weak light came from the apartment on the first floor. Upstairs, all the lights were out. She scanned the yard for any movement, but saw none.

She sprinted for the stairs.

Over the creaky gate and up the wooden stairs, her running shoes tapping lightly on each step. She was lighter than air. If she ran on snow, she would leave no footprints. At the top floor, she vaulted the low gate and landed on the deck like a gymnast. She glanced in the windows. The clock on the microwave oven gave some light to see by. If they were in there, they were hiding. She made for the door.

And saw the sign. Hand-lettered in Pamela's writing: 'Let's meet for dinner? 10 p.m.?'

She was alive. Lola had known she would be. Meeting for dinner could only mean one thing – meeting on the Maine State Pier like they had done so many times after work. So many times Lola had left a similar phone message or email for Pamela. So many times they had sat out there with sandwiches on sunny days in the summer, watching the boats come in and out, listening to the cry of the seagulls, admiring the passing men. Occasionally, harbor seals would frolic in the water right nearby.

These were happy memories.

Lola risked a look at her watch. She pressed a button on the side and the watch illuminated. It was 9.25 now. She had to hustle.

She vaulted back over the gate and took the stairs as fast as their rickety nature would allow.

* * *

Sticks stood in the dark shadows by the door to the laundry room. He watched Lola push her way through the hedge then force herself over the fence.

Moss was right. Even in the semidark, he could see she was a precious girl.

He waited until she was through the hedge on the other side and running for the street before he pulled out his cellphone and pressed the speed dial.

It rang exactly once.

'Yeah.'

'Mikey, you saw her?'

'She just went by.'

'She see you?'

'Nah, I'm all the way crouched down. You can't hardly see shit with all this fog, anyway. She's running for that parking lot all the way down the street.'

'All right. Be on her. We're right behind you.'

'Got it.'

Sticks rang off and walked briskly up the alley toward the street where the two other cars were parked. They had three cars to leapfrog sexy Lola with, and they probably had three or four marks to play with later on. At least Lola. Probably this Dugan character. Maybe the other girl. And the one Sticks personally looked forward to the most – the turncoat Cruz.

He reached the sidewalk and signaled like a man trying to hail a cab in Manhattan.

Headlights went on and an engine coughed into life. Jimmy pulled up, the passenger door already hanging open. Moss pulled up behind in his car. Sticks climbed into the cheap Saturn with Jimmy, a work car they had ganked from the long-term parking at La Guardia Airport before they rode up here. Shit, it had been a long fucking drive in this piece of shit, and fucking Moss was cruising around in a Mercedes.

Jimmy raised his eyebrows.

'We got her,' Sticks said. 'Let's hit it.'

It was going to be a fun night.

Lola pulled the Tercel up to the curb near the Narrow Gauge Railroad tourist attraction along the waterfront. In the fog, Smoke could just make out the old railroad cars sitting on their tracks, weeds growing up around them. He had often watched the tourists trying to stifle their boredom as they rode the train along East End Beach.

He had been able to convince her to let him go on this one. If it was a trap, he didn't want her anywhere near it.

'I'd say drive around for about ten minutes,' he said. 'Then pull right up to this spot again.'

'What if you don't come?'

He smiled. 'I'll come. Tell you what, though. If I don't, then don't wait around.'

She turned off the engine. 'I can't let you go alone.'

'Lola, this is my problem. I need to go and resolve it. You never should have been involved in this at all. Now start the car and get out of here.'

She hesitated.

'Start the car, little girl.'

She started it. A tear ran down her cheek. 'I love you, Smoke.'

'And I love you,' he said. He reached into his jacket and gave her an envelope. 'If I don't come back, then open that envelope.'

'What is it, a love note?'

'That, yes. And details on the location of the money.'

She looked up at him.

'There's quite a bit there – enough to last a thrifty girl like you for a good long time. If you don't see me again in the next half-hour, follow those instructions, get the money, and run like hell. Don't stop until you're far away from here, preferably somewhere exotic. That's what we should have done all along.'

She touched his hand, but he pulled away.

'Now go!'

He turned and walked toward Maine State Pier. He imagined himself disappearing into the fog, and indeed, when he turned around again, he could no longer see where the car had been parked. He heard the engine of his reliable old car as it shifted into gear and drove away. The damping effect of the fog made it unclear which way it had gone.

He kept walking.

His leg bothered him. He was limping without his cane. Despite the sleep and the simple rest he had gotten this afternoon, his body was surfing along the edge of exhaustion. He felt as if it might be weeks before he recovered from the beating he had taken. It would be years before he got over

Lorena, and if Pamela was dead, then years more. The carnage was too much for an old man to think about.

Well, there was no one to blame, unless he wanted to blame himself. If it seemed unfair that things should come to this pass, well then, wasn't life about unfairness? All of life, all of human history, was an ocean of unfairness and cruelty, with tiny desert islands of fair play and kindness dotting the endless vastness of it all. A children's soccer game might be engineered for fairness to some extent, but what was it when compared to 800,000 murdered innocents in Rwanda? No, there was very little fairness, and so he best get over the notion once and for all, and focus on winning this thing. If these were his wits, he would live or die by them.

It occurred to Smoke now that he didn't even have a gun. He had lost it in the commotion this morning. The cops probably had it by now. He had never even fired it.

To his left was a massive factory where once upon a time Bath Iron Works had built ships for the United States Navy. Now, the factory wall was painted with a gigantic mural of whales. There was a famous painter who traveled the world, painting whales on walls, and he had done his work here. Smoke knew this about the whales, but he couldn't see them in the fog. On a sunny day, they would be *right there*; tonight they were gone.

He passed the entry to the pier. A car was parked there at the vehicle barrier – a black Volkswagen Golf. Pamela's car. It looked like it was parked for a quick getaway. Now Smoke was out on the wide concrete island, shuffling painfully along in the gloom. He could hear the water gently lapping at both sides.

A fog horn blew deep somewhere out on the water.

Everything was wrapped in a death shroud. Everything was a mystery.

At least he had gotten to see Lola again.

He should have told her not to come back at all. Just get the money now and run. If they caught him, if they beat him again, if they — and here he didn't want to think about what they could do, so his mind stopped after the word torture — if they did what they could do to him, he didn't know if he could resist anymore. Sooner rather than later, he would just tell them where the money was.

Then it would be a race to see who got there first.

A bench loomed, appearing as if conjured by a magician.

A man sat on the bench, ostensibly gazing out at the water. There was nothing to see. He didn't look up, so Smoke slid onto the bench with him.

Lola stuffed the envelope into the glove box. She didn't even want to think about it right now. Smoke was coming back. Of course he was coming back. Even if she had to bring him back herself.

She drove around the block, going slow in the fog. The car rumbled over some cobblestones — delightful evidence of the city's authentic historic past for the tourists, a nuisance for the natives.

She drove through the Old Port for a few moments. Here

and there, knots of well-dressed drunks spilled out of the bars and into the fog. The whole thing had a spooky quality to it. The people looked like wraiths.

She made a left, rumbled over some more cobblestones, then made another left onto the wide avenue of Commercial Street. She had come full circle – she was on her way back to the pier. She had been away long enough that Smoke would think she was gone, but not so long that something terrible could happen in her absence.

She pulled into the entrance of the parking lot along the side of the ferry terminal. The pier was straight ahead, at the other end of this long parking lot. She couldn't see that end for the fog. All she could see were the weird yellow haloes around the sodium arc lights mounted above the lot.

She pulled the car off into a corner and parked. She killed the engine.

The fog pressed in, and she peered down to where she imagined Smoke must be, out on the Pier, meeting with . . . who? Pamela, it must be Pamela, still alive, still alive, still alive. Lola closed her eyes for a moment, willing it to be so.

She heard a sound, like someone rattling the chain-link fence behind her. She turned.

No one back there.

Moss appeared at the driver's side window.

'Hello, honey.'

She gasped and turned toward the passenger door. A man was in the window there, too. He was a skinny man in a leather jacket with a wild light in his eyes. He showed her his gun.

He smiled. 'Moss was right about you, Lola. You are a fine piece of ass.'

There were men at each of the back windows. They both had guns drawn.

Moss grinned and moved a toothpick around in his mouth with his big tongue. 'Now why don't you come on out of there and behave yourself?' he said.

He pulled the door open.

'Come on, baby. Be a good girl.'

Slowly, guns facing her, Lola climbed out of the car.

The two men sat together, several feet of space between them.

'Dugan,' the man said after a time.

'Cruz,' Smoke said. 'How have you been?'

'Since yesterday? Fair to middling, actually.'

'Yeah.'

They sat in silence for a moment.

Smoke shrugged. 'So I got a note from a friend of mine, asking me to dinner. I dunno. Thought maybe I'd see her here. But then again, after that double-cross and all the fireworks this morning, I guess that was foolish on my part.'

Cruz turned to him. The scar on his face stood out in some color like white. His eyes glittered, and Smoke didn't spend long looking into them. When Cruz spoke, it was with a quiet fierceness that barely rose above a whisper.

'I could kill you right now, Dugan. You know that? Then I could go back and kill Pamela too.'

'I hadn't thought of it that way. If anything, the past two

days have suggested to me that I'm harder to kill than I appear.'

'The goal wasn't to kill you.'

'Well, I guess that's two pieces of good news that I've gotten. One, you seem to be saying that Pamela is still alive. Two, you didn't actually plan to kill me. I can't tell you what a relief these two items are.'

Cruz turned and stared out into the mist.

'Man, this fog is fucked up. You live in this shit all the time?'

'We like it,' Smoke said. 'It keeps things hidden.'

'Listen, Dugan, here's the story. Pamela is fine. I've kept her alive this long, at some cost to myself and my credibility with my employers. She hasn't even been hurt. But I left her with Moss. If I don't come back there in two hours, Moss is going to kill her. We're through fucking around.'

Smoke nearly laughed. 'If *you* don't come back? What's the matter, Cruz? Are you afraid I'm going to hurt you?'

'We want half the money. It's that simple. We don't even want you anymore. We know you have the money, and we want to trade it for Pamela.'

'You want half the money? Cruz, forgive me, but things seem to have changed an awful lot since all the demands you were making yesterday. I gather you've lost quite a bit of credibility. A man who wants half the money sounds like a man on the run. What makes you think I even have any money?'

'You said so yourself.'

'You beat a man long enough, he's liable to say anything.'

Again, the conversation lapsed into a long pause. Smoke

heard himself sigh heavily, and was surprised by the sound of it. He made a decision.

'You'll let her go?'

'I will.'

'I want to see her first.'

'Do you have the money?'

'I do.'

'Where is it? In the bank, like you said?'

Smoke shook his head, then realized Cruz wasn't even looking at him. 'Uh-uh. Not in the bank.'

'Then where is it?'

'I'll tell you when I see her alive.'

Now it was Cruz's turn to sigh. 'Let's go.'

The two men walked back along the pier, Smoke lagging a few feet behind. There was no strategy to it. Cruz was in a hurry, Smoke was in a hurry, but Smoke couldn't keep up with Cruz's healthy legs. They reached the vehicle barrier and there was Pamela's car again. Cruz hit the button on the key chain. The headlights popped on and off, and Smoke heard the doors come unlocked.

Another car was parked a little way behind the Golf.

It was sleek and black, the big Mercedes logo on the grill gleaming in the fog like a malevolent smile. A man leaned against the side of the luxury sedan, idling there, like he had all the time in the world. He had a toothpick in his mouth. He was a very big man. Even in this light, Smoke could see his grin.

His voice was slow and thick like syrup. 'I been waiting

for you fellows,' he said. 'Thought maybe you were having a little, how should I put it, a little rendezvous back in there. A little romance.'

Smoke's mind raced.

Shit. It was a setup. Pamela was dead.

Run, Lola. RUN!

Smoke would tie them up as long as he could. He looked at the water. If he dove in now, it would take them a while to fish him out. If only he made it that far.

Then Cruz drew his gun.

But he wasn't even looking at Smoke. He was looking right at Moss. He slipped around the side of the Golf, gun in hand, eyes never wavering.

'Dugan, get in the car.'

Moss barely moved. 'Shit, Cruz,' he said. 'What are you doing, son? The game is up for you. Don't you know that by now? If you had left town this morning...' Moss made a gesture like maybe yes, maybe no, 'you might have lived a while longer. But you're still here. That was dumb.'

'Dugan! Get in the fucking car!'

Moss waved grandly. 'That's right, Dugan. Get in the car. Jump in the water. It don't fucking matter. The show's over anyhow.'

'Moss, I told you this morning I'd kill you if I saw you again.'

'Yet here I am.'

Smoke climbed into the passenger seat of the car. Cruz climbed into the driver's seat, gun pointed out the door. He fumbled the key into the ignition and started it, gun still pointed at Moss. The engine burst into life.

'Give it up, Cruz. You're dead, Fred.'

Two sets of headlights came on at the far end of the parking lot, blocking the entrance and exit. Fog swirled in the lights.

'See? I don't even need to draw my gun.' The satisfaction on Moss's face was that of a man who hated to tell you he told you so. 'Now, whyn't you turn that car off and let's go? You boys got a long night ahead of you.'

Cruz fired his gun into that satisfaction, two, three, four times.

And missed.

He hit the gas and slammed the door in the same motion, even as windows on the Mercedes shattered and Moss hit the deck. Smoke was thrown against the window as Cruz zoomed toward the two cars blocking the way. Then Moss was up and jumping into the Mercedes.

The two other cars came straight at them.

Cruz was steady, driving with one hand, gaining speed. He aimed the gun through the windshield at the oncoming disaster.

It was the end game, the final, apocalyptic, juvenile game of chicken.

'Go left!' Smoke screamed. 'Go left! There!'

Cruz glanced left, toward where Smoke pointed. He shrugged. 'It's an alley. We'll never fit.' The headlights ahead were blinding.

'I live here, you dumb shit! Go left!'

Cruz veered left, damn near a ninety-degree turn, and

Smoke was slammed against the window again. The little car plowed down the tiny airway between the office to the Peaks Island Ferry and a boat freight office that served the islands. The Golf scraped both sides against the brick walls. Sparks flew past Smoke's eyes.

On the other end of the alley, there was a small loading dock and then a canal.

'Right turn! Hard right!'

The car veered right, nearly putting Smoke in Cruz's lap. They zoomed along the boardwalk toward the street. This was where the passengers would line up to wait for their boats. A metal support beam loomed ahead. Cruz grazed it, shredding the right side of the car.

'Watch it!' Smoke said.

There were stairs just ahead, three or four of them, where teenage boys often jumped their skateboards in the warm weather.

The car leaped the stairs, throwing Dugan and Cruz around the cabin. They crossed the sidewalk, then barreled out onto Commercial Street.

'Left. Left turn here,' Smoke said. He glanced back. Nobody had come the way they did.

He looked to his right.

Here came the bad guys, piling out of the parking lot in three cars, coming hard, skidding as they turned left out of the entrance, their headlights piercing the fog. The first headlights shone blue – the xenon headlamps of a luxury car, a Mercedes.

'I thought you said Moss had Pamela,' Smoke said.

Cruz made a face. 'I lied. I do that sometimes. Pamela's back at our hotel room, watching TV.'

'*Our* hotel room?'

Smoke hadn't seen Cruz look sheepish. Not until this moment.

'It's a long story,' Cruz said.

Moss held the wheel lightly, with confidence, even with glee.

'Hold on, Lola!' he shouted, maybe loud enough for her to hear it in the trunk. 'Hold on, girl!'

This was what it was about. Hell, son, who cares if they missed 'em in the parking lot? That fireworks show alone as the Golf scraped through the alley was worth the price of admission. Now it was on and he, Moss, was gonna run them down like dogs.

He had the lead car. Sticks and them had been momentarily befuddled when Cruz took that left. They had come straight on, their momentum carrying them. Not Moss. Moss had already been going the other way.

He poured on the gas, foot not even to the floor.

The tiny VW came to him like it was on a fast moving conveyor belt. Up their ass in no time! This was driving. This was the car for it.

He checked the rearview. Sticks and them were coming along, coming just fine.

The Golf made a sharp right onto a narrow, cobblestone street. That little car could turn. It had some zip. Moss made the turn, a little slower, a little squishier in the big sedan. But still good, still responsive. All right, a rumble uphill on the cobblestones, drunken geeks leaping for the sidewalks.

'Out of the way, fuckers.'

If anything, the Golf speeded up. Moss followed suit. Lights, parked cars, and faces zipped by. Moss's eyes narrowed. His thoughts came in madcap shorthand.

Headlights in the rear. The boys still with me.

A right onto a two-way street.

More wandering dinks, eyes gone WIDE, jumping for cover.

Lots of bars on this strip.

A woman screamed.

The Golf zipped around a double-parked car, into the oncoming lane. A second later, Moss clipped the fucking thing, spun it, drove it onto the sidewalk like a linebacker driving a quarterback to the turf.

Headlights, blaring horns.

Shit.

The Mercedes was OK. Still rolling, headlight gone, side all scraped to shit.

THIS IS NOT A WORK CAR!

Aw fuck. Fuck it.

A high-pitched keening sounded in his head, like wind whistling through a mountain pass. It rose and rose and rose, a long ululating wail, then lowered and resolved itself into something more familiar. Sirens. Moss's head swiveled, looking everywhere at once. Looking for the cherry and blue.

Nothing yet. Good.

The Golf screamed left. Rammed a parked car, bounced off, kept going.

Moss did the same. Rammed the same fucking car.

The Mercedes had a pre-crash safety system. Moss had tripped it. The driver's seat moved up into crash position. Automatically. All by itself.

'Don't deploy!' he screamed at the air bags. 'Don't you dare fucking deploy!'

Where're my boys? He checked the mirror.

Still there.

Beating that fucking car senseless as they came around behind him. That thing was pulp. Some dink had parked too close to the corner.

It was a long, impossibly narrow street. Low-slung, three-story buildings. Charming. Historic. Parked cars all along, a wall of parked cars, a blur of chrome and reflected light. More eyes, more faces, frozen Os of horror.

Moss floored it.

The Golf was *right there*.

Some kind of building looming up ahead at the end of this street. Official-looking, a clock tower rising into the mist. City Hall, the State House, who the fuck knew?

A sharp turn coming, had to be.

Time to end it.

Moss pulled his gun.

His left window was gone. He stuck his hand out there, his left, not his best gun hand. Intersection coming.

'Go left, assholes.'

They did, not even braking at all. The car leaned to the right and nearly rolled, the turn was so sharp. Hand it to Cruz – no fear on these turns. Moss roared into the intersection. Two wide lanes, the steps to City Hall dead ahead.

The Golf came across his left side field of vision.

He fired, bang bang bang bang.

Windows shattered, a tire burst. The Golf kept going.

Time slowed. One more shot. BANG.

The rear windshield shattered.

One bang too many.

The building filled his windshield. He swung the wheel, skidded, lost control. He felt the Mercedes go sideways over the curb, ripping his two right tires off their axles. The car leaped, hit ground, spun hard and crashed backwards into the stately front stairs of City Hall.

All around him, the air bags exploded.

Smoke everywhere. Was there a fire? No, it was air bag dust. Talcum powder. Corn starch. Whatever they used nowadays. Moss hadn't been in a serious car crash in five years, and they still had this same shitty dust? He breathed the dust, hearing the sirens close now. He shook his head to clear the cobwebs. He glanced out the window.

Sticks and the boys roared around the corner in their two cars, leaning hard, holding it, making it. Not too fast, but the Golf was down at least one tire. Maybe he had hit somebody in there, maybe not. No time to wonder.

Gotta go.

He pushed the door open. At first it wouldn't go, but he forced it. He popped the trunk and limped around to the back of the car.

Jesus, that crash kind of hurt.

'Hey, baby, you alive in there?'

She was. Her head was cut, bleeding. She had been knocked unconscious, but she was breathing. He lifted her dead weight out of the trunk, groaning just a bit, then hoisted her onto his shoulder. He limped out into the middle of the street.

Headlights coming.

He stood right in their way, waving frantically with his free arm, hardly noticing he was waving a gun in the air. The car screeched to a halt. Terrified EYES looked out at him. King Kong with the hot babe hanging off him. The car was a little silver Ford Focus. Not too much in the zip department, but she'll do. He gimped over to the driver's side. Four people in there, kids really. The dink at the wheel had a goatee.

Come on.

He gave them the maw end of the gun.

Nothing but EYES looking down a big black cave. Hell, he'd been there himself a few times. Couldn't blame them.

'Folks, get the fuck out,' he said.

Cruz drove down the pedestrian mall, a cigarette dangling from his mouth. Smoke glanced over at him – no time to think about the sudden turn of events, no sense in pondering the new alliances. It was he and Cruz now, Cruz and Smoke.

People scattered ahead of them. The car veered in and out

of park benches and garbage cans. Smoke looked back. There were two cars still back there, doing the same sort of weird, slow-motion slalom.

Pamela's car shuddered and made a terrible noise, one that didn't bode well.

Fa-LUMP, fa-LUMP, fa-LUMP.

It sounded like a man running along with the rubber sole of his sneaker coming off, slapping the pavement every time he took a step. It felt a lot worse than that. It felt like the wheel was about to come off.

'Make a right down here at the bottom.'

Cruz did so, going much slower than before, but the Golf barely held the turn.

Headlights. Cruz veered, then went around.

'Jesus!'

'I forgot to mention – it's one way against us here.'

On the straightaway, the Golf did a little better. But the other two cars took the turn clean. They were right behind. There were sirens everywhere now. Smoke caught a glimpse of the street parallel and a little below them. Blue lights – just blue for Maine cops, Smoke knew, no red – going mad over there. Closing the net.

'We can't get arrested,' Cruz said. 'They get us inside, we're dead. All they gotta do is wait.'

'I know,' Smoke said.

Cruz reached inside his pocket. He pulled out his gun. 'Take this.'

Smoke took it. 'What am I going to do with this?'

Cruz nodded backwards. 'Get rid of those guys.'

Smoke glanced back at the pursuers. 'You know, when it comes right down to it, I really don't shoot people.'

'I know,' Cruz said. 'You just blow them up.'

Smoke shrugged.

They zoomed through an intersection. The two cars were right behind them. Smoke caught the lights in the corner of his eyes as they passed through. A second later, police lights appeared back there. A whole series of cop cars made the turn onto the street behind them. The sirens filled his ears.

Cruz scanned the empty streets ahead. 'Where are we going?'

'For the bridge,' Smoke said. 'Isn't that what you said?'

'Cape Elizabeth,' Cruz agreed.

They made a left, then a right, staying on side streets. It looked like they had their own parade behind them. High Street was up ahead, a major thoroughfare, three lanes of traffic coming one way off the bridge. Even at this time of night, it was bound to be crowded. Worse, it'd be crowded, but moving fast.

'OK, here's where it gets interesting,' Smoke said. 'This left coming up, it's the way to the bridge. But everything's coming at you.'

Cruz made the left without slowing down. Again, the car leaned, skidded across the lanes, but he held it. Headlights came, a line of headlights, horns blaring. Cruz plunged straight at it, jaw set.

They plowed through the traffic, oncoming cars scattering

like leaves, demolishing parked cars, jumping the sidewalk on either side.

Behind them, the bad guys did the same.

'Follow it around to the right,' Smoke said. 'Good.'

It was a long straightaway to the bridge, cars coming down off it in droves. Cruz plowed through like a boat cutting the waves. Smoke began to get that confident feeling – that humming, buzzing, we're-gonna-do-this-thing feeling he used to get right before a job. But then beneath all the noise – the horns blaring, the tires screaming, the Golf fa-LUMPING, and the sirens sirens sirens howling, he began to hear another sound. It was familiar, a sound he associated with something unpleasant.

Over and over it repeated, endless, insistent.

Clang, clang, clang, clang, clang, clang, clang.

It sounded like the bell they rang at a train crossing to tell you that the road was about to close. They always sounded that bell just before the safety arms came down.

They passed the approach to the bridge. Now they were about to go up and over.

Clang, clang, clang, clang.

Shit. It was the bridge. They were raising the drawbridge.

'Wait. Don't go up there.'

Cruz glanced at him.

'Cruz!'

Too late, they were going up.

'They're closing the bridge.'

Cruz peered ahead. In the fog, the red lights on the safety

arms blinked frantically. They started coming down. The bell sounded. Clang, clang, clang . . .

'We can make it,' Cruz said.

The Golf's engine roared as Cruz floored the gas. The car speeded up. Smoke felt the G-forces pushing him against the seat. Underneath them, the damn thing fa-LUMPED like demons were inside, pounding to escape.

'We will,' Cruz said. 'We'll make it.'

It sounded like Cruz was trying to convince himself.

The arms were already down. Behind the arms, the bridge was going up very fast, growing, growing, becoming impossibly huge, a giant gray monster.

'Duck!'

They burst through the safety arm, the windshield imploding onto them, tiny nuggets of safety glass spraying everywhere, the wrenching squeal of twisting metal in their ears. The safety arm bent and ripped the roof off the car.

The bridge was everything, a gigantic wall in front of them.

They skidded as Cruz must have slammed on the brakes.

Here came that wall.

They crashed, air bags deploying, the car bouncing backward.

Smoke sat stunned, air bag dust all around him.

'Are you all right?' he heard Cruz say.

He turned to look at Cruz.

'Have you lost your fucking mind?'

* * *

'Look,' Cruz said to the old man. 'If you're all right, if you can still move, then we gotta go.' Cruz himself felt OK. The drive had been exhilarating. He had enjoyed his brief glimpse of Moss going across that sidewalk.

But now they were out of time.

'Dugan.'

'Yeah, yeah. I'm OK. But where are we going?'

'I don't know yet.'

Cruz got out, then ran around to the passenger side and helped Dugan out. The car was wrecked. Beyond wrecked. The windshield was gone. The roof was shredded open. Steam poured out of the demolished front end. Cruz supported Dugan as they walked over toward the edge of the bridge. Behind them, the gangsters pulled up in the two tail cars. Far back, the cops were coming in their cruisers. It was a nice move, jamming through the oncoming traffic. The cops had to fall away rather than endanger the citizenry.

'I can't go over there,' Dugan said now.

'Over where?'

'Over to the edge.'

'Why?'

'The height. It makes me dizzy.'

Despite himself, despite everything that was happening, Cruz suppressed a smile. 'What's the matter, Smoke? You afraid of heights?'

The old man's answer was simple enough. 'Yeah.'

Cruz looked out at all that night and fog. Six stories below, it had to be that far, a massive oil tanker was coming along from further up the harbor. He could see its lights, its absolute monstrous size, approaching in the gloom. He felt a momentary twinge. They hadn't raised the bridge to stop him – there really was a ship coming through.

'We live and die out here,' he told Dugan. 'And the world doesn't care. It just goes on about its business.'

But that boat gave him an idea.

Smoke couldn't look in the direction where Cruz was dragging him.

He tried not to think about it – the height, the distance to the water, that feeling of falling – never in real life, but in a thousand dreams. Those fucking kids hanging him off that building. His whole body was already shaking.

So he looked back the way they came.

And saw the three guys had already climbed out of their cars and were walking this way, moving fast. They had their guns out. In the distance the cops had reached the base of the bridge.

Cruz dragged him all the way to the edge. He felt the guardrail behind him. It was higher than he thought. He used to think it barely reached his waist. Actually, it was nipple high. He couldn't imagine it would ever keep a car from going over. He looked down. There was a ship down there. The world spun.

'Step up on the first rung,' Cruz said.

If he stepped up on the first rung, then leaned back and pushed with his feet . . .

Never mind.

'Cruz. We got company.'

'I know. Get up on that rung.'

What Smoke didn't like, beside the height, beside the massive ship down there, beside the looming near certainty of death, was this bossy tone all of a sudden from Cruz. Who the fuck did he think he was? This little partnership was ten minutes old, and already Cruz was giving orders.

'Hey, Cruz? I'm a big boy, you know? I've been doing this shit since long before you came around.'

Cruz turned and looked at him. He seemed puzzled. 'What?'

Smoke held his ground. 'You're not the boss here.'

Light dawned in Cruz's eyes. 'Oh. Yeah. OK, do me a favor then, will you? Please get up on that rung.' He gestured with his hand, inviting Smoke to step up there.

Smoke did. He gripped the rail with both hands.

The three men walked up and stopped about ten feet away. The leader was a skinny guy in a leather jacket with a hat pulled down over his eyes. He flashed white teeth at them. Smoke marveled at these guys, as he always had. The guy was enjoying himself.

'Cruz?' the guy said.

Cruz raised a hand. 'Me.'

The guy nodded. 'Yeah. That's right. The scar.'

'That's right,' Cruz said.

'You know who I am?'

'Can't say that I do.'

'Ever hear of a guy they call Sticks?'

Cruz nodded.

'Know why they call him that?' The little guy glanced at the other guys with him. They giggled like kids. They were barely out of their childhood, the two of them. 'No? I'll tell you. Because he sticks sharp objects in your eyes. That's what he likes to do.'

The first police car pulled up, that powerful sound, that police car engine revving close. Doors opened. 'Freeze, assholes! Freeze! Raise those hands! Drop those fucking weapons right now.'

More cars screamed up. More doors opened.

'If we live, are you still going to honor our agreement?'

Smoke held the railing even tighter. 'Half? I'll honor it.'

'Don't worry,' Sticks said. 'You ain't gonna live.'

Still smiling, Sticks raised his arms in the air, gun still in hand.

His boys did the same.

'Drop the weapons!'

'I guess you're not going to kill us tonight,' Cruz said.

Sticks shrugged, teeth flashing. He had a certain charm, this guy.

'Not tonight. In the joint, maybe. Or after that.'

He let the gun fall from his hand. He turned his head slightly sideways. 'Officer,' he said. 'I'm a private bodyguard. I have a license to carry that firearm in the State of New York. So do these men with me.'

'This look like New York to you, asshole?'

Smoke glanced at Cruz. From the corner of his eye, far

below and to the right, Smoke could see the massive ship passing beneath the bridge. The dark water foamed along its side. Directly below them, a long way down, all was inky blackness. Smoke's knees were knocking together.

Cruz smiled. 'It's time to go,' he said.

He grabbed Smoke roughly by the jacket. He leaped backward, his ass landing on the railing, his momentum carrying him backwards and over the side. His grip was like iron, like the talons of an eagle. Smoke felt himself going over.

'No,' he said. 'No.' His grip on the railing slipped. 'No.'

He went head over heels. The world turned upside down. For no more than a second, he caught a glimpse of the man Sticks on his knees, cops around him. Then the light was gone and Smoke fell through the darkness. He closed his eyes and fell for what seemed a long time, a scream just behind his lips, but never quite coming to the surface. The ship was a shadow, a massive presence to his right.

Then he hit the cold black water and knew no more.

Moss pulled up slowly at the bottom of a dead end street.

In the back seat of the little Ford Focus, Lola squirmed and made a soft noise. He glanced back at her. Still out, but coming around a little bit. No matter. Her hands were cuffed behind her, her mouth was gagged, and she had been knocked silly by all that banging around in the trunk. Her whole face was smeared in dried blood. If she gave him any trouble, maybe he'd just give her a glimpse in the mirror. All that blood, she'd probably pass out again.

He smiled at the thought.

Across the wide-open park at the end of this street, he had an uninterrupted view across to the bridge. Uninterrupted except for the fog, which in any case wasn't as bad as before. The wind had picked up, and it blew the fog around in wisps. It still obscured things, but he could see well enough.

Perhaps four hundred yards from where he sat, the bridge was up like some kind of ancient megalith. There were swarms of cop cars out there, lights flashing, at the base of the thing.

It looked like they had some people in custody out there. With any luck, they had everybody. Wouldn't that be something? Cruz and Dugan spending the night trapped in the holding cell with Sticks and his boys. He could picture Sticks, quietly giving them the story about all the shit he was gonna do to them one day. Cruz and Dugan, knowing full well that it didn't matter what happened with the cops. If they let them go, we'd be there to get them. If they sent them up, we'd still be there to get them.

How's that feel, assholes?

Moss would probably get the whole story tomorrow. In a day or two at the very least. In the meantime, he had some business to attend to.

Behind him, Lola groaned. It was kind of a sexy sound.

'Whaddya say there, Lola? Let's go see Pamela, eh?'

8

Smoke was alive.

He didn't know how or why. He only knew that he was sitting on a chair, naked, but wrapped in a thick blanket. His entire body shivered uncontrollably. A dark room was close around him, and the room was gently rising and falling. There came the creaking sound he associated with a boat straining against its tie lines. Sure, he must be on a boat. He noticed he had a mug between his hands, and the mug was warm but not hot. There was a beverage in the mug. He sipped it. Warm apple juice.

Hmmm. That was good.

'Drink it slow,' a voice said.

Smoke looked up and across from him in the darkness sat Cruz. He was also wrapped in a blanket. His piercing eyes blazed away over there. A red light shone at the end of his cigarette.

'Where are we?' Smoke said.

'Somebody's yacht. Little boat club across the water from where we went in. It was a long swim. You were passed out, so I dragged you with me. Did the little lifeguard carry, grabbed you around the neck. Learned it in the youth center when I was a kid. Never forgot it.'

The shivering abated a little as the warm juice entered Smoke's system.

'Where'd you get the juice?'

'They have a refrigerator in this thing. Nuked it up in the microwave. Not too hot. Didn't want to drag you all the way over here just to kill you with a hot beverage.'

'Radical temperature change,' Smoke said.

'That's right.'

They sat for a little while in the darkness. Cruz smoked the cigarette he had scrounged from somewhere. Smoke settled into the lazy rise and fall of the boat. He felt like he could sit here for ever. He felt like he could fall asleep.

'You and Pamela an item now? Is that it?'

Cruz hesitated. 'Something like that.'

'Life is funny,' Smoke said.

'Yeah.'

More silence. Cruz blew a smoke ring that hovered in the air.

'You know how to drive one of these things?' Cruz said.

'Sure.'

'For real?'

'For real,' Smoke said. 'I bought my first boat right after I made my first big heist.'

Cruz smiled. 'Yeah? Which one was that?'

'In 1963,' Smoke said. 'You were probably in diapers. It was a food store, one that did a lot of business, and didn't bank its receipts until each Friday. This was a common thing back then. It made Thursday night a vulnerable night. Schulman's, the place was called. We had an inside guy, a guy who worked there but didn't know the combination. He described the safe to me. As soon as he started talking, I knew it was a good job. You know why? He was describing a fireproof safe. The safe was designed to withstand a fire, but not a crook. I knew I could beat it. We went in there and took out twenty-four grand in 1963 dollars. Split it four ways. The other guys were talking about cars. Me, I always wanted a boat.'

Cruz laughed. Smoke hadn't heard him laugh before.

It was the life. The life brought smiles to people's faces.

'Where *did* you put the money?' Cruz said.

'Roselli's money?'

Cruz nodded.

'Remember you asked me if I had a dog? I said no, it was the dog of the previous tenants buried there? I didn't have the heart to dig it up. Well, the previous tenants didn't have a dog. At least, not one that's buried back there.'

'Feel like getting that money right now?' Cruz said.

Smoke shrugged. 'Sure, why not? If Lola hasn't beaten us to it.'

* * *

Moss parked in the lot at the Ocean House Hotel, close to the building, but at the corner most distant from the front entrance, and very close to a high hedge. Why do a lot of walking, especially with Lola in her current condition?

The lot was mostly empty. A stiff breeze blew in from the water, rustling the sea grasses and making the hedge lean back and forth. Moss found himself wondering whether the cops ever did sweeps of this parking lot. It being private, they probably wouldn't unless someone called.

That was good. This car was hotter than hell. There might even be a description out on the TV and radio about him from the kids he had carjacked. If he had had it to do over, he might have just blown them all away.

In any case, better not to be seen.

He scanned the lot. He might just have to pull another carjacking later tonight to get out of this place. He was a lousy car thief.

He pulled Lola from the back seat and put her over his shoulder again. Then he walked around the building and out to the beach. It was dark back here, but the winds had blown away the remnants of the fog. The grass on the sand dunes waved crazily, like each blade of grass was a long skinny arm frantically waving goodbye. He dropped Lola onto one of the dunes.

He kneeled down by her and looked at her face.

He shook her. Her eyelids fluttered. Nothing more.

'Lola! Hey, cunt!'

Nothing.

He slapped her.

Her eyes opened wide, then rolled back into her head. Hell, she might have gotten fucked up back there for real. She didn't seem to have seen him at all. Well, we'd see in a little while. For now, though, she seemed like she'd be OK right here, hands cuffed behind her back, mouth gagged, out cold.

You know? Maybe one more bind would do the trick.

He shrugged out of his leather jacket. He had a dress shirt on, and under that, a T-shirt. He took off both shirts. Bare-chested, he could feel his skin tighten against the cold wind. He looked down at his erect nipples, proud of his massive chest and arms. He looked forward to capping off his night with these two ladies.

Was this gonna be something? What were those chumps gonna think when the staff found these two young ladies, naked, penetrated and dead together on a bed in this fine hotel? Man, how's that for a message? The very thought of it excited him.

He ripped his T-shirt down the middle, then put his dress shirt and jacket back on. He kneeled and tied the T-shirt around Lola's ankles, pulling it tight and knotting it.

OK. Only worry here was if somebody finds her.

He glanced around. After midnight. Pitch-darkness out here. Cold wind whistling and blowing. Ain't nobody gonna come out here and find her.

In any event, he wouldn't be gone too long.

'I'll be back for you in a minute, darling. Don't go nowhere.'

He stood and marched back across the sand toward the

hotel. Now I'm gonna take a guess here, he thought. I don't want to go into the building because I don't want anybody to see me. I want to go straight in through the balcony. They got balconies on the bottom floor, and that would be easy. But Cruz is gonna pick a room on the upper floor so that I can't come in through the balcony. OK. But little Pamela's gonna be there all by herself. She's gonna leave the light on all night, maybe all the lights in the room. So look for a room on the top floor with a lot of lights on — that ought to narrow it down.

And narrow it down it did. He scanned the length of the building and found only two rooms that fit his description. One of them was close to this end of the building. The other was more in the center of the building.

'If I was Room 215, which one would I be?'

Easy enough. The one closest to the end. He gazed at that one. It was less bright than the one further down, which didn't necessarily fit his idea of how it would go. But it didn't necessarily contradict it, either. A TV set flickered inside the room. He had no opinion on that one way or the other.

It would serve as a guess to work from, anyway. He'd go for that room. All that was left was figuring some way to get on up there.

All the way to the left was some kind of dinner patio on the ground floor. There was a decorative trestle over there. It looked flimsy from here, but if it was sturdy, he could go up the trestle like it was a ladder. At the top, the roof crossed back across the entire hotel. The roof sloped downward at a mild angle, and it stopped every ten yards or so at another room balcony.

It would be a cinch for him to move across that roof.

But how would he get Lola up there?

Don't worry. Verify first, then figure it out. Move forward.

He walked over to the patio. He stood at the bottom of the trestle and looked up at how it went straight up to the roof. The trestle was strong enough to hold his weight.

Well, well, well.

Moss started climbing.

Lola waited until she was sure he was gone before she opened her eyes again.

When she did, she saw that he had left her, bound and gagged, on a sand dune somewhere.

Jesus, what a pig.

She tried to put him out of her mind for the moment. She was cold, her head hurt, both a sharp pain where she had banged it while inside the trunk, and a dull ache that seemed to come from deep inside. She felt sick to her stomach. The ocean was right nearby – she could hear the waves crashing and smell the salt. Behind her, there seemed to be lights. She squirmed around and craned her neck. She saw the lights of hotel rooms maybe fifty yards away.

At some point, there must have been a car crash, but she didn't remember it. All she knew was she had been in the trunk of the big car. They had driven the damn thing like maniacs, and she had been tossed around like a doll. Then at some point later on, she was in the back seat of a smaller car, parked somewhere. And Moss had said, 'Come on, Lola, let's go see Pamela.'

Now here she was.

Maybe Pamela was in that hotel.

In any case, Lola needed to get out of here before Moss came back.

All right. Her hands were cuffed behind her back. Her legs were tied. Her mouth was gagged.

It couldn't be as bad as it seemed.

The legs seemed easiest, so she tried to kick them free. No luck. He had tied it tight. She just made herself dizzy through the effort. She thought about her hands. The thing about it was, years of training made her flexible. Try it. She sat on her hands at first, then bent from the waist and wriggled them down until they rested under her legs. Man, was she stiff from that trunk. Now came the challenging part. She bent all the way down, until her forehead touched her knees. She scooted her hands along until her wrists were at her ankles, then she pulled them over her feet and free.

Now her cuffed hands were in front of her body, a vastly improved situation to be in. Out of reflex more than anything, she brought her hands to her mouth and worked at the gag. It was knotted tight. It took a moment to pull the knot loose and get it out. She threw the gag to the wind and worked the muscle tightness in her jaw and neck.

One last job – she bent and untied her legs.

She stood, and immediately became dizzy again. She lost her balance and fell back onto the dune.

OK. That was too fast.

Moving slowly, she stood and started walking.

Up ahead, there was the big figure of Moss, framed by the glow of light from the hotel. Lola dove to the sand, then crawled up to the top of the next dune and watched. He seemed to be staring up at the building, thinking about something.

'Don't burn your wires,' she muttered.

Then he decided. He walked off toward the left side of the building. Lola kept low, moving parallel to him, crawling, keeping the same distance between them, but also keeping him in sight. She didn't want to get too close.

She watched him go up a trestle to the sloping roof of the second floor. A moment later, she saw him scooting along the roof from balcony to balcony.

'Well, hello darling,' Moss said as he strolled in from the balcony.

Pamela had been half asleep when she heard the loud thump outside the sliding glass door. Her eyes had popped open, thinking it was something on television. The TV was showing an informercial for skin products. A man was exhorting a young woman to rub some cream on her face in front of a studio audience.

Only as the big man snapped the lock on the door and pushed it open did Pamela realize what was happening.

Moss pulled a gun from inside his jacket. He raised a finger to his lips.

'Don't you scream or even say a word. If you do, I'll have to shoot you like I was gonna do yesterday. Remember?'

She nodded, the scream just behind her lips.

He studied her up and down. 'Now, what has Cruz done to you? Left you tied to the bedpost? With the telephone all the way over there? My word. And let's get a look at what he left for me.'

Moss pulled the bed sheet down and away from her. Pamela was conscious of wearing only a T-shirt and a pair of panties. In front of this monster. She was also conscious that Cruz had left her the gun and she had slipped it under the pillow earlier in the night. If she could reach under there and get it out . . .

Moss cupped his chin in his hand. And smiled.

'My, my. Ain't that pretty? I think I'll need a beer before I do anything.'

He walked across the room to the wet bar. He opened it and pulled out a bottle of beer. 'One for yourself?' he said.

She looked at him, shook her head.

'That's OK, you can go ahead and talk now. Once you're over that initial fear, that startlement, it's OK to talk. Just don't scream. So, can I offer you one?'

She could barely get it out. 'No,' she croaked.

He shrugged and opened his. 'Suit yourself.'

He took a long swallow and ambled back over to her. He pulled up a chair and sat down. His face was less than two feet from hers. 'You missed a hell of a night, Pamela. Car chases, kidnappings, shoot-'em-ups. And murder, did I mention that? Had to kill me two men tonight.' He shook his head sadly. 'Cruz and Dugan. They left me no choice.'

Pamela stared at him. She felt numb.

Could it be true? Could they both be dead?

She looked at his gigantic hand. The beer looked like a toy compared to that hand.

It could be true.

'But let's not dwell on unhappy things,' he said now. 'Let's talk about you and me. And Lola. She's just outside, waiting for me to bring her on in here. We're gonna have a big time, just the three of us. But you know, you're looking good enough right at this moment that maybe she could wait a little longer, eh? How tempting, that little outfit you got on.'

He ran his gun hand along her leg, up to her thigh.

'Mind if I take a look inside these little panties?'

Pamela felt her entire body start to shake. He put both his beer and his gun on the desk and his big hands *touched* her.

'Cruz treat you all right? Yeah, I bet he did. But you know what? I bet I'll treat you better than him.'

He stood.

'Don't you move,' he said. 'Don't you move an inch.'

He kicked off his boots. Then he undid his belt and removed his pants, eyes watching her all the time. He wore tight white BVDs, and he was already bulging under there. Above his right sock, he had a long-handled knife taped to his thick calf. He peeled off his socks. 'I see you looking at my knife. Tell you what. I'm gonna leave it on, make things a little kinkier for us.'

He climbed onto the bed with her, and his hands began to roam her body.

If Cruz was dead, and Smoke was dead, and all was lost, there was no reason not to go for the gun. Just reach back under that pillow slow and calm, pull it out, and shoot this evil bastard dead. Act like you were into it, this . . . defilement.

'Yeah, baby. Lean back. I'm gonna treat you real good.'

She leaned back, her free hand sliding under the pillow. She looked down at Moss's greasy hair as he kissed her stomach. She looked away.

OK. Do it.

Outside the window, a figure appeared on the balcony. It vaulted over the railing. The landing made a solid BANG.

Moss turned to look as Lola rushed into the room.

Her hands were cuffed together.

Moss jumped off the bed. Lola raised a kick but seemed to lose her balance. Moss blocked it and slapped her hard across the face. She flew backward and crashed into the TV, then fell to the floor. The TV quivered in its moorings.

Moss turned back to Pamela. 'She got here sooner than I thought.'

Pamela pulled the gun from under the pillow.

She aimed.

She squeezed the trigger.

The trigger was jammed. What the . . . ?

Shit. The safety was on. She looked down at the gun, looking for the lever.

Moss slapped the gun and it went flying across the room.

'Son of a bitch. Are you girls both crazy? Is that it? You know I ought to kill you both right now. But you got such spunk that I'm having too much fun.'

Behind him, Lola climbed to her feet. She leaped onto his back.

Moss spun around. 'Whoa! Ride 'em, cowgirl.'

Lola tried to slip her handcuff chain around Moss's neck. He grabbed the chain with one meaty hand. With the other, he reached back and playfully cupped Lola's ass.

'Careful with that chain, Lola.'

Pamela saw her chance. The one chance left. She dove to the floor. Her arm extended painfully behind her, still cuffed to the bed. With her free arm she reached for Moss's leg. She stretched, she reached.

He spun Lola around again.

Pamela grabbed the knife. She yanked it away, the tape making a ripping sound. Then, with all her might, she plunged it into his thigh.

He groaned and kicked her.

She fell back, stunned. The knife stuck from his leg.

He stood, eyes gone wide, staring down at the handle of the knife. He looked at Pamela in disbelief, then back at the knife again. He reached down, and ever so slowly, began to pull it out. The blade showed red as it came out an inch.

Lola slipped the chain around his neck and fell backward.

Moss slipped to his knees, one hand still on the knife.

Now Lola was behind him, her face a mask of concentration and effort, hovering above his face, choking, choking.

His face slowly went white. His hands came to his neck as his eyes bugged out of his head. The knife was still deep in his leg.

He sank face first to the floor, Lola riding him down.

'Keep killing him,' Pamela said. 'Make sure the bastard's dead.'

At 3 a.m., Cruz turned the key in the lock and entered his suite.

Dugan was just offshore with the boat, waiting. They had to hurry. They had more than two million in cash, but Dugan wanted to go back to the city and find Lola before he did anything.

Cruz didn't think anybody had seen him come in the hotel, but he couldn't be sure.

He turned the corner into the bedroom.

Everyone was on the floor.

Lola was here. Her face was a bloody mess. Pamela had that deer in the headlights look again. Moss was big and white and dead, with no pants on, his tongue lolling out.

Lola and Pamela both stared up at Cruz.

Lola smiled, then so did Pamela.

'Holy shit,' Cruz said.

Brian Knox stood at the payphone outside the dairy bar. The sun had just risen over the cove down the street – the cove where Knox had seen the bunch of them set out for open water.

It took a long time of waiting before the right voice finally came on the line.

'OK,' it said.

'OK,' Knox echoed. 'I just watched them leave on a medium-sized ocean-going powerboat. It's blue and white with a flying deck, but I couldn't get the name off the back. Going out from here, if they have the gas, and they get good weather, within a day or two they could be up the coast in Canada, they could be down in Cape Cod, Nantucket, maybe Rhode Island. They could go anywhere, really.'

'We got ya, kid. We're not idiots on this end.'

Knox waited.

'And Cruz?'

'That's the funny part,' Knox said. 'He got on the same boat. He had the women with him. They all left together.'

The voice sighed.

Knox waited some more.

'What about Moss?'

'Moss?' Knox said.

'He's the big guy. Huge. Kind of stringy hair.'

'I'm not sure who you're talking about.'

'You couldn't miss this guy. If you saw him, you'd know.'

What was Knox supposed to say? That he'd watched the guy climb a ladder to the hotel roof the night before, then cross over to a second- floor balcony and break into a room? That the guy looked like an ape, carrying a girl on his shoulder through the dunes like a twenty-pound sack of potatoes? That the same girl had followed him up to the roof, and gone into the same room?

That a couple of hours later, Cruz and the two girls had shoved the same ape's body off the balcony, then Cruz had come down to the beach, dug a shallow grave and buried the body in the sand? And Knox himself had witnessed all this and done nothing?

No thanks.

'Big guy? Doesn't ring a bell.'

'OK, kid. We'll take care of it. Do me a favor, will ya? Make a point of going into Boston next weekend. Get yourself a haircut or something. A good place would be Sonny's Barber Shop in the North End.'

'OK.'

'A man there has an envelope for you.'

'Thanks,' Knox was about to say, but the line had already gone dead.